Barbara McCauley has written more than twenty books for Mills & Boon, and lives in Southern California with her own handsome hero husband, Frank, who makes it easy to believe in and write about the magic of romance. Barbara's stories have won and been nominated for numerous awards, including the prestigious RITA® Award from the Romance Writers of America, Best Desire of the Year from *Romantic Times* and Best Short Contemporary from the National Reader's Choice Awards. Barbara loves to hear from her readers.

Maureen Child is the author of more than 130 romance novels and novellas that routinely appear on bestseller lists and have won numerous awards, including the National Reader's Choice Award. A seven-time nominee for the prestigous RITA® award from Romance Writers of America, one of her books was made into a CBS-TV movie called THE SOUL COLLECTER. Maureen recently moved from California to the mountains of Utah and is trying to get used to snow.

Katherine Garbera is a strong believer in happily-ever-after. She's written more than thirty-five books and has been nominated for career achievement awards in series fantasy and series adventure from *RT Book Reviews*. Her books have appeared on the Waldenbooks/ Borders bestseller list for series romance and on the *USA TODAY* extended bestseller list. Visit Katherine on the Web at www.katherinegarbera.com

Dynasties

Dynasties: The Danforths

BARBARA McCAULEY

MAUREEN CHILD

KATHERINE GARBERA

MILLS & BOON

First Published in Great Britain 2020
By Mills & Boon, an imprint of HarperCollins*Publishers*
1 London Bridge Street, London, SE1 9GF

DYNASTIES: THE DANFORTHS © 2020 Harlequin Books S.A.

The Cinderella Scandal © 2004 Harlequin Books S.A.
Man Beneath the Uniform © 2004 Harlequin Books S.A.
Sin City Wedding © 2004 Harlequin Books S.A.

Special thanks and acknowledgement are given to
Barbara McCauley, Maureen Child, and Katherine Garbera for
their contribution to the *Dynasties: The Danforths* series.

ISBN: 978-0-263-28103-3

MIX
Paper from
responsible sources
FSC™ C007454

This book is produced from independently certified FSC™ paper
to ensure responsible forest management.

For more information visit: www.harpercollins.co.uk/green

Printed and bound in Spain
by CPI, Barcelona

THE CINDERELLA SCANDAL

BARBARA McCAULEY

To my readers everywhere—thank you!
You are all special to me. I wish you much love,
laughter and happiness.

One

Sheets of icy January rain rippled across the Savannah countryside. Lightning exploded in the dark sky. Thunder rumbled through the magnificent oaks that lined the private stone drive, rattled the wide, sweeping branches and shook the moss-covered trunks.

The night wasn't fit for man nor beast, but when Abraham Danforth called his family to gather for a meeting, they came.

Though white-capped waves crashed on the beach below Crofthaven Manor, Reid Danforth was warm and dry inside the comfort of his car. Duke Ellington drifted quietly from the BMW's CD player, blended with the sound of the pelting rain on the car's roof and the *whish-whish* of the windshield wipers. After a long, hectic day negotiating a shipping contract with Maximilian Paper Products, one of Danforth & Co.'s largest clients in Austria, Reid was grateful for the peaceful thirty-minute drive to his family's house.

A drive, Reid thought as he pulled in front of the tall, black wrought-iron gates, that was about to come to an end.

Releasing a long breath, Reid pressed the remote inside his car, watched the massive gates slowly part. A flash of lightning lit the huge Georgian-style mansion at the end of the driveway; thunder boomed like cannon fire. Light shone through large, leaded-glass windows. Even to Reid, who'd been raised here in between semesters away at boarding schools, Crofthaven was an impressive estate. Built in the 1890s by Reid's great-grandfather, Hiram, the large mansion had been designed to survive. A trait Hiram had also firmly ingrained in his descendants.

Reid parked between two of the family's three limousines and shut off his engine, sat for a moment and listened to the rain battering the roof of his car. It always took a few moments to make the transition between the real world and Crofthaven. Tonight his father would expect the entire Danforth clan to be attentive while he laid out the game plan for his upcoming senatorial bid. Family unity and support were critical to a successful campaign. Abraham Danforth did not know the meaning of failure, a fact that had made the already prosperous shipping magnate more wealthy than his forefathers. Wealthy enough to step away from the day-to-day operations of Danforth & Co. Shipping and launch a new career in politics.

Because he was already late, Reid stepped out of his car into the piercing rain and strode toward the front entry. When he opened the oversize oak door, a gust of wind whistled around him, then swirled inside the white marbled hall. On a table at the base of the majestic sweeping staircase sat a large crystal vase filled with white roses that scented the air, as did the heavenly smell of roast lamb and oregano.

"Master Reid." Joyce Jones, Crofthaven's head housekeeper, appeared suddenly. Concern narrowed her brown eyes as she moved toward him. "I was worried about you."

"I'm fine," Reid reassured the woman he'd known the entire thirty-two years of his life. "Just finishing up some paperwork at the office."

Though the sixty-something housekeeper had never been especially demonstrative or affectionate, she at least had been a constant in Reid's erratic upbringing. The same black uniform, the same sturdy work shoes. Even the simple knot of brown hair at the base of her head hadn't changed, though lately Reid had noticed more than a few gray strands.

"It's nasty out there." Joyce moved behind Reid to help him out of his damp trench coat. Out of habit, she brushed a hand over the shoulders of his black business suit, then straightened the back of his collar. "Martin is serving spiced rum and martinis in the parlor. Your father's on a phone call in his office. I'll tell him you're here."

"Thanks."

Loosening his tie, Reid made his way to the parlor, then paused in the doorway. Two of his brothers, Ian and Adam were huddled by the fireplace with his cousin Jake, no doubt discussing the chain of D&D's

coffeehouses they'd started in the Savannah area. Beside the bar, Reid's youngest brother, Marcus—the lawyer in the family—was currently engaged in an intense legal discussion with their uncle Harold and cousin Toby, something about water rights on Toby's ranch in Wyoming.

Reid thought of his mother and wished she could be here now to see how her five children had grown. Though he'd only been eight when she'd died, he could still remember how she'd enjoyed cooking for the family, and how much she'd loved to throw parties here. Many a time he and Ian had sneaked downstairs and watched while all the beautiful people in their beautiful clothes laughed and ate and danced to a band. He would never forget the night of his mother's birthday party when Reid watched his father dancing with his wife under the silvery light of the ballroom chandelier.

She'd died the next week, and Abraham Danforth had never seemed the same since. None of them had been the same.

"Reid!" His sister Kimberly broke away from the conversation she'd been having with their cousin Imogene. "Look at you. You're all wet."

"I've been telling him that for years," Jake said from across the room as he lifted his martini glass in a toast. "The gang's all here."

"Where's Aunt Miranda?" Reid asked Kimberly as she rose on her tiptoes and kissed his cheek.

"Putting Dylan to bed upstairs." Kimberly smiled at the mention of Toby's three-year-old son. "I brought a scrapbook of fish I've been photographing and studying out at the island, and he wanted to look at them in lieu of a bedtime story.''

''Better watch out or we'll have another marine biologist in the family,'' Reid teased.

''If you'd have been here earlier and heard him playing the piano, you'd change your mind about that,'' Kimberly said. ''He'll be in Carnegie Hall by the time he's ten.''

''My money says he'll be there by eight.'' Imogene placed a vodka martini in Reid's hand. ''Hello, cuz.''

''Ah, the proud aunt.'' Reid grinned at Imogene, then leaned forward and kissed her cheek. ''How's the world of investment banking these days?''

''Two promotions in six months. Your tie's crooked.'' She tightened the knot he'd just loosened. ''Impression is everything, hon. Speaking of, where's Mitzi these days? You two are quite the handsome couple.''

''I have no idea where she is,'' he said dryly. ''Shopping, most likely.''

He hadn't seen Mitzi Birmingham in more than four months, thank the good Lord. For that matter, he'd been so busy at work putting things in order so he could take the next few weeks off and set up a campaign headquarters for his father, Reid hadn't been dating anyone. Which was just fine with him. When it came to women, he seemed to be a magnet for every money-hungry, status-seeking female in Savannah. As soon as a woman found out he was the son of Abraham Danforth, that he was the director of Danforth & Co. Shipping and that he lived in a penthouse, they either smothered him with compliments and giggled at everything he said or played coy games. Or worse, they did all three.

He knew that the lack of a warm, willing female in his bed would catch up with him soon, but for the moment, at least, he was content to concentrate on his work.

"Reid."

At the sound of his father's deep voice, Reid turned. Nicola Granville, Abraham's new campaign manager, stood by his side. "Dad. Miss Granville."

"Nicola, please. Nice to see you again, Reid."

Reid had met the tall redhead once at his father's office in town and spoken with her twice on the phone. At thirty-seven the woman had already made quite a name for herself in image consulting and politics, and Reid thought his father had made the right choice by hiring her. She was attractive, confident and hard-working. His father and Nicola would make quite a formidable team.

"Nice of you to join us," Abraham said evenly.

Though there hadn't been the slightest hint of irritation in his tone, Reid knew his father well enough to recognize a reprimand when he heard one. Reid also knew better than to offer excuses.

At fifty-five, Abraham Danforth had seasoned into a politician's dream. With his thick, dark-brown hair, deep blue eyes, broad shoulders and the famous Danforth smile, Reid had no doubt that his father would win the upcoming election, especially under the "Honest Abe" campaign slogan that Nicola had worked up.

"Everyone." Abraham's voice stilled the ongoing

conversations in the room. "For those of you who haven't met her already, I'd like to introduce my new campaign manager, Nicola Granville. After dinner she'll be outlining the upcoming campaign and family protocol."

While Nicola circulated around the room and met the family, Reid made his way over to his cousin Jake. "Where's Wes?"

"On a business trip." Jake lifted a brow. "Or so he says. You know Wes."

Reid smiled. Wes had been Jake's roommate in college, but the Danforths all thought of Wesley Brooks as one of the family. Despite Wes's reputation as a playboy, Reid knew that he would have been here if it had been possible.

Jake snagged a cracker with cheese as Martin passed by with a tray. "I heard you've found a building on Drayton to rent for campaign headquarters."

"Just the bottom floor," Reid said, sipping his martini. "I've spoken to the owner, Ivan Alexander, but I haven't signed anything yet. I'll meet with him tomorrow and take a look at the inside. He also owns the building and business next door, Castle Bakery."

Jake nodded. "They've got a good reputation. I've been meaning to get down there myself and check it out. We're always looking for new items on the menu at D&D's." Jake leaned in and wiggled one eyebrow. "And I've also heard that Ivan's got three daughters that look tasty, too."

"Since you're looking for some 'new items,'" Reid said with a grin, "maybe you should handle setting up the campaign headquarters."

"And deprive you of all the fun?" Jake dropped a hand on Reid's shoulder. "I wouldn't dream of it."

Before Reid could reply, Joyce announced that dinner was ready. As the family made their way to the dining room, the conversation turned to campaign strategies and procedures. The election was barely one year away, and Reid knew that the next twelve months were going to be busy. No doubt, there would be obstacles along the way, some predicted, some unseen. The entire Danforth family would be challenged, collectively and individually. Reid knew that he needed to stay focused and on track if he was going to help his father become a United States senator.

The last thing he had time for, Reid thought, no matter how "tasty," they might be, was Ivan Alexander's daughters.

With a sigh, Reid took his place at the table with the rest of his family and knew it was going to be a very long year.

Tina Alexander loved days when the chaos she called her life ran smoothly. The days when she didn't burn a single loaf of bread or an entire tray of apple Danish. The days when all the employees scheduled to work at her family's bakery actually showed up. The days when her sister Sophia wasn't having a man crisis and even managed to make her afternoon shift on time. The days that her other sister Rachel didn't lock herself in the back office and hide behind computer ledgers and sales accounts.

Tina especially enjoyed the rare days her mother

wasn't busy meddling in all three of her daughters' lives.

Today, however, was not one of those days.

"Sophia went to one of those dancing clubs again last night." Mariska Alexander gave a disapproving sniff while she boxed up a phone order for two dozen chocolate cupcakes. Mariska, with her aristocratic nose, strong European jaw and thick blond hair she always wore in a French twist, was definitely the queen of Castle Bakery.

"She did not come home until two in the morning," Mariska continued, even though Tina gave her mother no encouragement to do so. "Two o'clock! Without so much as a phone call."

Tina taped the lid shut on the box of Danish she'd just filled. The morning had been hectic, with only herself and their counter manager, Jason, working up front. There were customers to help, orders to fill and display cases to replenish before the noon rush hit. The last thing Tina needed right now was to listen to her mother lament her oldest daughter's transgressions.

"You placed an ad in the paper for a counter clerk," Tina said in an attempt to divert her mother's attention, then nodded at two young men sitting at a table in the corner of the bakery. The one with black spiked hair and ragged jeans appeared bored, while the one wearing a short-sleeved shirt and black slacks was reading a book. "Are you going to interview them?"

As if she hadn't even heard Tina's question, Mariska pointed to her face. "Look at my eyes. They are bloodshot from waiting up for your sister."

Tina sighed silently and slid the box of Danish

across the counter to Beverly Somersworth, the customer Tina had been helping. Like the majority of Castle Bakery customers, Beverly worked in the downtown Savannah business district. Every Thursday the plump, sixty-year-old brunette bought one dozen Danish for the legal office where she worked as a receptionist.

"Sophia is twenty-eight years old, Mom," Tina said as patiently as she could manage. "You don't need to wait up for her."

"My daughter is out until all hours of the night." Mariska shifted her attention to Beverly. "How could I sleep?"

"Eight or twenty-eight, a mother worries about her children," Beverly agreed as she fished around her purse for her wallet. "More than one night, I remember pacing my living room until my Eleanor came home. Thank goodness she finally got married and settled down. Have I shown you pictures of my grandchildren?"

Only ten times, Tina wanted to say, but she didn't, of course. She simply smiled and nodded when Beverly whipped the pictures out with the speed of a policeman flashing a badge.

"Ah, so lucky you are." Mariska sighed with envy. "I fear I will never be a grandmother. Sophia is dating too many young men, Rachel spends all her time at the movies and museums, and my Tina—" Mariska tweaked Tina's cheek "—she is just a baby herself."

I'm twenty-four, for God's sake, Tina thought and gritted her teeth. Because she was the youngest, she knew her mother saw her as the baby and, no matter what her age, probably always would. But she supposed it made no difference, anyway. Tina knew she could never accept a proposal.

Any man who would actually *want* to marry into the Alexander family couldn't possibly be right in the head.

Not that she didn't love her family. Her two sisters, mother, father and Aunt Yana were the only family she had. She loved them with all her heart.

But they were all just so…overwhelming. Her father looked and acted more like he was in collections for a loan shark than a baker. With just a look, Ivan Alexander had scared off every man who'd come to date his daughters. The ones who'd managed to survive Ivan never made it past Mariska, who asked endless questions regarding their job status, their family lineage and the question that really sent them running—did they like children?

Tina figured the only way she'd ever be able to marry was if she were witness to a mob murder and testified, then put under the witness protection program. Then, by some miracle, if she found Mr. Right, he would never be able to meet her family.

A little extreme, but it just might work.

Tina helped the next customer while her mother continued to ooh and aah over the baby pictures. When Beverly finally left, Mariska slipped off her apron and reached for her purse.

"The chamber of commerce has ordered twelve dozen muffins and ten dozen Danish for a breakfast tomorrow," Mariska said, pulling her sweater out from under the counter. "I have to run to the market for pecans and blueberries."

Tina glanced at the two young men sitting at the corner table. "But you were supposed to interview the applicants."

"Be a good girl and do that for me, dear." Mariska patted Tina's cheek.

"But—"

"Oh, and we need you to come in early tomorrow," Mariska said. "We have a heavy load of orders in the morning. Your father and I could use your help."

It wasn't a question, so Tina didn't bother to answer.

"I will be back shortly." With a quick wave Mariska disappeared down the hallway leading to the offices and back exit.

Tina stared after her mother, then sighed. It wasn't as if it was a problem to come in to work early. The most exciting thing going on in her life this evening was apartment-sitting for her aunt Yana while she was out of town for the next three weeks. Tina's hot date for the night was a cat and a video copy of *Sleepless in Seattle*.

"Sorry I'm late, T." Sophia breezed through the front entrance of the bakery. "I stopped to gas my car and darn if I didn't break a nail, so I just had to run by and see my manicurist."

The two applicants took one look at Sophia dressed in her black leather skirt, low-cut sweater and tall boots, and they snapped to attention. Sophia, who'd just recently put highlights in her already-blond hair, smiled at the young men. They puffed their chests out and sucked their guts in.

Tina frowned at her sister when she came behind the counter and reached for a black apron. ''Must you torture every male you see?''

''I'm the one in torture,'' Sophia said smoothly. ''So many men, so little time.''

Tina rolled her eyes at her sister's foolishness. They were all so different. Sophia, the gorgeous green-eyed, blond man-eater; Rachel, the pretty, though timid, hazel-eyed brunette.

And then there's me, Tina thought.

Not blond like her mother, not dark like her father, but with her sandy-brown hair and light-brown eyes, somewhere in the middle, a mix of them both. She was the smart daughter, the level-headed daughter and—the label that Tina hated the most—the responsible daughter.

But what she really hated was the fact that it was true.

There was a crash from the kitchen, followed by a mumbled string of Hungarian curses. Sophia gnawed on her shiny, red bottom lip. ''Ah, I'll be right back. I've got to go ask Rachel something about, ah, reimbursement for petty cash.''

''Chicken,'' Tina said, but Sophia merely clucked as she hurried away.

Walking into her father's kitchen when he was in a foul mood was like entering a lion's den. You never knew if you'd come out alive.

With a lull in the storm, Tina knew she'd have to hurry and do the interviews before the lunch crowd flowed in. Slipping out of her black apron, she looked at Jason, who was ringing up an order for a cappuccino and a chocolate muffin.

The twenty-six-year-old counter clerk had a boyish charm about him: unruly dark-blond hair, deep-blue eyes, a lean, athletic build. Teenage girls and young women had a tendency to giggle and bat their eye-lashes when he waited on them, and even older women seemed flustered by the counter clerk's good looks.

But Jason, much to Tina's distress, had eyes for only one woman.

With a sigh, Tina forced her mind back on business and asked the applicant with the spiked hair to follow her down the hall to her father's office.

The sidewalks in front of the narrow, three-story red-brick building were damp from the previous night's rain. Over the wide, bevelled-glass storefront window, drops of water still clung to the forest-green awnings.

Reid stared past the For Lease sign and scanned the empty office space. The location and square footage were exactly what he'd been looking for, and the rent was in the ballpark. Public parking two doors down and heavy traffic only sweetened the deal.

And speaking of sweet—Reid glanced at the build-ing next door. The most incredible smells were coming from Ivan Alexander's bakery.

Based on the number of customers Reid had watched coming and going in the past few minutes, the business was doing very well. Housing his father's campaign headquarters next to the busy bakery would not only bring a lot of foot traffic, the staff and volunteers working the campaign would have easy access to food and drink.

By the end of the day Reid intended to have a lease signed and a key in his hand.

An overhead bell tinkled when he opened the oak-framed, bevelled-glass door of Castle Bakery. The scent of warm cinnamon, rich chocolate and freshly baked bread assaulted his senses. Reid glanced at the polished display cases of neatly stacked cookies, fancy cakes and assorted fruit pastries. His mouth literally watered. The place had an old world feel to it, he thought as he closed the door behind him. Stone floor, suit of armor in the corner, framed pictures of famous castles in Europe. Glass-topped tables with wrought-iron chairs allowed seating for customers, though currently only two of the tables were occupied: a man drinking a cup of coffee and munching on a muffin while he talked on his cell phone and a teenage boy reading a physics book.

Reid approached the counter and stood behind an elderly couple who couldn't make up their minds between prune Danish or apple tarts.

"Excuse me." Reid caught the counter clerk's attention. "I'm here about Mr. Alexander's ad for—"

"In the office—" the clerk raised a thumb toward a hallway "—third door on the left, across from Merlin."

Merlin? Reid followed the direction in which he'd been pointed and rounded the corner, then came face-to-face with a life-size statue of King Arthur's magician. Wand in hand, dressed in deep-blue velvet and wizard's hat, the whimsical, white-bearded figure greeted customers on their way to the rest rooms. Reid studied the realistic figure for a moment, then knocked on the office door.

"I'll be right with you."

The voice was distinctly female, Reid noted, and had a smooth, smoky quality. Fantasies, immediate and extremely erotic, pinballed in his brain. Reid hoped it wasn't Mrs. Alexander; he sure as hell didn't want to have the kind of thoughts he was having over another man's wife. Still, he couldn't wait to see if the voice matched the face.

Merlin seemed to glare at him.

"I'm only human," Reid said with a shrug, then folded his arms and leaned against the wall.

The door opened a moment later and a young man dressed in ragged jeans and a blue T-shirt that read, No Flash Photography, came out of the office.

"Hours suck," the guy muttered.

Lifting a brow, Reid watched him walk away, then turned back to the still-open door and stuck his head inside. A woman wearing a long-sleeved white blouse sat bent over a small, cluttered metal desk. Her sandy-brown ponytail cascaded down her long neck and skimmed one narrow shoulder. She held a pen between slender fingers while she made notes on a piece of paper.

"I was looking for—"

"One second." Her gaze still on her scribbling, she waved him in. "Would you mind closing the door, please?" Reid moved into the office and shut the door behind him. Because he couldn't quite see the woman's face, he studied her hands. Smooth skin. Nails short and neat. No polish, no rings.

"Before I have you fill out an application," she said without looking up, "I'd like to ask you—"

That's when her gaze lifted.

With the large-framed eyeglasses she wore, Reid might not have said that the woman was beautiful, but she was definitely pretty. Her skin was porcelain smooth over high cheekbones, her eyes wide and expressive, the color of smooth whiskey. Her lips, parted in midsentence, turned up slightly at the corners.

"—a few questions," she finished after a moment's hesitation.

Though it was brief, Reid saw the unshielded surprise in the woman's eyes, heard the breathless edge to her voice.

Just as quickly the moment was gone.

"I'm Tina Alexander." She straightened her shoulders and held out her hand. "Thank you for coming."

Tina's heart lurched when the man's large hand enclosed her own, and she struggled to hold on to her composure. She'd interviewed dozens of applicants before, but never one who looked quite like this.

And certainly none who'd made her brain cells turn to dust.

He was just over six foot, she assessed, and from what she could tell by the jeans, black crewneck sweater and denim jacket he wore, he was lean and muscular. *Handsome* was too easy a word to describe him, Tina thought. With his dark hair and good looks, he was more complicated than that simple word. Eyes so deep blue, so intense, that they had quite literally stolen her breath. Add to that a square jaw, a strong slash of brow and a firm mouth, and he had her pulse skipping.

Of course, the fact that her fingers were still enclosed in his wasn't helping, either.

She pulled her hand away and gestured to a chair on the other side of the desk. Though she was absolutely certain she'd never met this man before, he looked strangely familiar.

She shook the thought off. No matter. She couldn't possibly hire him, anyway. He would be too big a distraction for Sophia and, if she were going to be completely honest, for herself, as well.

But she could hardly tell him that, of course. Better to let him decide the position wouldn't be right for him. She'd start with a few basic questions, then discourage him with a job description.

"So, Mr.—" She hesitated, realizing she hadn't asked him his name.

"Reid Danforth," he finished for her. "Reid will be fine."

The name was familiar, too, she thought, but she couldn't place it. She wrote his name on the top line of the application.

"Reid." She pushed her glasses up with her index finger. "Do you have any problems getting to work on time or working early morning hours?"

Confusion furrowed his brow, and it took him a beat to answer. "Not usually."

"Do you have any medical conditions that prohibit you from lifting or doing physical labor?"

He narrowed his eyes. "No."

She made a note on the application that he was in good physical condition. As if she hadn't already noticed. Darn it, though. She'd been hoping for an easy way out.

She moved on to the next question. "Do you have any experience working in sales or with a cash register?"

He stared at her for a long moment, then one corner of his mouth slowly turned upward. It was really quite annoying what that casual half smile did to her stomach.

"I have some experience in sales," he said with a nod. "I've never worked a cash register, but I'm a fast learner."

I'm sure you are, Tina nearly said out loud. She also had no doubt that he would be quite good at sales. Lord knew she'd certainly want to buy something from him.

They hadn't talked about wages, she realized. Though the job was good pocket money for a teenager or college student, it was hardly enough for a more mature man to live on. "Is the hourly wage we advertised acceptable?"

To her discomfort, he leaned forward and leveled his gaze with hers. She caught the faint, spicy scent of his aftershave, and could hear her pulse beating in her ears.

"Let me just ask you this," he said, his voice smooth and deep and edged with amusement, "if I said the wage was irrelevant, would you hire me?"

Her first instinct was to say yes, but Tina knew it

would be wasting her time and his to give him false hope or continue this interview. "No."

"Why not?"

"Because—" she hesitated "—for one thing, you're...a little older than most of our applicants."

Irritation narrowed his eyes. "I'm too old for you?"

"Of course you're not too old for me," she said, then quickly tried to sidestep. "I mean, you're not too old." Oh, hell. She'd certainly gotten herself into a corner on this. There were laws against age discrimination. "It's just that we mostly hire teenagers and college students, that's all."

"You wouldn't hire me because I'm not a teenager or college student." He crossed his arms and looked down his nose at her. "So what else is wrong with me?"

"It's not that there's anything wrong with you." She chewed on her bottom lip. "Exactly."

He lifted a brow. "Exactly?"

"Well, there's also my sister, Sophia."

"What about her?"

"She is easily—" Tina searched for the right word "—distracted by good-looking men and vice versa."

"So you think I'm too old and too good-looking," he said dryly. "What else?"

When he repeated it all back, Tina knew it sounded absurd. She cursed herself for not having had him just fill out an application and leave. "You're overqualified."

"How do you know that?"

"You're obviously educated," she said. "You

speak well, exude confidence, and you look like you just stepped off the cover of *Fortune 500* or—"

It felt as if a lightbulb had flashed on.

Danforth. Of the Savannah Danforths. Shipping magnates. Big estate. Lots and lots of money. There'd been rumors that Abraham Danforth would be running for the Senate.

Everyone who lived in Savannah, and most everyone who didn't, had heard of the Danforth family.

Unable to speak, Tina continued to stare at Reid. That's why he looked so familiar. He *had* been on the cover of a magazine, *Savannah Business*. The issue Reid's face was on had been sitting in the customer magazine rack of the bakery for the past three months.

"You—" her voice was a ragged whisper "—you're...Abraham Danforth's..."

"Son," he finished for her, and stuck out his hand again. "Reid Danforth. I'm here to rent the building next door."

Two

Reid let the words hang between them while the woman digested her mistake. Her eyes had widened behind her glasses, and her cheeks bloomed a pretty shade of pink. She hadn't even released the breath she'd inhaled when she'd realized who he was.

He supposed he could make the situation easier by simply shrugging it off and assuring her there was no harm done. A simple misunderstanding. No big deal at all. It would certainly be the gentlemanly thing to do.

But, hell, it wouldn't be nearly as much fun.

He decided he would enjoy watching her squirm for a minute or two. Something told him that Tina Alexander was used to being composed and in control, and he rather liked the idea of ruffling this woman's feathers.

Especially after the crack about him being old. Dammit, thirty-two was not old!

But when she continued to stare at him with alarm in her eyes, he began to feel a little guilty. He just wanted to rattle her a bit, not humiliate her.

He opened his mouth with the intention of easing her embarrassment, but when the breath she'd been holding came rushing out like an icy snowstorm, he realized it wasn't embarrassment on her cheeks but annoyance.

"You knew perfectly well I was interviewing you for a job," she said tightly. "Why didn't you stop me?"

Well, well, he thought, raising a brow. The kitten definitely had her back up now.

"I suppose it was like watching a train wreck," he said with a half grin. "I just couldn't seem to tear myself away."

It was also refreshing not to be recognized, he realized. He'd always hated that people treated him differently when they knew he was a Danforth, either turned extremely helpful or absurdly friendly.

Though at this moment *friendly* would hardly be a word to describe Tina Alexander, Reid thought. The mouth he'd thought so soft only a moment ago now pressed into a thin line.

He wondered for one insane moment what those lips would feel like under his own.

"I'm glad I've given you a few minutes of entertainment." She crumpled the application under her fingers into a ball and tossed it into a trash can beside the desk. "Since you're obviously not here looking for a job, is there something else I can do for you?"

Well now, *that* was a leading question, Reid thought, but certainly not one he could honestly answer without getting thrown out of the office. "I'm here about the space next door."

She glanced up sharply. "What about it?"

"My real estate broker spoke to a man named Ivan Alexander about leasing it."

"Ivan is my father." Tina's eyes narrowed cautiously. "But there must be some mistake. That space isn't for lease."

"That's odd, since I was told to stop by today so I can look at the inside and pick up a key."

"But—" Her voice faltered, broke. "That can't be."

"I've already put a deposit down, Miss Alexander."

"A deposit?" she repeated, her cool tone now one of disbelief.

"My broker gave your father a check yesterday." Reid couldn't help but wonder why it should matter to Tina one way or the other who rented the space. "Is there a problem?"

Is there a problem? Tina stared at the man sitting across from her, felt a bubble of hysteria lodge in her throat. This can't be, she told herself. Surely her parents would have told her if they'd rented the space.

Her space.

But it was true. She knew it in her heart. Reid Danforth would not be sitting here if it weren't.

Slowly she slipped her reading glasses off, then

spread her hands on the desk and rose. "Will you excuse me a minute?"

Without waiting for him to answer, Tina walked stiffly from the room, then headed directly for the double doors of the kitchen entrance. Her father was bent over a work table, frosting the bottom layer of what was going to be a three-tier, whipped cream, strawberry shortcake.

Hands on her hips, she faced him. "How could you do this?"

"Very easy," he said without glancing up. "Slice the strawberries very thin and just the right amount of gelatine in the whip cream. Perfect every time."

"That's not what I mean and you know it." She snatched up the bowl of whipped cream sitting on the counter and held it away from him. "When the antique store moved out next door, you promised to rent the space to me."

"I make no promise." Frowning, he straightened and faced her, then folded his beefy arms over his wide chest. "I told you I think about it."

"It's a perfect spot for a sandwich and coffeehouse." She struggled to control her voice and her temper. "I poured my heart and soul into that project. Design plans for the interior, a prospectus, potential menus. You told me you were impressed."

He nodded. "I was."

"Then why?" Her voice trembled as she hugged the cold metal bowl close. "Why would you do this to me?"

"You are too young to open your own business,

Katina.'' His voice softened a bit. ''When you are older, we will talk.''

''Stop treating me like a child. I'm twenty-four,'' she said through clenched teeth. ''Me, Rachel, Sophia. We *are* older. Why can't you see that?''

''I am your *apa*,'' Ivan said firmly. ''It is my duty to take care of my family. We have only each other.''

''Dad.'' She struggled against tears. ''*Apa*. I've worked in this bakery with you since I was ten. You know I can do it.''

''It is too much money.''

''Aunt Yana is going to help—''

''This is not Yana's decision.'' Ivan's voice rose. ''My sister has the blood of the gypsies, running from city to city, country to country. What does she know about business and responsibility?''

''She's dedicated to her work,'' Tina defended her aunt. ''Just because she travels doesn't mean that—''

''Enough!'' He lifted a hand to silence her. ''It is done. I have rented the space for one year. We will talk again then.''

''But—''

''Be a good girl, Katina.'' Ivan patted Tina on her head. ''Now you will take Mr. Danforth next door and show him what he has paid for.''

''What?'' Her mouth dropped open. ''You expect me—''

''You will do as I say.'' He snatched the bowl of whipped cream from her arms. ''And you will be nice to this man. Do you understand?''

Tina opened her mouth to protest, then closed it again. She knew it was useless to argue at this point.

The deal with the Danforths had obviously been made. It was too late to change that, and if she pushed her father too far, he would never rent her the space.

And now she was supposed to be nice?

Setting her teeth, she marched back to the office. Outside the door she paused, then drew in a long, slow, calming breath. She'd already made a big enough fool of herself in front of Reid Danforth. She refused to add pathetic to his opinion of her, as well.

Certain her face might crack under the strain, she forced a smile and opened the door.

"Well," she said, breezing into the room and plucking a key from a hook beside the door. "It appears there was a wrinkle in our line of communication here, Mr. Danforth. When do you plan on moving in?"

"Tomorrow."

In spite of her determination to be calm, Tina felt her jaw go slack. "Tomorrow?"

"We're announcing my father's candidacy in a few days," he explained. "It's taken quite a while to find a space that meets our requirements, so I have to move quickly."

"I see." Regaining her composure, she nodded. "Well, shall we go have a look, then?"

The woman had certainly come back with a different attitude, Reid thought as he followed Tina into the hallway. She'd gone from Miss Tempest to Miss Hospitality in the space of about five minutes.

Not that he was buying her facade of serenity. Reid could see just a trace of tension in her eyes, hear the edge of stress in her silky-smooth voice. Under the surface of all that so-called calm, a storm was brewing.

No doubt about it, she intrigued him. Made him wonder what all that pent-up energy would be like in bed.

They stepped out the back door of the bakery into a lovely garden framed by high walls of aged brick and stucco. Lush ferns and plants surrounded stone benches, statues of smiling cherubs and a small rock pond.

"There's a private alley between the buildings," she said as they walked across the patio, her tone clipped and matter-of-fact.

She opened an iron gate and they stepped into the alley. Reid noted the wrought-iron stairs leading to the second and third levels above the space he'd rented. "Are the upper levels rented out?" he asked.

"My aunt's apartment is on the second floor and she has a photography studio on the third." They moved past the alley, stepped through a second gate into another garden. "She's traveling most of the time on shoots, if you're worried about her disturbing you."

As Reid followed Tina through the second garden to the back entrance of the building, he couldn't help but notice the sway of her slender hips and the fact that she had nice legs. Something told him that it wouldn't be Tina's aunt who would be disturbing him, he thought.

He forced his attention back to Tina, realized he'd missed part of what she'd been saying, something about the buildings being built in the early 1800s, then renovated in the 1970s.

Over the next year, there'd be numerous receptions

for donors and volunteers, Reid knew. For the smaller, more private gatherings, the brick patio, with its stone benches and two-tiered fountain, would be perfect. "Will I have use of the garden area?"

"Of course."

She moved to the bevelled-glass back door of the building and inserted the key into the lock. He watched her visibly square her shoulders and draw in a breath as she turned the knob.

The smell of fresh paint filled the cool and damp air inside the wide hallway they stepped into; Reid realized that the layout was very similar to the bakery's. The afternoon sun spilled in through the back door and glowed golden off the recently refinished hardwood floors. "The back half is split into two offices, a bath and a kitchen." Tina moved stiffly down the hallway. "The front half is one large room."

As they stepped into the front area of the building, Reid saw the longing in Tina's eyes as she glanced around the room. A sense of possessiveness, he thought. It suddenly dawned on him why she was upset.

"You wanted this space, didn't you?" he asked quietly. "For yourself."

She stilled at his words, then lifted her chin. "What I wanted is unimportant at this point." She held the key out to him. "The space is yours for one year. Congratulations."

"I'm sorry." He closed his hand around hers as he took the key. Her skin was soft and warm against his. "I didn't know."

"Would it have mattered to you if you had?"

"I wouldn't have changed my mind, if that's what you mean." They both knew he'd be lying if he said anything different. "What were you going to do with it?"

"Nothing that won't keep." Determination shone in her eyes as she glanced around the room. "For another year, anyway. Good luck to you and your father, Mr. Danforth."

When she tried to pull her hand from his, he held tight. Arching one brow, she leveled a questioning gaze at him.

"We are going to be neighbors, Tina," he said. "How 'bout you call me Reid?"

She cocked her head and studied him, and though he wouldn't exactly call it a smile, her mouth wasn't quite so firm, her eyes so cool.

"Good luck, Reid," she said with a nod, then added, "I'll be counting the days."

"So will I, Tina." He grinned at her, then released her hand. "So will I."

From the second-story window of her aunt's apartment, Tina watched the moving van—Miller's Home and Office Rental—pull out of the busy, early-evening traffic and slide into a parking space on the street directly below. A burly, bald-headed man carrying a clipboard and wearing lead-gray overalls stepped out of the van's cab, then disappeared into the first floor.

"Grass certainly doesn't grow under Reid Danforth's feet, does it, Delilah?" Tina said to the long-haired tabby currently winding its sleek, lithe body around her bare legs. "It's hardly been five hours

since I handed him a key, and here he is, bringing in
furniture.''

Damn him.

Logically, Tina knew she shouldn't blame Reid. It
was, after all, her parents' decision. But the fact was,
she wasn't feeling especially reasonable—or forgiving—at the moment. Besides, it was much easier to be
angry with a stranger than her mother and father.

Tina had made one last-ditch appeal to her mother
to reconsider leasing out the space to the Danforths,
but her effort had proven futile. Convinced that Abraham Danforth's campaign headquarters would be a
hotbed of handsome, wealthy bachelors, Mariska was
practically doing handstands.

And speaking of handsome, wealthy bachelors,
Tina's pulse jumped when Reid stepped out onto the
sidewalk with the burly man.

He'd stripped off the denim jacket he'd been wearing earlier, and looking at his wide shoulders and
thick-muscled arms under the T-shirt he wore, she
might have thought him one of the movers. When he
dropped one large hand on a lean, denim-clad hip and
gestured toward the doorway, her eyes traveled down-
ward over his tall, well-sculpted body, then back up
again.

She told herself the flutter in her stomach was hunger, not lust.

''Most mothers would warn their daughters about a
man like Reid Danforth,'' Tina huffed, then knelt
down and picked Delilah up in her arms. ''My mother
is already planning a wedding.''

Bored, Delilah twitched her whiskers.

Though she knew she shouldn't be peeping out the blinds, Tina watched Reid walk to the back of the van with the movers. In spite of herself, she couldn't help but admire the confidence that radiated from the man. His stance, his walk, the tilt of his head. Even now, in her mind, she could hear the steady, deep tone of his voice, could feel the firm grasp of his hand over hers.

And that smile, she thought. That smile should be banned from public display.

"All the more reason to stay away from the man," she said emphatically to Delilah. "He knows perfectly well the effect he has on women. I, for one, have no intention of encouraging his already inflated ego."

Still, Tina watched Reid glance at his wristwatch, she could look, couldn't she? As long as he didn't know she was looking, what was the harm?

That's when he glanced up.

With a gasp she jumped back, praying he hadn't been able to see her through the half-open blinds.

Darn it, darn it.

"That's what I get for being nosy," she told Delilah. "And you know what they say about curiosity."

As if annoyed by the comment, Delilah jumped from Tina's arms and strode away with a flick of her pretty tail.

"It's just an expression," Tina called after the cat. "No need to be waspish about it."

Resisting the urge to creep back to the window again, Tina headed for the bathroom, stripped off her work clothes and stepped into the shower. It felt good to let the hot water pound on her shoulders and neck. Slowly, her tension from the day eased.

A year, she told herself. Surely she could manage twelve short months. Fifty-two weeks. She smiled, remembering the look on Reid's face when she'd told him she'd be counting the days. When he'd looked her in the eye and told her he'd be counting them, too, she'd almost felt as if it were a challenge.

God help her, she couldn't resist a challenge.

Yes, you will resist, her mind yelled at her. Determined that she'd spent enough brain space on the man, Tina stuck her head under the spray of water. The time would pass quickly enough. Before she knew it, the man would be out, and she would be in.

The thought lightened her mood immensely.

After she toweled off and passed a blow dryer over her hair, she slipped into a pair of jeans, a pink cotton T-shirt and, because she was going out this evening, a bra. Dinner and a movie with Rachel would take her mind off Reid, Tina told herself.

She found a black leather ankle boot under the end table beside the sofa and was searching for its mate when she heard the sound of muffled voices drifting up from a floor vent. She could almost make out what the men were saying. Was that Reid's voice, too? she wondered, then got down on her hands and knees and listened. They were saying something about turning the desk at an angle.

It was utterly rude to be eavesdropping, of course, and she started to move away until she heard a deep voice say something about the blond babe at the bakery. They were talking about Sophia, Tina knew, but when the man made a crude comment and the rest of the men laughed, Tina gasped.

How dare they talk about her sister like that!

''Hey—'' she shouted into the vent ''—you down there. That's right, I'm talking to you.''

She waited a beat to get their attention, but before she could say anything else, she heard Rachel's voice behind her.

''Tina, what on earth are you doing?''

Startled, she slammed the top of her head on the end table and swore. Rubbing her head, she crawled out backward. ''Rachel, for heaven's sake,'' Tina said, glancing over her shoulder, ''you could at least—''

She froze.

Standing next to Rachel, his brow lifted and a smirk on his face, was Reid Danforth.

Please let this be a dream, was her first thought, the next one was to compose herself as quickly as possible.

''—help me look for my shoe,'' she finished her sentence, though that wasn't what she'd been about to say.

When Reid's gaze drifted down and lingered a moment on her behind, Tina scrambled to her feet.

Why should she be embarrassed he'd caught her on all fours, yelling like a crazy woman down an air vent? He'd invaded her space—again—and she could act any way she wanted. What this man thought about her didn't matter in the slightest.

''Mr. Danforth needs the key to the service panel,'' Rachel said awkwardly.

''Reid,'' he corrected Rachel, then smiled.

Rachel blushed and glanced away.

Tina was certain she could bean him with her boot at ten paces and wipe that smile off his face.

"I'm not sure, but I think it's in the kitchen somewhere." Tina hooked an arm through her sister's and smiled. "Rachel, why don't you help me look?"

"I—" Rachel blinked, then met Tina's glare and nodded. "Ah, okay."

When they rounded the corner and were out of sight from Reid, Tina dragged her sister to the laundry room on the opposite side of the kitchen and closed the door. "Why didn't you warn me?"

Rachel furrowed her brow. "Warn you about what?"

"That you were bringing him here," Tina hissed.

"I actually did call, but you didn't answer the phone." Rachel chewed on her bottom lip. "I'm so sorry, T. Did I do something wrong?"

Shame had Tina releasing the tight grip on her sister's arm. "I'm sorry, Rach," she said with a sigh. "I'm just a little upset over losing the space downstairs, that's all. It makes me crazy that Dad and Mom both treat me like a child."

"At least our mother isn't constantly looking to find you a husband, a man that she approves of." Rachel's eyes filled with tears. "Why can't I marry the man I want?"

"You can and you will," Tina said firmly.

"I'm not strong like you," Rachel said quietly. "Or independent like Sophia. I don't know how to say no."

"Then you'll learn." Tina hugged her sister. "We'll go out tonight and work on a—"

Rachel shook her head and stepped away. "I can't go out tonight, T."

"Rachel, if this is because of—"

"I don't want to talk about it." Rachel put up a hand and shook her head. "Please."

"Rachel, please, don't—"

"I've got to go." Rachel wiped away a tear, then opened the door and hurried out of the laundry room.

Frustrated, Tina started to follow, then realized she still had Reid standing in the living room. The key, she remembered. He'd come here for a key to the service box.

She pulled the key from a hook inside the laundry room, drew in a slow breath to steady her nerves, then returned to the living room.

She found him studying the wall where several of her aunt's personal photographs were displayed. Purring loudly, Delilah was weaving her way in and out of Reid's legs. Hussy, Tina thought and frowned at her aunt's cat.

"These pictures are amazing," Reid said when Tina walked into the room. "Your aunt has quite a gift for capturing a mood."

"She's extremely talented." To Delilah's annoyance, Tina scooped the cat up and dropped her on the sofa. "She just had a book of her work published."

"Any of these?"

Tina shook her head. "These are personal. Mostly of my family."

"I like this one of you sitting by the pond reading

a book,'' he said, pointing to a black-and-white photo. ''How old were you?''

It embarrassed her a little, felt strangely intimate looking at photographs of herself with a man she barely knew. Especially Yana's pictures, which seemed to capture the very soul of a person.

''Eighteen, I think.'' She shrugged. ''It was a candid shot, taken with a telephoto lens from my aunt's studio. She's always sneaking around taking pictures of the family when we're not looking. It drives us crazy.''

To distract him, she pointed to another picture. ''That's my aunt.''

''She's a beautiful woman.''

With her dark hair and exotic looks, Yana Alexander, even at forty-eight, could still make men forget their own names and stumble over their feet.

''She was in Spain at the time, photographing bull fighters,'' Tina said. ''One of the toreadors took her camera and shot this picture of her.''

The man had also been her aunt's lover, Tina knew, but she didn't think she needed to mention that.

''I see a resemblance,'' Reid said thoughtfully.

It was all she could do not to roll her eyes. She had to give it to him. He was smooth as glass. ''I don't look anything like my aunt, Mr. Danforth.''

''You have her eyes.'' He turned to study her face. ''And her mouth.''

Tina felt her pulse shudder when his gaze lingered on her mouth. *Very smooth.* It irritated her to no end that she was not immune to the man's charm. But, in all fairness to herself, Reid Danforth was certainly not your average man. He was a prime male specimen, with just enough of an edge to make him a touch mysterious.

Working at the bakery, she came into contact with a lot of the local businessmen. Occasionally there'd be an exchange of harmless flirting or innocent banter. She'd even dated a couple of the men. She'd never thought it a big deal or wanted to take it any further.

With Reid, though, something told her it wouldn't be quite so innocent or harmless. Warning flags were waving in her head, signaling her to take another road.

Still, she thought, lifting a brow and meeting his steady gaze, as long as she didn't lose touch with reality—reality being the fact that there was no chance of any kind of relationship between them—then she had no reason to worry. She could hold her own against the likes of Reid Danforth.

She held out the key in her hand. "I believe you came here for this."

"Are you hungry?"

"What?"

"Are you hungry?" he repeated. "I'm going to grab a burger down the street."

Not only smooth, she thought in disbelief, but he moved fast.

But then, she already knew that.

"I made plans." The fact that they'd been changed were none of his business. "But thanks, anyway."

One corner of his mouth tilted up, then he took the key and nodded. "See you tomorrow, T."

She frowned at the closed door after Reid left. How did he know her nickname? Unless…

She glanced at the vent beside the sofa. It *did* back up to the laundry room, she realized. On a groan, she closed her eyes. Had he heard her conversation with Rachel? If he had, then he knew she'd been lying about having plans.

Well, so what if he had? She crossed her arms and pressed her lips together. It wouldn't hurt the man to find out that there might be a few women left in Savannah who weren't completely taken in by that damn smile of his. You're being ridiculous, she told herself. He'd asked her to get a burger with him. That was hardly what anyone would call a date, for heaven's sake.

She knew she was overreacting and decided that was another reason to keep her distance. She'd known him less than a day, and already he'd seriously slanted her equilibrium.

But as she moved past an oval, wood-framed mirror on the wall, she stopped and looked at herself. Her eyes, then her mouth.

Just for a second she wondered.

Oh, for heaven's sake. She shook her head and frowned.

"Idiot," she said out loud, and wasn't certain if she was speaking to herself or Reid.

Three

A cup of coffee in his hand, Reid stepped out of his car the next morning and breathed in the titillating smells wafting on the cool, predawn air. Though the lights were not yet on in the bakery or the Open sign in the window, it was obvious that while most of the city was still sleeping, Ivan Alexander was busy baking for the day ahead.

On the deserted sidewalk, Reid paused and glanced up at Tina's apartment. A soft light edged the closed blinds, and he wondered if she'd already left for work or if she was still up there.

He had an odd feeling that she was.

It was strange, but he'd had the same feeling yesterday, when he'd been standing on the sidewalk with the furniture rental people. The blinds had been partially open, and though he hadn't actually seen her, he'd felt her. Sort of a prickling sensation at the base of his neck.

Weird, he thought, then laughed at himself.

Letting himself in the front door, he flipped on the overhead lights and glanced around. The movers had brought in ten desks yesterday, plus filing cabinets and tables. Phones lines would be hooked up this morning and computers would be installed in the early afternoon. He had set up two private offices in the back, one for himself and one for Nicola. Since she was his father's campaign manager, she'd be the one running the show.

Hands on his hips, he stood in the middle of the room that would soon be filled with volunteers and family and he listened to the absolute quiet.

A floorboard creaked above his head and he looked up, followed the sound across the ceiling. So she *was* upstairs. Leaning back against a desk, he sipped on his coffee and stared at the ceiling.

Had she just gotten out of bed? he wondered. An image of tangled sheets, tousled, golden-brown hair and sleepy eyes came to his mind.

His blood stirred at the thought.

Was she the cotton pajama or silk nightie type? Or maybe, he thought with a smile, she slept in the buff.

That thought stirred more than his blood.

Maybe it was for the best that she'd turned down his offer to get something to eat last night. The woman was a distraction, something he didn't need right now. Something he didn't want.

Still, he thought, listening to the sound of her moving around upstairs, a guy could dream, couldn't he? He took another swig of coffee. No harm in that.

Movement on the sidewalk outside the front window caught Reid's attention. A man who looked familiar hurried past, and Reid recognized him as one of the counter clerks from the bakery. The guy with the blond ponytail. A moment later the sound of a door buzzer filtered down through the vent upstairs. The man hadn't gone to the bakery, Reid realized. He'd gone upstairs.

Reid frowned. A little early to come visiting, wasn't it?

He heard the sound of footsteps moving to the door, muffled voices, then movement again toward—Reid furrowed his brow to remember the layout of the apartment—the sofa, he guessed. Or the bedroom?

Pushing away from the desk, Reid moved closer to the vent and listened. Though it was hard to hear everything, he could distinguish between Tina's voice and the man's, and was able to catch snippets of what they were saying.

"I can't go on like this..." Man's voice.

Tina's voice. "Jason, please be patient and I'm sure we can..."

Man's voice again. "...been patient and nothing has changed..."

Heavy footsteps started, back and forth across the ceiling. The man—Jason—was obviously pacing.

"...a solution," Tina said. "I promise."

Reid concentrated, trying to hear more than bits and pieces of the conversation. He wanted to yell up at them to talk louder.

"I'm going to tell them," Jason said, the frustration heavy in his voice. "We're in love. They'll have to accept it."

Reid went still. Tina and the counter clerk? In love?

The vent was too high to get any closer. He considered dragging a desk chair over and standing on it, but that was a little extreme. Besides, it might be a little difficult to explain if someone saw him with his ear pressed up to the vent.

"…to get to work now," Jason said. "…not giving up."

Footsteps moved back toward the door, then silence.

Confused, Reid stared at the vent for a long moment. He didn't know what, but something wasn't quite on the mark here.

You heard what you heard, pal, a voice in his head said. *Let it go.*

Still…

Oh, hell. He shook his head, wondered why he was having such a difficult time believing that Tina was in love with the bakery clerk. Because of something he'd thought he'd seen in her eyes yesterday? Because of something he'd thought he'd felt when he'd taken her hand in his?

Frowning, he downed the rest of his coffee and crumpled the paper cup in his hand. Maybe it was because he didn't want to believe it. Because he had designs on her himself.

But if she'd been so in love with this guy, then why hadn't she simply said she was seeing someone when he'd asked her out? Reid knew he hadn't exactly been subtle letting her know he was interested.

Who the hell could figure women out? he thought, dragging a hand through his hair. He should be glad she was involved with someone else. He'd known her one day, and already she'd occupied way too much of his brain space. He had a hundred things to do if he was going to have this office up and running by tomorrow. Not one of those things involved a pretty, golden-eyed temptress whose image had kept him awake half the night.

Tossing his crumpled cup into a trash can, he headed for the back office to unload the dozen or so boxes of office supplies that had been delivered yesterday afternoon.

Suddenly, the day—the year—stretching out ahead of him seemed very long, and very boring, indeed.

That entire morning the bell over the bakery door never stopped ringing. Currently a line of customers stretched six deep. Nearly every table and chair were occupied. It wasn't even eleven, Tina realized, and the muffins were gone, the Danish nearly depleted and only a few loaves of bread remained on the shelves.

But still, the biggest seller for the morning at Castle Bakery wasn't baked goods or even the coffee bar, Tina noted while she crammed blue icing into a pastry bag.

It was gossip.

"Mariska Alexander, I declare, y'all must be dizzy with delight." Sharie Jo Sullivan pressed a bag of chocolate *rugala* to her chest, then glanced at her sister, Louzanna. "Imagine, Lulu, right next door to Abraham Danforth's campaign headquarters."

"The *Savannah Morning* calls him Honest Abe II."
Louzanna handed three bills to Mariska, then dug in
her coin purse. "I hear he intends to run a clean, scan-
dal-free campaign."

"What do I know about politics?" Mariska said
with indifference. "They will be good tenants. Anything else is of no interest to me."

Louzanna lifted a dubious brow. "And I suppose
the fact that Abraham's sons and nephews and all
those other eligible bachelors gathered in one place,
no more than a few yards from here, doesn't interest
you, either."

Mariska shrugged, then slowly smiled and leaned
across the counter. "Like fish in a barrel," she said,
wiggling her eyebrows.

The women all laughed.

Tina's grip tightened on the pastry bag, and blue
icing exploded onto the middle of the sheet cake she'd
just frosted. Gritting her teeth, she reached for a knife
to scrape off the errant icing.

"We saw Rachel talking with Reid Danforth on the
sidewalk last night," Sharie Jo whispered. "*After* the
bakery was closed."

Tina glanced over to the coffee bar where Jason was
steaming milk for a latte. Every time Reid's name had
been mentioned this morning—which had been numerous times—Jason's eye had started to twitch. She
wanted to tell him that Reid was no threat to him, but
she knew Jason wouldn't believe her. Especially now,
after listening to the female customers expound on the
Danforth attributes.

Tina could only hope that the novelty would wear

off after a few days and the gossipmongers would find something—or someone—else to occupy their minds. But considering the high profile of the Danforth company, Tina seriously doubted that was going to happen anytime soon. While her mother, Sharie Jo and Louzanna prattled on, Tina forced her attention back to writing ''Happy Birthday, Randy'' on her cake, determined not to let their conversation bother her.

''All those eligible bachelors,'' Louzanna said with a sigh. ''Ah, if only I was ten years younger.''

Sharie Jo rolled her eyes. ''Then you'd still be ten years too old.''

''Don't be sassy, Sharie Jo,'' Louzanna said with a sniff, then tucked an imaginary loose strand of blond hair behind her ear. ''Besides I wasn't thinking of the younger Danforth men, I was talking about Abraham.'' Her eyes took on a dreamy quality. ''A handsome widow in his fifties. Surely the man must be lonely.''

''Don't kid yourself, Lulu,'' Sharie Jo said. ''Rich, powerful, handsome men are never lonely. Bored, maybe. Lonely, no.''

In the middle of writing the *t* in birthday, Tina went still. Is that why Reid had asked her out last night? she wondered. Because he was bored? To say that she was different from the women he usually dated was probably the understatement of the century. Blue-blooded Savannah socialites and debutantes were more up his alley. Women with names like Caroline or Blair or—what was the name of the woman in the magazine article she'd plucked from the magazine rack and read this morning? Oh, yeah. She curled one corner of her lip. Mitzi.

Like Sharie Jo said, rich, handsome, powerful men were never lonely. Reid had probably dated dozens of women. Tina shrugged a shoulder, annoyed that she was wasting brain space wondering about the man's love life. Who Reid Danforth did or didn't date certainly had no bearing on her life. They were neighbors for the next year, that was all.

After he'd left her apartment last night, she'd seen him walk across the street and order a pizza at D'mores. Later in the evening, long after she'd gone to bed, she'd heard him working downstairs. She'd done her best to concentrate on the mystery novel she'd been reading, but her mind had kept wandering, wondering what he was doing.

Wondering what might have happened if she had gone out with him.

"Maybe I would have been the one bored," she muttered out loud.

"Did you say something, Katina?" Mariska glanced over.

"No," she said quickly. "Nothing at all."

When her mother turned back to her customers, Tina shook her head at her foolishness. She doubted Reid even remembered her name today, and here she was, talking to herself about the man.

Determined not to let thoughts of Reid Danforth distract her further, she finished the *y* in Randy, then looked at her work.

Happy Birtday, Randy.

Birtday?

So much for her determination not to be distracted.

Scowling, she reached for the knife again to fix her mistake, then added more white frosting to smooth the top of the cake. Completely focused now, she grabbed the pastry bag and concentrated on her work.

When every letter was perfect, Tina gave a satisfied nod. Lifting the pastry bag to dot the *i*, she happened to glance over as Reid walked in the door.

His gaze met hers and held, and though it was only for a moment, it felt like minutes. Hours. If a fire had broken out and she was surrounded by flames, she couldn't have moved.

When one corner of his mouth lifted, her heart did a somersault, her hand tightened.

And blue icing oozed all over her cake.

Chastising herself, she looked away. Darn it! She'd been so proud of herself that she'd managed to resist the man's charm, then he walks in the door with that you-want-me-you-know-you-do grin, and suddenly she can't breathe? How did he do that? she thought irritably.

Every head had turned. Conversation had died. When he walked through the crowd, it was like some-one had rolled out a red carpet. And when he flashed that smile on the women in the bakery, they all but swooned.

He owned the room, Tina realized. His confidence, his demeanor, his presence. And his looks, she thought, appreciating the stretch of broad shoulders under his black polo shirt and the low slung worn jeans across lean hips and long legs. A woman didn't stand a chance.

Well, except her, of course.

It took all of five seconds for the bakery to erupt into chaos and converge on Reid, another forty-five seconds for Tina's mother to come around the counter and push her way through the crowd like a linebacker at the Super Bowl.

"Let the man sit." Mariska shooed everyone away. "Jason, bring our new neighbor a cup of coffee."

When Jason mumbled something under his breath, Tina shot him a warning glance. Nothing but trouble and heartache would come from any kind of public confrontation between the two men. A scowl on his face, Jason turned away, certainly not appeased, but for the moment, at least, contained.

"Thank you." Reid plucked a ticket from the number machine. "But I can wait my turn."

"Of course you will not wait," Mariska said and everyone who still had tickets in their hand nodded their approval. "Latte, cappuccino, espresso?"

Tina rolled her eyes, surprised her mother didn't add, *my daughter's hand in marriage?*

"Black would be great," Reid said. "But—"

"We have strudel still warm from the oven." Mariska didn't give Reid a chance to protest as she pulled him to a chair. "Tina, a slice of strudel for Mr. Danforth. And a nice apricot *rugala.*"

"Please, call me Reid," he said to Mariska, then looked at Tina with a grin that clearly said he was enjoying himself. "I really don't want to be any trouble."

"It is no trouble," Mariska said cheerfully. "Is it, Katina?"

Though it hurt, Tina smiled. "No, of course not. No trouble at all."

"So tell me." Mariska sat in the chair beside Reid. "Will your wife be helping you with the campaign?"

Oh, for heaven's sake. Tina turned to slice the strudel. Her mother couldn't have been less subtle if she'd pulled out a calendar and asked him what day he was available to plan a small wedding for four or five hundred.

"I don't have a wife," Reid said. "But I'm certainly looking for volunteers."

Tina's head shot up. Every female in the room drew in a breath.

But before Mariska—or any of the other women in the room—could offer their services, Reid said, "To help with the campaign, of course."

Disappointment rippled through the bakery.

"Ah." Mariska's shoulders sagged, then straightened again as she smiled brightly. "My daughters will help," she said with enthusiasm. "We are all big supporters, you know."

What! Since when were they supporters of any political campaign? Tina stared at her mother in horror.

"That's very generous of you, Mrs. Alexander." Reid slid a glance at Tina. "But maybe you should ask your daughters how they feel about that."

"Sophia and Rachel will be happy to volunteer," Mariska said, waving a don't-be-silly hand at him. Then she added as an afterthought, "And my Tina, of course."

Tina clenched her jaw at the murmurs and nods from the customers who weren't even pretending not to listen. It wasn't bad enough she'd lost out on her restaurant to Reid and his family, now she was supposed to *help* them? She had to stop her mother before this got out of hand. Snatching up the plate of strudel and the cup of coffee Jason had poured, Tina hurried over to the table.

"Mom," she said as sweetly as she could muster. "I'm sure Mr. Danforth is looking for volunteers with some political knowledge."

"Not at all." Leaning back in his chair, Reid glanced up at her. "We're having a volunteer welcome gathering tomorrow night at seven-thirty. Why don't you and your sisters come by?"

Tina opened her mouth to say she was busy, but her mother was much too fast.

"They will be there. We will all be there," Mariska said firmly. "I will bring cookies and *rugala.*"

When Mariska rose, Reid stood, as well, smiling as he extended his hand. "Thank you, Mrs. Alexander. You are an extremely generous woman."

When Reid smiled, Mariska's cheeks bloomed red and she giggled. Tina's jaw went slack. Her mother never blushed, and she most certainly did not giggle. Disgusted, Tina watched her mother hurry back into the kitchen.

Did all the Danforth men have the ability to make women act and feel stupid? she wondered, glancing back at Reid. If they did, Tina could only hope that one day some brilliant female scientist would be able to isolate that gene and come up with a vaccination.

She'd be first in line.

''Your strudel,'' she said tightly, sliding the plate onto the table and setting the coffee beside it.

''Thanks.''

''Don't mention it.''

When she turned, he surprised her by reaching for her arm. *Darn it.* There it was again. That jolt of electricity. She looked at him, prayed he couldn't feel it, too. Prayed that he couldn't see the effect he had on her. With so many people watching, it would really be embarrassing if she swooned.

''Here.'' He took her hand and laid a key in her palm. ''I had a copy made.''

To anyone watching it was a completely innocent exchange. To Tina it felt personal. The touch of his fingertips on her skin, the press of the key in her palm. The almost imperceptible lingering of his hand against her own.

She closed her fingers tightly around the key and pulled her hand away. ''Thanks.''

''Till tomorrow, then,'' he said with a nod.

''Right. Tomorrow.'' When she turned and walked away, she could have sworn she heard him chuckle.

She hoped he choked on the strudel.

Lying on his back under the desk, Reid struggled to wiggle the printer cable into the back of the computer. If he'd had another inch of cable, along with another inch of space to reach into, he would have been done ten minutes ago.

But that would have been easy, he thought irritably. And after the morning he'd had, why should he expect his afternoon to be any better?

He'd scraped his knuckles changing a flat tire, dropped a cup of coffee on the press release he'd told Nicola he'd fax to the *Savannah Morning News,* misplaced the sign-in book for the orientation tonight and just five minutes ago, reaching blindly into the back of the desk, drove a splinter the size of a screwdriver under his thumbnail.

It still hurt like hell, dammit.

But what really aggravated him the most, what really set his teeth on edge, was the slender, curvy, sassy-mouthed woman he couldn't get out of his mind.

What was it about Tina Alexander that had him tied up in knots? he wondered. With her velvet, amber-brown eyes, heart-shaped face and turned-up nose she was pretty, but not necessarily what most men would consider beautiful. She was average height, a little thin for his taste and icy as an Arctic breeze.

Damn if he didn't want to get his hands on her.

It was as if she'd gone out of her way to alienate him, and perhaps that was what intrigued him the most. But he wasn't stupid, and he certainly wasn't blind. He'd seen the way she'd reacted every time he'd touched her. He'd felt her shiver, watched her eyes widen. Something told him that under that cool exterior was heat and plenty of it.

Damn if he didn't want to taste that heat.

When the cable slipped from his fingers for the tenth time in fifteen minutes, he swore like a truck driver in a skid, then narrowed his eyes and threaded the cable through the hole in the wall of the desk again. He'd be damned if he'd let a stubborn printer cable—or woman—make him lose control.

When the cable plug finally dropped over the inlet, Reid smiled, grabbed his bottom lip between his teeth while he wiggled the cable into place…

"Hello?"

At the sound of the feminine greeting, Reid sat up sharply and slammed the top of his head on the underside of the desk. He wasn't certain if the crack he heard was wood or his skull.

Dammit, dammit, dammit…

Through the stars swimming in his blurred vision, Reid watched a pair of shapely legs appear from around the corner of the desk.

"Sorry if I startled you." Tina peered down at him. "You okay?"

Grunting, he pulled himself from under the desk, winced at the rocket of pain that shot through his brain when he sat. "Sure. I slam my head into desks every day just for fun."

His sarcasm earned him a smile. She dropped down on her knees and leaned close. "Here, let me look."

"I'm fine." When she reached out and took his head in her hands, his heart slammed against his ribs.

"I don't see any blood," she said, gently sliding her fingers through his hair.

That's because it's all dropped to the lower half of my body, Reid wanted to say, but wasn't willing to risk her letting go of him just yet.

His head tingled; heat rushed through his veins. He'd never felt anything like it before. Maybe I'm hallucinating, he thought. Or maybe he'd knocked himself out and this was one hell of an erotic dream.

If so, he didn't want to wake up.

"Where does it hurt?" she asked.

Her fingernails lightly brushed over his scalp, and Reid's throat turned to dust. He doubted he'd be able to speak if he tried, so he simply pointed.

"I did knock," she said, softly touching the area he'd indicated. "I guess you didn't hear me."

He could barely hear her now, through the buzzing in his head.

"The door was open," she went on when he didn't respond. "I thought maybe you were in the back."

When her fingertips moved in a soothing, circular motion, Reid bit back a groan. Less than a foot separated their bodies; the press of her breasts against the white blouse she wore made it difficult to breathe, let alone think.

Surely the torture this woman was putting him through had to be some kind of karmic payback for something he'd done in his life, Reid thought. Some wrong he'd caused someone. The sweet scent of her—a mix of vanilla and cinnamon—the soft, incredibly erotic touch of her hands, the seductive, provocative tone of her voice. It was all he could do not to drag her in his arms, right here under this desk, on this dusty floor, to taste her, to shove her skirt up those long, slender legs until he touched warm, soft flesh and—

Gritting his teeth, he clamped his hands around her wrists. He didn't pull her to him. He didn't push her away.

Her eyes widened; her lips parted with surprise. She didn't move.

He held her gaze with his own. Slowly, his intent clear, he tugged her closer…closer….

When his mouth touched hers, he watched her lashes flutter down, felt the release of her breath on his cheek. Her lips were soft as rose petals. He nibbled, cautiously, lightly, eager to taste her more fully. And while she didn't respond, she didn't pull away, either.

It was all the encouragement he needed.

He deepened the kiss, though just barely, tracing her bottom lip with his tongue. Sweet, he thought. Unbelievably, seductively sweet.

He wasn't at all surprised at the need coursing through his body; he'd been attracted to her from the beginning, had wanted this since he'd laid eyes on her. Nor was he surprised by her response. He'd sensed her attraction to him, as well.

What surprised—no, annoyed—him was the unexpected, niggling question chipping away at the edge of his desire.

"What would Jason think about this?" he murmured the words, cursed himself for wanting to know.

She stilled, then her eyes slowly opened. "Jason?"

"Yeah," he said dryly. "Remember him?"

Confusion furrowed her brow, then suspicion. "What do you know about Jason?"

"Not much." Obviously, she didn't appreciate being reminded that she and Jason were an item while she was kissing another man, Reid thought irritably. "I was hoping you would tell me."

It was fascinating, as well as frustrating, to watch the heat in Tina's eyes turn to ice. With a regal lift of her chin, she pulled back, then stood and smoothed the front of her skirt. ''I was sent over here to find out how many people to expect this evening.''

''Look, I'm sorry.'' Reid stood, reached for her arm, but she yanked it away. ''I shouldn't have—''

''Fifty?'' she said coolly. ''A hundred?''

''Around fifty.'' He dragged a hand through his hair, was instantly reminded of the bump he'd taken. ''Tina, dammit, I know it's none of my business, I—''

''You got that right, mister,'' she said, tossing her hair back over her shoulders. ''Now if you'll excuse me, I really need to get back to work.''

Reid watched her turn on her heel and march stiffly out the door.

''Smooth, Danforth,'' he muttered. ''Real smooth.''

Resting a hip on the desk, Reid stared at the door Tina had just disappeared through. It would be easier to just let it go, he told himself, to forget about her and keep his mind completely focused on his work.

But, he thought, smiling slowly, remembering the feel of her mouth against his, it wouldn't be nearly as interesting.

Four

Tina didn't make it to the alley before her knees buckled. Struggling to breathe, she stumbled around the corner of the passageway between the buildings and leaned against the wall.

Reid had kissed her.

She'd kissed him back.

Closing her eyes, she laid her head against the cool bricks. A groan rolled deep in her throat.

And what a kiss.

Her lips still tingled, her head still reeled, her pulse raced. She glanced down at the tips of her shoes to see if smoke was rising.

She'd certainly been kissed before, she wasn't completely inexperienced with men. But she'd never been kissed like that. Never been so overwhelmed. And if he hadn't asked her that ridiculous question about Jason, she'd probably be rolling around on the floor with Reid at this very moment.

The thought made her cheeks burn.

She wasn't certain if she was glad that they'd stopped before things heated up even more, or if she was irritated.

Of course I'm glad, she thought, narrowing her eyes. Deliriously glad.

She touched her mouth. She could still taste him there, could still feel the press of his mouth on hers. An involuntary shudder coursed through her, and she knew she'd be lying if she didn't at least admit she'd been curious. And maybe, at an unconscious level, she'd actually *wanted* him to kiss her. After all, she *had* been the one who'd touched him first. He must have thought she'd been asking—begging—for it, the way she'd put her hands on his head, then combed her fingers through his hair and lightly stroked his head.

Remembering the soft, thick texture of his hair sliding through her fingers and the touch of his scalp under her fingernails sent a wave of heat shimmering over her skin. She still couldn't believe she'd done something so...*intimate.*

Couldn't believe her fingers itched to do it again.

A welcome breeze rippled through the alley, cooling her blood and her skin, finally bringing her overloaded senses back to a manageable level. Once again, reason prevailed.

You're making too big a deal about this, she told herself. Men like Reid kissed women all the time. It didn't mean anything to him, for heaven's sake, and it shouldn't mean anything to her, either.

"It doesn't," she said, needing to hear herself say it out loud. Reid had caught her off guard, that was all. In the future, she'd be more careful around him.

She'd also have to warn Jason to be more careful, she realized. If her parents found out about him—Tina shuddered at the thought—there would be hell to pay.

But there was no reason for them to find out, she told herself. Reid didn't know anything. He'd been fishing, and he'd come up with an empty hook.

She intended to keep it that way.

At seven forty-five that evening, Abraham Danforth's campaign headquarters had officially been open for fifteen minutes. The scent of fresh-brewed coffee and still-warm cookies wafted through the already crowded room. Music, upbeat instrumentals meant more to inspire than entertain, flowed from an overhead sound system, but could barely be heard over the excited conversations of volunteers and newly hired campaign staff. Because the man of the hour hadn't arrived yet, anticipation increased with each passing minute.

Reid, arms folded, leaning against the back wall of the room, watched the activity buzzing around him. His family was scattered throughout the room: Kimberly sat at a guest book table; Adam manned the volunteer schedule; his cousin Jake was currently charming Matilda Henning, the president of the Savannah Women's Historical League. Nicola Granville, wearing an Honest Abe II campaign button on the lapel of her navy blue blazer and a straw Danforth for Senator hat tucked neatly over her red hair, made her way through the throng of people and personally greeted each and every one of them.

Abraham might be the heart of the campaign, but the volunteers were the lifeblood. Without them, no amount of publicity or money could win an election.

But there was really only one volunteer—albeit a reluctant one—that had caught Reid's attention and he shifted his gaze to Tina.

Wearing tan linen slacks and a black turtleneck, she stood by the refreshment table with Jason, a cup of punch in her hand, listening politely to an animated, balding man dressed in an oversize gray suit. She appeared cool and composed and even interested in what the man was saying to her, but when he turned away from her to grab another cookie from a tray, Tina's boredom flashed in her eyes.

Reid smiled, even considered saving her. It would be easy to make his way over there and tell her she had a phone call in the back office. But he wasn't so sure she would appreciate the gesture, not with Jason standing there, and especially not after what had happened between them this afternoon.

Not that he was really sure what had happened. He'd kissed her, she'd kissed him back, they'd both enjoyed it—that much he knew. Everything else was just a little fuzzy. Maybe he had hit his head too hard, he thought, though it certainly hadn't knocked any sense into him.

Because all he'd thought about since he'd kissed her was kissing her again.

From the moment Tina had walked into campaign headquarters with Rachel and Jason a few minutes ago, Reid had been very aware of the fact that she'd kept her distance from him. She hadn't even glanced in his direction. It would certainly make sense that with her boyfriend here, she might want to avoid the man she'd been in a lip lock with just a few hours earlier.

But what she couldn't avoid was the unspoken tension still lingering between them. It didn't matter that she was on the other side of the room, it was there nonetheless. He knew it, and he knew that she knew it, too.

Whether she would admit it or not was another issue.

"A friend of yours?"

Reid turned at the sound of Ian's voice, annoyed that his brother had caught him staring. "Who?"

Ian took a sip of his coffee, then grinned that annoying I'm-your-brother-you-can't-fool-me grin. "Not the type you usually go for, is she?"

Refusing to answer his question or rise to the bait, Reid simply lifted a brow. "And exactly what type is it you seem to think I go for?"

"Dim-witted debutantes," Ian said, cocking his head. "High-society heiresses, soporific society girls."

Reid frowned. So maybe a few of the women he'd dated had been a little shallow, he thought irritably. Or maybe just a little low in the brain cell department. So what? He'd been looking for company, not commitment. And Ian, of all people, who'd avoided any kind of relationship since his divorce, was hardly one to talk.

''For your information,'' Reid said dryly, ''her father owns Castle Bakery.''

''Ah. One of the Alexander daughters.'' Ian nodded, then sipped his coffee again as he glanced across the room at Tina. ''Jake and I have talked about adding some new items to D&D's. Maybe I should go introduce myself.''

Reid slid a dark look at his brother. ''She's not on the menu, Ian.''

''Is that so?'' Grinning, Ian returned his attention to Reid. ''Not on my menu or yours?''

Reid would have liked nothing better than to wipe that smirk off his brother's face, but considering the time and place, it would have to wait. ''Neither. She has a boyfriend.''

Ian shrugged. ''I don't see any ring on her finger. You getting soft in your old age?''

''Why don't we go out back and see who's soft?'' Reid said irritably.

''You're too pretty in that new suit to mess up.'' Ian slapped a good-natured hand on Reid's shoulder. ''And besides, I hear she's got sisters. Good Lord, please tell me that's one of them.''

Reid followed the direction of his brother's gaze. The tall, leggy blonde had just stepped through the front door. Curls spilled from a silver clip on top of her head and tumbled around an oval face, lush mouth and pale-green eyes. The long-sleeved ruffled blouse and black leather pants she wore showed off a body that most men could only fantasize about.

And right now, Reid noted, just about every man in the room was doing some serious fantasizing.

''Daughter number one, Sophia,'' Reid said. He'd met her yesterday at the bakery. ''Why don't you go introduce yourself?''

Keeping his eyes on the blonde, Ian straightened his tie, then handed Reid his coffee. ''I think I'll do that.''

Reid watched his brother move in on Sophia like a panther, but he had the feeling that the woman could handle herself. He took a moment to appreciate her beauty—he was human, after all—but it simply wasn't the eldest Alexander daughter he was preoccupied with at the moment.

And even though he didn't want to admit it, not even to himself, he knew that Ian had been right about Tina. She *was* different from the other women he'd dated or been interested in before. It was strange how she annoyed and fascinated him at the same time. Something about her had caught his attention and refused to let go. Despite his better judgment, he intended to explore what that something was.

''May I have everyone's attention, please,'' Nicola said over the noise in the room, then waited until the crowd slowly quieted. ''I'd like to thank you all for coming this evening. I speak for Abraham and myself when I say how grateful we are to each and every one of you for so generously donating your time and money to this campaign. With your support, there is no doubt in our minds and hearts who the next senator of our beautiful state of Georgia will be—Abraham Danforth!''

Cheers and applause exploded from the crowd, and a few zealous volunteers held up Honest Abe II bumper stickers that Nicola had distributed a few minutes ago.

"And a special thank you," Nicola said when the crowd quieted down, "to Ivan and Mariska Alexander from Castle Bakery for so generously providing refreshments for us this evening."

Mariska beamed and waved at everyone, while Ivan, clearly not liking the attention, nodded stiffly.

"At this time I'd like to invite everyone to mark the date for a cocktail party at Crofthaven in two weeks." Nicola waited for the excited murmur to settle down, then smiled and went on, "For now, while we're waiting for Abraham to arrive, please help yourself to drinks and desserts and introduce yourself to your fellow volunteers."

Reid sipped on the coffee his brother had left him while the crowd moved in on the sweets. And speaking of sweet…Reid glanced back to where he'd seen Tina standing a few minutes ago, but she was gone. Slowly he scanned the crowd, but didn't see her amongst the mass of people crowded in the room.

He didn't see Jason, either.

They hadn't gone out the front door, Reid was certain of that. Which meant they'd either gone into the back offices, rest room or out the back door.

What the hell does it matter? he thought, though he already knew the answer. It did matter, dammit. And he was suddenly in a bad mood because he didn't want it to.

If she and Jason really were an item, then fine. But if that were true, Reid asked himself, then why, just a few hours ago, had she been kissing *me?* And why, when he'd asked her point-blank what the deal was, had she turned so indignant?

Something didn't jibe. Reid wasn't certain what it was, but once and for all, he wanted an answer.

It took several minutes to make his way through the crowd, but when he finally stepped into the back hallway, Reid could see the offices and the rest room were empty.

Questioning his sanity, not to mention his lack of common sense, he stepped outside.

The air was crisp, the cloudless night sky filled with stars. An iridescent ring shimmered around a nearly full moon. In the far distance, a ship's horn sounded from the river. A perfect night for a tryst, Reid thought, closing the door behind him.

When he saw the couple standing in the shadows of the garden, their arms entwined, Reid's hands balled into fists and he nearly turned back around. But then he heard Ian's voice in his head, accusing him of being soft. Like hell I am.

Relaxing his hands, he shoved them into his pockets and strolled casually over. "Nice evening."

The couple jumped apart. Jason stepped in front of the woman in his arms, shielding her from view. "We were just…getting a little fresh air."

Why the hell was Tina hiding behind this guy? Reid wondered. The woman he'd met wasn't the type to cower in a corner when confronted. Unless she was worried about Jason finding out she'd been kissing another man.

"Sorry if I interrupted." In an attempt to see around

Jason, Reid moved a couple feet to the left. Jason moved, too.

"No problem," Jason said, though his voice gave away his nervousness.

"Look." Reid sighed. "Why don't we just—"

"What in the world are you doing out here? Are you crazy?"

Startled at the sound of Tina's hushed shout from behind him, Reid turned. She hurried across the patio toward them. Confused, Reid looked back at Jason, then watched a woman step hesitantly from the shadows.

Rachel.

"Mom is looking for you both," Tina said to her sister. "You've got to get back inside before—"

"What is going on out here?"

At the sound of her mother's voice, Tina froze, then slowly turned. Hands on her hips, eyes narrowed suspiciously, Mariska looked at the group assembled on the patio.

"I was just—" Tina faltered. "We were just—"

"Rachel said she had a headache," Reid said easily as he moved closer to Rachel. "I brought her out here for some fresh air."

Stunned, Tina looked at Reid, wasn't quite sure why he was lying for them, but was thankful nonetheless.

"That's right," Tina added quickly. "Jason and I just came out to see how she's doing."

"Oh." Mariska glanced from Rachel to Reid, then her eyes widened with delight. "*Ohh.* I see. Yes, well, fresh air is good for a headache, is it not?"

Nodding, Rachel glanced hesitantly at Reid, then smiled stiffly. "I...I'm feeling much better now."

Her mother was obviously hearing wedding bells, Tina knew. What her mother didn't know, was that she was looking at the wrong groom.

"Well, then," Mariska said, already turning. "I will just go back inside and tell your father that you are all right."

"We'll be right there," Reid called after her.

When Mariska disappeared back inside, Jason glared at Reid, then took Rachel's hand in a blatant display of possessiveness. "Rachel, we've got to settle this now. I'll talk to your parents and—"

"No." Rachel pulled her hand from Jason's, then looked at Reid. "We didn't mean to involve you. I'm sorry."

Tears shining in her eyes, Rachel quickly followed after her mother. Jason started after her.

"Jason." Tina touched his shoulder and shook her head. "Please. Not now."

Jason stopped; a muscle jumped in his jaw. Shaking off Tina's hand, he turned on his heel and stomped out the side garden gate, slamming it behind him.

Tina slowly released the breath she'd been holding. That had been close. Too close. Forcing a smile, she turned to Reid. "Thank you. You have no idea what kind of disaster you just diverted."

"Why don't you tell me?"

Though her first impulse was to hold back, Tina reminded herself he had helped, after all. She supposed she at least owed him the truth. "Jason and Rachel are in love."

The look he gave her said, "Duh."

"Rachel doesn't like confrontation," Tina explained. "She knows my parents wouldn't approve of her dating Jason, so they've kept it a secret."

"Why wouldn't they approve?"

"For one thing, he's an employee. That's always been absolutely forbidden."

"So why doesn't he just quit?"

"It's not that simple." Tina sighed. "He's also the lead singer in a band called Controversy."

"The struggling musician," Reid said thoughtfully.

"A double whammy," Tina said with a nod. "Even if he quit the bakery, my parents still wouldn't approve. And Rachel won't let him quit the band. She knows how much his music means to him."

"Is he any good?"

"Rachel says so." Tina hugged herself when a cold breeze swirled leaves around her feet. "But it's a tough business."

"You're cold." Reid shrugged out of his suit jacket and dropped it over her shoulders. "Here."

"No, really, I'm fine, you don't have to—"

When he took hold of the lapels and tugged her closer, Tina's protest died on her lips. She could feel his warmth inside the jacket, could smell his masculine scent on the brushed wool. When he tugged her closer still, her pulse skipped, then raced.

"When I came out here tonight," he said, gazing down at her, "I thought you were the woman Jason was kissing."

If she'd had any air left in her lungs, Tina might have laughed. "Me?"

He nodded. "I thought you two were involved."

She did laugh now, though it was such a throaty, deep sound that she wondered where it came from. "That's why you asked me about Jason earlier, after—" She stopped, felt her cheeks heat up.

"After you kissed me," he murmured.

"I kissed *you?*" Lifting an indignant brow, she angled her head and met his dark gaze. "That's not the way I remember it."

"Yeah?" His gaze dropped to her mouth. "How do you remember it?"

Ignoring the voice in her head that told her to run, Tina placed her palms flat on Reid's chest and leaned into him. She felt the steady thud of his heart under her fingertips and the heat of his skin through his cotton dress shirt. "Remember what?"

Smiling, he lowered his mouth to hers.

It was the same as before. The same wild rush. The same build of heat.

The same insanity.

His lips moved over hers, gently at first, barely tasting. Certainly not a kiss that should overwhelm or overpower, she thought dimly. Nothing that should make her knees weak or her mind numb.

But it did all of those things. All that and more.

A lot more.

He changed the angle of the kiss, traced the seam of her lips with his tongue, then dipped inside to meet hers. Her breath caught, quickened. He tasted like coffee, dark and rich and hot. His hands slid inside his jacket and around her waist, pulling her body flush with his. His thumbs brushed over her rib cage, no more than a whisper from the underside of her breasts. Desire shot through her like an arrow, hummed deep in her throat.

Afraid she might sink to the ground if she didn't hold tight, Tina slid her hands upward. His shoulders were wide and strong; she felt the ripple of muscle as she circled his neck with her arms.

A tiny part of her brain fought to regain control of reason. This could go nowhere, could lead to nothing but heartache, that tiny voice screamed at her. She'd be way in over her head with a man like Reid. But it seemed that her body had a mind of its own, determined to enjoy the moment, consequences be damned.

When he deepened the kiss, when the tips of his thumbs barely brushed the curve of her breasts, even that tiny voice shut up. She heard the sound of her own soft moan, but was too immersed in the sensations swirling through her to be embarrassed. His touch thrilled her, consumed her, and she knew she was lost.

Reid felt the shudder roll through her body into his. He was no stranger to desire, to need, but this was something different, something stronger, deeper, than anything he'd experienced before. The urgency grew like a storm, dark and swirling, heavy. His pulse pounded in his head, in his body.

Lifting his head, he gazed down at her, watched her slowly open her eyes. Passion smoldered there. Her lips, swollen and moist, enticed him to dip down and taste her again.

''So sweet,'' he murmured against her lips. ''So soft.''

Desperately he wanted to drag Tina upstairs to her aunt's apartment and finish what they'd started here, but the faint sound of laughter from inside the building reminded him where they were. Frustration had him tightening his hold on her, then mentally cursing his lack of timing.

With a willpower he didn't know he possessed, he pulled away, then pressed his forehead to hers.

"We should go back inside," he said with a sigh.

She blinked. "What?"

"My father will be arriving any minute," he explained. "They'll wonder where I am."

"Oh, yes, of course." She stepped back, slipped his jacket from her shoulders and handed it to him. "Thanks."

"Tina—"

"It's no big deal, Reid." She tilted her head and smiled. "We got a little caught up in the moment, that's all. It happens."

It happens? Annoyance tapped at his pride. "Twice now, if you're counting," he said dryly, and she at least gave him the satisfaction of appearing embarrassed.

"I…I'm sorry." She dropped her gaze and folded her arms. "I'm not handling this well at all. I just don't want to give you the wrong impression, that's all."

"And what impression was that?"

"That I—that we—" She shifted awkwardly. "That this would go anywhere."

"So what you're trying to say is," he said, keeping his voice even, holding her gaze and watching her eyes widen as he stepped close to her, "you aren't going to sleep with me."

She drew in a slow breath. "No."

"No, you aren't trying to say that?"

"No—I mean, yes." Flustered, she shook her head. "I'm not going to sleep with you."

"The thing is, Tina." He touched her earlobe with his fingertip, heard her soft intake of breath. "I haven't asked."

Thoroughly satisfied at the surprise in her eyes, Reid dropped his hand.

"See you inside," he said casually, then wished to God he could see the look on her face as he strolled away.

Five

Saturday afternoon, with her shift finished and the bakery closed, Tina made her way up the stairs to her aunt's apartment. All day she'd been dreaming of a quiet evening at home. Alone. In her mind she'd planned an hour-long bubble bath, with scented candles and a glass of white wine. Next came her favorite sweatpants, a cotton tank top, soft slippers and the mystery novel she'd started two weeks ago.

And maybe, just maybe, she might even get some sleep, instead of tossing and turning all night thinking about Reid.

Her cheeks still burned every time she remembered what he'd said to her last night before he'd walked away. *I haven't asked.*

She'd managed to get through the rest of the evening, had even smiled and held her voice steady when her mother had dragged her over to meet Abraham Danforth. It was like looking at an older version of Reid. The same piercing deep-blue eyes, the same thick, sable-brown hair. The same charm. Like Reid, he exuded power and masculinity. And like Reid, the women, young and old, couldn't take their eyes off him. Suddenly Tina completely understood why Reid hadn't asked her to sleep with him.

Because he didn't have to.

He had his pick of any woman he wanted. Anytime.

Tina knew she was no femme fatale. Men might have shown an interest in her from time to time, but they weren't exactly dropping at her feet.

So the question she'd asked herself repeatedly since she'd met Reid was, why is he interested in me?

Still mulling that thought over, she slipped her key into the lock and opened the door.

In front of her eyes, Tina's dreams of a quiet evening dissolved like sugar in water.

"Tina, it's so wonderful." Rachel met her at the door and dragged her inside the apartment. "You won't believe what Sophie's done."

Rachel glanced at Sophia, who was sitting on the sofa, making an old pair of jeans and oversize white tunic top look like high fashion. She had an incredibly smug look on her face. "Swallowed the canary?"

"No, silly." Excitement danced in Rachel's eyes. "She got Jason's band booked at Steam. Tonight!"

Tina stared wide-eyed at Rachel, then Sophia. Steam was the newest, hottest, most-difficult-to-get-into blues dinner and night club in Savannah. Though Tina had never been there herself, she knew that Sophia went often, that she'd even done some interior designing in the owner's office.

Tina also knew that it took nothing short of a miracle for a band to get a booking there. "And how, pray tell, did you manage that one?"

Sophia casually shrugged a shoulder, but there was a twinkle of a smile in her eyes. "The band booked for tonight had to cancel. The owner owes me a favor."

Tina lifted a curious brow. "What kind of favor?"

"Not that kind, dear," Sophia said with a pretty tilt of her head. "Though Clay Crawford is quite a catch. We just decided we'd make better friends."

"Could we please not discuss Sophia's love life for once." Rachel took hold of Tina's hand and pulled her to the sofa. "We have to talk about what we're going to wear."

"We?" Tina swiveled a look at Rachel.

"Of course 'we,'" Rachel said. "I told Jason we'd all be there. And this is the perfect night for us all to go out with no questions from Mom and Dad."

Saturday night was her parents' date night out to Buddy's Buffet and Bingo on the waterfront. Unless one of them was sick, they never missed it. It was the perfect night for her and her sisters to all go out and not have to worry about any inquisitions. Tina's fantasy of a bubble bath began to pop, one scented bubble after the other.

"Just think." Rachel clasped her hands to her chest. "Jason, my Jason, singing at Steam! You have to come, Tina."

The happiness on her sister's face disintegrated the

last of Tina's resolve. "Of course I'm coming," she said, surprised at her own sudden rush of excitement. "I wouldn't miss it."

"I love you both so much!" Laughing, Rachel threw her arms around Tina and Sophia. "This will be the best night of my life!"

Maybe this was exactly what she needed, Tina reasoned. She hadn't been out with her sisters like this in a long time. A little music, a little wine. It would be fun. Maybe she'd meet someone nice. Someone who could make her forget about Reid Danforth.

Who knows, she thought, maybe this would be her lucky night.

Starting at nine every night of the week, Steam featured only the best in live blues music. On a Saturday night, without a reservation or a connection, it was nearly impossible to get in either the posh second-floor restaurant or the trendy club on the first floor.

Unless, of course, your last name was Danforth.

"Are you dining this evening, Mr. Danforth?" The hostess, a pretty brunette in a black cocktail dress smiled at Reid. "Or would you like a table in the club?"

"In the club." Smiling back at the woman, Reid slipped her a bill that made her eyes widen. With the skill of a magician, the money disappeared. "I'm meeting my brother."

"Thank you, sir. Just give me one moment to find the best seat for you."

While the hostess scribbled on a seating chart in front of her, Reid took in the decor of the large, dimly lit reception area. Deep-red velvet draperies hung from the floor-to-ceiling windows; the walls were pale gray, with thin red stripes. A lavish Oriental rug in hues of red, gray and black graced the highly polished, dark mahogany floor. Behind the hostess, a large mahogany staircase led to the restaurant upstairs. To the right, the bar area vibrated with conversation and laughter.

"Right this way, sir."

Still not certain why Ian had insisted on meeting him here tonight, Reid followed the hostess through an entrance to the left which led to the stage and dance area. "Let's Give Them Something to Talk About" blasted from the dj's speakers and bodies moved on the dance floor in rhythm to Bonnie Raitt's raspy tune while cocktail waitresses in black slacks and button-down red blouses hustled through the crowd, balancing trays and taking orders.

Settling in at a stage side table, Reid ordered a beer then munched on a spicy mix of pretzels and nuts the waitress had left him. Since his college days, he'd spent very little time in night clubs and bars, but some things never changed. And though Steam was much too high class for the average college frat boys, the draw was still the same: music, food, drink and, of course, the women.

He glanced around the packed room at the slinky dresses and low-cut tops. A great deal of skin and cleavage were on display, and he'd have to be dead not to notice it. Still, other than a mild flicker of appreciation, he wasn't interested in engaging any of the glances a few of the women were sliding his way.

It irritated the hell out of him that he couldn't get

Tina out of his mind. Frustrated him to no end that since he'd kissed her, all he could think about was kissing her again.

And more.

At least he knew now it was Rachel, not Tina, who was involved with Jason. And while Tina hadn't exactly waved a green flag, it also helped to know he was the only car on the course at the moment. He had the feeling there would be stop signs and detours, but he was determined that sooner or later he'd encounter a yield sign.

He hoped like hell it was sooner.

"So what do you think?" Ian asked over the hum of noise as he sat in the chair across from Reid. "Nice place, huh?"

Reid nodded. "And we're here because…?"

"Sophia invited us." Ian gestured to the waitress that he'd have the same as Reid.

The bottle of beer in Reid's hand paused halfway to his mouth. "Sophia Alexander?"

Ian grinned. "You know, the sister of the woman who's 'not on the menu,' as you put it."

"When did you talk to Sophia?"

"I called her today to see if she was busy tonight. She said she was coming here and suggested I stop by."

"You said she invited *us*."

"She's bringing Tina." Ian's grin widened. "Ah. I thought that might get your attention."

It more than got his attention. Carefully Reid set the bottle back down on the gray marble tabletop and scanned the room. He didn't see Tina or Sophia at a table or on the dance floor. Scanning the crowd again, he spotted Rachel walking into the room through an exit door behind the stage. Sophia came next.

Then Tina.

The black, Mandarin collar dress she wore emphasized her long neck and heart-shaped face. The knee-length hemline was conservative, the short sleeves demure. Nothing that should make his pulse jump or his mind stutter.

And yet it did—*she* did.

Keeping his gaze on Tina, he watched the sisters hurry to a front-row-center table as the dj announced that Controversy, the performing band for the evening, would be out in five.

Controversy. That was Jason's band, Reid remembered. So that's why Tina was here. Lifting the bottle of beer, Reid took a long pull, then sat back and waited for the show to begin.

"Stop fidgeting and relax." Tina handed Rachel a glass of ice water. "And breathe, for heaven's sake. It won't help Jason if you're passed out on the floor."

"You're right. I know, I'm sorry," Rachel said in a rush and sipped at the water. "But did you see him? Did you see how handsome he looks in his black satin jacket? And his hair, all that wonderful blond hair, loose around his shoulders."

"I saw him," Tina said. They'd just come from backstage where the band was waiting to come out. "He looked very handsome."

When the lights dimmed, Rachel turned white. "Oh, God, I think I'm going to be sick."

Rolling her eyes, Sophia dipped her fingers into the ice water, then flicked Rachel's face.

Rachel gasped, then scowled at Sophia. "Hey!"

"Got you breathing, didn't I? Now be quiet, sit still and let's see what your man can do."

But even Tina held her breath when the dj announced the band. Five men strolled out, everyone wearing sunglasses, looking very cool and very hot at the same time. They took their places, paused a moment, then the drummer tapped his drumsticks and said, "One, two, three, four!"

The lead guitar started solo, strong and loud, the drums rolled in a moment later. The sound was hard-beating southern blues. Like a living, breathing entity, the heavy bass and keyboard joined in, pulsating through the crowd, pulling them to their feet and moving them to the dance floor.

Then Jason stepped to the microphone.

"Tell me why…"

His voice trembled through the room, a smoky, raspy sound that was uniquely his own. A sound that echoed a hundred years of soul and sorrow, all the life of every blues singer who'd stepped on that stage before him. He sang of deception and lies, lost love and heartache. Passion flowed like lava from his words and set the room on fire.

This was Jason? Tina thought in stunned amazement. She'd never heard him sing before, had never dreamed he was this good. The audience and dancers moved to the beat, and Tina couldn't stop herself from moving with them. He was better than good, she thought. He was terrific.

Tina glanced at Rachel, saw the love shining in her eyes, and felt her chest swell with happiness for her sister. To be that deeply in love with someone, and to have them love you back, was a dream come true. Of course, in this case, the dream came with a few difficulties. But surely, Tina thought, when two people were that deeply in love, there was no difficulty that couldn't be resolved.

Tina could only hope that someday she'd find that kind of love, too. That someday there'd be a man who'd look at her the way Jason looked at Rachel.

Remembering Reid's kiss yesterday and the way he'd looked at her made Tina's stomach flutter. She knew it was just physical between them, but that didn't seem to discourage her thinking about the man constantly. If anything, it simply fueled the fire he'd lit inside her. Made her wonder what it would be like if he'd done more than kiss her, more than lightly brush his hands against her breasts. Her breasts ached just thinking about it, her skin felt tight and hot, and—

The room exploded with applause and cheers at the end of the band's first song. Thank goodness, Tina thought, shaking off the tingling sensation that had been curling through her blood. That kind of thinking was only going to lead to more sleepless nights.

While the applause continued, Rachel grabbed Tina's hand and squeezed. To say that Controversy had been well received was a bit of an understatement.

''Isn't he wonderful?'' Rachel shrieked over the noise. ''Isn't he?''

Laughing, Tina and Sophia hugged Rachel, then Sophia said, "I have to go say hi to someone. I'll be back in a little while."

Jason started his next song, a slower, soulful tale of forbidden love. Couples melted together on the dance floor, swaying gently to the music. Tears in her eyes, Rachel leaned forward in her chair and kept her eyes on Jason. Why he hadn't received a recording deal already amazed Tina, but she knew it was a tough business, that even the most talented singers and groups were often passed by. She hoped this would be Jason's chance to make his dream come true.

At the touch of a hand on her shoulder, Tina glanced up. A man flashed dimples and a diamond earring stud. His build was lean, his biceps the size of tree trunks. He nodded toward the dance floor.

She hesitated, though for the life of her, she didn't know why. She was at a club, for heaven's sake. A nice-looking man was standing here asking her to dance. Didn't she tell herself she was going to cut loose and have a good time?

So why was she so…uninterested? "Uh—"

"Sorry, pal, she's with me."

At the sound of the deep, familiar voice, Tina snapped her head around.

Reid?

Maybe this wasn't her lucky night, after all.

She watched the man who'd asked her to dance move away. Frowning, she looked back at Reid.

"I am not with you, and that was very pushy." She sipped from her water glass, wishing it were the wine she'd passed on earlier. "Maybe I wanted to dance with that man."

''Did you?''

Oh, why pretend? She was a lousy liar, and coy simply wasn't her style. She shrugged. ''Not really.''

Grinning, he sat in the chair Sophia had vacated. ''Hi, Rachel.''

''Hi, Reid,'' Rachel replied without taking her gaze off Jason. She had a dreamy, faraway look in her eyes.

''The wine you ordered, Mr. Danforth.'' A cocktail waitress set a bottle of wine and three glasses on the table, then filled the glasses. ''Can I get you anything else?''

Tina didn't miss the suggestive tone in the waitress's voice. Or the lack of response from Reid when he shook his head.

''What are you doing here?'' she asked him when he handed her a glass of wine.

''Same as you, watching the show.''

She lifted a dubious brow. ''Why do I have the feeling there's more?''

Reid slid a second glass of wine across the tabletop to Rachel, who didn't notice. ''Sophia invited Ian.''

''Really.'' Why did he have to look so handsome in his black leather blazer and sage-green T-shirt? And why did her pulse have to do somersaults every time she saw him? Gathering her wits, forcing her hand to stay steady, she took a sip of the wine. ''And you just happened to come along?''

''Actually, Sophia told Ian to bring me.''

Wine nearly sloshed out of her glass when her hand wobbled. My own flesh and blood conspiring against me. Wondering where her dear sister had disappeared to, Tina scanned the crowd, then spotted Sophia standing with Ian at the back of the room. When Sophia waggled her fingers and smiled knowingly, Tina glared back.

The band slipped into another fast number, and with the music so loud, it was easy to avoid any kind of serious conversation for the next few minutes. What she couldn't avoid or ignore was the proximity of Reid's body. His aftershave was woodsy, masculine, and she resisted the animal urge to slide closer and draw the intoxicating scent into her lungs.

When the music shifted back to a slow number, he leaned in, making her heart skip when he brought his mouth to her ear.

"With a voice like that," Reid said, nodding at Jason, "why's he working in a bakery?"

"The hours leave his afternoons and evenings free for writing and practicing with his band." His warm breath on her ear made it hard to think. "Mostly, he stays because of Rachel. They can see each other every day, and manage to sneak in a little private time, too, especially when my mother's not there."

"So your parents really don't know what's going on?"

Tina shook her head. "My father's kitchen is his own little world, and my mother—" she sipped at her wine, then shrugged "—well, her vision is skewed by her aspirations."

"What aspirations are those?"

With the wine cooling her nerves and Reid's voice warming her insides, Tina felt herself relaxing. "To see Sophia and Rachel married into prominence and wealth, and at least one grandbaby on the way. That's the real reason she bumped my restaurant and rented the space to your family. She sees the campaign headquarters as a hunting ground for potential husbands.''

''What about you?'' Reid asked. ''Doesn't she want to see you married, too?''

''Heavens, no.'' The laugh in her throat quickly faded when she realized that if she moved just a smidgen, Reid's mouth would be touching her neck. The very thought of it made her shiver and inch away. ''It doesn't matter that I'm twenty-four. I'm her baby. She doesn't think of me that way.''

He shook his head slowly. ''You're no baby, Tina.''

Something in Reid's voice, in his eyes, something dark and smoldering, sent heat pulsing through her veins. Was this a game to him? she wondered. And if it was, did she want to play? It would be dangerous and very foolish and she'd lose. She hadn't the experience or the skill to take on a man like Reid.

She'd be the one left hurting, she was certain of that. Was that a chance she could take?

Before she could even consider her answer, he'd already tugged her to her feet and was pulling her toward the dance floor. And when he drew her into his arms, she wasn't thinking at all.

The song was slow, smooth, as sexy as it was soulful. Her body molded to Reid's, and they moved as one. They were close, a blending of soft against hard. Even if she'd wanted to, she couldn't have pulled away. She cursed the fact that she didn't want to. She could have stood like this forever with Reid, her head on his shoulder, his arms tightly around her.

But there was no forever, not with Reid and not with

the song. When it ended, she sighed and lifted her head.

"Come home with me."

Her breath caught at his words. Her heart drummed. *Come home with me.* It would be so simple to leave here with him. To fall into his bed. She was certain it would be a night to remember.

But nothing would be simple tomorrow. She was just as certain about that, too.

While the dance floor began to clear and the band left the stage for a break, she imagined what it would be like. No man had ever made her feel like this before. Made her hot and cold at the same time. Made her ache. Made her yearn.

She needed space. Standing here, with Reid still holding her, she couldn't breathe, let alone think.

"Rachel is…"

"Backstage with Jason."

Tina glanced at the table where they'd all been sitting. The seats were all empty now. "Reid, I—"

He dipped his head, brushed his lips over hers. She forgot what she'd been about to say.

"I…I need a minute," she said breathlessly, shivered when he touched her cheek with his hand.

"I'll wait for you at the table."

Nodding, she turned, and on weak knees headed for the ladies' room. What kind of spell had he woven over her? she wondered. Whatever it was, it was as potent as it was formidable. A heady mix of excitement and fear.

Anticipation shivered through her.

Inside the rest room, Tina squeezed her way through

the mass of buzzing females and made her way to a sink. Dampening a paper towel, she pressed it to her cheeks and neck while the women around her slicked on fresh lipstick, smoothed their hair and adjusted their low-cut dresses and tops.

She looked at her own dress, and though it was pretty and she thought she looked nice enough, she still felt like a sparrow in the midst of swans. A daisy next to roses. For the hundredth time she wondered why Reid would want her. Even if all he wanted was a one-night stand, he had his pick of the most beautiful women in Savannah. For that matter, in the world. It simply made no sense to her.

But did it have to?

For once, did she have to be so damn logical, so sensible? she asked herself. While the women chattered and laughed and pressed all around her, Tina stared at her own reflection, not even certain who she was anymore. For once, couldn't she just let herself *be?* Let herself *feel?* Just enjoy the moment, the night, and not worry so much about tomorrow?

She felt a hand on her arm and blinked.

"Tina," Rachel said, her voice quavering. "We have to go."

"What?" When tears spilled from Rachel's eyes, Tina quickly pulled her sister into a stall and closed the door. "Rachel, honey, what's wrong?"

"We have to go. Please."

"What's happened? Are you all right?"

"I—" Rachel swallowed, then choked on a sob. "I broke up with Jason."

Six

He sat at the bar, nursing a beer, but he wasn't drunk. Not yet, anyway. At 2:00 a.m., the night was still young.

Reid figured he wasn't the first man to close down a bar thinking about a woman, and was even more certain he wouldn't be the last. In the ongoing battle between the sexes, womankind would forever remain a confusing and incredibly frustrating creature.

Reid decided that no woman could possibly be more confusing, or more frustrating, than Tina Alexander.

''Mind if I join you?''

Reid swiveled a glance at Jason. If the singer's face dropped any lower, it would be scraping the wood floor. After two encores his group had finished a few minutes ago. The club was starting to thin out, and even Ian had left after the music ended. But there were still plenty of late-nighters scattered in the bar. "You buying?"

"Sure." Jason slid onto the stool beside Reid, then gestured to the bartender for a new round.

"That was a hell of a performance."

"A record producer was in the audience." Based on Jason's tone, he might as well have said his best friend had died. "He wants the group to come to Los Angeles next week and cut a demo."

"Congratulations."

Jason shrugged, took a long pull from the beer bottle that appeared in front of him. "I asked Rachel to come with me."

Reid waited, didn't think he needed to ask the obvious question.

"She broke it off." Jason dragged a hand through his hair. "Told me she was happy for me, but she didn't want to see me anymore. She asked me if we could just be friends. Friends, for God sakes! Why the hell would she say something like that?"

Reid shook his head. As if he had any answers when it came to women. But he realized it just might explain why Tina had left without even saying goodbye.

When she hadn't come back from the rest room, he'd assumed she'd made up her mind about coming home with him and the answer had been no. He'd also considered it might be payback for the way he'd left her in the garden the night before. Somehow, though, he didn't think that was Tina's style, and when Rachel hadn't come back, either, even after the band started playing again, and Sophia seemed to disappear, as well, it hadn't taken a rocket scientist to figure out something was up. Now he at least had an inkling why the Alexander women had all vanished like smoke in the wind.

His expression dark, Jason looked at Reid. ''I wanted to put a fist in your face. Nearly jumped off the stage a couple of times. You're bigger than me, but I figured the element of surprise would be in my favor, in the short run, anyway.''

Reid lifted a brow. ''What did I do?''

Jason shrugged. ''I see you sitting with my girl, then she breaks up with me. What would you think if you saw the woman you love with another guy?''

''I have no idea,'' Reid said honestly. ''I've never been in love.''

''Lucky you.'' Jason shook his head. ''It hurts like hell. Walking around with your heart on your sleeve, it's damn embarrassing.''

Reid might have agreed, but why kick a guy when he was down? And anyway, if that's what love felt like, he wanted no part of it.

''Anyway—'' Jason sighed ''—once I calmed down a little, I figured out she didn't break up with me because of you. I've just been jealous since you showed up. Everyone's talking about seeing you and Rachel together, and what a great pair you'd make. I know she wouldn't cheat on me, but the thought of you making a move on her made me crazy.''

''Women do that to a man,'' Reid said with nod.

They clinked bottles and drank.

''All Mariska talks about is having a Danforth for a son-in-law.'' Anger narrowed Jason's eyes. ''How's that supposed to make a guy feel?''

Not so good, Reid figured. Unless the guy happened to be a Danforth and had a thing for one of Mariska's daughters. Not that he was interested in marriage, of course, Reid thought. Hell, no. Maybe one day he'd settle down, but that was way in the future. He was attracted to Tina, very attracted, but he sure wasn't ready for picket fences and baby carriages.

When Jason indicated another round to the bartender, Reid could see that an already long night was going to be even longer. What the hell, he thought with a sigh. There were taxis outside and he didn't have any better place to be, anyway. He'd pay for it in the morning, as would Jason, but somehow getting drunk tonight seemed to beat the alternative of being alone.

"If I live to be a hundred, I'll never love again." Her nose red, her eyes swollen from her tears, Rachel stared unseeing at the cup of peppermint tea that Tina set on the kitchen table. "My life is over."

After two pots of coffee, and because it was nearly three in the morning, Tina had brewed a pot of organic tea. With all the caffeine buzzing in her system, she doubted she'd be able to fall asleep for three days. In the corner, Delilah slept peacefully in her cushioned basket.

"Your life is not over," Tina said. "We'll figure something out."

Rachel shook her head. "The minute he told me he was going to Los Angeles, I knew we had to break up. He's going to be a star, Tina. A big star. I'd only be in his way."

Tina sighed. They'd been over this a hundred times since they'd left Steam, but Rachel was being ridiculously stubborn. "He loves you, Rachel. You know he does."

"Did you see the way all those women were looking at him tonight?" She reached for another tissue from the nearly empty box on the table. "Why would he stay with me, subject himself to all the hassels from Mom and Dad, when he could have any woman he wants?"

"He wants *you*, Ray." Tina couldn't understand why her sister had suddenly become so incredibly unreasonable and emotional. "He adores you. Don't give up so easily. We'll call Jason tomorrow."

"And you." Delicately Rachel blew her nose. "I ruined your night, too. You should have gone back to the club with Sophia."

"For one thing, I only went there for you," Tina said firmly. It killed her to see Rachel like this, frustrated her that she couldn't talk any sense into her. "And for another thing, do you think I'd leave you alone when you're hurting like this? If Sophia hadn't already promised the owner she'd help him close tonight, she wouldn't have gone back, either."

"Still, if it wasn't for me," Rachel said forlornly, "you'd be with Reid right now."

Tina's pulse jumped. "What are you talking about?"

"For heaven's sake." Rachel rolled her reddened eyes. "I'm not blind. I saw the way he was looking at you."

Hoping her hand wouldn't shake, Tina calmly picked up her cup of tea. "What way was that?"

"Like he wanted to cover you with whipped cream and lick it all off."

"Rachel!" Tea sloshed out of Tina's cup. "You didn't just say that!"

A smile, the first one since they'd left the club, curved Rachel's lips. "Why shouldn't I say it? It's true, isn't it?"

Reaching for a napkin, Tina wiped up the spilled tea. "He looks at every woman that way."

"He never looked at me that way, or Sophia." Rachel pulled her feet up onto the chair and wrapped her arms around her knees. "And *every* man looks at Sophia that way. So did he ask you?"

"Ask me what?"

"To spend the night with him."

"Rachel!" Tina's cup clattered onto its saucer.

"Stop saying my name." Rachel dropped her chin on her knees. "Besides, it makes me feel better to talk about your love life. You want me to feel better, don't you?"

"Okay, okay." Tina rolled her head back. "So he asked me. But I assure you, it has nothing to do with love."

"I knew it." Rachel hugged her legs tighter. "So what did you say?"

"I never exactly got around to answering."

"And then I pulled you away," Rachel said on a sigh. "Oh, T, I'm so sorry. To think you've had to sit here all night and listen to my problems, when you could have had a glorious night making love with Reid Danforth.''

''Sex.'' Her tea had a bitter taste when she swallowed. ''Nothing more than that. You saved me from a big mistake.''

''You don't know that.'' Rachel covered Tina's hand with her own. ''I saw you two dancing together. There was something there, T. Something more than just sex.''

If only that were true, she thought. But she couldn't let herself believe that, couldn't let herself even think it. If she did, she'd be the one sitting here with red eyes and a broken heart, emptying a box of tissues.

Shaking her head, Tina smiled at her sister. ''It's for the best, Ray. Reid and I just aren't meant to—''

A scuffling from the stairwell outside had both women turning.

''Rachel! Open up.'' A loud knock rattled the front door. ''I know you're in there. Open up this door.''

''Jason!'' Rachel's eyes widened in horror. ''Ohmigod, Tina, don't tell him I'm here. Please!''

The pounding continued, and despite her sister's pleas, Tina rose and headed for the door. ''You're going to have to face him sometime, honey. It might as well be now.''

''No, Tina, I can't.'' Rachel followed, pulling on Tina's arm. ''I'm not ready. Maybe tomorrow.''

''It *is* tomorrow,'' Tina said and opened the door, prepared to face a lovesick Jason.

At the sight of Reid standing on the doorstep holding up an obviously inebriated Jason, Tina's heart slammed in her chest.

"Sorry." Reid's smile was apologetic. "He was insistent."

Rachel rushed past Tina and threw her arms around Jason. "Jason, oh, sweetie, what have you done?"

"Rachel, sugar, I love you." Clumsily, Jason reached for Rachel. "I won't go to L.A., baby. I won't go anywhere without you. Come here and kiss me."

"You idiot." But she did kiss him. "You big fat idiot. I'll take you home."

While Rachel slipped her heels back on and tugged on her coat, Reid held Jason on his feet. When he started to sing to her, Rachel's eyes filled with tears and she kissed him again. Tina shifted awkwardly and met Reid's gaze. He simply grinned.

"I'll help you downstairs," Reid said to Rachel when she managed to pull her lips from Jason's.

She shook her head. "Thanks, we'll be all right."

"That's right, baby," Jason mumbled, kissing Rachel's neck. "We'll be all right."

Arms around each other, they stumbled out the door, closing it behind them.

"Well." Tina let out a long breath when it was quiet again. "You want to tell me how you two ended up together?"

With a shrug, Reid slipped his hands into his pockets. "Guess he needed someone to talk to."

She couldn't imagine a more unlikely coalition. "No offense, Reid, but Jason doesn't like you."

"Only because he thought I was interested in Rachel." He leveled his gaze on hers as he slipped off his jacket. "Now that he knows it's you I want, we're pals."

His words thrilled her, made her pulse leap and her skin heat up. When he tossed his jacket on the sofa and moved close, her throat turned to dust. ''Reid, I...this is not a good idea.''

''Maybe not.''

''We barely know each other.''

He nodded. ''You're absolutely right.''

''We should just say good-night now.''

''Probably.''

''Oh, for heaven's sake.'' Fisting her hands in the front of his shirt, she yanked him close. ''Must you be so damn agreeable?''

Smiling, his arms came around her. ''I aim to please.''

And he did please, she thought dimly when his mouth covered hers. Senses reeling, she melted against his strong chest, slid her arms up his broad shoulders. When he deepened the kiss, she met the thrust of his tongue with her own, and the minty, hot taste of him made her knees weak and her toes curl.

She could stop this, she *should* stop, but she didn't want to. Since the day she'd met Reid they'd been moving toward this moment like a runaway train. They were careening out of control and it was as exhilarating as it was exciting. All she could do was hold on for the ride; she knew it would be a wild one.

She squirmed against him, anticipation vibrating through her. She'd waited so long—a lifetime—for this moment. Now that it was here, impatience had her clutching at his shoulders, moaning. She wanted to remember every moment, every thrilling touch, every glorious taste.

His breath was as ragged as her own; she could feel the heavy beat of his heart against her aching breasts. How she wanted him to touch her there, she thought. And other places. And how she wanted to touch him, too. Her hands, her fingers itched to explore his body.

He dragged his mouth from hers, his midnight-blue gaze seared her to the core. "Bedroom," he managed, but was kissing her again before she could answer.

Slowly but steadily, their bodies still molded to each other, their mouths still fused, they inched their way across the living room, through the hall. So far, she thought, so incredibly far…

Had he ever wanted a women like this? Reid wondered while they made that long journey to the bedroom. If he had, that woman, that moment was lost to him forever. There was just here and now and Tina.

It had required tremendous willpower not to take her right there on the living room floor. Only the thought that he might hurt her had him reining in the raw need clutching at his gut. If it killed him, he'd take his time with her. Slow, he told himself. He'd take it slow. He wanted her underneath him, writhing with need, pleading, and just the thought of it nearly made him lose it before they'd even stepped into the bedroom.

He trailed kisses down her neck, reveled in the soft sounds she made deep in her throat. When he nipped at her earlobe, she shivered.

"So sweet," he murmured.

They moved through the doorway, into the bedroom.

Soft light shone from a beaded lamp on a nightstand, shimmered through drops of clear crystals and reflected on the walls. Pillows of all shapes and sizes adorned the deep-green comforter on the large, four-poster bed. The faint smell of lavender hung in the air, mixed with the heady scent of desire.

Standing next to the bed, he lifted his head, gazed down at her. Her lashes fluttered open, and her eyes, glazed with passion, met his.

Keeping his gaze on hers, he reached for the embroidered closure at the base of her neck, flicked it open, then slid his hand underneath. He felt the wild beating of her heart under his fingertips, the warmth of her bare skin, then slid the soft fabric off one creamy-white shoulder. He pressed his mouth to the curve of her neck and nibbled. On a soft purr, her head rolled back.

Tina wondered how she would survive the sensations consuming her. She felt as if every nerve, every cell, were exposed, a pleasure so intense it bordered on pain. Heat pumped through her veins, a rushing, hot river of need. Dizzy, she swayed against him, and the intimate press of her body against his startled yet thrilled her at the same time.

While his arms held her steady, his lips moved down her neck to nuzzle her shoulder. The light scrape of his teeth, the hot slide of his tongue over her skin made her whimper. She wanted that mouth on her, she realized, wanted his mouth and his hands everywhere.

As if he'd read her mind, he slipped both hands under the loosened neckline of her dress and slid the garment completely off her shoulders, then down her arms to her waist.

"Sexy," he murmured when his gaze dropped to her skimpy black lace bra.

The flicker of shyness she felt dissolved when she saw the dark, intense look of need in his eyes. When he cupped her breasts in his large hands and lightly kneaded, she drew in a deep breath. When he brought his mouth to her lace-covered nipple and suckled the beaded tip with his hot lips, she gasped.

Burrowing her fingers into his hair, she arched upward, clutching at him. A meteor of white-hot pleasure streaked from her breast to the ache between her legs. The need she felt turned to a burning throb.

"Reid," she whispered, not even recognizing the sound of her own voice. She had no idea who this wanton stranger was who had invaded her body, but she welcomed the intruder with open arms. She'd never felt so alive in her entire life. So aware. The smooth texture of Reid's hair between her fingers, the masculine scent of his skin, the ragged sound of his breathing. There were colors and textures behind her eyes, and wonderful, ever-changing shapes and images.

While he moved his attention to her other breast, his hands guided her dress down her hips. The fabric pooled at her bare feet. She squirmed, wanting him with a desperation that was driving her mad. When he lifted his head, circled her waist with his hands and brought his mouth to her stomach, she moaned.

"So pretty," he murmured, sliding his mouth across the bottom of her rib cage. "So delicate."

His mouth and words aroused her even more and the urgency grew. As he trailed hot kisses across her belly, her hands pressed against his skull. She didn't think she could take much more; she was certain a person could die from feelings this intense.

"Reid," she whispered hoarsely. "Please."

She helped him drag his top over his head. Wanting desperately to touch him, she reached out and slid her hands over the hard muscles of his shoulders and chest, felt the raw power and strength under her fingertips. When she leaned closer and pressed her mouth to his collarbone, he sucked in a sharp breath.

His taste, salty and warm, intoxicated her. She felt his heart pounding under her fingertips, felt the coiled energy rippling through his muscles. *Mine,* she thought. Even if only for this one night, he was really hers.

And she was his.

He lowered her to the bed, and the weight of his body pressed her into the soft mattress. He crushed his mouth to hers, demanding, insistent. She quivered when his hand found her breast again, arched upward when his mouth replaced his hand.

Every touch, every taste, every sensation, each one more intense than the one before, rolled through her, building and building. She wanted, needed, him inside her. Needed to end this incredible, wonderful torture. But when his hand slid down her stomach, then slipped under her lace panties and dipped to the pebbled heat between her legs, she knew the exquisite torture had only just begun. He stroked her, matching the rhythm of his tongue against her own. She moved with him, frustrated at the pace he had set. Determined to speed things up, she slid her hands between them and loosened his belt, then reached for the zipper of his slacks.

Every thought of going slowly raced out of Reid's mind when Tina closed her hand around him. He knew she was ready for him; she was wet and swollen, arching her body to his. With the last thread of control, he moved away from her.

"Reid." She whimpered in protest and reached for him.

"Don't worry, sweetheart, I'm not going anywhere." While he tugged off the rest of his clothes and took the extra moment to protect them both, he kept his gaze locked with hers.

Her eager arms welcomed him back. He kissed her deeply, tenderly, let the passion rise to the same fever pitch before he slipped her panties off, then moved between her thighs. She opened to him, wrapped her long, silky legs around him and pulled him into her.

When she stiffened and softly cried out, he went still.

"What…?"

Her arms and legs tightened around him, held him close. "Don't stop," she said raggedly. "Please, Reid."

"But you…but I—"

She reared up, kissing him, moving her hips against him, making it impossible for him to think, impossible to do anything but hang on to the growing wave of sheer, raw need. Helpless, he moved inside the tight, hot velvet glove of her body. Blind pleasure, dark and uncontrollable, took over. The wave rose, then rose higher still, until it finally crested. She hovered there, shuddering, a moan on her lips.

His own climax slammed violently into him and broke apart, crashed and rolled.

Lungs burning, he pulled her close while his mind struggled to pull words into a coherent sentence.

"Tina." His voice was raspy, strained. "Why didn't you tell me?"

While her hand moved restlessly over his chest, she snuggled in his arms. "I didn't think about it."

"You didn't think about it?" His voice cracked. "How could you not think about it?"

"I was a little busy." Her hand stilled. "Would it have made a difference if I'd told you I was a virgin?"

"Yes. No." He jerked a hand through his hair. "Yes."

"I'm twenty-four years old, Reid," she said thinly. "I waited to be with a man until it felt right to me. I'm sorry if that's a problem for you."

When she started to move away, he hauled her back and pressed a kiss to her temple.

"I didn't say it was a problem. I just would have been more careful," he said quietly. "I hurt you."

Slowly she relaxed, then shook her head. "A twinge, that's all, just for a moment. Everything else was wonderful. You were wonderful."

"Yeah? How wonderful?"

"Oh, stop grinning at me like that." She pushed at his chest. "As if you don't hear that all the time."

He rose on one elbow and frowned at her. "What's that supposed to mean?"

"I've seen your name in magazines and newspapers,'' she said with a timid shrug. "There's usually a woman's name attached somewhere.''

"Don't believe everything you read, sweetheart.'' He gathered her close again and lay back on the bed. "I've dated a lot of women, had a few I'd even call girlfriends. I may not be a saint, but I sure as hell didn't sleep with them all, either. Okay?''

Silence settled around them like a soft blanket. Somewhere in the room a clock tick-tocked; warm air hummed through an overhead duct.

"Why me?'' she asked quietly, stroking her finger-tips back and forth across his chest.

Would this woman ever stop surprising him? he wondered. Strangely, he realized that was part of the attraction.

Because the way she was touching him was a big distraction, he took hold of her hand, then hauled her on top of him. She gasped at the unexpected move-ment, and the fact that he was hard and ready for her again, wanting her as much now as he had only a few minutes ago.

"You really don't know, do you?'' He was defi-nitely enjoying the new position of her body on top of his, not to mention the view of her bare breasts. "You really are completely unaware of how sexy and utterly captivating you are.''

Her cheeks turned pink and her lashes fluttered down. "I figured you were just bored.''

"Bored?'' He nearly choked. "Good Lord, woman. Where would you get an idea like that?''

"Sharie Jo Sullivan.''

"Who?''

"Sharie Jo Sullivan. A customer at the bakery. She said men like you get bored easily. That you're always looking for a challenge."

"Is that what you think you are to me?" He couldn't believe he was hearing this. "A challenge?"

"I was probably the first woman who ever said no to you," she reminded him.

"I didn't hear you say no tonight." Reid skimmed his hands down Tina's back, then brought his mouth to hers and nibbled one delicious corner. "In fact, I believe I heard a lot of 'yes' and 'please,'" he teased.

"You're going to need a new head to fit that ego if you aren't careful, buster," she said with a prim sniff.

"I'll be careful." He cupped her firm behind, watched her eyes widen when he moved his hips against hers. "Very careful."

"Darn you, Reid Danforth. You've turned me into a loose woman." Lifting her hips, she took him inside her. "Remind me later to thank you."

Later turned out to be close to ten in the morning, with food the motivating force that finally pulled them out of the bedroom. While Reid showered, Tina had her omelettes cooking and her own special recipe of breakfast potatoes warming in the oven. Considering the night they'd had, she was certain he was going to be one hungry man.

Lord knew, she thought with a smile, he certainly was a man with an appetite.

They'd dozed on and off throughout the early morning hours, waking briefly enough for a kiss or a touch...sometimes more. Remembering how eager she'd been for him brought a blush to her cheeks. And though she had no idea what today, tomorrow or next week would bring for her, she had no regrets at all. She'd waited twenty-four years for last night, and even now, in the light of day, she was so glad.

It had been amazing. *He* had been amazing. But there'd been no whispered promises, no mention of the future, and though it pained her to think that last night might be their only night together, she'd gone to him with her eyes wide open.

Unfortunately, her heart had been wide open, as well.

Sometime during the night, or maybe the first time she'd laid eyes on him, she realized, she'd fallen in love with Reid. She'd fought it, of course. It was, after all, very foolish and completely reckless. But clearly, reason did not prevail when it came to love. It simply was.

At the sound of the shower turning off, she slipped her omelettes onto plates, loaded on potatoes and was setting them on the table when he walked into the kitchen wearing nothing but a knotted towel slung low on his hips. Her heart jumped at the sight, and that ache she'd become so familiar with last night pulsed through her veins. The intensity of it startled her, had her wondering, and worrying, about tomorrow.

She couldn't think about that now, refused to let herself give in to fear. She would accept what they had and be happy for it.

And then he smiled at her and her heart shattered.

"Hey."

"Hey, yourself." She swallowed the lump in her

throat and forced herself to smile back. "Breakfast is ready."

"Smells great."

He walked toward her, made every piece of her heart vibrate with longing.

"It'll be on the breakfast menu of my restaurant in one year." She hoped her voice sounded as easy as she intended. "As soon as I have my space back from you, of course."

When he moved beside her and leaned close, her breath held, waiting for his kiss. But he reached past her to the table and snatched a slice of potato instead, then popped it in his mouth.

"Tasty."

"Thanks."

She was about to turn when he tugged her to him, then covered her mouth with his. She melted into the kiss, felt it sing through her entire body.

"Very tasty," he murmured against her lips and pulled her closer. "You know what they say, don't you?"

"What?" she whispered, sliding her arms around his neck.

"If you can't stand the heat—" he scooped her up in his arms "—get out of the kitchen."

Laughing, she wrapped her arms around him and held on as he headed for the bedroom. At the sound of keys jangling in the doorknob, Reid stopped and turned. Tina froze, watched in horror as the door swung open.

"Well, now, what have we here?"

Ohmigod.

Clutching her robe together across her bared breasts, Tina blinked, then sucked in a lungful of air and managed a weak smile. "Hi, Aunt Yana."

Seven

Aunt Yana? Reid glanced at the photo of Tina's aunt hanging on the wall, then back at the woman standing in the doorway. Yep. Aunt Yana, all right.

She wore a deep-blue, long, flowing duster over silk ivory pants. Colorful stones dangled from her ears and circled a long, slender neck. In spite of the incredibly awkward moment, it was impossible for Reid not to be stunned by the older woman's beauty. A short crop of thick, straight sable-brown hair accented high cheekbones, aristocratic nose and gypsy-green eyes.

Her mouth, wide and full, slowly curved up at the corners as she closed the door behind her.

"You…you're home early," Tina sputtered.

"My shoot finished ahead of schedule." Yana slid a large straw handbag from her shoulder and dropped it on the entry table along with her keys, slid her gaze from the tip of Reid's bare toes to the towel draping his hips, then up to his face. "Aren't you going to introduce me to your friend, Katina?"

"I—oh, of course." Tina gulped. "This is Reid Danforth. Reid, my aunt, Yana Alexander Dimetri Romano."

Not quite certain what the proper etiquette was for the situation, Reid simply nodded. "A pleasure, Ms. Romano."

"I think just Yana would be more appropriate." Folding her arms, Yana glanced back down at the towel. Amusement danced in her eyes. "All things considered."

"Yes, ma'am."

"Reid," Tina whispered, her voice strained. "Could you, ah, put me down?"

"Oh. Right."

When her feet touched the floor, Tina tightened the belt of her robe. Her face had gone from pale to rosy pink. "We were just…ah, going to have breakfast."

"Of course you were." Yana's smile widened. "It smells wonderful."

"I'll set another plate." Tina shifted from one bare foot to the other. "Just give me…us, a minute, to ah—"

"I believe I hear something buzzing." Yana glanced at the sport coat lying on the sofa, then looked back at Reid. Though the sound was faint, it was definitely a buzz. "Yours, I assume?"

He'd have to kill whoever was calling him, Reid decided. Holding tightly to the knot of the towel, he stepped to the sofa and retrieved his cell phone from his jacket.

"Excuse me." He backed toward the bedroom where he'd left his clothes.

"Take your time, dear," Yana called after him. "My niece and I could use a minute alone to say hello."

Closing the bedroom door behind him, Reid snapped the phone to his ear. "Yeah."

"Reid, where have you been? I've been trying to reach you all morning."

"Kimberly?" He heard the stress in his sister's voice. "Are you all right?"

"You have to come to Crofthaven right away. In the attic. They, they were working there this morning, and found—"

At the sound of her quiet sob, fear snaked through him. "Found what, Kim?"

"They found a body."

At least a dozen patrol cars were already at Crofthaven when Reid pulled in front of the mansion's main entrance. Several uniformed officers standing outside turned at the sight of the black BMW screeching to a halt, then quietly returned to their conversations after Reid hurried past them.

The first officers on the scene had carefully taken in every detail of the activities at Crofthaven. Later they would have the inside scoop to give to the rest of the station, not to mention their friends and family. And if they were really lucky, they just might find their faces on TV or in the newspapers.

The public, not to mention Abraham's rival candidates, would eat up every tasty morsel of the juicy story.

"Reid." Ian was coming down the stairs as Reid stepped into the foyer. "Thank God you're here."

"Tell me what's happened." Reid met his brother at the base of the stairs. "Kimberly called and said they found a body in the attic, but I didn't get much more out of her."

"She's pretty shook up." Ian dragged a hand through his hair and sighed. "Reid, we think it might be Victoria."

It was like taking a punch in the gut, and it was a moment before Reid could speak. "Vickie?"

"'Fraid so."

Victoria Danforth had suddenly disappeared five years ago and, though there'd been a nationwide hunt and several private detectives had been hired, no one had ever found a trace of their cousin.

"How is that possible?" Just the thought of it made Reid's stomach clench. "How could she be up there all this time? We searched everywhere."

"That section of the house has been closed up for years," Ian said. "And it also appears there was some kind of hidden compartment. If Dad hadn't decided to reopen that wing and renovate, we might not have ever found the body."

"Are they sure it's her?"

Ian shook his head. "The coroner's up there now, taking pictures and running a few preliminary tests. It could be days or even weeks before we have a positive ID."

At the sound of hushed voices, Reid glanced toward the living room. "Uncle Harold and Aunt Miranda?"

"They're in the living room with Dad and the rest of the family. If it is Vickie, they want to know as soon as possible."

All the years of not knowing if their daughter was alive or dead. He couldn't even imagine the agony his aunt and uncle had gone through. But even through their devastating loss, even as the months and years had passed without a trace of what had happened, they, and the entire family, hadn't given up hope that one day Vickie would be found alive.

And they wouldn't give up hope now, either, Reid thought somberly. Not until they had tangible, physical proof.

"What about the press?" Reid was surprised they weren't already swarming the mansion like locusts. "What do they know?"

"Nothing yet. Dad's called in a couple of favors to keep this quiet for a day or two, but I doubt we can contain it much longer. Nicola will put together a statement today."

"And the police?"

"They want to speak with the entire family," Ian said. "Right now they're questioning Joyce."

Reid frowned. "Why Joyce?"

"Procedure." Ian shrugged. "I guess they figure the housekeeper always knows everything, sees everything."

"That's certainly true with Joyce," Reid said with a nod. "When we were kids, I always swore that woman had eyes in the back of her head and superhero hearing.''

Ian furrowed his brow. ''Doesn't she?''

Reid managed a grin, then sighed. ''We might as well settle in with everyone else. Looks like it's going to be a long day.''

''Based on the fact you're still in the same clothes I saw you in last night—'' Ian took in his brother's rumpled appearance ''—it looks like your night was a long one, too. Want to tell me about it?''

''Not really.'' He wasn't ready to talk about Tina yet. Wasn't certain what his feelings were, though there was no question he had them. Stronger than any feelings he'd ever had for a woman before.

It was just as well that Tina's aunt had come in when she had, Reid thought. After the night they'd had, a little distance might be a good thing.

But even as Reid followed Ian to the living room, even as he told himself that his family needed him now, that there was a much bigger issue than anything happening in his own personal life, he still couldn't get Tina Alexander out of his mind.

''These potatoes are delicious.'' Yana speared a small slice and popped it in her mouth. ''Your creation?''

Freshly showered and dressed, Tina sat down at the kitchen table. It was just like her aunt to avoid the most obvious question and discuss something as innocuous as potatoes. ''Aunt Yana, I can explain—''

''I don't need the recipe.'' Yana waved her fork.

"You know I never cook unless I'm absolutely forced to."

Tina almost smiled. It was also like her aunt to make light of an awkward situation. "You know what I mean."

"I'm forty-eight years old, Katina," Yana said. "I've been married twice. There's very little you could explain to me that I don't already know."

Tina dropped her gaze. "I...I just don't want you to think that I was...that I—"

"Katina. Look at me." Yana slipped a finger under Tina's chin and lifted. "I was there the day you were born. Such a pretty baby, all pink and bright-eyed. Now you're a beautiful woman. All grown up."

Tina shook her head. "You have to say that. You're my aunt."

"I say it because it's true." Lovingly Yana touched Tina's cheek. "I can see you don't believe me, but one day you will."

She didn't believe her, of course, but still it felt good to hear the words. Tina smiled at her aunt, then said shyly, "It was my first time."

"You always were the cautious one," Yana said with a nod. "And I can see you are still being cautious. What is it you're afraid of, Katina?"

"I—" It was one thing to think it, Tina realized, but to say it out loud was quite another. She drew in a steadying breath. "I think I'm falling in love with him."

"And why is this such a bad thing?"

"I don't know how I'll survive when he...when it's over," she said quietly. "But just thinking about it makes my chest ache. I'm not sure I'm strong enough.''

''You're strong enough.'' Yana's expression was as patient as it was thoughtful. ''But is he?''

Tina furrowed her brow. ''What do you mean?''

''Never mind, my dear.'' Yana patted Tina's hand and smiled. ''Now tell me, was he a good lover?''

Tina nearly choked, felt the heat of a blush race up her neck and across her cheeks. She couldn't believe she was sitting here having this conversation with her aunt. But then, she still couldn't believe that last night had really happened at all.

Smiling slowly, she met her aunt's eyes. ''He was wonderful.''

''*Nagyszeru,*'' Yana said, smiling. ''He is also very handsome. I would have liked to photograph him, especially in that towel.'' Her aunt's smile turned lusty. ''Or without. Maybe you will ask him for me?''

Tina gasped at the outrageous request. But the thought of it also warmed her blood. She knew what that incredible body looked like firsthand, what it felt like against her own.

''Oh, Aunt Yana.'' Laughing, Tina threw her arms around her aunt and hugged her tightly. ''I'm so glad you're here. Welcome home.''

Every Sunday Mariska spent most of her day cooking a six-course meal for her family while Ivan watched sports from his easy chair in the den. From the time they were tall enough to see over the kitchen counter, all of the Alexander daughters helped in the preparation. Though the menu varied, the tradition was strict. Attendance was mandatory, no excuses accepted.

Today was no exception.

''Your mother wants the good silverware and china tonight.'' Carrying the wooden box that contained the silver set, Yana came through the swinging kitchen door. ''Are we celebrating something?''

''She wants the crystal candle holders, too,'' Tina said, smoothing the wrinkles from the white linen tablecloth. She and Yana had walked in the front door only minutes ago and there'd been no time to find out what was going on.

''Maybe it's because she won at bingo last night.'' Rachel pulled plates from the cherrywood buffet and set them on the table. ''She made chicken paprika and has a bottle of Putonos chilling.''

''She's definitely got something she's happy about.'' Yana handed the silverware box to Tina, then winked at both her nieces. ''I'll go see if I can pry it out of her.''

When Yana went back into the kitchen, Tina moved close to Rachel. It was the first time since she'd walked in the door that they'd been alone. ''Are you all right?''

Rachel nodded. ''I sneaked in late last night after Mom and Dad were asleep.''

Shaking her head, Tina sighed. ''We're too old for this, Ray. We've got to talk to Mom and Dad, both of us.''

''I know, I know.'' Then Rachel's eyes widened. ''Both of us? Are you saying what I think you're saying?''

"Yeah." Tina smiled slowly. "I am."

"What's going on?" Sophia swung through the door carrying the candlesticks. She looked at Tina, then Rachel. "No fair. You're telling secrets without me."

"Not me, Tina," Rachel whispered. "She and Reid—"

"Oh, heck—" waving a hand, Sophia moved next to her sisters and formed a circle "—tell me something I don't know."

Tina's jaw dropped. "How do you know?"

"I saw it on your face the minute you walked in, T. Your feet weren't even touching the floor."

"Don't be ridiculous." No one could tell something like that, Tina thought. Lord, she certainly hoped not. Shaking her head, she stepped away from her sisters and opened the silverware box. "But I will admit, it was a little interesting when Yana came home this morning and found Reid wearing nothing but a towel."

Gasping, Rachel clasped a hand to her chest and Sophia lifted a brow. When their father looked over at them from his easy chair, they all quickly turned their attention back to setting the table, then glanced up at each other and started to laugh.

Tina realized how important all this was to her. Family. Tradition. Sharing secrets with her sisters. She knew that no matter how much their lives might change, they would always be there for each other, all of them. Through thick and thin, through happy and sad. Tina could only pray that the happy times would be more plentiful than the sad.

They were nearly finished setting the table when Yana came back out of the kitchen carrying a marble trivet.

"Did you find out anything?" Tina asked.

"As a matter of fact, I did," Yana said. "Rachel, grab another plate and put it on the table, please, and another set of silverware, too."

"I already have six," Tina said, recounting to be sure.

"You'll need seven."

"Seven?"

When the doorbell rang, every head turned.

Yana smiled. "I'll get it."

Tina had a bad feeling as she watched her aunt walk across the living room. A bad, bad feeling.

When Yana opened the door, the bad feeling became a reality.

Reid.

He stood on the front step, the bouquet of roses in his hand bright pink, the dress shirt under his sport coat slate blue. Tina's heart stopped, then began to race.

"What's he doing here?" Rachel grabbed Tina's arm.

"I...I don't know."

Tina and Rachel and Sophia all looked at each other, then said at the same time, *"Mom."*

"Reid." With all the grace of a queen, Yana held out her hand. "What a pleasure to see you again."

"Ms. Romano." Reid handed the roses to Yana, who lifted them to her nose and breathed in their scent.

"How lovely. Please, come in. Mariska will be out in a moment."

"Thank you."

The house was open and warm, Reid noted as he stepped into the foyer of the living room. Beige walls, hardwood floors, a large burgundy sofa covered with tapestry pillows. Lots of framed family photos. The delicious scent of spices and chicken made his mouth water and reminded him he'd barely eaten anything since he'd left Tina at Yana's apartment that morning.

"Girls." Yana slipped her arm through Reid's. "Look who's here."

"Rachel, Sophia." When his gaze shifted to Tina, their eyes met and held. "Tina."

Lips softly parted in shock, she nodded back. It didn't take a genius to figure out that his visit had not been expected.

Though fewer than eight hours had passed since he'd seen her, it felt like days. He wanted to tell her how pretty she looked in a cardigan the same rosy blush as her cheeks and a simple black skirt, but he held himself in check. Knowing that he couldn't just walk up to her and kiss her, he shoved his hands into his pockets. "Reid!" Carrying a steaming casserole, Mariska burst out of the kitchen. "You are just in time."

"Thank you for inviting me, Mrs. Alexander."

"Please, you must call me Mariska," she reminded him. "I am so glad you could come at such short notice."

He glanced at Tina again, who was staring at her

mother in disbelief. "I assure you," Reid said with a smile, "it's my pleasure."

When Ivan yelled something rude from the other room, Mariska shook her head. "My husband and football. I have to pry him out of his chair if there is a game on."

Mariska set the casserole on the table, then frowned at her daughters. "Why do you all stand there like stones? Sophia, get our guest a drink. Yana, will you please tell your brother that supper is ready."

When Rachel started to move toward the kitchen, Mariska stopped her. "Rachel, you keep Reid company while Tina and I bring out the food."

"But—" Rachel cast a nervous glance at Tina, who shook her head "—all right."

When everyone scurried off, Reid leaned down and whispered, "Jason was great last night."

Rachel's nerves seemed to calm at the mention of Jason's name, and her eyes brightened. "Thank you for taking care of him."

While he and Rachel quietly talked about Jason and his band, Reid sipped on the glass of beer Sophia brought him and watched as dish after loaded dish of food came out of the kitchen. Wine and water glasses were filled, crisp white linen napkins were laid beside each plate.

Every time Tina came into the room, their eyes would meet. Every time she would blush, then hurry back out.

"Dinner is ready." Mariska came out of the kitchen carrying a platter of chicken. "Reid, you sit in the chair beside Rachel."

Reid was beginning to have an understanding of what Jason had been going through by needing to hide his feelings for Rachel. It was killing him, Reid thought as he pulled out Rachel's chair for her, that he couldn't touch Tina, or slip an arm around her waist, or even kiss her cheek. Though this might not be the right time, he was determined to make it clear—very soon—that it was Tina he wanted to be with, not Rachel.

Ivan sat at the head of the table, the expression on his face not exactly what Reid would consider cordial. While a bowl of watercress salad made its way around the table, Mariska said to Yana, "Reid's father is going to be our next senator."

Yana held up her wine glass. *"Gratulalok."*

"Thank you, but it might be a little early for congratulations." Reid scooped up a spoonful of dark, fragrant rice with vegetables. "We'll need to have an election first and make it official."

Yana met his gaze, her smile knowing. "One should always hold hope."

"I agree." Reid glanced at Tina, who quickly reached for her wineglass.

"So are you interested in politics yourself?" Yana asked.

He shook his head. "I'm just taking a month off from the family business to help establish a campaign headquarters."

"So, Reid," Mariska said, clearly wanting to steer the subject in a different direction, "I understand you come from a big family. Do you see yourself having children one day?"

He felt Rachel stiffen beside him, while Tina softly coughed. Ivan glared at his wife.

"I'm sure I will," Reid said evenly. "One day."

"When you find the right woman, of course." Mariska handed him a platter. "Chicken?"

Tina's cough turned to a choking sound, and Sophia slapped her on the back.

"Thanks." He speared a leg and set it on his plate. "This all looks and smells delicious. You must have been in the kitchen all day."

"It is nothing." Mariska waved a hand. "Rachel helped with most of the preparation. She is a wonderful cook, you know."

Rachel furrowed her brow. "I chopped the celery and onions, Mom."

"And so beautifully," Mariska said. "Every piece perfect."

Ivan's mouth pressed into a hard line as he stabbed a chicken breast.

"Tell Reid about your bingo win last night, Mariska," Yana said, sipping her wine. "It's such an interesting story."

Thrilled to repeat the story everyone else had already heard five times, Mariska leaned close to Reid. "I have only one number left, B7. Ivan, he has one, as well, B1."

In spite of being distracted by Tina's presence, Reid was truly trying to listen to Mariska. Until he felt a bare toe slide up his pant leg. He froze and looked at Tina, who appeared completely absorbed in her mother's story, then glanced at Sophia, who was casually sipping on a glass of ice water.

When the toe slid higher, Reid grabbed his own water glass to ward off the threatening cough, careful to keep his gaze on Mariska.

"The ball comes up, it is blue, so I know it is a B, and what number do they call?" Mariska slapped a hand to her chest. "B7!"

"It was a hundred dollars." Scowling, Ivan took his knife to his chicken. "You would think she won the lottery, the way she carries on."

"It is a hundred more than you won, Ivan Alexander." Mariska waved a fork at her husband.

The argument was without heat, but it was enough to distract Tina's parents for the moment. Reid looked at Tina, watched her gaze slowly lift to his. Though it was only for a split second, the look she flashed him was as hot as it was arousing.

He really needed to get this woman alone, he thought, taking a gulp of his wine. He hoped like hell it would be soon.

Mariska was serving strudel and coffee when the phone rang. When she started to rise, Rachel sprang out of her chair.

"I'll get it."

"If it is a salesman, hang up on him," Ivan yelled after Rachel, then looked at Reid. "A man cannot have a meal in peace with his family."

Not sure if the comment was directed at him, Reid simply nodded.

"Since when has this family had a peaceful meal?" Mariska said. "You are always grumbling about something."

Ivan frowned at his wife, then forked up a bite of strudel. "I do not grumble. I make observations."

Reid drew in a breath when Tina—he hoped it was Tina—ran her toes up his pant leg again. She was intentionally torturing him, he realized, and was already planning payback when Rachel returned.

"Salesman?" Ivan asked.

"Hang up." Rachel slid back into her seat.

A moment later, while Ivan and Mariska were still discussing how incredibly rude and inconsiderate some people were, Rachel cleared her throat, then looked at Reid and said, "Would you like to go to the movies?"

Phone call forgotten, Mariska beamed. "That is a wonderful idea."

Ivan scowled. "My daughter does not ask a man on a date."

"It's not a date," Rachel said quickly. "There's a new comedy at the cinema. Tina and Sophia said they wanted to see it, too. After we did the dishes, I thought we could all go."

He was beginning to get the picture, but Reid realized it had nothing to do with the movies. Obviously that phone call had been the source of Rachel's unexpected invitation. "I'd love to go."

"You and Reid go." Mariska was already rising from her seat. "Tina and Sophia will help me with the dishes."

"Katina and Sophia will go, too," Ivan decreed.

"Sorry." Sophia shook her head. "I'll help with the dishes, but I promised I'd help out in the office at the club tonight."

"Then Katina will go," Ivan said firmly. "It is settled."

Thank you, Ivan, Reid thought, and when he glanced at Tina, could see she was thinking the same.

It took a while to say their goodbyes, but once they were outside and away from the house, Rachel looked at Tina and Reid. "I'm sure you realize we aren't really going to the movies."

"I figured it out," he said with a nod.

When headlights flashed from a parked car down the street, Rachel hugged Tina, then hurried off.

Left alone in the darkness behind a tall hedge, Reid dragged Tina into his arms and kissed her. Placing her palms flat on his chest, she leaned into him and kissed him back.

"You taste like apples," he said against her lips.

"So do you."

He kissed her again, then whispered, "Well, that was interesting."

"Kissing me?" she teased. "Or having dinner with my parents?"

"Both."

"*Interesting* is not exactly the word I'd use." She blew out a breath. "More like horrific."

He grinned at her. "So you want to tell me exactly what you were doing back there at the dinner table?"

"What do you mean?"

"You know what I mean," he said, lifting a brow. "Sliding your toe up my leg. I nearly had a heart attack."

Furrowing her brow, she met his gaze. "I didn't touch your leg with my toe."

He felt a moment's panic, then saw the smile in her eyes and frowned at her.

"Very funny," he said, then pulled her close and slid his mouth to her neck. The hitch of her breath, her soft sigh, the slight trembling in her hands made his own pulse stutter.

"I asked you a question last night," he murmured, lifting his head. "I don't believe you ever truly answered me."

Her fingers moved restlessly over his chest. "What was that?"

"Will you come home with me?"

Her lashes slowly fluttered up. Smiling, she looked into his eyes. "I thought you'd never ask."

Eight

The penthouse was spacious. Marble foyer, high ceilings, rich, glossy hardwood floors. Antiques—an impressive, and expensive, mix of eighteenth- and nineteenth-century pieces—were artfully arranged throughout the large living room and parlor. Softly lit paintings, mostly oils, graced the hunter-green walls. From an art history class she'd taken at the local college, Tina knew that several of the paintings were nineteenth-century Southern artists.

More than a little intimidated, she stood in front of the wall-to-wall leaded windows overlooking Forsyth Park. A full moon shone silver on the thick treetops; downtown city lights twinkled in the dark. She could only imagine how spectacular the view from here would be during the day.

Wondering briefly if she would ever see that view,

she turned and strolled around the room, paused to admire a walnut Chippendale sideboard table, then moved on to examine the intricate leaf carvings on a mahogany framed mirror.

Engrossed in the detail of the frame, she didn't notice Reid come up behind her. He wrapped his arms around her before she could turn.

"Sorry. I had to return a call from Ian."

Her pulse jumped when she met his gaze in the mirror. "Everything all right?"

On the drive from her house, Reid had told Tina about the body being found in his family's attic and their suspicions that it might be his missing cousin, Victoria. Tina couldn't imagine what the entire Danforth family was going through right now, not knowing the truth and having to wait for days or even weeks before the results of the tests could be verified. Her heart went out to all of them, especially to Reid's aunt and uncle.

"Ian wanted to warn me that there's a hotshot reporter named Jasmine Carmody sniffing around." Reid's arms tightened around Tina. "Nicola wants to keep this situation quiet for as long as possible. Even the hint of a scandal so soon in the campaign could blow the election for my Dad."

"Can you really keep something like this from the press?"

"Not for long." He sighed. "Especially with an army of reporters skulking around every corner just waiting for the tiniest speck of dirt. But we might be able to hold off until we at least get some preliminary results from the DNA testing. That will help Nicola decide how to best handle the press.''

''I can't imagine living under a microscope like that,'' she said quietly. ''I don't think I could stand it.''

''It's part of who I am.'' He shrugged. ''Who my family is. I guess I just accept it.''

''I can certainly understand that.'' She smiled at him. ''After spending the evening with my family, you probably wonder how I manage to get through a day without going crazy.''

He brought his face beside hers, grinned at her in the mirror. ''I think your family is terrific, though I don't think your dad likes me too much. You know the saying 'if looks could kill'? It's amazing I made it out of your house alive tonight.''

She laughed softly at the absurdity, yet truth, of his statement. ''My dad doesn't like any man who wants to date one of his daughters. He says that men just want one thing.''

''Smart man.'' Reid brushed his mouth along her neck, then moved up to nuzzle her ear.

The closeness of his body, his mouth just a few inches from her own, made it hard for Tina to think. She desperately wanted to turn in his arms, press her lips to his and ask him to take her to his bed, or just simply take her, but watching what he was doing to her in the mirror absolutely mesmerized her.

''I thought about you today,'' he whispered.

''Did you?'' Her breath quickened when his tongue flicked over her earlobe.

''Did you think about me?''

"No." Every nerve ending along her neck quivered.

He glanced at her in the mirror and smiled smugly. "Liar."

"Maybe a little," she admitted, heard the breathlessness in her own voice.

"Just a little?" He moved to her neck, rubbed his lips up and down the slender column of soft, sensitive flesh.

Her skin grew hot and tight, her bones soft. Afraid she might slide to the floor, she leaned back against his chest. "Maybe more than a little."

Keeping his eyes locked with hers, he smiled against her neck. "What did you think about?"

"Towels."

He lifted his head. "You thought about towels?"

"Actually, it was more about the expression on your face when my aunt walked in and that's all you were wearing."

"Me?" His smile widened. "You should have seen *your* face."

Just thinking about it now made her cheeks warm. "It's not every day a member of my family walks in and finds me with a naked man."

"I'm glad to hear that." He nipped at her neck. "Very glad."

His teeth on her skin sent shivers through her. His breath was hot on her throat. She felt her eyelids grow heavy, her blood thicken. Each and every beat of her heart echoed like a drum inside her brain.

"My aunt wants to photograph you," she managed to say, even as a whirlwind of heat spiraled through her mind and body.

He stilled, looked at her doubtfully. "Me?"

"In your towel." She watched him lift one brow. "But preferably without."

"Maybe some other time," he said, though his expression said more like "never." "I'm going to be a little busy for a while."

"Doing what?"

"This," Reid murmured, and turned his attention back to Tina's neck.

He couldn't get enough of the taste and feel of her. Watching her in the mirror aroused him like nothing he'd ever experienced before. The flutter of her thick lashes, the rise and fall of her breasts, the soft flush of desire on her cheeks. He slid his hands under her sweater, felt warm skin and soft cotton. She shivered when he cupped her breasts.

She fit perfectly. Firm, yet soft, and when he caressed her, he felt her nipples harden against his palms.

"Reid." She said his name on a ragged whisper, tried to turn in his arms.

"Don't move." He held her against him. "I want to look at you."

She stilled, held her breath when he reached for the hem of her sweater, then slowly pulled it over her head and tossed it aside.

Her bra was baby pink, simple cotton, and he didn't think he'd ever seen anything sexier in his life. Gently, he kneaded the firm, soft flesh, then slipped the fabric down and bared her breasts.

Her cheeks darkened with a blush, and she dropped her eyes.

"Look at me, Tina," he said hoarsely. "Keep your eyes on me."

He watched her lift her gaze to his, saw the fire in her eyes, the same fire that raced through his own blood and over his skin. He lowered his gaze and had to remind himself to breathe. She was so beautiful, her skin so soft and smooth. He brushed his thumbs over her rosy nipples, saw and felt them grow tighter under his touch.

Every inch of him wanted to take her now, right this second, standing right here. But he couldn't let go of this moment, not yet. He felt intoxicated by the sight and touch of her, wanted this feeling to last as long as he—as they both—could possibly stand it. Not a simple task when he wanted to touch her, kiss her everywhere at once.

So he concentrated on her breasts. Stroking, caressing, teasing. Pushing fabric away until there was only skin against skin, soft against rough, ivory against tan. He thought he might die if he didn't taste her soon, if he couldn't take her pearled nipple in his mouth, feel the hardness of her against his tongue.

On a moan her head fell back against his chest. And then her hands got busy.

She slid her hands up and down the outsides of his thighs, a slow, rhythmic movement…up, down, up again…gradually inching her way to the inside. When her fingertips skimmed the edge of his hardness, he sucked in a breath.

It shocked Tina that her knees were still able to hold her. Like warm wax, her body melted against Reid's, molding intimately so she felt every muscle of his chest against her back, the curve of her hips against his, the press of his erection against her buttocks. Watching what he was doing to her, with his hands on her breasts, his mouth on her throat and neck, was more than she could bear.

Didn't he know that? she thought, squirming against him. Didn't he know how much she wanted him, how desperately she needed him?

She took comfort in knowing that the sweet torture was not hers alone. His eyes had darkened with need, as well. His body had grown hard and tense, his breathing had turned ragged. If this was a contest as to who could last the longest without begging, she would surely—gladly—lose.

"Reid," she breathed his name, pressed herself firmly against him and moved back and forth, felt him grow harder still.

His hand moved down her stomach to the button on her slacks and popped it open. Tugging her zipper down, he slid his fingertips over her belly, then cupped her in his palm. When he pressed his lips to her ear and whispered what he wanted to do, she thought, *Yes, yes!* Please do that and more!

Moaning softly, she could only wonder when and how she'd become so shameless, so wanton. She felt as if she might burst into flames any moment, and when he began to stroke her, she did. A firestorm swept over her, and the fury of it consumed her.

"Look at me," she gasped.

His eyes, glinting dark with need, met hers.

"I need you," she whispered roughly. Taking hold

of his wrist, she moved her hips against him. "Inside me."

His jaw tightened, then he turned her toward him, dropping his mouth down on hers at the same time he lifted her up in his arms. She slid her arms around his neck and held on tight, the urgency overwhelming her ability to think of anything but satiating the raw, consuming need.

While walking with her to the bedroom, his mouth never left hers for more than a second. Kiss by kiss, touch by touch, their clothes fell away. Arms entwined, they tumbled onto the bed. She felt the mattress give beneath her, the downy cushion of a comforter, the slide of soft cotton on her back. The hard press of man.

Her breath caught, and she wrapped her arms around his shoulders as much to brace herself as to pull him closer. He bent his head to her neck, her shoulder, then to her breast. She arched upward on a moan when he took her into his mouth and suckled, arrows of white-hot pleasure shot from her breast to the V of her thighs. He used his tongue and teeth and lips on her; one moment he was gentle, the next he was rough. She couldn't decide which she liked better. Both thrilled her, aroused her to the edge of insanity.

When he finally moved between her legs and entered her, she slipped over that edge.

After what they'd shared the previous night, Tina wouldn't have thought it possible that this joining could be more. But somehow it was. This time she felt as if he took more than her body, more than her heart, but her very soul. In every way she was absolutely and completely vulnerable. She held back nothing, willingly gave all she was.

He thrust deeply inside the tight, hot glove of her body. Again and again. Long, slow strokes that gradually quickened. Like a drum beating faster, then faster still, pounding fiercely. They moved as one, the urgency now gripping them both.

She cried out when the first shudder rolled through her, dug her fingernails into the rippling muscles of his damp back. He took her hips in his hands, held her still as the second shudder shattered inside her.

She felt his climax stiffen his body. On a deep, harsh groan, he crushed her to him and shuddered.

Too spent to move, to speak, to even think, they sank into the mattress together. After minutes or hours, it was hard to say which, he rolled to his side and pulled her into his arms.

Laying her head and hand on his chest, she listened to, and felt, the heavy beat of his heart.

And she smiled.

When Reid woke, he had no sense of time. He glanced at the bedside table, then realized they'd only been asleep a few minutes. Tina stirred at the movement, then murmured a complaint when he slid out from under her.

"You're cold." He pulled down the bedclothes, then tucked her under the warmth of the covers.

Her eyes fluttered open as she rolled to her side and tucked her hands under her face. "I wasn't until you moved."

Light from the moon washed the walls in shades of

gray, sent shadows sliding across the floor. An over-whelming sense of peace and...wholeness? settled over the room.

Climbing under the covers beside Tina, he stretched out and leaned on an elbow, gazed down at her and grinned. ''You look good in my bed, darling.''

Her eyes met his as she slid a fingertip from his shoulder to his hand. ''You have such a big one.''

His grin widened. ''Thanks.''

Rolling her eyes, she slid her fingertip to his chest and pushed. ''Bed.''

''Oh.'' He feigned a hurt look.

''Very masculine.''

His heart lurched when her fingertip slid down his chest to his rib cage. ''I'm glad you like it.''

It wasn't so much what she was doing to him as it was what she *wasn't* doing. With her finger tracing the outline of his bottom rib, she seemed quite content to touch him, but stay within the parameters of ''safe'' territory.

Not that her touching him anywhere was exactly what he'd call safe, Reid thought.

When she ever so slightly inched her way down-ward, he sucked in a breath and covered her hand with his. ''Tina, look at me.''

She lifted her gaze to his, and he realized she didn't have to touch him at all to turn him on. All she had to do was look at him with those languid bed-room eyes.

''I'm not going to pretend I'm interested in Rachel anymore.''

Her hand stilled, then she rolled to her back. ''I

know," she said, closing her eyes. "I don't want you to."

Leaning over her, he brushed his mouth against hers. "We can talk to your parents tomorrow and—"

"No!" Her eyes snapped open. "I'll need to talk to Rachel first, to prepare her. Then I'll talk to my parents."

"I understand that family dynamics can be complicated. Lord knows mine gives new meaning to the word. But you're twenty-four years old."

She shook her head. "You don't understand my father. When it comes to Sophia and Rachel and me, he's more than unreasonable—he's irrational and inflexible."

"What could he object to?" Reid asked, then cocked his head and grimaced. "Well, other than the fact I've seduced his youngest daughter and taken her virginity. So how big are the knives in his kitchen, anyway?"

"Just be glad he's a baker, not a butcher." Smiling, she pressed a kiss to his jaw, then dropped her gaze. "Reid, I want you to know that just because you... because we, ah, slept together, I'm not expecting, I mean, I'm not asking for any kind of—" She blew out a breath. "You know."

"Commitment?" The word felt odd on his tongue. He had to roll it around in his mouth, found the taste wasn't as bitter as he'd thought it would be.

If anything, he suddenly realized with startling clarity, the taste was just right.

Yet here Tina was, Reid thought irritably, intently trying to explain to him that she wasn't expecting, or asking, for a relationship. He frowned at her. "Are you dumping me, Tina?"

"No, of course not." Her gaze snapped back up. "I just think you, *we,* should be open and honest with each other."

"Haven't we been?"

"I just don't want any misunderstanding between us."

"Looks to me like there already is, sweetheart." She gasped when he took her by the shoulders and rolled to his back, bringing her on top of him. "Look, I don't know exactly what's going on here between us, but I do know I want to be with you, openly and publicly."

"I'd like to be with you, too," she said softly, then pressed her smile to his mouth. "But your family, your father's campaign—"

"My father's campaign has nothing to do with you and me, Tina. Who I see personally and what I do in my private life is my business."

"And every newspaper and magazine reporter's in Savannah," she added.

"That's always a possibility," he said with a nod. "I'm a Danforth. I can't stop being who I am."

Her eyes softened as she touched his cheek. "I wouldn't want you to, Reid."

Her hand on his cheek, such a simple, gentle gesture, made his chest hitch. He couldn't remember any woman who'd ever made him feel this way. No woman who had ever mattered so much.

He took her lovely, delicate face in his hands and

brought her mouth to his, wondered if he would ever get enough of the sweet taste of her.

He certainly intended to try.

Tracing the seam of her lips with his tongue, he slid inside the honeyed softness. Her tongue met his, mating, stroking, slowly growing more urgent. He felt more than heard the moan from deep in her throat, and the slight forward thrust of her hips heated his blood.

Wanting, needing more, he deepened the kiss, slanted his mouth against hers over and over. He ran his hands down her back, cupped the round softness of her firm bottom, arched his hips up to press intimately into the V of her legs.

They were both breathing heavily when she rose upward, then slowly came back down onto the hard length of him, inch by torturous inch. He pressed himself deeply inside her, his hands tightly gripping her hips.

And then she began to move. Slowly at first, drawing out the intense pleasure until it became unbearable. With every thrust of her hips, the rhythm built, spiraled. The fever swept through them like a storm, wild and fierce. Powerful.

Eyes closed, hair tumbling around her shoulders, she tossed her head back on a sharp cry as her climax shuddered through her. He crushed his hips to hers, driving himself into her again and again, until his body convulsed with the same release.

She collapsed on him, gasping for breath, murmuring something incoherent. Struggling to breathe, himself, he wrapped his arms around her, brushed his mouth over her temple and kissed her cheek.

While their hearts and breathing slowed and their minds cleared, he held her close, smiled when she sighed and snuggled against his chest. "No more sneaking around," he reminded her.

"Tomorrow," she murmured on a nod. "I'll talk to my parents tomorrow."

Nine

Tina came into the bakery through the back entrance, winced at the bright tinkling of the bell that signaled the opening of the door. On a daily basis, she never even noticed the sound. But today, considering the fact she was an hour late, that little brass bell seemed to blare with the fervor of a bastille trumpeter.

Once, Tina remembered, when Sophia was sixteen, she'd managed to wrench the clangor out of the bell so she could meet a boyfriend in the back garden. But their father had caught on quickly enough. The boyfriend had been banished, Sophia grounded, and the bell replaced with a stronger, louder, daughter-proof model. While Mariska held charge at the front door, from the kitchen, Ivan kept track of the comings and goings through the back door. No one sneaked in, no one sneaked out. As teenagers, it had driven the Alexander girls crazy, but as adults, Tina had never given it much thought.

Until today.

Today, she thought with a smile, she'd overslept in the arms of the man she loved.

A shiver ran through her that had nothing to do with the cool air coming in through the still-open back door. When she'd wakened this morning in Reid's penthouse, with his broad chest pressed against her back and his muscled arm draped possessively around her waist, she'd had to pinch herself. *Enjoy the moment,* she'd told herself. Don't think about the future. Don't let yourself hope, or wish, for too much. Be happy with what you have now.

But what if, she thought. What if maybe, just maybe…

A breeze whispered over her neck, and an unreasonable dread shivered through her. She closed the door, wincing again at the bell's clanging, then glanced at her watch. Rachel would be in her office already, and even though Tina knew they needed to talk, she didn't dare take the time now.

Hurrying down the hallway, she stuck her head around the corner and cringed at the sight of the long customer line. Her mother was working the register while her aunt helped fill orders. Billy, the counter clerk Tina had just hired, was working the coffee counter.

She wondered briefly where Jason was, then realized he was probably already preparing to go to Los Angeles with his band.

Terrific. One more straw on the camel's back.

At least Yana had come in to help this morning, Tina thought. That would save the day from being a complete calamity. Tina caught her aunt's attention and gave her an is-it-safe-to-enter look. Yana nodded, then pressed a finger to her lips.

Sucking in a breath to calm her nerves, Tina walked behind the counter and grabbed an apron.

"Katina." Her mother frowned at her. "Where have you been?"

"I'm sorry, I—" She glanced at her aunt, who shook her head.

"Never mind." Mariska cut Tina off with a swipe of her hand. "We will talk about this later. Take the register while I package Mrs. Green's brioche."

A crash from the kitchen, then mumbled cursing, had Mariska shaking her head. "There will be no living with that man today."

"I'll go talk to him," Yana said, then winked at Tina. "He'll be fine."

Tina swallowed the lump of tension in her throat, grateful for the temporary reprieve. Even though this was not looking like the best of days to have a father/daughter talk, she'd made a promise to Reid, and for both their sakes, she was determined to keep that promise.

It was another fifteen minutes before the morning rush finally thinned out, and with only two customers in the bakery, both of them sitting at tables, and her mother and Yana in the kitchen, Tina knew she had to "seize the moment," as the saying went. It was time for her, and for Rachel, to tell their parents the truth. It was time for them to realize that their daughters were not children anymore, but adults.

"Billy, watch the counter," she said to the new clerk. "I'll be back in a minute."

She was already heading for Rachel's office when the bakery door opened and Reid walked in.

No! she wanted to say. *You can't be here yet.* She was torn between throwing her arms around him or throwing him out.

When he walked straight toward her, her heart stopped.

For a moment she almost thought he was going to kiss her, but he didn't, just looked at her and smiled.

Her insides turned soft and warm.

Quickly she looked at the customers to see if they'd noticed who had walked in. When it appeared they hadn't, she grabbed his hand and pulled him into the hallway out of sight.

"Reid—"

His mouth caught hers, and for a moment she leaned against him, her pulse quickening as she returned the kiss. Oh, he smelled so good, a woodsy aftershave, and he tasted like mint. She wanted to kiss him all over.

Somehow she managed to come to her senses and stepped back.

"You shouldn't be here now," she said, still breathless from his kiss.

"I know." Sighing, he shoved his hands into his pockets. "I couldn't help myself."

In spite of her nerves, she smiled, then folded her arms and took another step back before she did something she'd regret, like wrap herself around him and kiss him again.

"This isn't a good time." Keeping her voice low, she glanced over her shoulder toward the kitchen. "I'm not sure what's going on, but my father's on the warpath this morning."

"Have you told him about us?"

She shook her head. "I got to work so late I didn't have a chance, and he's been in such a mood, I think it's better to wait."

"Why don't you and I go now?" he said quietly. "Together."

"It's not that simple." She closed her eyes and hugged her arms tightly around her. "You don't know what it's like when—"

"*Katina.*"

At the sound of her father's voice in the hallway behind her, Tina's heart dropped. Slowly, very slowly, she turned and faced him. The look of fury on his face turned her blood to ice.

Ivan's gaze snapped to Reid. "You. In my kitchen."

"Yes, sir."

Tina touched his arm as he moved past her. "Reid," she whispered. "You don't have—"

"It's all right," he said with a nod. "It's time."

Heart racing, she followed Reid and her father into the kitchen, where her mother and Yana were dusting powdered sugar on cooled nut cookies. "Dad—"

"Quiet." Her father pointed a finger at her. "This is not your concern, Katina."

Not my concern? Too stunned to even respond, she simply stared at her father.

"Were you with my daughter last night?" Ivan demanded.

"Yes, sir."

"Ivan, keep hold of your temper." Wiping her hands, Mariska stepped closer to her husband. "We should discuss this calmly."

"Calmly!" He broke into a string of Hungarian phrases that Tina had never heard before and couldn't make out. "You think I should be calm when our daughter spends the night out with this man?"

"With all respect, sir," Reid said without raising his voice or batting an eye. "I'd like to say—"

"Please." Tina looked at Reid. "Let me explain."

"How can you explain for your sister?" Ivan narrowed his eyes as he looked at Tina. "When she gets here, she will speak for herself."

When she gets here? It took a beat to sink in. They were talking about *Rachel,* Tina realized. And what did they mean "when she gets here?"

"Rachel's not here yet?" Tina asked carefully.

Mariska bottom lip quivered. "She did not come home last night, or to work this morning. She did not even call."

Tina looked from her father, who had his beefy arms folded over his wide chest, then to her aunt, who shook her head.

"This is unbelievable." Tina looked up at the ceiling and sighed, then squared her shoulders. "Mom... Dad, Rachel's fine, but she didn't spend the night with Reid."

"The man just admitted it," Ivan shouted, then glared at Reid. "I demand to know where my daughter is."

"She's right here. With me."

All heads turned at the sound of Jason's voice. He stood at the back kitchen entrance, his arm locked securely around Rachel's waist.

"She was with me last night," Jason said, meeting Ivan's eye.

Uh-oh. Tina heard her mother gasp, then watched her father's face turn deep red and his eyes bulge. Here it comes.

"We got married." Beaming with happiness, Rachel held up her left hand to display the gold band on her third finger. "I'm Mrs. Jason Burns."

Rachel's announcement seemed to suck the air out of the room. No one spoke, no one moved.

"I love your daughter." Jason looked at Rachel and smiled. "And she loves me. I want to spend my life with her."

"Please be happy for us," Rachel said, her eyes filling with tears. "Please. I love him so much."

Breath held, Tina waited for her parents to say something, *anything,* but the shock hadn't worn off yet. They were still frozen in place, their eyes wide.

Maybe this wasn't going to be such a good time to tell her parents about Reid, after all, Tina thought.

It was Yana who moved first. Wiping her hands on a towel, she moved across the kitchen and wrapped her arms around both Rachel and Jason. "May you be blessed with happiness, health and many children."

"Well, that's the rest of the good news." Rachel

hugged her aunt back, then looked at her parents timidly. "We're going to have a baby."

Gasping once again, Mariska clutched a fist to her chest. Ivan went from red to purple.

A baby? Rachel was having a baby?

Her parents forgotten for the moment, Tina rushed to her sister and new brother-in-law and threw her arms around them. "When…how…"

"I wasn't sure until yesterday." Rachel wiped at her tears. "That's why I didn't get a chance to tell you, and then last night, when you went with Reid and I—" Rachel bit her lip when she realized what she'd said.

"Stop!" Ivan's bellow rattled the pans. "Everyone stop right now."

They all froze.

His fists on his hips, Ivan stomped across the kitchen and narrowed his eyes at Rachel. "You got married to Jason and are having a baby."

Rachel nodded hesitantly.

Ivan swung a look at Tina. "And *you* were with this man—" he glared at Reid "—last night."

Tina swallowed the lump in her throat and nodded.

A muscle twitched in Ivan's jaw. He turned slowly and looked at his wife. "How could this happen?"

"What's happened?"

It was Sophia who spoke. She stood in the kitchen doorway, took in the look on everyone's faces, plus the way Rachel and Jason were wrapped around each other, then arched a brow and said, "Oh."

Calmly, so calmly it frightened everyone, Ivan removed his apron and walked out of the room.

No one moved or spoke for a full ten seconds, then Yana let out a breath and said, "Well. I'd say that went well."

"My baby." Eyes overflowing with tears, Mariska opened her arms and rushed to Rachel. "I am going to be a grandmother."

And then Mariska was hugging everyone, including Reid, though she did grab his arms and frown at him for a moment before she sighed heavily, then hugged him again.

"Reid." Tina touched his arm. "I'm going to go talk to my father."

"I'll go with you."

"It's better if I go alone right now," she said, shaking her head. "Please."

He sighed, then nodded. "I'll be next door."

She found her father in the garden, standing by the small pond, staring down at the rippling water. The morning air was beginning to warm as the sun rose higher, and somewhere overhead in the branches of a magnolia tree, a songbird called to its mate.

He didn't turn when she approached, and she wasn't certain if he hadn't heard her, or if he was avoiding her. She stood quietly, several feet away and watched him, realized how long it had been since she'd truly looked at her father. He had always been a big man, strong, with shoulders broad enough to carry the world, she'd thought growing up.

Looking at him now, with those shoulders slightly bent and a distinguished touch of gray at his temples, her heart swelled with love. She couldn't bear it if he turned away from her, or from Rachel.

She stepped closer, was about to speak when he said, "Do you remember when we built this pond, Katina?"

His question stopped her. "I was ten," she said after a moment. "We lived upstairs, over the bakery."

"I mixed the cement, you and your sisters placed every rock exactly where they are now."

Nodding, she moved beside him. "You took us to the riverfront fair and let us each win a fish at the ping-pong toss."

"You named yours Gilbert." He turned then. "But you called it Gil."

She stared at him in wonder. "That was fourteen years ago. How could you remember that?"

"You are my baby," he said evenly. "You, your sisters. All of you. How can I forget?"

Tears welled in her eyes as she met his gaze. When he opened his arms, she moved into the comfort there. She couldn't remember how long it had been since he'd held her like this. Since she'd wanted him to.

"How can you, and Rachel and Sophia, how can you do this to me?" he said, his voice edged with anger. "To your mother."

Her heart sank. She'd wanted so desperately for him to understand and to accept she wasn't a child anymore. Lifting her head, she looked up at him, searching for the words.

"How can you grow up?" he said more softly, then touched her cheek and shook his head. "It is not right."

Relief poured through her. "I love you."

"And do you love him?" he asked.

She hesitated, then slowly nodded.

Her father sighed. "Does he love you?"

"I know he cares for me," she said. "But his family, our lives, are so different. I don't know if there's a place for me there."

"Ah. I see. This can be a problem." It was a long moment before her father spoke, as if he were carefully considering what Tina had said. "When your mother married me, your grandfather never spoke to her again."

Confused, Tina looked up at her father. "But I thought he died when Mom when a teenager."

"Your mother was eighteen, I was nineteen when I asked for her hand." Ivan's mouth pressed into a hard line. "A common man marrying a woman whose great-grandmother was a countess. He thought I was arrogant."

Tina had never heard there was a countess in her lineage, but as intriguing as it was, she realized this wasn't the time to ask. "You *are* arrogant."

"And you are impudent," he said, frowning. "But that was not the only reason he would not speak to your mother."

"Then what was?"

Ivan met his daughter's gaze, then sighed heavily. "Come sit, Katina," he said softly. "It is time I tell you the truth."

Reid paced the length of the back office in the campaign headquarters, wondering what was taking Tina so long. There hadn't been any explosions next door yet, nor had Ivan charged through the door breathing fire, so at least that much was a positive.

He wasn't used to waiting and it was driving him crazy. In fact, the operative word here was *crazy*. Everything about this entire situation was insane. A smarter, wiser man would have stayed away, he thought, would walk—no *run*—away. There were bound to be endless complications, and who the hell needed complications?

"Not me," he said to himself, then turned to pace the length of the office again. "I like things simple and easy," he told himself, and glanced at his wristwatch.

So what the hell was taking her so long?

He supposed she had her hands full at the moment. With her father finding out she'd spent the night with a man, then Rachel getting married *and* being pregnant, Reid imagined the dust was still flying.

What he found odd was that he hadn't wanted to leave, that he'd wanted to stay and be a part of all that dust. And that was *really* crazy.

Turning to pace again, he shoved his hands into his pockets. Dammit, where was she?

He started for the door, then stopped himself. He couldn't go back over there. Not yet. He'd give her another half hour, maybe even forty-five minutes. It wasn't as if he didn't have anything to do. He had five messages to return, one from Ian warning him that Jasmine Carmody had been snooping around at one of D&D's coffeehouses, the rest were from his shipping office regarding a lost container coming in from the Maximilian Paper account overseas. He knew he should handle that problem first, before he went back to the bakery.

He reached for the phone, punched in his office number, then slammed the phone back down.

Dammit!

He was heading for the door when he heard the light knock. Annoyed, he threw it open. "What!"

Startled, Tina took a step back. "I…I'm sorry. I can come back late—"

Grabbing her arm, he dragged her inside his office, kicking the door closed as he pulled her into his arms.

She stiffened when he caught her mouth with his, then relaxed and slid her arms around his neck. Her lips parted and he flicked his tongue over hers, a rough, deep, demanding kiss. Possessive. He could have tasted her forever like this, held her forever, but he finally, reluctantly, lifted his head and gazed down at her. "I had to do that first."

Her lips were still damp and rosy from his kiss, so tempting. He bent his head again.

"No." She placed a hand on his chest and he could feel her fingers trembling.

"You okay?"

"I…I don't know what I am."

Her voice was so distant, so strange, it worried him.

When she stepped out of his arms and turned away, he clenched his jaw. "Look, I know this is hard on your parents and it's a lot for one day, but dammit, we aren't kids. Just because they don't want you to see me—"

"No." She turned back, leveled her gaze with his. "That's not it at all."

What he saw in her eyes, the bleak emptiness, made his gut twist. "Then what?"

She sighed heavily, then folded her arms close. "When my father was a teenager, he was an apprentice in his country. He worked at the Castle Marcel under a man named Wilheim, who was the head baker."

"Why are you—"

"Please." She put up a hand. "Just listen."

Though he thought he might explode, Reid pressed his lips tightly together.

"There was no king or queen at the castle," Tina said. "Just a duke. But that's not relevant. Wilheim is."

When she paused, it took Reid every ounce of willpower he had not to rush her, but clearly she was struggling to gather her thoughts.

"According to my father," she finally went on, "Wilheim hated him, humiliated him every chance he got, publicly and privately. After four years, when my father turned nineteen, he'd decided he'd had enough and left. Wilheim lied and told the constable that my father had stolen Castle Marcel's secret recipes, recipes that had been passed down for generations. There was a warrant issued for my father's arrest."

In the corporate world, Reid knew that recipes of any food business were highly guarded, kept under lock and key and sophisticated alarm systems. And though it was a white-collar crime, it was still a crime.

"Isn't it a little extreme for Wilheim to have your father arrested?" Reid asked.

"Wilheim hated my father," Tina said. "Even

though all the recipes my father took were his own, they were recipes that Wilheim had taken credit for. Wilheim was worried he would be found out.''

''Surely your father could have proven himself innocent,'' Reid argued. ''The courts would have exonerated him.''

''Maybe, maybe not.'' She sighed. ''Wilheim had connections in high places. My father was young and afraid he would rot in prison. So he and my mother left the country on a merchant ship and were married. He worked in the galley to support them. When they came to America, they changed their name, moved from New York to Florida, then ended up in Savannah just before Sophia was born.''

She looked so pale, Reid thought. Her eyes so empty. And for the first time, he felt the fear snake through him.

''Tina. Sit.'' She stiffened when he took her arm, but he held on and tugged her to a chair, then knelt beside her. ''That was thirty years ago. Wilheim is probably dead by now.''

She shook her head. ''He's not dead.''

''So, what difference does it make?'' Reid said. ''He couldn't possibly still be angry.''

''Oh, but he is,'' she said quietly. ''When my father left, he did take something of Wilheim's.''

''What was that?''

''My mother. Wilheim is my grandfather.''

Whoa. Reid whistled through his teeth, then sat in the chair beside Tina. ''Oh,'' was all he could manage to say.

''Yeah. Oh.''

They were both silent for a moment, then Tina said, "My mother has called my grandfather several times over the years and tried to mend the rift, but he refuses. He insists he can still have my father arrested. My mother has never told him their new name or where we live, in case he tries to cause trouble."

"It will never stick, not after all this time. A good lawyer will clear him."

"My father is worried that even an accusation of being a thief will bring shame to his family. It's one of the reasons he's always been so protective of us, worrying that someday he might be found out."

"But your mother was happy when she thought I was interested in Rachel," Reid insisted.

"She was too excited at the prospect of one of her daughters marrying a Danforth to think about repercussions to the family," Tina said. "My father is innocent but innocent people are ruined everyday, Reid. I don't have to tell you that."

What she was saying was true, Reid knew. No matter how innocent a person truly was, accusations hung around like a bad smell. "Look, Tina, I know how difficult this might seem to you, but we—"

"It's not difficult, it's impossible. And I'm only telling you all this so you'll understand." She stood, looked down at him. "I can't jeopardize my family, and I won't jeopardize yours, either. If we continued to see each other, the media would be just as interested in my family as they are yours, and they'd be looking for dirt. Everyone would be hurt."

"Dammit, Tina." He rose and took hold of her arm. "We'll find a way to—"

"There is no 'we,' Reid," she said quietly, pulling her arm back. "There can't be. Not now. Not ever."

He wanted to shake her. Wanted to argue, to yell, throw something, even. But the cold conviction in her eyes told him that nothing was going to get through to her.

So he said nothing. Just felt his gut tighten and his stomach clench as he watched her turn, open the door and walk out of his life.

Ten

"It will not be too big, I have decided. No more than two hundred. Tina and Sophia, you will help me with the menu. Yana, you will take the pictures, of course."

Even though ten days had passed since Rachel and Jason had gotten married and left for Los Angeles, Mariska had not stopped talking about the impending reception. No one bothered to mention to her that she'd repeated herself at least a hundred times. She was too caught up in the excitement of her daughter's marriage to listen to anyone but herself. And the baby, good heavens! Mariska Alexander was going to be a grandmother, and she made sure that everyone knew.

While her mother rattled on and her father cleaned his oven, Tina dried the cake pans that Sophia and Yana had washed. It was the end of a long, busy day at the bakery, and rather than go home, Tina had stayed to help clean. If she kept busy, she didn't think as much.

It hurt to think. For that matter, it hurt to breathe.

"And the cake! Ivan, you must create something special, so special that people will cry at the mere sight of it, let alone the taste."

Just the mention of Rachel's wedding cake *did* make Tina feel like crying. She was happy for her sister, of course, and for Jason, but with her own heart shattered into tiny pieces, it was more than a little difficult to get excited about a wedding reception.

Reid had made several attempts to talk with her since she'd walked out of his office, but she'd coolly and quickly ended any discussion he'd tried to have with her. What was the point in discussing what could never be? It was impossible to date openly, and dangerous to date secretly.

Maybe it was for the best, she thought. They hadn't known each other that long. Surely it would only hurt more later when he decided to move on, she told herself. But it didn't make her feel any better, and she couldn't imagine any pain worse than what she felt in her chest right now.

"Abraham Danforth's secretary called this morning and ordered three hundred pastries for Saturday," Mariska said to everyone. "We will need extra hands to have them ready for delivery by four."

Tina's fingers tightened on the towel in her hand. Just hearing the name Danforth made her heart skip, but she forced herself to remain calm. She knew her family was concerned about her since she'd ended her relationship with Reid. She didn't want them to worry

or fuss over her, was afraid she might break down if
they did.

She'd convinced them all she'd be fine, that Reid
had understood why they could never be more than
friends. It was ridiculous, of course. She knew she
could never truly just be friends with Reid. Not when
every time she saw him she wanted to wrap herself
around him, wanted to feel his heartbeat against hers,
his mouth on her lips.

She shook the dangerous thoughts off, set down the
pan she'd dried, then picked up another without missing a beat.

"We will all have to be ready for the party by six-
thirty," Mariska continued. "Cocktails are at seven
and dinner is at eight."

Party? Tina's hand stilled on the cake pan.

The party. At Crofthaven. What seemed like a lifetime ago, Nicola had invited all the volunteers at the
orientation meeting to come to a campaign-kick-off
celebration. Tina silently groaned. She'd completely
forgotten. And when she realized the party was only
two days from now, her heart jackhammered against
her ribs.

Oh, dear God! She couldn't possibly go. Couldn't
look at Reid, couldn't even be in the same room with
him. Here at the bakery was one thing, but at a party?
Without the formality of work and the solid wall of a
counter between them, she would fall apart for certain.

"Tina?"

She glanced up sharply and looked at her mother.
"What?"

"Will you be all right?" Mariska asked softly. "You do not have to go if you do not want to."

"Of course I'm going." The way everyone was watching her, with sympathy in their eyes, she knew she *had* to go. She needed to prove to her family that she was over Reid. This would be the perfect opportunity. She would laugh, she would smile, maybe even flirt a little, though she'd rather pick blackberries in high heels, naked.

She imagined the feeling would be somewhat the same.

"Are you sure?" Sophia asked softly.

"I told you." Tina shrugged casually and reached for another pan to dry. "Reid and I are still friends. I'll be fine."

Her father grunted, and she wasn't sure if the sound was directed at her or the oven he was cleaning.

It didn't matter, she told herself. As difficult as it would be, she would go to the party, and for everyone's sake, she would pretend she was having a wonderful time.

It was nearly midnight when Reid walked through his front door. He'd spent the day at his father's campaign headquarters, but the escalating crisis with the lost container had kept him at his Danforth & Co. office until after eleven. Maximilian Paper Products' shipping department had been screaming at Reid's office to find the container immediately, and Reid had decided to handle the problem himself. Fortunately, the error had turned up on Maximilian's end when Reid discovered that one of the office workers had transposed a docking number. Once the mistake had been cleared, Reid had finally been able to go home.

Not that it much mattered to him where he went. If anything, he'd rather stay at work and deal with angry clients. It was much easier than coming home to an empty apartment. Much easier than sleeping alone in his bed, thinking about Tina. Remembering the way she'd looked lying in his bed, with her hair tousled and her eyes glazed with passion.

He missed her smile, the way her brow arched when she was surprised. The way she said his name. When she was annoyed, it was "Reid!" short and clipped. When she smiled, it was "Reid," warm and soft. When they'd made love it was breathless, "Reid..."

He couldn't get her out of his head, though God knew he'd tried. Other than a polite hello every time he'd gone into the bakery, she hadn't actually spoken to him for ten days. Ten days, dammit!

He dropped his keys on his entry table and dragged a hand through his hair. If she refused to talk to him, how the hell were they supposed to work out this problem?

But the real question was, could they?

Sighing, he slipped out of his coat, tossed it over a living room chair, then sank down on the sofa. He'd gone over what she'd told him a hundred times, looking for a loophole somewhere, but he hadn't found one. Any kind of open confrontation with her grandfather would put her family in peril, and if he and Tina continued to see each other, the press would most certainly find out and dig into her family's background. Ultimately they would find out something. They always did. And no matter how small something was, how insignificant, it would be sensationalized. His father's campaign would be hurt, and though Reid seriously doubted Tina's father would be deported or go to jail, he still stood the danger of his reputation being tarnished.

The media and the gossipmongers would have a field day.

Unbuttoning his shirt, he closed his eyes on a weary sigh and laid his head back. He could almost smell her sweetness, could almost taste it, could almost hear her laugh, her sigh. Everything about her lingered here.

On an oath, he rose and walked to his liquor cabinet, pulled out a bottle of Glenlivet, then put it back. Too smooth, he thought, and grabbed a bottle of cheap whiskey instead. He needed something with more of a bite, something he could sink his teeth into.

Pouring a healthy shot, he tossed it back, felt it burn all the way down, then poured another, hoping like hell it would wash away the lump in his chest that refused to go away.

Crofthaven received its guests with uniformed valets and thousands of twinkling white lights on the front lawn trees. Once whisked inside and coats checked, they were greeted by a five-piece band playing soft pop music and white-gloved waiters serving shrimp toast, salmon-mousse-stuffed cherry tomatoes, melted brie in puff pastry and spicy meatballs in wine sauce. Drinks were available from a full-service bar, while roving wine and soda attendants offered refills for the thirsty crowd.

By Crofthaven standards, 150 people was not a large party. Abraham and Nicola had invited only the first group of volunteers from the main campaign headquarters and a dozen or so of the campaign's largest donors. The press, a carefully selected few, had also been treated to the evening's festivities. They swarmed through the crowded ballroom like hornets, buzzing with questions disguised as casual conversation, hoping, praying, for the tiniest piece of breaking news, good or bad, though any reporter worth his or her salt knew that bad always made bigger, more interesting headlines.

Standing by the closed patio French doors with Ian, Reid took in all the people, their smiling faces, bright eyes and animated conversations. Though he'd never much cared for parties, he'd never especially detested them, either. Until tonight.

Tonight his neck hurt from sleeping on his sofa for the past week; his vision was blurred from sitting at his computer all day while he'd entered docking manifests into a log; and to top it off, he had an annoying twitch in the corner of his left eye.

When Albert Johnson, one of his father's wealthiest contributors and staunch supporters walked by, Reid forced a smile and thought his face might break.

"Hard to believe that only a week ago police lines and the coroner's office were center stage here," Ian said quietly to Reid. "It almost seems as if we dreamed the whole thing."

Nodding, Reid snagged a glass of red wine from a

passing tray. He felt that way about Tina, too. As if being with her had never truly happened. That he'd had the ultimate dream that had turned into a nightmare.

Getting drunk the other night hadn't helped, he thought, taking a gulp of his wine, but what the hell, maybe he'd try it again. "What's really hard to believe is that it hasn't leaked to the press yet."

"Nicola has a statement ready to go. Two, actually, one if we discover it is Vickie, and the other if it isn't. In the meantime," Ian said somberly, "we wait."

Reid glanced at his aunt and uncle, who were on the other side of the ballroom. Though they were both smiling and shaking hands with people, Reid knew that on the inside they were anxious and more than a little afraid of what the coroner's results would show.

He also knew they would have preferred not to show up tonight but had worried that their absence might have led to questions, questions that always led to suspicions that there were problems in the Danforth family. Problems that the other candidates would love to pounce on and blow out of proportion.

Which is the exact same reason I'm here tonight, Reid thought. He sure didn't feel like shaking hands and making idle conversation, either. What he felt like was putting on a pair of boxing gloves and punching off some of the rage that had been building in him since Tina had walked out of his life.

He was going absolutely crazy.

He'd hoped that as each day passed and he stayed away from her he wouldn't miss her so much, that he wouldn't think about her every minute of the day and dream about her at night. What had happened was he missed her more. Not even burying himself in his work and the campaign had eased the tension burning his blood.

And though he'd told himself he didn't want to be here tonight and he'd only come for appearance's sake, he knew the real reason he was here. The only reason he was here.

He'd hoped that Tina would come.

When Ivan and Mariska had walked in several minutes ago without their youngest daughter, Reid's hope had disintegrated. He supposed he understood why she hadn't come, but dammit, if he couldn't do anything else, he'd at least wanted to *talk* to her. To *see* her. At this point he was willing to take whatever crumb he could find.

While he continued to scan the ballroom, just in case he'd missed her come in, he sipped the glass of wine and did his best to listen to Ian discuss a new coffee he'd added to the already extensive menu at D&D's.

"…full body and the taste is a little sweet…"

Tina has a sweet taste, Reid thought. And her body…hell, that body drove him mad.

"…and a smoothness about it that should make it…"

Smooth. Tina's skin was silky smooth, like rose petals.

"…blended is selling well, though there seems to be a preference to hot…"

Definitely a preference to hot. The image of Tina

lying naked under him, whispering his name, her body moving in rhythm with his—*dammit!*

He missed everything about her.

"Something wrong with your eye?" Ian asked, interrupting Reid's wayward thoughts.

"No." Scowling, Reid touched the corner of his left eye.

Ian leaned closer. "It's twitching."

"It's nothing."

"Nothing." Ian chuckled. "Right. Unless nothing is about Tina."

"Let it rest, Ian."

"Sure you don't want to talk about it?" Ian grinned. "Since you're looking like a lovestruck pup, might as well get it off your chest."

"Are you intentionally trying to provoke me?" Reid asked tightly. "Or does it just come naturally?"

"Neither." Ian's grin widened. "I just want to watch the look on your face when I tell you that Tina just walked in with her aunt."

Reid's head snapped around at Ian's comment. He thought for a moment that Ian was messing with his mind. But then he saw her, standing at the ballroom entrance, and his heart stopped, along with his ability to think or breathe.

She wore red. Not siren red, but deep, deep red, more the color of a fine claret. The dress shimmered snugly around her slim shape, scooped low over her breasts, but stopped demurely at her knees. Her heels were high and shiny black, open at the toes and wrapped around her narrow ankles. She'd done something different to her hair, sort of swept half up and let the other half tumble around her soft shoulders. Her lips were red, too, but her eyes were smoky.

When she turned and he saw the back of her dress—a lace-up, corset look that exposed just enough skin to make a man need to see more—his heart jumped up into his throat.

"Can I have her?" Ian sounded hopeful. "'Cause if you're not going to—"

"Shut up, Ian," Reid growled. "Don't say it, don't even think it, unless you want us to be headline news on the *Savannah Morning* tomorrow."

Laughing, Ian rocked back on his heels. "Whatever you say, bro."

Keeping his gaze on Tina, Reid shoved his glass of wine into Ian's hand and made his way through the crowd.

"Tina, for heaven's sake—" Yana slipped an arm through her niece's "—if you don't breathe, you're going to pass out."

"I *am* going to pass out." Tina clung to her aunt's arm, turned them both and made an attempt to drag Yana back to the door they'd just come through. "Please, I can't do this. I know I told you and everyone else I was over Reid, but I lied."

"I know, Katina." Yana patted Tina's arm and turned them back around again. "We all know. We lied when we told you we believed you."

"You did? They did?" So much for her acting abilities.

"Of course, dear."

"Then you know I can't do this." Tina felt the

panic rise as her aunt pulled her into the crowd of people. "If I see him, I'll melt into a puddle."

"Don't be silly. Alexander women do not melt into puddles at men's feet." And then she added with a wink, "At least, not in public."

Walking with Yana was like the parting of the Red Sea, Tina thought. One look at how beautiful her aunt was, and people just naturally stepped aside. But tonight, Tina also felt that there were eyes on her, as well. Several of the men smiled and nodded as she passed, and the look in their eyes was clearly one of appreciation. She nodded back politely, but without interest.

There was only one man she was interested in, and he was the one man she couldn't have.

"Smile, Tina," Yana whispered. "I didn't spend the past two hours fitting this dress to you and fixing your hair for nothing. You are too stunning not to show off."

"What's the point?" Tina asked quietly. "What does it matter what I look like now? You know Reid and I can't be together. I might as well have come here wearing a sweatsuit, for all that it matters to me."

"Reid will be the one wearing a sweatsuit," Yana said with a smile. "Believe me, once he takes a look at you, he'll need a nice, long, cold shower."

"I'll be the one needing a shower," she muttered, and let her aunt lead her to the bar and order them both white wine. Since she knew she was going to have to face Reid tonight sooner or later, it just might help take the edge off her nerves.

When a hand closed around her arm, she turned.

Looks like it was going to be sooner, she thought, staring into Reid's deep-blue gaze.

"Buy you a drink?" he said softly.

Her heart was too busy doing somersaults to listen to her brain telling her not to fall into his arms. "Okay," she said, more than a little breathless at his touch.

"Don't be impressed, Katina." Yana stepped between them and gently removed Reid's hand from Tina's arm. "The drinks are free. Hello, Reid."

Without taking his eyes off Tina, Reid nodded. "Yana."

Torn between distress and relief at her aunt's interference, Tina barely managed a smile. "It's a lovely party."

"It is now." He took Tina's arm again. "Why don't I show you around?"

"I believe you've already done that, dear," Yana said firmly. "And smile for the camera, would you?"

The hard line on Reid's mouth curved into a smile, and he let go of Tina's arm at the same moment the photographer stepped in front of them. Smiling, Yana moved in closer to Reid, blocking Tina just as the flash of the camera went off. When the photographer moved on, Reid reached for Tina again.

But Yana was too quick. She slipped her arm into Reid's and smiled at him. "Why don't you take both of us on a tour?"

He glanced from Yana to Tina. "Sure."

Trying not to chew off her lipstick, Tina followed hesitantly behind her aunt and Reid. What she should do was run, but she was too weak. Too foolish.

Too much in love.

She half listened while Reid gave a brief history of Crofthaven, that it was built over a hundred years ago by his great-grandfather, Hiram Danforth, and was considered a historical landmark. The chandeliers and marble were imported from Europe, the grounds meticulously cared for by an army of gardeners. As they walked through the main entry, Tina marveled at the high ceilings and white columns, the spectacular staircase, the glossy hardwood floors and beautiful furnishings.

But mostly she marveled at the pleasure of simply being with Reid.

Pulling her gaze back to the tour, Tina followed Reid and her aunt down a hall off the main entry. They glanced into the music room, which held an elegant baby grand, then moved on to the library. The floor-to-ceiling shelves were mahogany, he explained, the books an ever-growing collection of classic, contemporary and reference.

Being so close and not being able to touch him, to stand close and breathe in the familiar scent of him was driving her insane. To distract herself she moved to the opposite side of the library and examined a leather-bound collection of twentieth-century Southern poets. When she heard the click of the library door, she turned and realized that Yana had left.

Alone. She and Reid were alone.

Her hand shook as she carefully slid the book back into its place on the shelf, then turned to face him. He watched her, his gaze so intense it took her breath away.

"I've missed you," he said evenly.

She glanced away. "Reid—"

He started toward her. She took a step back.

"This isn't over." He kept moving, making her pulse skip, then race. "*We* aren't over."

If only she knew what to do with her hands, maybe she wouldn't want so badly to reach out to him, to tell him she missed him, too, that she didn't want it to be over. All she could do was shake her head.

"I've made a decision, Tina."

He never once took his eyes off her, just kept coming. This time when she moved away from him, she ended up in a corner. With nowhere to go, she pressed her back to the shelves and held her breath.

"Tina." He said her name again so softly, so longingly, she wanted to cry. "I love you."

Her breath shuddered from her lungs. Had she heard him right? "You…you love me?"

"Yes."

When he touched her cheek, she closed her eyes, knew she was trembling, but couldn't stop. How was it possible to feel so wonderful, when she felt so awful at the same time?

Dear God, help me. For this one moment she couldn't lie, couldn't hold back. Just this one moment.

"I love you, too."

"Good." He moved in so close his thighs were touching hers. "It helps when people get married if they love each other."

Married! Her eyes flew open. He wanted to marry her?

Her heart soared, then immediately took a nosedive

and she looked away. "You know that's not possible."

"I won't be without you." He tucked a finger under her chin and brought her face back to his, gazed down at her with a determination that almost had her hoping, almost had her believing. "I can't be without you," he added softly.

"Nothing has changed," she said, struggling against the moisture burning her eyes.

"Then *we'll* make the change. We'll go to Europe." He placed a hand on the wall on either side of her head and leaned in. "It would take months for anyone to track us down there, if ever. We'll live in a villa off the coast of Spain. It's beautiful there. Let me take you. Let me marry you." His mouth brushed hers. "Let me love you."

How wonderful it sounded. She felt herself sway against him, felt her lips soften against his.

Then she pulled back, shook her head.

"How long could we be happy like that?" she said, even as she pictured how beautiful it would be. "How long before you resented me or we missed our lives here?"

She slipped under his arm, wasn't certain that her knees would carry her to the door. "I'm sorry, Reid. I want to marry you, more than you can imagine. But not like this."

At the sound of a deep voice clearing his throat, Tina spun around, gasped when she saw Abraham Danforth and her parents standing in the doorway.

"Dad." Jaw tight, Reid looked at his father, then

Mariska and Ivan. "Mariska, Ivan. Would you excuse us, please?"

They all looked at each other, then stepped into the room. Abraham closed the door behind them.

"I'm afraid this concerns all of us, son." Abraham locked the door. "We simply can't let this happen."

"For God's sake, Dad." Reid blew out a breath, then shook his head. "I love this woman. I want to marry her. I'm *going* to marry her, dammit."

"How romantic." Tears in her eyes, Mariska stepped to Tina and cupped her face in her hands. "So strong, he is. What fine children you will have."

"Mom, Dad, Mr. Danforth, I know that you all—" Tina snapped her gaze back to her mother. "What did you say?"

"I said what fine children you will have, *edes sziv-emn,*" Mariska repeated, this time adding the endearment. "We did not come to tell you that we object, but to give our blessing."

"But, Dad—" She looked at her father, then at Abraham. "I can't, we can't…"

"Did you really think I would stand by and do nothing?" Ivan said with as much irritation in his voice as love. "That I would let you sacrifice yourself for me?"

With the way her head was spinning, she couldn't think at all. "Everyone gets hurt," she insisted. "Our family, the Danforths. How can Reid and I—" she looked at him, felt her throat thicken with tears "—how could we possibly have any kind of happiness if we've hurt the people we love?"

"And what kind of happiness could *we* have—" Mariska said, shaking her head "—if we stole yours?"

When Reid stepped beside her and slipped an arm around her, Tina let herself lean into him, wondered how she could ever leave the safety and strength she felt there.

But they were still caught in a vicious circle, and she saw no escape.

"It did seem like quite the challenge when Ivan and Mariska called me this morning," Abraham said, moving into the room. "Until I learned one interesting bit of information. Does the name Maximilian strike a cord?"

Not to Tina it didn't, but from the expression on Reid's face, the name meant something to him.

"Johann Maximilian?" Reid asked.

Abraham glanced at Tina. "Johann Maximilian is one of our largest shipping clients in Austria. I've known the man for twenty years."

"I handle his accounts," Reid explained to Tina, though clearly he was as confused as she was by the direction of the conversation. "I've been talking with his office almost every day for over a week, trying to straighten out a mistake with a docking number."

"Which Johann was very apologetic about when I spoke with him a little while ago," Abraham said.

"I don't understand." Tina desperately wished someone would get to the point. "What does this man have to do with any of this?"

"My mother was a Maximilian before she married my father," Mariska said. "Johann is my cousin."

"You—we—have other family, too?" Tina asked. "Other than your father?"

Mariska nodded. "We left our past behind us, so that we could have a future."

"But what does all this have to do with Wilheim?" Reid asked.

"My father was always an unhappy man," Mariska said sadly. "From what I have been told by my family, when my father married my mother and went to work at Castle Marcel, he became obsessed with his own importance. He was a tyrant, in his work and at home. This I know from my own life. He kept my mother and me separated from friends and family, but he also used her family name to elevate his own reputation. When my mother died, he cut all ties to the Maximilians but still retained his status in our town. He was so furious with me when I wanted to marry your father that he would have done anything to stop me."

"So we left." Ivan stepped beside Mariska and took her hand. "Once we were settled in America, we contacted Yana. She came to the states two years later and took the name Alexander, as well. I am not proud that I did not face Wilheim," he said, looking at his wife, "but I did what I needed to do for my Mariska."

Tina put her hand to her chest, struggling to absorb everything she'd just heard. There were too many emotions coming at her at once, and her head literally reeled. Only the strong pair of arms wrapped around her kept her knees from giving out.

She glanced at Reid, then her parents and Abraham. "And now?" she asked carefully. "What now?"

"Now nothing." Abraham shrugged. "If anyone

should happen to discover that Ivan Alexander was once Ivan Savar, the records will show a clerical error. A thirty-year-old arrest warrant no longer is in force, and there is no record of any complaint ever filed.'' Abraham smiled. "Johann is a very thorough man."

"I talked to Johann this morning," Mariska said. "He will make sure that no one listens to the incoherent ramblings of an old man."

Still holding on to Tina with one arm, Reid held his other hand out to his father. "Thank you."

When he shook his father's hand, Reid felt something pass between them, an awareness of each other that he'd never felt before. An understanding that they faced each other man to man, not just father to son. Strange that it had taken thirty-two years to come to this moment and this place. It felt good, he realized.

It felt right.

Just as it felt right to be here with Tina at his side, and even Ivan and Mariska. He turned to Tina's parents and offered his hand to Ivan. "Sir."

Ivan's grip was like a bear's, filled with emotion. Blinking back the moisture in her eyes, Mariska leaned forward and kissed Reid's cheek. "I wish you all the happiness that my Ivan and I have shared." Dabbing at her tears, she kissed Tina, then stepped back. "My baby," she mumbled, then turned and hurried from the room.

Abraham turned to Ivan. "I have a full bottle of Palinka on ice. Would you care to join me?"

"How could I refuse such an offer?" Ivan bowed and gestured for Abraham to go first.

And then, once again, they were wonderfully, blissfully alone.

Reid turned Tina in his arms and gazed down at her. "You okay?"

"I...I think so." Then she smiled slowly. "Yes, I am. Better than okay, I'd say. More like wonderful."

Smiling back at her, he lowered his mouth to hers, kissed her lightly. "Do you know that I fell in love with you before I even met you?"

Surprise widened her eyes. "Before you met me?"

"Yep." He brushed his lips against hers again. "I was standing outside your office door at the bakery and I heard your voice. And then, when you turned me down for a job, well, that cinched it."

"So are you saying—" her hands slid to his chest and she ran a fingertip along the edge of his tie "—that I have to turn you down to keep your interest?"

"Too late for that, sweetheart." He grinned at her. "I've got you now, and I'm not letting go."

He kissed her again. Long and deep. A kiss of promise and love. When he finally lifted his head, they were both breathing hard.

"Will you marry me?" He brought her hand to his mouth and kissed her fingertips. "Our parents are expecting it, you know. You have to say yes."

"I suppose we shouldn't disappoint them, should we?" she murmured. "They did go to quite a bit of trouble."

"Yes, they did." He nibbled on her wrist now, couldn't wait to get her alone and nibble on other areas. "I think we should invite Johann to the wedding, too."

"Absolutely." She drew in a breath when he touched his tongue to the pulse at her wrist. "I love you, Reid. I don't know how I would have ever lived without you."

"I wouldn't have let you." He lifted his head and smiled down at her. "Please don't make me wait too long, sweetheart. I want to give you my name, make love to you every night, wake up beside you every morning."

"I don't want to wait, either," she said softly. "It's just all so overwhelming. To think I have family I never knew. And now Rachel is married and expecting a baby, too. Sophia will never forgive me."

He furrowed his brow. "For getting married?"

"For making her the last one. With Rachel and me both married, our mother will completely and whole-heartedly focus on Sophia now."

Chuckling, Reid pulled Tina close again. "I want you to have your restaurant, too," he said. "When the campaign is over and the headquarters are shut down, I'll help you any way I can."

"That's a year away." She slid her arms around his neck. "It seems like a lifetime."

"A lifetime is what we're going to have, sweet-heart. Babies. A home. Grandbabies, great-grandbabies. That's a lifetime. God, how I love you, Katina Alexander."

"And I love you, Reid Danforth."

He leaned down to press his mouth to hers; she reached up. The kiss was sweet. Tender.

Timeless.

"What do you say we go announce it now?" he said when he finally lifted his head. "While the press is here. They're gonna love having the scoop on this one."

"The press?" She bit her lip. "Now?"

"Better get used to it, darling," he said with a grin. "You're going to be a Danforth."

"That," she said, smiling back as she pressed her mouth to his, "I can get used to."

*   *   *   *   *

MAN BENEATH THE UNIFORM

MAUREEN CHILD

One

Zack Sheridan scowled at the streetlights shining through the wide window, then glared at the man sitting opposite him in the booth.

"She studies *fish?*" Danny Akiona, a full-blooded Hawaiian and a Navy SEAL, looked at his friend and laughed.

Irritating as hell, Zack told himself. Especially since, if the shoe had been on the other foot and it was Danny facing this assignment, Zack would be the one laughing.

Zack took another long swallow of his beer. But even the crisp bite of the alcohol couldn't quite take the sting out of his friend's laughter. Leaning back in the red leather booth, he turned to look at the crowd filling the waterfront bar.

Couples sat in booths and singles prowled the edges of the mob, looking to catch someone's— anyone's—eye. Music blared from an ancient juke-box loaded with everything from golden oldies to hip-hop. The waitresses, decked out in skintight, black leather miniskirts, red, belly-baring halter tops and red spike heels, dipped and swayed through the crowd, balancing trays full of drinks.

Zack sighed as he checked out an especially appealing blond barmaid with a size forty chest packed into a size thirty-four top. If he'd been a free man, he'd have made a play for her and enjoyed his first night of leave. But since he was facing thirty days of pure hell, he just didn't have the heart for it.

"Oh, man." Danny chuckled and shook his head. "This is just too funny."

Zack shot him a look hot enough to cook bacon. "I'm glad somebody's getting a laugh out of this."

"It's perfect, man." Danny's dark brown eyes glittered with humor and his perpetually tanned face split into a wide grin. "We get a month's R and R and *you* get sentenced to baby-sit a scientist." He lifted his beer in a toast. "Here's to the women I'll get now that you're out of action for a while."

He'd be out of action, all right, Zack thought

miserably. Thirty long days of riding herd on some babe born with a silver spoon in her mouth and a yen to play with fish.

"Gonna be a long month." Zack shifted a glance out the front window of the bar to the bustling street beyond the glass.

Even on a chilly February evening, Savannah was crawling with tourists. With cameras slung around their necks and guidebooks clutched like the Bible, visitors wandered narrow streets and the waterfront. Gift shops did a bumper business year round and the locals tidily counted their pennies and waited for summer, when even *bigger* crowds would show up.

Savannah was a small Southern town disguised as a bustling city. It had a great harbor, beautiful old homes and a couple of really terrific bars. Ordinarily, Zack would be looking forward to a little down time here. He'd be wandering the town looking to pick up a couple of Southern belles. But this trip was all business.

Or punishment, rather.

"It's no surprise, man," Danny said, bringing Zack's attention back to the matter at hand. "Hell, you knew you'd have your ass kicked the minute we got back home."

Zack moved his glass through the water rings it had left on the highly varnished wood table. Glancing at his friend, he asked, "So, do you think I should have done it differently?"

"Hell, no." Danny straightened up in the red leather seat and leaned both forearms on the table-top. "If you hadn't gone back for Hunter..." His voice trailed off and he shook his head. "Unacceptable. No way. We had to go back for him. Orders or not."

"Hoo-yah." They lifted their glasses and clinked them together.

Zack nodded to himself. He knew he'd done the right thing—the *only* thing he could have done. But it was good to hear his friend back him up on it. The rules were simple and he lived by them. A Navy SEAL didn't leave a man behind. If a team of six men went in, then six men had better damn well come back out. Dead or alive, every SEAL *always* came home.

Memories rushed through his brain. Instants, moments, rose up, were recognized and then faded into the next. He remembered it all clearly. That mission two weeks before had gone bad from the beginning. His team had been sent in to infiltrate, rescue, then exit, fast.

But someone had screwed up the intel. The hostage wasn't where he was supposed to be. By the time Zack and the others had found their man, time was short. With only a couple of hours left before extraction, their cover was blown and Hunter Cabot had been shot. Zack and the rest of the team had made it back to the Zodiac boat with the hostage before they'd realized Hunter was missing.

Zack had reported in and had been given the order to cut Hunter loose and get the hell out of Dodge. Just remembering the easy dismissal of a SEAL's life made him furious all over again. Zack's hand tightened around his beer. No way in hell would he agree to leaving one of his team behind. So he'd disregarded orders, left the team to guard the hostage and went back in himself to drag Hunter's ass out.

Now Hunter was recovering in the hospital, surrounded by gorgeous nurses and Zack had been sentenced to serve as nursemaid to a geek.

Yeah, life was fair.

"What kind of fish, you think?"

"Huh?" Frowning, Zack looked at Danny.

"I mean," his friend said, "maybe its something interesting like sharks. Back home I saw a shark once, big enough to—"

"Please." Zack held up a hand and winced. "No Hawaiian folk tales today, okay?"

Nothing Danny liked better than telling tall tales about the beauty of Hawaii, the big waves, the gorgeous women and just how many of those women were nuts about Danny Akiona. Zack wasn't in the mood.

Danny grinned. "Fine. When do you go see the fish woman?"

"I'm a free man until tomorrow morning, 0800."

"Hell, brudda," Danny used the island slang for "brother," and his voice was almost musical as he added, "that leaves us all of tonight."

Zack smiled, feeling a little better. Eight o'clock was hours away yet. No point in acting like he was in prison until the cell door actually slammed shut. "You're right."

"Damn straight." Danny signaled the waitress for another round of drinks, then looked at Zack. "I say we find us a couple of ladies and then pack in a whole month's worth of R and R into one night. If it's your last, let's make it count, brudda."

One night. Hell, they'd done it before. He and Danny had torn up towns and welcomed the dawn in too many countries to count. No reason why he couldn't have a big blowout the night before starting a new assignment.

Whatever Kimberly Danforth—God, what a snooty name—was like, the fish geek wouldn't have to be faced until tomorrow. And as any SEAL knew, you lived life one moment at a time, 'cause you never knew if you'd get another.

"I've said it before, I'll say it again," Zack said, ordering himself to relax and enjoy the rest of the night. "Hula," he said, using Danny's team nickname, "I like your style."

Kim Danforth glared at the telephone receiver in her hand and then slapped it back against her ear. Frustration bubbled inside her, blending with the blossoming sense that she was losing this battle. "Dad, this is ridiculous. I don't want a guard dog and I certainly don't *need* one."

Abraham Danforth's voice, fluid, strong and commanding, came across the line. "Kimberly, do this for me. These threats are not to be ignored."

Fear for her father's safety took the edge off her frustration and she winced. "Dad, first of all, it's only one threat and it was made against *you,* not me."

There was a long pause and she heard him inhale slowly, deeply. She counted to ten, knowing he was doing the same. Always careful about what he said, Abraham prided himself on his self-control. Even around the family dinner table, he'd always weighed every word, thinking carefully before speaking. Which was only one of the reasons why he made such an excellent senatorial candidate.

"Kimberly, whoever is behind this would know that the surest way to hurt me would be to hurt my family."

Kim sighed. Her father hadn't always been the most involved, caring parent. A man of business, he'd spent most of his energies growing the Danforth bank balances rather than spending time with his five kids. But he loved his children, and she knew he worried most about her, his youngest child and only daughter.

She also knew that a part of her father was using this situation as an attempt to be the kind of father he wished he'd been when she was growing up. The stalker sending threatening e-mail messages to Abraham hadn't threatened his family. Kim knew perfectly well that she wasn't in any real danger—which made the idea of having a bodyguard that much harder to accept. But she couldn't bring herself to turn her father down and give him one more thing to worry about.

Besides, her dad's younger brother, her uncle Harold, had asked her to go along with her father's request. Uncle Harold had said the entire family would be relieved if she was safe.

"Give the old man a break, will you?" he asked.

She smiled and shook her head. There was simply no way out of this. Between her father and her uncle, she was outnumbered and she knew it. Harold Danforth had been a substitute father to her and her brothers. Without the responsibilities of running the Danforth business interests, he'd had more time to give to both his own children and Abraham's.

"Fine," she said. "He can protect me. But he's not living here."

"There's room." Abraham's voice became abrupt as if now that he'd won the argument, he was ready to move on. "Just put him up in your spare room."

"Dad, I'm not letting a stranger stay in my house."

"He's not a stranger. He's the son of—"

"Your old navy buddy, I know," she said interrupting him before she heard the old war stories again. The only war she was interested in at the moment was the personal war for her own independence.

"Zack should be there any minute," her father was saying. "I expect you to cooperate."

"Dad—"

"Have to run now."

The dial tone ringing in her ear kept her from arguing further. "Nice chatting with you, Dad," she said tightly, wishing that just once, she could have gotten in the last word.

When the doorbell rang a few minutes later, Kim was still primed for battle.

She opened the door to a grim-faced man in dark glasses. He seemed to take up a lot of space on her small, flower-filled front porch. Was this Navy SEAL supposed to be her protector? Weren't military men a little better groomed? "Yes?"

The man frowned and reached up to rub his forehead. "Do you have to shout?" His voice sounded creaky, careful.

"I wasn't shouting."

"You're *still* shouting," he told her and reluctantly took off his sunglasses, wincing at the brightness of the day. "Man, morning sucks."

Kim stared up at him. *Way* up. A couple of inches over six feet tall, the man was broad in the shoulders, had a narrow waist and legs long enough for two men. His reddish brown hair was cut militarily high and tight. His ancient jeans were threadbare at the knee and faded. The collar of his dark red shirt was twisted, one side up, the other tucked beneath the neck of the shirt. He also wore a dark blue sweatshirt that looked as worn as his jeans. His narrowed eyes were a mixture of blue and green—and the red streaks surrounding the irises told her he'd had a late night.

This couldn't be the man her father was sending, she told herself. Zack Sheridan was a Navy SEAL—not a man she'd expect to show up with a hangover and two days' worth of stubble on his square jaws.

She wished suddenly for a steel security screen door.

"What do you want?"

"Loaded question," he said, his voice a low rumble that seemed to vibrate right through her without even trying. "What I want," he said, "is aspirin, a dark room…and to be anywhere but here."

"Charming," she said, clutching the door in a tight grip, ready to slam it home and lock it. "Why don't you go get those things? Start with the last one and go away."

She swung the door closed, but he shoved one sneaker-clad foot between the door and the jamb.

Kim narrowed her eyes on him and ignored the curl of fear in the pit of her stomach. Naturally, she didn't let him know it. "Move that foot mister, or I'll break it."

"Let's start over," he said, not moving the foot an inch.

"Let's not." She pushed the door harder.

His mouth tightened. "That hurts, you know."

"That's sort of the point."

He sighed. "You Kimberly Danforth?"

"Is that supposed to ensure my trust? You knowing my name?" She put her whole weight behind the door now and thought she felt it budge.

He slapped one hand on the door and pushed back. With very little effort, he managed to shove the door open a crack farther.

"Hey. Let go of my door."

"I'm Zack Sheridan."

"Good for you."

"Your father sent me."

She released her hold on the door and his heavy hand pushed it wide open until it swung back and slammed into the wall behind it.

"Damn, you're loud," he muttered, reaching one hand to his forehead again as if trying to hold his skull together.

Kim was rethinking this whole proposition. The man was obviously hungover, not exactly inspiring a lot of trust. He looked more like a pirate than a navy SEAL. Danger emanated from him, reached out toward her, and gave her nerves a little shake.

If there was a trickle of pure female appreciation mixed in with the trepidation rolling through her stomach, she chose to ignore it.

Sure, she'd agreed to her father's request. But she had a feeling that Abraham Danforth wouldn't be so in favor of Zack staying with his little girl if he could get a good look at the man.

So she went with her instincts.

"I don't want you here," Kim said, lifting her chin and meeting his gaze squarely. "I don't need you here, either, despite what my father thinks."

"Lady, I just take orders."

"A centuries-old claim of innocence."

"Huh?" Those blue-green eyes of his narrowed.

"Look." She pulled her glasses off the collar of her V-necked blue T-shirt and put them on. She only used the glasses for reading, but she'd found out long ago that wearing them gave her a little distance. "I don't need your help, so why don't you just go?"

"Wish I could," he said and stepped into her house, practically sighing at the cool shade of the room.

"Well, please. Come in," she said dryly.

He glanced around the room as if she hadn't spoken and Kim followed his gaze, looking at her home through a stranger's eyes.

The small, two-bedroom cottage was more than a hundred years old, with all the charm and foibles of an antique. The plumbing wasn't the greatest, but there were built-in bookshelves and a built-in china hutch in the kitchen. There were niches cut into the walls for vases of flowers, but the bathroom was pitifully small. The yard was no bigger than a postage stamp, but the tree in the front yard was eighty years old and gave much-needed shade in summer.

The living room was, like the rest of the place, tiny. But the soft blue walls looked like a cloudless summer sky. A blue-and-white plaid sofa sat in front of a miniature tiled hearth and brightly colored rag rugs dotted the glistening wood floor. On the walls, she'd hung framed photos from her travels and a couple of paintings done by a marine artist. It was home. It was all hers. And she didn't want to share it.

Not even temporarily.

"Nice place," he said.

"Thank you. Now, if you don't mind—"

"Lady…" He folded his arms across his pretty impressive chest and stared down at her through bloodshot eyes. "Whether you like it or not, we're in this together."

The room suddenly felt a lot smaller and the air a little warmer. "I don't like it."

"If you think my idea of a vacation is riding herd on a fish geek—"

"Excuse me?" Kim straightened up to her less-than-impressive five feet seven inches and tried to look down her nose at him. Not easy to do when she had to tilt her head back all the way to meet his gaze. "I happen to be a Doctor of Marine Biology."

"Yeah? So?"

"So I prefer that term to *fish geek*."

"Who wouldn't?" He chuckled, then the sound trailed off as he caught her irritation. "Fine. *Doctor* Danforth…"

She nodded.

"Climb down off your high dolphin because for the next little while, you and me are gonna be best friends."

Something hot and sharp and really annoying blasted through her. "I don't—"

He cocked his head and gave her a patient smile he probably reserved for small children and half-wits.

"I'm calling my father." A bluff, but it was all she had.

He nodded. "Give him my best."

Kim's small flicker of irritation burst like a Fourth of July firecracker. No way was she going to be able to have this man living in her home for thirty days. "I'll call your commanding officer to complain."

Zack plopped down onto one of her chairs, sighed and stretched out his long legs in front of him like a man settling in and getting comfortable. "He'll be happy to know I reported to duty on time."

Kim was losing control. She felt it slipping from her fingers like the string of a helium balloon on a windy day. Of course his commanding officer wouldn't listen to her. Her father had already seen to that.

"I'll call the police. They'll arrest you."

For one brief moment, hope lit up his eyes. "You think?" Then he shook his head. "Nah. Forget it, darlin'."

She stiffened. "Don't call me darlin'."

He slipped his sunglasses on, rested his head on the chair back and sighed. "No darlin'. Got it."

"This isn't going to work out," Kim said tightly.

Tipping his shades down a fraction of an inch, he gave her a warm look and a smile that sent something completely unexpected scuttling through her. ''Baby, I'm a SEAL. I can make anything work.''

Two

Zack watched her stalk around the small room, phone in hand, muttering a string of complaints to whoever was unfortunate enough to be on the other end of the line.

She was hopping mad.

And damn, she looked good.

He smiled to himself. Slitting his eyes as a defense against the morning sunlight flooding the room, he admired the woman who was somehow more than he'd expected. Who would have thought a fish geek would be so nicely put together?

Her sky-blue, V-necked shirt clung to her small, high breasts like a lover's hands. Her long legs were hidden from him in a pair of khaki-colored drawstring pants that dipped beneath her belly button, giving him a tantalizing glimpse of smooth, tanned skin. Her long, straight, midnight-black hair was gathered into a ponytail that swung in a wide arc across her back as she marched furiously around the room.

"I don't care if he's in a meeting," she said, louder now. "I want to speak to my father, *now*." A pause, then, "Fine. I'll hold."

"Won't work," Zack muttered and she flipped him a quick look.

"What won't?"

"Getting rid of me." When her frown deepened and her big, grass-green eyes narrowed on him, Zack almost chuckled. Damn, she got prettier the madder she got. And he was just ornery enough to enjoy the show. "I tried to get out of this, but no way."

"You tried?"

Another dry chuckle sounded from his throat. "You think this is my idea of a good time?"

Thoughtful, she cupped one hand over the mouth of the phone. "Why'd you agree to it?"

"Long story." He folded his hands atop his abdomen and drummed his fingers. Zack wasn't going to get into the whole sad tale about his too-many-to-count futile stands against authority. It was none of her business and besides, he didn't

want to think about it. "Let's just say it beat the
hell out of the alternative."

"Must have been some alternative."

"Trust me."

"That's the point here," she said. "I don't."

"Bottom line," Zack said, fatigue dragging at
him, "I go against this order, and I kiss my com-
mission goodbye. I'm not willing to do that."

"Fine." Clearly coming to a decision, she hung
up the phone then turned to face him. Folding her
arms beneath her breasts, she hitched one nicely
rounded hip higher than the other and tapped her
bare toes against the rag rug. "If this is going to
work, I think we should come up with some
ground rules."

"Yeah?" Zack smiled. Couldn't help it. Her
small, wire-framed glasses glinted in the sunlight
and her full lips thinned into what she probably
considered a firm line. Black eyebrows were
arched high on her forehead and her glasses
slipped a bit down her small, straight nose. Not
exactly the intimidating picture she was no doubt
hoping for.

"Shoot."

"Don't tempt me."

He snorted a laugh. "Damned if I couldn't start
to like you."

"Why, my little heart's just fluttering."

He grinned.

She almost smiled back and Zack felt a solid but invisible punch in his midsection. Damn, the fish geek had some secret weapons other than that trim, compact body.

"Okay, here's my suggestion," she said.

Zack waited.

"I'll put up with you and you can fulfill your orders to protect me during the day…"

"And?"

"And at night, you'll go away."

"Tempting, but no deal."

She threw both hands up and let them slap against her thighs. "Why not?"

"Because," he said, pushing himself up from the chair that was way too comfortable for a man as sleep-deprived as he was. "My orders say I stick to you like a stamp on a letter for the next month. That's what I'm gonna do."

"It's not necessary."

"And if you were an admiral," Zack told her, "I'd take your word for it."

She practically vibrated with impatience. "Surely you can see this house is too small for two people."

"It's a little…cozy." He'd dug foxholes with more maneuvering room.

"It's not even a real two-bedroom. It's a one-bedroom house that somebody broke up into two rooms with a few two-by-fours and a couple of sheets of plywood.''

''Your point?''

''There's no room for you.''

''The couch'll do me.''

''It won't do for me.''

''You don't get a vote.''

''How do I not get a vote?'' she echoed and he could actually see the fury mounting in her eyes. ''This is my house.''

''And I'm your guest.''

She fumed silently for a long minute and Zack wondered if she was planning to make a break for it. But he didn't think so. She seemed too stubborn for a surrender.

He was right.

''I don't take orders well.''

He smiled. ''Me, neither. We'll probably make a good team.''

''I doubt it.''

Zack studied her for a long minute, until he had the satisfaction of seeing her shift uncomfortably. He was willing to make nice—but he'd be damned if he'd be stonewalled by some scientist.

''Doctor Danforth, I don't want to be here any more than you want me to be here.''

''Then—''

''It doesn't change the fact that I am here. And here I stay until my superior orders me to get out.''

* * *

Kim tiptoed through the dark house, grateful that she'd had her floorboards treated six months before. They didn't squeak anymore, so her progress through the tiny house was absolutely silent.

Careful not to breathe too heavily, she clutched her house keys tightly in one fist so they wouldn't rattle together. A sly smile curved her mouth and she hugged her deception to her. It was almost fun, she thought. Putting one over on the mighty SEAL who'd been assigned to watch her every move.

She hadn't had fun in a very long time, and if it wasn't necessary to be quiet, she might have given in to the urge to chuckle. After all, to anyone looking in through a window, she would have appeared ridiculous. Sneaking through her own house like a burglar.

Inching past the door leading to the tiny second bedroom she used as an office—and for now, a makeshift guest room for the invader—her heart slowed to a more reasonable beat. As she stepped quietly around the hall corner leading to the living room, it occurred to her that she'd never sneaked before in her life.

Girls at her private high school used to talk about slipping out of their houses to meet boys. And then having to slip back in before dawn to avoid both parents and servants. But Kim had never done it herself. She'd always been the "good" one. The obedient one. The respectful one.

The boring one, she thought now.

Shaking her head, she gritted her teeth and pushed those old memories to the back of her mind. No point in reliving them now, for heaven's sake. Besides, Johnny-come-lately or not, she was finally doing a little sneaking. Even if it was out of her own house.

Moonlight slid through the white curtains at the windows and lay like God's nightlight over the room. Eyes accustomed to the dim lighting and so familiar with her own house she could have walked through it blindfolded, Kim headed for the front door. Carefully, she turned the deadbolt until it snapped clear with an audible click.

She winced at the sound and held her breath, waiting.

When she didn't hear anything, she smiled to herself again and closed her fingers over the cold brass knob. Slowly, she turned it and the soft sigh of the door coming away from the jamb sounded like a shriek to her anxious ears. But again, there was no sound from her guard dog. Another step or two and she'd be clear. She could go about her nightly routine without worrying about being followed. Without having to put up with a man she didn't want or need in her life.

Kim eased through the doorway, pushed the

screen door open, then stepped onto the porch. She turned around and relocked the deadbolt with a nearly silent *snick* of sound. After all, she didn't want to leave the guard dog unprotected.

Pleased with herself, she eased the screen door closed, turned around—and crashed into a broad, hard chest.

Her screech, set at a level only dogs should have been able to hear, rattled Zack's brain and, he was pretty sure, made his ears bleed. Before he could check, though, she recovered.

Lifting her right leg, she slammed her heel down onto his instep. While the dazzling pain of that move was still fresh, she whirled and rammed her elbow into his midsection. Surprise, added to the blow, had all of his air leaving him in a rush.

Stunned, Zack tried to figure out how a fish geek had gotten the drop on him.

But as she moved again, lightning fast, his own survival instincts kicked in—just in time to save his esophagus from being speared by her rigid fingers.

Zack grabbed her wrist and held on. ''Damn it, Doc, it's me.''

She fought against his grasp, tugging and pulling until slowly, she eased off and he knew his words had gotten through. She stared up at him, and he saw her pulse pounding raggedly at the base of her neck. Breath rushed in and out of her lungs and her wide green eyes looked huge in the moonlight.

"You?" One word, strangled out from a throat obviously still tight with fear.

"Yeah, so cool your jets, huh?"

"Cool my…" She sucked in air, then drew her free hand back and jammed her closed fist into his abdomen.

This time though, he'd been ready for the attack. Tensing his muscles, he felt her blow glance off his body like a rock off the still surface of a lake.

"Hit me again," he muttered as he grabbed her other wrist, "and I just might hit you back, darlin'."

"Don't call me darlin'."

"Don't hit me."

She kicked him.

He winced. Shouldn't have challenged her, he thought wearily. "Fine," he admitted. "So I won't hit you back." Still holding on to her, he eased back far enough that kicking him would take some real effort. "But I *will* tie you to a chair."

She ignored that and wriggled in his grip like a worm trying to escape the hook.

"What the hell do you think you're doing?" she said, her words coming fast and furious. Fear still stained her voice and smeared the air between them. "You scared me to death."

"I didn't mean to. I only meant to stop you."

"Well, you did both. Happy now?"

He grinned down at her. Scared or not, she'd done all right. Way better than he'd expected. And standing here in the dark, watching her breasts rise and fall with her rapid breathing, was giving him a few ideas about seeing if other things about the fish geek would be better than he'd expected, too.

"Fight pretty good for a corpse," he said.

She blew out a breath. "That's not funny."

"Not a lot of laughs from where I'm standing, either," he said, releasing one of her wrists to rub one palm over his stomach.

She caught the action. "Did I hurt you?"

Let's see, he thought. A one-hundred-twenty-pound female throws a lucky punch and actually hurts him? Not a chance. But damn, she looked so hopeful, he heard himself say, "Yeah."

"Good." She yanked her other hand free and rubbed at her wrist long enough to make Zack worry that he'd hurt *her*.

"You okay?"

"I'm fine." She stepped a wide path around him, then turned her head back to level a long look at him. "What I want to know is what are you doing out here?"

"Waiting for you."

Her eyes narrowed on him.

"You heard me?"

He'd been awake and alert from the moment she

started moving around in her room. Her attempt at "stealthy" wasn't all that great. Of course, maybe it would have worked on some regular guy who didn't always have one ear cocked and ready for the sound of a threat coming out of nowhere.

For Zack though, waking from a dead sleep to red-alert status was nothing new. He'd been trained to sleep with one eye open. And that ability had saved his ass on more than one occasion. Once he'd gotten used to the night sounds of her house, her neighborhood, the small, subtle sounds coming from her room had told him she was on the move.

He hadn't figured her for the type to try an escape in the dead of night. He'd looked at her wire-rimmed glasses and trim, tight figure and the stacks of books she surrounded herself with and told himself she'd be no trouble at all.

Which only went to prove that it was possible to surprise a SEAL.

"Yeah, I heard you." No point in telling her that he'd slipped out the window in his room, scooted around the edge of the house and waited on the front porch while she made her escape. The evidence was here in front of her. Besides, if he told her what not to do, she'd only use it against him at another time.

He was beginning to see that riding herd on Kim Danforth wasn't going to be the walk in the park that he'd expected.

"You must have ears like a bat," she muttered and went down the front steps without another look at him.

"I heard that well enough." He was just a step behind her. Far enough back not to crowd her, but close enough that he got a real good view of her excellent behind. She wore black jeans and a black jacket over a black sweatshirt. Her midnight-colored hair was coiled into a tight knot at the back of her neck.

Zack's night vision was good enough to notice just how well those jeans fit her. And his imagination was good enough to picture everything that was hidden beneath the too-bulky jacket and sweatshirt.

"Any particular reason you're dressed like a burglar?" he asked conversationally as he kept just a step or two behind her.

"You've discovered my secret life," she said, sarcasm dripping from every word. "I'm a cat burglar."

He grinned and shook his head. "Then you can answer a question for me. I've always wondered why somebody would go to all the trouble to break into a house just to steal a cat."

She stopped, looked back at him and smirked. "I had no idea SEALs were such comedians."

"See? Learn something new every day."

"Then since your lesson plan is concluded, go away."

"Nope." Zack's long legs closed the distance between them quickly and he fell into step beside her. "Where you go, I go."

"I don't want you."

"I don't care."

She stopped under a streetlight and glared up at him. And damned if Zack wasn't starting to like the look of those green eyes firing sparks at him.

"You don't seem to understand," she said and her voice adopted the standard professor's this-is-a-lecture-pay-close-attention tone that used to put him to sleep at the Naval Academy. "I don't need you here. I don't want you here."

Zack stared down into those eyes and then let his gaze move over her features. Her cool, creamy skin gleamed like porcelain in the pale wash of the streetlight. She looked a damn sight better than he'd expected a scientist to look. And she was more stubborn than he'd been prepared for. Not to mention she had a real nasty, sharp-edged tongue on her when her temper was on the boil. She was sneaky, underhanded and a dirty fighter.

Add all of that to great legs, an excellent behind and a pair of small, high breasts that he was itching to cup, and you had a hell of a package.

"Doc," he said when he could tell by the tightening of her lips that she was on the edge of temper again, "you don't have a say in this."

"But—"

"Now." He cut her off, dropped one arm around her shoulders and started walking in the direction she'd been headed a minute or so before. "We can stand here and argue, or we can keep walking and argue as we go. What'll it be?"

She pushed his arm off her shoulders. "I can walk and talk at the same time. You sure you're up to the challenge?"

"Damned if I'm not getting real fond of you, darlin'."

Three

___

Kim completely ignored the still-sizzling sensation of heat that was rocketing through her body. She'd pushed his arm off almost instantly, and yet, despite the cold night air, her skin hummed and her blood was bubbling in her veins.

She couldn't even remember the last time a man had had that sort of effect on her. In fact, she was pretty sure it had never happened before.

This was probably not a good sign.

He walked beside her, his long, jeans-clad legs moving in time with hers. She felt him watching her from the corner of his eye and in response, she kept her own gaze locked straight ahead. She wouldn't let him know that he was getting to her.

"So where're we going?" he asked.

"I'm going to the riverfront. I have no idea where you're going."

"Wherever you go, sweetheart. Just consider me your shadow."

She glanced at him, then away again. "Shadows are quiet."

"I can do quiet, but what's the point?" He shrugged and she caught the movement from the corner of her eye. "We're stuck together, peaches. So we may as well be friendly."

Friendly? He wasn't her friend. Kim didn't have many of those and the ones she did have weren't six foot tall, gorgeous, greeny-blue-eyed guard dogs. And they certainly didn't set her blood boiling with a simple touch. In fact, she didn't have any male friends. Strange, now that she thought about it, but true. She'd never been the kind of woman men paid attention to.

She'd been the studious one. The one with straight As. The one who, when she was at college, spent her Friday nights at the library instead of attending frat parties. Maybe it was having grown up with four older brothers, she thought.

They'd been great, but with the Danforth brothers standing between her and boys, there hadn't been many willing to risk running the gauntlet. As a teenager, she'd hoped for a boyfriend, but had finally settled for the Principal's

Honor Roll. When that situation continued through college, she'd slipped into the rut she found herself in now. No real life. Just her job. She was thankful it was one she loved…but that didn't change the whole lack-of-a-life thing.

But she was better off than some of the women she knew. Working on their third or fourth husbands, fighting custody battles and going to spas to maintain the figures they hoped would win them another trip down the aisle.

She didn't envy them the lawyers and hard feelings and bitter divorce settlements. Kim was still enough of a closet romantic to believe that marriage should last forever. Which probably explained why she was still single.

"Look," she said, coming at the current problem as she did everything else in her world, with calm logic. "I have things to do. I don't need an escort or a guard. I don't want your company and I'm not your friend. So why don't you go back to the house and wait for me?"

"Does that usually work?"

"What?"

"That quiet, teacher-to-student voice," he said, one corner of his mouth tilting into a smile that nearly curled Kim's toes. "Do the men you date actually go for that? Just roll over and do what you want?"

"I don't—"

"Know?"

"Date," she corrected.

"Never?"

Kim stopped and stared up at him. They were in between streetlights, so his face was mostly in shadows. But why did she know he was smiling again?

"That really isn't any of your business."

"Call it curiosity."

"Call it intrusive."

"Big word."

"Need a dictionary?"

He laughed and the deep, rolling sound of it washed over her. Stunned, Kim just looked at him. Normally her sarcasm put people off. Or scared them off. Apparently, Zack Sheridan was different.

But she'd known that right from the start, hadn't she?

"You've got a hell of a mouth on you."

She blew out a breath. "I tend to say whatever I happen to be thinking at the time."

He shook his head. "I wasn't talking about what you said. I was talking about your mouth."

Her breath lodged in her throat. "What?"

He reached out and rubbed his thumb over her bottom lip. "Wide smile, great snarl and lush, full lips."

She pulled her head back. Too late to stop the jolt of electricity ricocheting around her blood stream, but quick enough to keep her from asking him to touch her some more.

Oh, wow. Where had that come from?

Too much alone time, Kim thought. Just way too much. She should get out more. Join a bowling league. Take line-dancing lessons. *Something.* Then she wouldn't be bowled over by a man who probably had a string of women trailing in his wake.

That image straightened her up.

"I really have to go," she said and started walking again.

Wind off the river brushed past her, the cold damp of it sliding into her bones and wiping away the lingering heat Zack's touch had ignited. Good. That was good.

The houses they passed were dark but for the occasional glimpses of lamplight pooling behind curtains. Ordinarily, on her late-night walks, she indulged herself with wondering what was going on behind those curtains. What kind of people lived in the well-tended old homes. Were they laughing, crying? Wondering how to pay the bills or planning a vacation?

She told herself she didn't mind always being on the outside looking in, but once in a while, when she heard a baby's cry or a child's laughter, she would wish that there was someone at home waiting for her. Someone she could talk to, turn to in the night. Someone to worry about. Someone to love.

Tonight, someone *was* with her. For all the wrong reasons. Indulging in flights of fancy was impossible, too. How could she wonder about strangers when she had her very own personal stranger walking right beside her, ruining her routine?

"Do this often?" he asked.

"Hmm?"

"Stroll around in the dead of night all by yourself?"

She slid him a glance. "I'm a big girl."

"I noticed," he pointed out, then let his gaze drift across the darkened street. "Most other red-blooded guys would notice, too."

That had never really been her problem, but he didn't have to know that. "Darn. I forgot my stick."

"What stick?"

"The one I use to beat all the men off me."

"That's real cute, honey. But the point is, a woman walking alone at night is looking for trouble."

"Excuse me?" Kim stopped again, this time directly under a streetlight, with a three storied, gingerbread covered Victorian beauty behind her. Tipping her head back, she told herself to pay no attention to the way the light and shadow fell on his features, making him look both unreasonably attractive and dangerous. "Because I'm taking a walk at night it would be my fault if I get attacked?"

"Not your fault, but you do present a window of opportunity."

"Right. Well, I can take care of myself."

"I remember." He rubbed one hand over his stomach again.

"Oh, please. I didn't hurt you."

"True. Surprised me, though."

"I grew up with four brothers. You learn a thing or two."

"They taught you that instep move?"

"Among other things." She let her gaze slip down to his groin briefly.

He grinned. "Now that would hurt."

"Supposed to."

He gave her an approving nod. "Your brothers were thorough."

Not to mention the self-defense courses she'd taken. But Kim didn't think he needed to know that. She wasn't an idiot. She knew how important it was for a woman to be able to protect herself. Especially a woman who up until today had lived alone.

"I told you, I don't need a bodyguard."

"Uh-huh. But I'm willing to bet a Navy SEAL

knows a few more things about defense than you do.''

Yes, but could a Navy SEAL tell her how to protect herself against a Navy SEAL? That was the real question. And one she didn't think she could ask Zack.

"Fine." She threw up her hands in surrender. "Let's just go, all right?"

"We're making progress," he said, falling into step beside her again. "At least you admit you're not going to shake me."

"For now." But she had hopes, Kim told herself. In the morning, she'd call her father again. Try to talk to him about this rationally, calmly. And if that didn't work, she'd call Uncle Harold and whine. And if that didn't work...well, a person could only have so many plans at once.

She walked along the river's edge, moonlight glinting off the darkness of her hair and the creamy coolness of her skin. She seemed to notice everything—from the trash she picked up as she walked, to the stray cat hiding in the oat grass near the water's edge.

She ignored him for the most part and that was all right with him. He didn't need to get to know her. She was just an assignment and after thirty days, he'd be moving on. But he couldn't help no-

ticing things about her. Hell, he was a trained ob-
server.

Her hands were small, fine-boned and delicate
looking. Her legs were long and looked damn good
in those dark jeans. Her sneakers were battered and
her jacket was new, but had two missing buttons
and a torn pocket. She was a contrast, he thought.
A woman who came from more money than he'd
likely see in a lifetime, but who spent her nights
picking up litter and wandering a riverbank alone.

Why wasn't she out on a date with some good-
looking, fast-talking guy with a bank balance
higher than his IQ? Why wasn't she at a party in
some sleek black dress with diamonds at her
throat?

Why did he care?

He didn't.

Zack shoved his hands into his jeans pockets and
kept a step or two behind her. A cold, damp wind
rustled in off the water and tugged at her hair, teasing a few long strands free of the knot at the nape
of her neck to swirl about her face. She stared out
at the river as if looking well beyond the dark water into the distance. When she took a deep breath
and blew it out, he nearly felt her distraction.

Hell, he sympathized. He didn't like anyone
hanging around cramping his free time, either—
when he had some. But sometimes, life just

smacked you in the face and you had to deal with it.

His sharp gaze moved across the area for the hundredth time in the last half hour. He was a man used to trouble and he liked to be ready and waiting when it came knocking.

But this small slice of Savannah was quiet and nearly deserted. One or two couples wandered along the river walk, hand in hand, stopping now and then for a kiss that made Zack think wistfully about things other than baby-sitting a beautiful nerd. But then the couples moved on and it was just the two of them in the darkness.

Wrought-iron grillwork lined the river walk, with low-lying shrubs and now-dormant flowering plants crowded close together at the base of the trees. In another month or two, the flowers would be blooming and the night air would already be starting to steam up in anticipation of summer. Moonlight glittered on the surface of the river, and the sound of the water rushing past was almost like a whisper in a quiet room.

Kim swiveled her head, looking first up the river and then down again.

Zack moved in closer.

"Are you looking for something?"

"No."

"So why come down here?"

She turned her face to his. She looked cool and

remote and somehow incredibly appealing. "I like the water."

It made sense. Why be a fish geek if you preferred dry land?

"Me, too," he said and briefly studied the surface of the dark, swiftly moving river. "Give me an ocean and I'm a happy man."

"Makes sense for a Navy SEAL."

He glanced back at her. "Or a marine biologist. So what's a woman who studies ocean life doing down at a river in the middle of the night?"

She turned her face back toward the water and Zack caught the far-off look in her eyes. As if she was, at least mentally, a long way from Savannah.

"The ocean's eighteen miles away. I don't like driving at night."

"You don't mind walking for miles."

She smiled. Just a slight lift of her lips and it was gone again but for that one instant, Zack felt the slam of that smile hit him low and hard. He knew the signs of attraction. He just hadn't expected to feel them for a fish geek.

"Walking's different." She shrugged. "Relaxing. Driving, I'd be all tense and gripping the steering wheel."

"You do this often?"

"Every night."

"A routine?"

She looked at him again. "I guess. Why?"

He shrugged, but the movement belied his suddenly more alert status. "Routines can be dangerous. Anyone watching you would know in a couple of days of surveillance that he could find you here. Alone. At night."

Her shoulders hunched and she stuffed her hands into her coat pockets and drew the fabric tight across her middle. "Nobody's watching me."

"Can't be sure."

"I'd know."

"So you're a psychic fish doctor?"

"I'm not a fish doctor."

"But you are psychic?"

"No. Are you always this annoying?"

"Yes. So you don't know if somebody's watching you."

She paused, her gaze narrowed on the river and her mouth worked as if she wanted to argue with him. Eventually though, she sighed. "I guess not."

He admired her independence and her willingness to fight to protect her own space and way of life. But damned if he didn't also admire her for being willing to admit when she was wrong. In his experience, not many people were big enough to handle that. "Wasn't so hard, was it?"

"What?"

Her gaze was turned up to him again and he noticed that even in the dark, her eyes were a clear and startling green. Made a man wish he could just let himself fall into their depths and sink. That thought brought Zack up short. "Admitting you might need help."

"I didn't actually admit that," she corrected primly. "What I said was, I don't know if someone's watching me. But I'm betting, no."

"Willing to bet your life on that?"

"You're here, aren't you?"

"So I am."

"Look," she said, "my father's worried, that's why I'm letting you stay. There is no danger to me."

"Not as long as I'm here," he said, one corner of his mouth tilting up in a crooked smile.

She frowned. "I like taking care of myself."

"Me, too," he admitted and reached out to tug the collar of her jacket up higher around her neck. The backs of his fingers brushed along her throat and she shivered. Before that shiver could slide into him, Zack let her go again and stuffed his hands into his pockets. "We have something in common."

"Maybe," she conceded.

"Maybe'll do for a start." He took a step back, not sure why exactly, just knowing that a little distance wouldn't be a bad thing. But as he looked into her eyes, he felt himself wanting to look even deeper. Over the next thirty days, he was probably going to require a hell of a lot more distance than a couple of feet.

Four

The next day, their first battle was fought over breakfast.

Early-morning sunlight streamed in through the kitchen window, lying across the blue-and-gray linoleum, the blue granite counter and then glinting off the sparkling, stainless-steel refrigerator. A trio of small clay pots lined the windowsill and boasted tiny herb seedlings. Through that same window came the sounds of birds singing, kids laughing and, from a distance, a lawnmower growling.

Life in the neighborhood was ordinary, normal. Life in Kim's house was anything but.

Bent over double, head in the refrigerator, Zack asked, ''Where's the bacon?''

''There isn't any.'' Kim stirred honey into her herbal tea, then lifted it for a sip.

''Eggs?'' His voice was muffled, hopeful.

''Nope,'' she said, then offered, ''There's a carton of egg substitute on the top shelf.''

He straightened up, still holding the fridge door open and looked at her, clearly appalled. ''Does that come complete with taste substitute?''

She ignored that. ''I have some whole wheat bagels and low-fat cream cheese.''

He shuddered and closed the refrigerator. ''That's what you eat?''

''It's healthy.''

''So's grazing in a field,'' he pointed out. ''And just about as tasty.''

She smiled. If he was less than comfortable at her place, maybe he'd leave. ''You're cranky in the mornings, aren't you?''

He reached up and pushed both hands along the sides of his skull, skimming his palms over his short, neat hair. Kim's gaze drifted briefly to his broad chest hidden beneath a clean white T-shirt. Even through the fabric, she could see the play of his muscles, shifting, flexing.

Heat rushed through her, so she took another sip of tea in an attempt to cool herself down. Oh, yeah. That made sense.

When Zack's hands dropped to his sides again, he gave her a disgusted look before shifting his

gaze. He took in the kitchen, with her tidy coun-
tertop, the toaster, the blender and the microwave.
Finally, he shifted that steady gaze to her.
''Where's the coffee pot?''

''I don't have one. I don't drink coffee.''

His eyes bugged out. ''No coffee?''

''There's tea.''

He considered that for a minute or two. ''Is it
caffeinated?''

''No. Herbal.''

''Good God, woman,'' he muttered, crossing the
tiny, galley-style kitchen to sit at the small, round
table opposite her. ''How can you get going in the
morning without a shot of caffeine?''

''Wake up, get up, get dressed and go.''

''That's not human.''

''Jolting your system with caffeine is crazy.''

''Bet you don't drink beer, either, do you?''

''For breakfast?'' She smiled.

He shook his head, scowled darkly and leaned
back in his chair, folding his arms over his chest.
''You're a hard woman.''

Not at the moment, she thought as she felt his
gaze lock on her. In fact, everything inside her was
soft and squishy and sort of like a marshmallow
toasted over an open fire.

Kim watched him and wondered how she was
going to get through the next month. The house
was too small. Too confined. And with Zack Sher-

idan in residence, it felt downright Lilliputian. He not only took up a lot of room—being as big as he was—but there were the constant reminders of his presence.

For instance, having to stand in the hall and listen to him shower.

Fine, she could have gone into the living room where the rush of water would have been more subtle. But once her mind had drawn the image of Zack, naked, under a stream of hot water, steam rising all around him, she'd been caught. Mesmerized by her own imagination.

Which was really ridiculous.

He wasn't even her type.

But then, she didn't have a type, did she?

Most men walked right past her as if she weren't there. Or, if they did stop to talk to her, it only meant that they'd discovered her last name was Danforth. They never looked at her and saw Kim. They took one look and saw a bank account.

Frowning, she stopped that train of thought and lifted her tea for another sip. Over the rim of the fragile china cup, she watched the man now drumming his fingers on the table top.

He looked like a chained tiger. Energy coursed around him in an aura that was practically vibrating with the need to move.

"Okay, I'm willing to put up with a lot. But I'm gonna need coffee in the mornings."

"There's a D & D coffee bar on the next block."

"Thank God." Then he looked at her thoughtfully. "D & D. Doesn't your family own those places?"

Here it comes, she thought and she willed away the tiny twinge of disappointment. The speculation. The mental addition all men did when they tried to work out just how much she might be worth. She'd be able to see it in his eyes, she knew. He'd wonder, consider and try to decide if the money was worth hitting on her.

A long moment ticked past.

Her fingers tightened on her teacup.

"You own coffee bars and don't drink the stuff."

"I don't have anything to do with the shops."

"Not even as a customer."

"No."

"Weird." He pushed up from the table and looked down at her. "If my family owned those joints, they'd have a hell of a time getting rid of me. I'd be drinking the profits all day."

He walked around her and snagged his heavy sweatshirt out of the hall closet. Yanking it on, he zipped it up and she saw the faded white capital lettering spelling out NAVY. He slapped one hand to his back pocket as if checking for his wallet, then turned and headed for the front door.

Stunned, Kim watched him. He wasn't going to say anything? No caustic jokes about her being rich? No teasing proposal of marriage? No half-joking pleas for an all-expense paid trip to the Bahamas?

"That's it?" she asked. Now that he hadn't said anything that she'd assumed he would, she was too intrigued to let it go. "That's all you have to say?"

He stopped with his hand on the doorknob and turned to look at her. "What were you expecting?"

She pushed her glasses higher up on her nose and stared at him. He'd surprised her. She hadn't seen a glimpse of speculation in his eyes. Not even the slightest sheen of greed. "I don't know." She hedged a bit, not willing to admit that she thought a little better of him for not looking at her and seeing dollar signs. "Most people want to know how rich I am."

He shook his head. "It's none of my business."

"True," she said. "But that doesn't stop anyone else from asking."

"Money doesn't mean a hell of a lot to me," he said and opened the front door, allowing a wide slash of sunlight to spear into the room. "If it did, I damn sure wouldn't have joined the navy. Military bank balances are just downright embarrassing."

She opened her mouth, then closed it again. She

didn't know what to say, so it would be better all the way around if she just kept quiet.

"So," he asked when she simply stared at him, "you want me to bring you some tea?"

After filling up on coffee, Zack kept busy the rest of the day by installing new locks on her doors and windows. Naturally, she'd objected, but he'd reminded her that it was now his job to see to her safety. And damn it, he was good at his job.

He sure as hell hadn't requested this assignment, but now that he had it, he'd do his best.

The window guard locks would never stop a man determined to enter, but it would sure as hell make the task a little more difficult. The dead bolt locks on the front and back doors, however, were strong enough to keep out just about anyone. And as he walked the perimeter of the little house, he told himself it still wasn't enough.

Disgusted, he looked at all the window panes glistening in the afternoon sunlight. Pretty, to be sure. But all it would take was a brick through the glass and whoever was stalking Kim's father would be in her house in an instant. She shouldn't be staying here. She should be in lockdown somewhere if her old man was that worried about her.

But no one had asked his opinion and, he admitted silently, he'd be willing to bet cold, hard cash that Kim would never stand for being pulled out of her house. The woman had a head like a rock.

And a body like a goddess.

"Whoa," he muttered, stepping through the side gate into the tiny backyard. "When you start daydreaming about fish geeks, Zack, old boy," he whispered, "you've been too long at sea."

That was the problem.

He hadn't been with a woman in too damn long. No wonder the doc was looking good. Hell, that one last night on the town with Hula hadn't produced more than drinking and dancing. He should have spent some quality time with a willing female. Then his hormones wouldn't be on overdrive.

It was the only explanation as to why he found himself watching Kim so closely. Or why he'd suddenly decided that glasses slipping to the end of a short, straight nose were so damn sexy.

Still grumbling, he came around the edge of the house and stopped, staring at the garden she'd made for herself. A brick patio with irregular borders drifted in and out of a patch of grass and low-lying shrubs. A few spears of green were beginning to spring from the freshly tilled dirt and he idly wondered what kind of flowers she'd planted. Judging from everything else he'd seen though, he was willing to bet they were tidy blossoms. Probably stood up straight, like little soldiers marching along the edges of the flower beds. They'd have one or two perfectly aligned leaves and would bloom and then die with predictable regularity.

The woman was wound so tight, she practically gave off sparks. Even her refrigerator was ruthlessly organized into food groups. None of which were the least bit appetizing. Plain yogurt for God's sake. Who ate that stuff?

"Who're you?"

He spun around on his heel to face a woman peering over the fence at him. Gray hair stuck out around her head like well-used steel wool and her sharp blue eyes were narrowed suspiciously on him. Her face was wrinkled, lined deeply from too many years in the sun, and her hands, propped on top of the fence, were grubby with dirt.

"Ma'am," Zack said, nodding.

"Your manners are good, boy," she said, "but that doesn't tell me who you are."

"Zack Sheridan, ma'am," he said, stepping closer and holding out his right hand. "I'm a…friend of Kim's. Staying with her awhile."

She grabbed his hand and shook it, transferring a good portion of the dirt clinging to her skin to his. "Friend, is it?"

"Yes, ma'am." He wasn't about to tell someone he'd never met before that he was here as a body-guard. Probably just a nosy neighbor, but Zack had learned early that it wasn't wise to throw trust around too easily.

"Well, she could use a friend, I'm thinking." The woman nodded. "You just call me Edna, son. It's good to see Kim having a 'friend' over. Alone too much. Not good to be alone. Start talking to yourself and then where'll you be?"

"I—"

"Locked up," she finished it for him. "That's where. Talk to yourself and people start thinking you're peculiar. It's all right when you're old like me. Supposed to be peculiar. People expect it. Colorful. That's what I am."

"Yes, ma'am." Zack grinned. The more she talked, the higher her voice went, as if she was preaching to rows of interested listeners.

"Young people got to get out sometimes. Go to a dance. I'm always telling Kim she should find herself a handsome man. Kick up her heels a little. Looks like she listened, finally." She looked him up and down, then narrowed her steely eyes again. "You see that you take her dancing, you hear?"

"Yes, ma'am." Edna would have made a good admiral. All talk and no listening.

"Good. Now I've got to get my daffodil bed loosened up." She slapped her grubby palms down on the top of the fence. "Nearly spring, you know. Can't wait till the last minute."

"No, ma'am."

When she was gone, Zack chuckled and headed for the back door. But he hadn't gone more than a step or two before he really thought about what Edna had said. So Kim was alone too much, huh? Didn't go out? See people?

Why?

He stopped on the back porch and looked through the window in the door and spotted Kim, still sitting at the tiny table, working on her research. The woman had hardly moved from that spot all day. She flipped through books, rifled through papers and did her best to ignore him— well, except for the glare she'd shot him while he was "making too much noise" installing the locks.

She was pretty much cut off—at least from him. And Zack wondered just why it was a pretty woman like Kim would prefer fish to people.

When the phone rang an hour later, Kim reached for it and, distracted, mumbled, "Uh-huh?"

"Hey, Kim."

"Reid." She dropped her pen and leaned back in her chair. Her older brother's voice was warm and rich and slow, as any good Southerner's would be. Just hearing it made her relax a little. She realized suddenly the day was gone and she'd spent hours hunched over her work. Her back ached and her eyes were throbbing.

Plucking her glasses off, she set them aside and

rubbed her eyes with her fingertips. It wasn't just the day of work that had her tired, though. Having Zack in and out of her house all day had kept her on edge. Even when he was trying to be quiet, she knew he was there. She felt his presence in the room with her and her concentration had been slipping all day. It had taken her twice as long as usual to get half as much work done.

"How are you, Kim?"

She smiled into the phone, despite the unsettling feeling rippling through her. The second oldest of Abraham Danforth's children, Reid was quiet, and just as seriously minded as Kim. Though, she thought, he had lightened up considerably since falling in love with Tina.

"I'm okay. How's my favorite newly engaged person?"

"Fine."

The clipped, one-word answer immediately told Kim something was up. These days, Reid was normally only too willing to be chatty and to let everyone know just how happy he was with Tina. He wasn't an easy man to shake, so when she heard the tightness in his tone, Kim braced herself.

"What's wrong?"

"Thought you should know," her brother said, measuring each word as he spoke it, "Dad got another threatening e-mail."

Kim's stomach twisted, knotted, then coiled into a vicious ache. "Like the last one?"

"Close enough."

Kim's hand fisted on the telephone until her knuckles whitened. Why was this happening? All of a sudden, her family's lives had been thrown into turmoil and nothing was the same anymore.

Zack stepped into the room. She didn't hear him. She *felt* him. Breathing deeply, evenly, she shot him a quick look. Questions filled his eyes, but she couldn't give him any answers yet. She had to hear the rest.

The first threatening e-mail her father received had been short and to the point.

I've been watching you.

Just enough to throw a pall over her father's senatorial campaign—and the family, not to mention her own life into chaos. As far as Kim knew, the police were still investigating. But it wasn't as easy as someone might think to track an anonymous e-mail message. Thanks to technology, stalkers had more freedom than ever to maneuver.

"What did this one say?"

Reid sighed. "Three words. 'You will suffer.'" Signed the same, Lady Savannah."

Fear tickled the back of her neck, then skittered down her spine. One letter might be a crank. This second one was a little more determined. She sighed and looked up as Zack came around to take a seat beside her at the table. Kim didn't even want to think about how much better she felt just having him close by. If she'd been alone in the house, she would have been worried about nightfall and everything that could hide in the dark.

"How's dad taking it?" she asked.

Reid chuckled wryly. "Like you might think. He's all set to tear through the computer himself and track every wire. He's frustrated, angry…"

"And scared?"

"Not so much for himself." Reid blew out a breath that seemed to echo over the phone. "He's really worried about you."

"He doesn't have to be," she said, picking up her pen to doodle mindlessly on the paper in front of her.

Zack plucked the pen from her nervous fingers and closed his hand over hers. She didn't question it. Didn't wonder if it was a good idea or not. She simply folded her hand into his and held on, grateful for the warmth.

Reid sighed and she heard the fatigue in his voice as he said, "Let's not argue that one, all right?"

"You're right. No arguments."

"Dad just wanted me to check and make sure your bodyguard was there. In your house."

"Oh," Kim said, lifting her gaze to Zack's stony features. "He's here."

Holding her hand. Keeping shadows at bay. Making her think things she shouldn't be thinking. Making her feel things that she'd be much better off not feeling.

Yeah, he was there.

He was everywhere.

"Good," Reid said, oblivious to the turmoil churning through his sister. "That'll take one worry off the old man's mind."

Kim nodded and let her own mind wander while her brother continued, telling her about the private protection the Danforths had put in place around Crofthaven, the family home. She imagined the world shrinking. Tightening up into a small, encapsulated ball, with the Danforth family gathered inside and the world locked out.

It wouldn't last.

Couldn't hold.

You couldn't stay apart from the world forever. Sooner or later, that world would find a way through the cracks. And you'd better be able to deal with it.

Zack's fingers tightened on hers as if he'd read her mind and knew that she needed that one extra squeeze of reassurance.

"Let me talk to Zack a minute, will you?" Reid said abruptly.

She stiffened. "There's no reason to—"

"Give me a break, Kim."

Everybody wanted a break. But, it seemed, nobody wanted to give her one. Sighing, she held the phone out to Zack. As he took it, she pulled her hand free of his, instantly missing not only the warmth of his skin, but the sense of connection. "My brother wants to talk to you."

Walking into the kitchen, Kim stared out her window at the street beyond the glass. She'd made her home here. Set up her own life just the way she wanted it. A part of her family, sure, yet separate and distinct. Here she wasn't just one of the Danforths. Here, she was Dr. Kimberly Danforth. She'd worked hard to earn her degree and for the small successes she'd had and the respect she'd acquired from colleagues.

And now it felt as though everything was being threatened. Some anonymous sneak was throwing invisible darts at her father and the ripples of that action were drifting all the way down to her.

And darn it, she wanted it all to stop.

She wanted her life back the way it had been just two days ago.

Kim hardly noticed when Zack came up behind her.

"Your brother's worried."

"They're all worried about me," she said, never taking her eyes off the limbs of the oak tree in the middle of her yard. Sunset streaked the sky with ribbons of gold and crimson, drifting into pink and orange at the edges. Clouds banked in the distance and the twilight breeze ruffled the leaves of the oak, sending its gnarled limbs dancing and swaying.

From two doors down came the regular thump of a basketball bouncing off the Johnson's garage and a snatch of music drifted from a neighbor's open window.

"They don't have to be worried," Zack said softly.

She turned and looked up at him, standing just an inch or two away from her. He was big and solid, and his features were set in lines of stubborn determination. She missed the feel of his hand on hers and that worried her a little. Not enough to wish him gone just now, but enough to make her wonder if things would ever be able to go back to the way they were before he showed up on her doorstep.

Worry and frustration blended together inside her and bubbled to the surface. "I just want this all to go away," she admitted, then lifted one shoulder in a half shrug. "I suppose that makes me a coward."

He leaned one hip on the granite counter and looked down at her. Reaching out, he speared a stray lock of her hair and gently tucked it behind her ear. She shivered lightly as his skin brushed over hers.

"You're no coward," he said, smiling. "You didn't even want a bodyguard, remember?"

One corner of her mouth tilted. "But I've got one, don't I?"

"Damn straight, peaches," he said, his smile carrying the unmistakable sheen of self-confidence. "And as long as I'm here, you don't have to worry, either."

Five

The latest threat on her father's life had affected Kim whether she wanted to admit it or not.

Her eyes were haunted, shadows drifting across their grass-green surfaces. She jumped at unexpected noises and darted anxious glances behind her when they were out on her nightly walks.

It bothered the hell out of Zack.

He was forced to stand by and watch, as daily, she became just a little more tightly wound. And for the first time in years, he was unsure about what to do.

Usually, he had no doubts. He had a target and he did what he had to do to accomplish his goals.

But this enemy was nebulous. Hiding in shadows, moving behind the scenes, using fear as a weapon. He felt helpless and he didn't like the feeling.

But he had to admire Kim's handling of the situation. She didn't surrender to the fear. She rose above it, going on with her life as if nothing was wrong. She insisted on keeping up with her routines, refusing to give in to his suggestions to stay close to home—or better yet, get the hell outta Dodge.

He wanted to take her somewhere. Anywhere, really. A safe house. Someplace that no one else knew about. Where whoever was threatening her father would never find her. But she wouldn't go. She'd already made that perfectly clear and he didn't feel like having the same old argument with her again.

"So," he muttered, "how am I supposed to protect her from something I can't see?" He reached for a coffee cup. "Can't hit? Can't stop?"

Damn unsettling for a man used to action to be trapped in a holding pattern that showed no signs of letting up. And the longer they were trapped together in that little house, the crazier she made him. It wasn't only worry that had him walking a razor's edge, delicately balanced between sanity and madness.

It was Kim herself.

Zack groaned and poured himself a cup of coffee from the new coffee maker as he stared out the kitchen window. Gray clouds had scuttled in off the ocean and hung low over Savannah like a cold steel blanket. Wind whipped through the trees and every once in a while, a distant rumble of thunder rolled out like a pack of snarling dogs.

He took a sip of the steaming, rich brew and told himself the weather suited his mood. Grim. Damn it, she was pushing him way beyond the point of no return.

Worse yet, she was doing it without even really trying.

Every night, he stretched out on a narrow day bed she kept in the small second bedroom she used as an office. And every night, he lay awake, listening to the sounds she made during the night. Her damn bed squeaked loud enough to be classified as a scream. When she turned in her sleep, that shriek of sound carried to him and he wondered if she was lying on her back or her stomach? Was she wearing flannel pj's or something silky? Or, God help him, nothing at all?

The wall dividing the two rooms was a flimsy barrier of two sheets of pine paneling nailed to a few two by fours.

Which meant it was no wall at all.

He heard her breathing. He heard her soft sighs and the whisper of bed covers as sheets slid along her body. And he imagined, all too clearly, storming through those flimsy walls and showing her just how loud her bed really could squeak.

He was only averaging a couple hours sleep a night and it didn't do a damn thing for his temperament to know that Kim didn't seem to be bothered by his presence in the slightest.

Just his luck.

The fish geek was getting to him.

And for the first time in memory, the woman he wanted didn't want him.

"Just as well," he muttered and took another sip of the steaming coffee, wincing when he burned his tongue. Kim Danforth wasn't the kind of woman Zack went for. She practically reeked of permanence. He liked his women a little more temporary. He liked going into a relationship knowing that neither he nor the woman in question had any plans for a future.

Three years ago, he'd tried planning a future. An old, tired ache pinged briefly in his heart, then disappeared. He'd thought himself in love, popped the damn question and had his own balloon popped when the lady said no. It seemed a Navy SEAL was good enough to sleep with, but she'd wanted more out of life than a military paycheck and a husband who was gone more than he was home.

The worst of it was, once the hurt had faded, Zack couldn't even blame her for saying no.

Zack had made it a point to keep his distance

from the kind of woman who was currently making him nuts. Revolving-door relationships were a lot easier on the heart. He had no intention of giving up his military career—and really, what kind of life was that to offer a woman? SEAL spouses spent most of their time worrying. Who the hell would readily agree to that?

His gaze focused on his own reflection in the window and he narrowed his eyes at himself. "There's nothing for you here, man. So pull it together already. You've only got three weeks left on this mission. Hell, you can do three weeks."

He'd made it through SEAL training. Finished top in his class. He'd dived in shark-infested waters. He'd had a ship blown up under him. Hell, he'd survived a four-day trek through a desert armed only with a quart of water and a GPS.

Zack straightened up.

"Hoo-yah," he muttered. "You can live through all that, you can live through Kim Danforth."

He turned his back on his own reflection and let his gaze wander the confines of his cozy prison.

His newly purchased coffee maker sat on the gleaming kitchen counter alongside Kim's blender. While she whirled together disgusting concoctions of carrots and peaches and whatever else she found lying around, he enjoyed the rich scent of ground D & D coffee beans being brewed.

She ate plain yogurt and bagels with enough stone-ground wheat in them to be still growing in a field somewhere. He ate frozen waffles dripping with maple syrup.

"Complete opposites," he murmured, underlining their differences as he shook his head. So why, then, did he want her so bad?

"They say talking to yourself is the first sign of dementia."

Her voice, silky, soft, sly, brought him up short.

"There're those big words again," Zack commented and pushed away from the counter. Damn good thing she couldn't read minds.

She gave him a quick smile and he sucked in a gulp of air, hoping to ease the punch of it.

Didn't help.

"So what is it exactly that we're doing today?"

She glanced up at him. "I'm driving to Tybee Island to take some pictures."

"Of?"

"The ocean. Kelp beds. Whatever."

"Is this for your research project?"

"Nope." She straightened, then reached up, gathered her long, black hair into a ponytail at the back of her head and carelessly whipped a rubber band around it. "This is for me."

"Probably not a good idea, Kim," he said.

Her hands dropped to her sides and fisted. "I need to get out of the house, Zack."

"We're still going for those walks at night."
Though he was planning on cutting them down to
a couple of nights a week. Didn't pay to lay down
a routine for a stalker, no matter what she'd like
to think.

"I'm starting to feel like a vampire," she
snapped, then sent him a long look. "I know
you're going stir crazy, too."

"Does feel like the walls are closing in sometimes," he admitted. Although, he'd keep to himself the fact that she was the main reason for his
jumpiness. Hell, he could be on an aircraft carrier
and if she were somewhere aboard, the ship would
feel too small.

"Then let's go." She tilted her head and looked
up at him.

"Gonna storm."

"I won't melt."

Zack stared at her for a long minute. Most
women he'd known wouldn't even think of going
outside without layering on a coat of war paint.
But Kim hadn't even checked a mirror to see if
her ponytail was straight. She didn't have a trace
of makeup on, yet her skin nearly glowed. Her eyes
looked huge with her hair pulled back off her face
and her stubborn chin looked a little more fragile
than usual. Her eyes met his and he saw the skitter
of nerves in their depths and he knew what it was
costing her to hold it together. Maybe she was do-

ing it out of pure stubbornness, but however she was managing it, she was close to the breaking point.

Her gaze drilled into his and he felt that solid punch of awareness hit him low and hard and this time he didn't even flinch. He didn't have a clue as to what to do about his body's response to her...but he sure as hell couldn't seem to stop it.

''What the hell.''

She grinned and relief flickered in her eyes just long enough to make him glad he'd relented.

''Thanks.''

He grabbed up her black tote bag and his eyebrows lifted. ''Weighs a ton.''

''Need help?''

''Not likely,'' he quipped, swinging the straps of the bag up and over his shoulder. Heading to the front porch, he said, ''I've carried fully loaded packs through jungles so thick you can't see and so dense you can't take a step without catching your foot on roots bigger than your arm...this little pack is no problem.''

''Jungles, huh?'' Kim followed him out and stopped to lock the door behind them. ''Is that where you were last? I mean before coming here?''

''No,'' Zack said, remembering that last mission. No jungles. Just hills and forests and rivers and gunfire.

"No? Just no?" She looked up at him. "You can't tell me where you were?"

"I could," he said amiably, taking her elbow in a firm grip as he led her down the steps. "But then I'd have to shoot you. And you're just too damn pretty to shoot."

She stopped and pulled her arm free.

Frowning, he looked down at her. "What?"

"Don't do that."

"Do what?" He waited, wondering what the hell she was talking about. "Already told you I wouldn't shoot you."

"No." She pulled in a sharp breath and blew it out again in a rush. "Not that. Don't tell me I'm pretty."

A cold wind kicked up out of nowhere and tugged a few long strands of black hair free of her ponytail. They whipped across her eyes and she plucked them free with an impatient hand. Thunder rolled in the distance and echoed ominously around them.

Zack shook his head. "Why not?"

"Because I'm not pretty," Kim told him, lifting her chin and looking him dead in the eye. "And I know it. So I'd rather not hear your standard lines or recycled flattery, okay?"

Well, he thought, so much for friendly banter and a nice release of tension. Looked like they were stacking up for a fight. And hell, a fight was as good a way as any to loosen up.

He swung the bag off his shoulder and let it drop to the grass. The equipment inside the bag rattled in protest at the treatment, but he hardly noticed. "I wasn't giving you a line."

"Right." She planted both fisted hands on her hips, cocked her head and glared up at him. "'You're too pretty to shoot.' Good Lord, Zack. That's right up there with 'what's your sign' and 'my wife doesn't understand me.' But you don't even realize you're doing it, do you? It's practically unconscious."

"Now I'm sleepwalking?"

"That's not what I meant."

He glared at her. "Then say what you mean. You usually do."

"Fine." She nodded sharply. "I have a name, you know. It's *Kim*. K.I.M."

His eyes narrowed on her but he kept his voice low, quiet. "You know, I heard that somewhere."

"Funny." Her eyebrows winged up sharply. "I didn't think you knew it."

"Why's that?" Zack couldn't look away. First, it would have been dangerous to not keep an eye on her at the moment. She looked as though she was suddenly mad enough to chew him up and spit him out. But more importantly, she made a hell of a picture in her fury.

Her eyes were giving off sparks. Fire flashed in those green eyes, until they looked like emeralds under a spotlight. She practically shook with the coiled tension inside her. What had he done to get her so damn mad? One minute, she's all smiles, talking about the ocean, the next she's jumping down his throat, kicking and scratching the whole way down.

And what was wrong with him that he liked seeing her so damn mad?

"Because you rarely use my name." She shifted position slightly, folding her arms beneath her breasts and Zack was just male enough to notice the movement. She noticed him noticing and gave a derisive snort. "Women are just interchangeable to you, aren't we?"

"What the hell—"

"It's like we're an all you-can-eat buffet—"

His eyebrows lifted and Kim practically snarled. She'd stepped right into that double entendre.

"You know what I mean," she snapped, then continued before he could speak again. "Blonde, brunette, redhead. Doesn't really matter as long as we have breasts, right?"

"Hold on a damn minute," he countered, looming over her, trying for steely intimidation. It didn't seem to be working.

"No, you hold on. You think I don't notice you calling me peaches or darlin' or honey or sugar?"

She reached out and poked him in the chest with her index finger. "You think I don't know that it's your way of talking to a woman without actually having to remember her name?"

He inhaled sharply, deeply, and then closed his mouth tightly.

Irritation swelled inside her and mingled with the tension that had been coiled tight in the pit of her stomach for days. She'd felt like a tightrope walker trying to keep her mind on the research project due in little more than three months, while at the same time trying to keep her mind *off* the fact that someone out there was threatening her family.

Then there was the whole Zack issue.

She kept watching him. Couldn't seem to help herself. He was big and handsome and *there* all the time. She knew darn well that she wasn't the type of woman a man like him usually went for. Hadn't she been generally ignored by the male population for years? But that knowledge hadn't stopped her imagination from kicking into high gear when she least expected it.

She imagined his hands on her. She pictured him, sweeping her up into his arms and carrying her off to her bedroom and making her feel all the things she wanted to feel.

But the last time she'd given in to her fantasies, surrendered to her wants, she'd crashed into a wall of betrayal that still stung if she let herself think about it.

So she wasn't about to stand here and let him say things he didn't mean only to have her heart dredge them up in the middle of the night just to torture her.

"I'm not one of your little shore-leave SEAL groupies," she said quietly. She met his eyes, those greenish blue eyes that she spent way too much time thinking about, and told herself not to look away. "I'm not your latest bed warmer and I'd appreciate it if you'd keep that in mind."

"Number one," he said tightly, "I don't have groupies, darlin'. I have women friends. Occasionally, I have lovers...."

She winced. Oh, she really didn't want to think about him with other women. But men like him had women falling at their feet all the time.

"Unlike you," he added, "I actually prefer people to fish."

Her gaze narrowed. "I never said—"

"You had your say, peaches," he interrupted, keeping his gaze locked with hers. "Now it's my turn. If I say I think you're pretty, then I mean it. I don't have to lie to a woman to get her attention."

"No ego problems here," she whispered.

"None at all," he agreed, giving her a quick,

but lethal grin. "You want to believe I'm lying, there's nothing I can do about it."

"Fine," she snapped. "You're not lying. You just need your eyes checked."

He snorted a laugh. "You're a piece of work, babe."

Kim gritted her teeth and swallowed the twinge of pain. Babe. Darlin'. No one had ever called her by an endearment. Not once. And to hear it now, when she knew it meant nothing, tore at her. Stupid, she thought, to let it hurt. To let it disappoint. To wish, even for a moment, that the words had meaning.

She was a scientist.

She, more than anyone, knew that wishes didn't equal facts.

Zack started talking again and she told herself to listen. "For whatever reason, you decided to take a swing at me. Well, I'm not gonna stand here and get skewered because you're mad at Daddy for siccing a bodyguard on you."

That stung, too. Mostly because it was true. "I'm not mad at—"

"The hell you're not. Now who's lying?" Zack countered, grabbing her upper arms and dragging her close as the first few spattering drops of rain pelted them both. "But you know what the main problem is, darlin'?"

"What?" She squeezed the word through a tight

throat and told herself to ignore the blasts of heat skittering through her.

He gave her a slow smile and let his gaze run over her features. "You want me bad."

Damn it, he was right.

Lightning flashed, thunder crashed overhead. Rain erupted and drenched them both. Kim blinked up at his watery image, and thought again that he looked like a pirate. Dangerous.

And way too good.

Her blood was boiling despite the damp chill snaking right down to her bones. His fingers dug into her upper arms and felt like ten separate little match heads. Her insides curled up and whimpered, and a low, throbbing ache pulsed in time with her heartbeat.

Her breath caught in her throat, her lungs straining for air she couldn't seem to deliver. His eyes gleamed and even though her vision was blurred, she read the heat in those blue-green depths and shivered in anticipation.

His breath dusted her face as he leaned closer, and closer and—

He grinned, shook his head and let her go. Surprised, Kim stumbled backward.

"Oh, you want me. And you can have me," he said, bending down to pick up her bag before giving her a wink and another smile. "As soon as you admit it."

He bent down, picked up her bag of equipment and stared at her while the rain pummelled her. Shaking with want and frustration and trembling with a need so huge she hardly knew what to do with it, she watched him walk away from her.

There would be no walk on the beach during a thunderstorm. Instead, they'd be trapped together in a house that seemed to be shrinking daily. It was going to be a long day.

But she could do it. She could survive the wanting. She could be in that house with Zack and never admit just how much she wanted him. She wouldn't give him the satisfaction. Inwardly, she winced as she admitted that she'd be cheating herself of satisfaction as well.

Soaked to the skin, Kim swallowed that regret, stared up at him and said, "It'll be a cold day in hell before I admit any such thing."

Grinning again, he swiped one hand across his face, wiping the water off his skin. "Darlin', it *is* a cold day in hell."

Six

The storm raged outside, trapping them inside. For two hours, the wind howled and rain pelted the windows like thousands of arrogant fists demanding entry. The assault finally ended as the rain became a cold mist and the wind died into a soft moan that sighed around the edges of the house.

Kim curled into one corner of the sofa and balanced a book she wasn't reading on her lap. Her gaze slid from the pages to Zack, staring at the television with all the concentration of a neurosurgeon tackling a brain tumor.

He wasn't fooling her.

She knew darn well he wasn't paying attention

to the mindless chatter spewing from the TV. His hands, fisted on the arms of the chair were a big clue. And the grim set to his mouth. Her gaze fastened on that mouth and she wondered, as she had for the last few hours, just what it would have tasted like. What his mouth would have felt like, pressed to hers. She had a feeling that being kissed by Zack Sheridan was like nothing she'd ever experienced before.

But she wouldn't be finding out anytime soon, since he'd said she'd have to initiate anything between them. And she'd be blasted before she'd inflate his ego that much more.

Still, she wasn't going to sit in silence for the rest of the night, either. It was bad enough having a constant companion foisted on her. A surly, silent companion was even worse.

"Storm's over," she said.

"Thanks for the update." His gaze never left the TV.

Well, that was nice. Scowling at the inane game show, Kim thought, just for a minute or two, about throwing something through the television screen. She happened to know that she was way better company than the idiot woman cooing over a new refrigerator.

"How can you watch that stuff?" she finally blurted.

He slid a long, lazy look at her, swept her up

and down, then settled on her gaze. One dark brown eyebrow lifted. "There some fish show you'd rather be watching?"

She met his gaze and ignored the little jab. "You know, there's no reason why we have to be enemies."

"Nope. No reason. Some things just *are.*"

"And that's how you want to leave it?" Kim challenged, watching him. She was sure she saw a flicker of emotion run through his eyes and then disappear.

One corner of his mouth tipped up and Kim's stomach did a quick flip-flop.

"Doc," he said, his voice caressing each word, "I already told you. You want things to change, all you have to do is say so."

Her body jittered with anticipation, but Kim's brain willed it into submission. "I'm never going to—"

He cut her off. "Never say never, darlin'."

She took a deep breath, hoping to quell the fury that nearly blinded her. "You are the most—"

A knock at the door interrupted her and Kim shot to her feet. Anything was better than trying to talk reasonably with a man who was so clearly unwilling to be reasonable.

Edging around the couch, she headed for the door. But Zack moved even more quickly than she did. He stepped in front of her, holding up a hand to keep her back.

"It's probably a neighbor," she muttered.

"Just in case," he said. "I answer the door, got it?"

"For heaven's sake..."

He ignored her muttered complaints, checked the peephole, then laughed and yanked the door open. Kim looked over his shoulder at the men grouped on her porch.

"Hey, boss."

Three men, wearing worn, faded jeans and T-shirts in a variety of colors, stood on the porch, grinning.

"What the hell are you guys doing here?" Zack asked.

"Figured you must be missing us by now," one of them said.

"Like a rash." Zack snorted a laugh.

Amazing. Kim instantly felt the difference in Zack's mood. Pleasure colored his voice and the tension that had been gnawing at him for the last two hours drained away. In the glow of the porch light, the three men stood on her porch, aligned together in a small wave. And they seemed to snake out invisible arms to draw Zack into their center.

The men were clearly military, despite their casual clothes. They stood as if at attention, broad shoulders squared, hands behind their backs. And if that weren't enough, their military buzz cuts screamed out their identities. Zack and these men were more than friends, she thought. They were… family of a sort. Connected by something she'd probably never fully understand.

Zack suddenly seemed to remember that she was there. When he turned to look at her, his eyes were warm and friendly. Unguarded. Their fight earlier and the squabble just moments ago were clearly forgotten. His wide smile drew her into the circle of men, including her, and Kim was grateful.

"Kim," Zack said, sweeping out an arm to indicate all three men, "this is my team. Hula Akiona—"

A tall, dark man with black hair and dark brown eyes grinned at her and nodded. "Ma'am."

"Mad Dog Connelly."

The next man, just as tall, with pale blond hair and deep blue eyes gave her a smile that was both wicked and deceptively innocent.

"And Three Card Montgomery."

"'Lo," the last man said. He was shorter than the others, but with a quiet intensity streaming from his brown eyes.

Kim stared at them all, then shifted her gaze to Zack before saying, "Why don't you all come in and sit down?"

"Thank you, ma'am." Hula said and started inside, leading the way.

"Call me Kim."

"Nice place," Mad Dog muttered as he punched a quick fist into Zack's middle in greeting.

"Don't mean to impose," Three Card whispered, then stepped inside.

Zack looked at her and gave her a smile that made Kim glad she'd gone with her first instincts and invited his friends in. She would have slipped away to her bedroom, to give him some time with his friends, but Zack grabbed her hand and drew her into the living room with him.

"So what's with the visit?" Zack asked.

The men were sprawled comfortably on her furniture and for the first time, Kim realized just how feminine and dainty her surroundings were. These muscular men looked like tigers crouched in cat carriers. One of them was sprawled on her couch, the other draped bonelessly across one of her chairs and the third had plunked down in front of the hearth, where a fire snapped and hissed.

"Wanted to give you the word on Hunter." Three Card spoke up, leaning his forearms on his knees and flipping idly through a magazine on the table in front of him.

"Who's Hunter?" Kim asked no one in particular.

"Hunter Cabot. The last member of our team," Zack said tightly. "How is he?"

"Sitting up and driving the nurses crazy." Hula chuckled and scooted a little farther back on the stone hearth, edging closer to the screened-in fire. "One of 'em's thinking about a sexual harassment suit. A redhead."

"Always his weakness," Three Card said from the chair.

"Then he's gonna be okay," Zack said, relief coloring his voice.

"Got a weakness of your own now, don't you, man?" Hula said, grinning at Three Card.

"Funny."

Zack glanced at Kim. "Three Card just got married a while back."

"Congratulations," Kim said automatically.

The intense man nodded at her. "'Preciate it." He looked at Zack again. "Hunter keeps askin' for his pants and a beer—not necessarily in that order." Three Card reached out one leg and shoved Hula farther to the side. "Shift, man. You're hoggin' the fire."

Hula swatted the man's big foot out of the way and didn't budge an inch. "The doctors are threatening him with restraints."

"Wouldn't hold him, anyway. He's just as ugly and mean as ever," Mad Dog offered.

''What happened to him?'' Kim asked, looking from one man to the next.

''Nothing,'' Zack said tightly.

''Nothing?'' she repeated. ''Your friend's in the hospital recovering from a bad attack of nothing?''

''Boss is just being modest, ma'am,'' Hula said.

Mad Dog snorted and gave Hula another good-natured push.

Zack scowled at all of them.

Kim ignored him. ''If he's so modest, why don't you tell me,'' she said and moved around Zack to take a seat on the couch opposite Hula.

''Be happy to, ma'am,'' the man said, then slid a look at Three Card. ''But why don't you get the supplies out of the car first? I'm feeling a little dry.''

''Supplies?''

''Beer,'' Zack muttered.

Three Card vaulted over the back of the sofa in a quick, fluid move, then slipped through the front door. While she was staring after Three Card, Hula started talking. Zack took a seat behind her, on the arm of the couch. His thigh, hard and warm, pressed into her back and Kim leaned into him. She felt Zack shift uncomfortably as his friend talked, telling her about their last mission.

Hula's words painted a vivid picture. The darkness, the danger. She felt their victory when they rescued the hostage and shared in their fury when they were told to leave one of their own behind.

"That's terrible," she blurted.

"Yes, ma'am," Hula said, mouth grim. "That's what we thought."

"Damn politicians," Three Card murmured, as he walked in and set the twelve pack of cold beer atop a magazine in the center of the table. Pulling a few out, he passed them around, first handing one to Kim.

"She doesn't—" Zack started to say.

"Thank you," Kim said and accepted the beer. Lifting the can to her lips, she took a sip and Zack grinned.

"So, what happened?" she asked.

"Hunter's in the hospital," Zack reminded her, "we got him."

"Thank God."

"No, ma'am," Hula said, staring at Zack. "Thank the boss. Shooter told the big guns to go to hell, then he doubled back, scooped Hunter up and carried him out on his back."

"Shooter?" she asked.

"The boss's code name."

"Shut up, Hula."

"Keep talking, Hula," Kim said.

"Yes, ma'am." He grinned at her and ignored Zack. "Shooter carried Hunter out on his back, under enemy fire and got him back to the Zodiac in time to be evacuated.''

''Alone?'' She stared up at Zack and wasn't surprised to see him shift uncomfortably again. She couldn't imagine going into danger alone. Yet he did it all the time. As routinely as she walked to the beach to take photos of starfish.

Pride filled her as she looked up at him. She'd never known anyone like him. The men she'd grown up around would take credit for the simplest of tasks. Hailing a cab in the rain. Landing a successful account. But Zack faced down guns to help a friend and didn't want to be reminded of it. Apparently, he had no problem doing what needed to be done. He simply didn't want to be praised for it. Even if the praise was well deserved.

Three Card laughed. ''Shooter does best on his own, ma'am. It's how he likes it.''

Zack scowled at him.

Kim was fascinated. She'd known that Zack was a warrior. He carried an innate sense of self-confidence that she envied. She'd never really been sure of herself. Oh, she was confident in her work. She knew oceans and marine life. But put her on dry land and throw her into a situation where she'd be forced to talk to people and she was lost. At parties she could be most often found standing in a corner, talking to a plant. Or better yet, sneaking out early and heading back home. To her nest. Her cave.

Her sanctuary.

At least, that's what it had been until Zack had invaded it. And now, she doubted that it would ever feel the same to her again. He'd imprinted himself on the walls. He'd made himself a part of her daily life and she wasn't sure how to get him back out again.

Or even if she wanted to.

"You saved him." She looked up at Zack until he met her gaze and when he did, she saw embarrassment color his eyes. Something she hadn't expected. And for some reason, she liked him even more for it.

"The team goes in," he said simply, "the team comes out."

"Hoo-yah," the three other men muttered all at once, lifting their bottles of beer in salute.

The evening slid past in a rush of conversation and laughter. Forgotten, the TV provided a background current against the ebb and flow of stories being told. Kim laughed and talked more than she had in years. The men, closer than brothers, teased and joked and drew her into their camaraderie, made her one of them, and she loved it. She felt a sense of belonging that she'd never really felt before. She drank beer until her head swam, and then she ate pizza. She hadn't had pizza in years, but when Hula had two huge pies delivered, she'd dug right in with the rest of them, fighting and grumbling over every slice of pepperoni.

It felt…good. It felt comfortable. She felt Zack's approval as he watched her fit in with his friends.

By the time she was on her fourth beer, the stories had turned to scuba diving and they were all recounting their favorite spots. Here, Kim joined right in, telling her own version of war stories.

These men understood her love of the sea. The dangers and the attractions of visiting a world far below the surface of the everyday. They'd seen the beauty and experienced the unbelievable silences of deep-water diving. They knew what she knew. They'd each known the magic of descending into darkness and finding life teeming around them in the frigid waters.

"Oh, man, here's the best part," Hula shouted, splintering conversations and grabbing everyone's attention at once.

"What?" Kim turned her head too quickly and saw the room spin. Probably not a good thing.

"The movie—" Hula pointed to the TV and Three Card groaned.

"The man never gets tired of this."

"Tired of what?" Confused, Kim blinked to bring the men into focus, then turned her gaze on the television set where an old movie was playing.

The characters were sitting around a scarred table aboard a disreputable boat in the middle of the ocean. Drinking themselves silly, they were comparing scars as a giant shark circled their small ship, looking for revenge.

"I can beat them," Hula said and lifted his left leg, propping one foot on the edge of the table. Pulling his jeans up, he displayed a vicious scar. "Barracuda, Florida Keys."

"Hell," Three Card said, then winced. "'Scuse me, ma'am. That's nothin'." He stood up, lifted the tail of his shirt and displayed a flat, tanned abdomen with a circular scar over his ribcage. "Tiger Shark, Gulf of Mexico."

Kim grinned as Mad Dog rolled the right sleeve of his shirt up. Slapping one hand to the long, thin scar wrapping around his bicep, he proclaimed, "Stingray, Malibu."

Zack, not to be outdone, pulled his shirt up and turned around, exposing the long scar waving across the small of his back. "Moray eel, Thailand."

Four pairs of eyes shifted to Kim in silent challenge. She thought about it for a long minute, then decided, she was a part of this group, now. They'd welcomed her in, and now she could pay her dues. Propping her left leg up on the coffee table in front of her, she pulled up the hem of her jeans and displayed a set of small, circular scars running up the inside of her calf. "Octopus, Sea of Japan."

"Hoo-yah!" all four men cried, lifting their beers in a salute to her.

Kim grinned and for the first time in her life, felt as though she really belonged.

Hours later, Zack was stretched out on his narrow bed, staring at the ceiling. The guys were long gone in the cab Zack had called for them. Kim was tucked up in her soft bed and every time she shifted, he winced at the creak of her bedsprings.

Watching her all night, it had taken everything in him not to grab her and kiss her senseless. He never would have believed that the fish geek would pull up the leg of her jeans and match scars with a bunch of SEALs. Miss Whole-Wheat-Bagels-and-Blended-Carrot-Juice had sucked down beer and fought him for the last slice of pizza. She'd laughed and told stories and that grin of hers had hit him hard enough that his heart was still a little rocky.

She'd made him want her more than ever.

Damn it.

From the room next door, the bed creaked again and Zack told himself not to think about it. He closed his eyes, but that didn't help, since he kept seeing her in his mind, smiling up at him.

"Zack?"

His eyes flew open. Turning his head to the wall, he stared at the paneling as if he had X-ray vision. "Yeah?"

"I like your friends," she said, her voice clear and soft through the wall that wasn't a wall at all.

He scrubbed one hand hard across his face. "They liked you, too."

"They did, didn't they?"

Frowning now, he said, "That surprises you?"

A long pause before, "Well, yeah."

"Why?"

"You don't like me. I figured they wouldn't, either."

"I never said I didn't like you."

"Do you?"

He pushed himself up onto one elbow and stared at the damn wall. "Why am I talking to a wall if I don't?"

"I like you, too," she said after another long moment. "I didn't think I would, but I do."

"Thanks." He's dying of want and she "liked" him. That was just great.

"If I tell you something, will you promise to stay where you are?"

"I never make promises without all the facts," he said, dropping his head back onto the pillow. The ceiling tiles were dotted with thirty-four speckles of green paint and seventy-five speckles of gray paint and one hundred and twenty-seven dots of blue paint. He knew. He'd counted them all in the last two hours. Desperate to get his mind off Kim, he'd resorted to math, for God's sake.

And now she wanted to have a heart-to-heart chat from behind the safety of a sheet of paneling?

"Just promise," she said and he heard her teeth grinding.

"If it'll get you to shut up and go to sleep, I promise."

Seconds ticked past. Wind kicked up outside and rattled under the eaves of the old house.

"You were right before," she said finally, her voice softer now, a little more hesitant.

"I never get tired of hearing a woman say that to me, Doc," he said, smiling a little. "But right about what, exactly?"

"Earlier today," she said. "When we were outside?"

His insides coiled, tightened. "Yeah?"

"You said I wanted you."

"And..."

"You were right."

Kim's bedroom door flew open and Zack was silhouetted in the open doorway. She shot straight up in bed, clutching the rose-patterned quilt to her chest. Glaring at him, she shouted, "You promised to stay in your own room!"

"I lied."

Seven

Kim leaped off the bed, dragging the sheet and quilt with her. Clutching both to her chest, she stared at him in dumbfounded shock and... appreciation.

He was really built. His muscled, well-defined chest gleamed like warm, golden honey in the slash of moonlight spearing through her room. The waistband of his jeans hung open, giving her a tantalizing glimpse of slightly paler flesh. Deliberately, she looked away and lifted her gaze to his.

"You said you never lied."

"Not about the big things."

She nodded her head sharply. "This is pretty big."

He grinned quickly, devastatingly. "Thanks."

Kim's stomach quivered even while her sense of humor tickled. "I didn't mean that."

One dark eyebrow lifted.

She scooped her hair back with an impatient hand. "You're impossible."

"It's been said before."

"Oh, I'm sure of that." She inhaled deeply and blew out a surprisingly shaky breath. He was so much more than she'd expected. So much more dangerous a man than she'd ever known before.

Not dangerous physically, of course. But the threat to her heart kept growing. She didn't want to care about him. Didn't want to feel anything for a man she knew was only there because he'd been ordered to protect her. And she knew that the moment his "sentence" was lifted, he'd be gone. She'd be a memory and he'd be on to the next woman.

And despite that, a part of her wanted to cross the room, step into his arms and enjoy what he was offering, anyway. But a larger and, she hoped, smarter part of her knew better. The line between brains and desire was blending, though, and if she didn't act quickly, it'd be too late to stop the inevitable. Lifting one arm, she pointed at the doorway and said simply, "Out."

He didn't budge. "I'm not in yet."

God, he could affect her this much and he

wasn't even within reach. What would he be able to do if he actually got his hands on her? *Oh, boy.* Her blood did a quick boil and her breath staggered from her lungs. "You're not going to be in, either."

He gave her a slow, lazy smile. "You said you wanted me."

Oh, yeah, she thought. Big-time. "I want lots of things."

He grinned. "I'll see what I can do."

"Cut it out, Zack."

He put one hand against the doorjamb and leaned his weight into it. His chest rippled and Kim sucked in a breath. But the air in the room felt thick and hot and she couldn't seem to make her lungs work.

He took a step into the room and Kim's heart skittered in her chest.

His gaze drilled into hers and even in the darkness, she saw the heat, the desire, the glint of pure need shining in their depths. "All teasing aside," he said, his voice soft and warm, "I want you to know, I didn't technically lie."

She opened her mouth to argue, but he kept talking.

"It's important to me that you know I won't lie to you."

"You're here. You promised to stay in your own room."

He smiled and shrugged slightly. "A promise made under duress."

"Duress?"

"And I had my fingers crossed."

She laughed shortly. "What are you, twelve?"

"Only in my heart," he said, smiling.

"Right."

"So, we're clear on the not-lying thing?"

Kim looked at him closely and saw that despite the teasing note in his voice, his eyes were dead serious. This was clearly important to him and the fact that it was meant a lot to Kim. "We're clear."

"Good." He took another step closer to her and stopped. "Now. About the other thing."

"Yes?"

"I told you before that you'd have to ask."

"I know." Her voice sounded creaky, unused, as if she'd been mute for years and was only now attempting speech. She swallowed past the knot in her throat and told herself to get a grip. But it wasn't easy when everything in her ached. Need pumped through her body, leaving flash fires in its wake. Her knees went weak and her blood pumped in a furious rush, making her head spin.

If she had any sense at all, Kim thought, she'd tell him to leave again, and this time, she'd mean it. But while her brain argued with her hormones, Kim couldn't help thinking, *why not?*

They were adults. There was an obvious attraction. Neither one of them was looking for anything more than an end to the need rocketing around the room like a Ping-Pong ball. There was an easy answer to all this. All she had to do was make a move and she could feed the fires within. She could enjoy Zack and then have her life back when he was gone.

All she had to do was speak up.

So what was stopping her?

Reality, that's what. She took a deep breath in a desperate attempt to steady herself, but since that was useless at this point, she simply started talking.

"Okay, I can admit this much."

His eyes darkened, his mouth tightened, but he didn't speak. He waited.

"I do want you."

"Atta girl," he muttered and started around the edge of the bed.

"But…" That one single word had the desired effect. It stopped him cold.

"How did I know that was coming?" he asked, shaking his head.

"Maybe you're the psychic."

"Yeah, that's it."

"There has to be a 'but,' Zack," she said, clutching the quilt and sheet just a little closer to her chest.

"With you?" he murmured. "Naturally."

"What's that supposed to mean?" she demanded.

He held both hands up, palms out. "Cool down, Doc. All I meant was, there's nothing about you that's easy."

Kim smiled as her temper eased and the feelings she'd expected would be stomped on were instead soothed. "I think that was a compliment, Zack."

A long moment passed before he nodded. "Yeah, I guess it was."

"Thanks." Warmth stole through her, softer, gentler than the heat that had burst through her body only moments before. That flash fire of need and hunger was exciting, but this slow slide of warmth was more…tempting somehow. More… intoxicating.

Which meant she was in serious trouble. "I'm really tempted to just have an affair with you," she blurted.

"Go with your urges, babe."

"That's what you do, isn't it?" she asked, tipping her head to one side as she watched him.

"Mostly, yeah." He grabbed hold of the spindle post at the end of her bed. Even in the moonlight, she could see his fingers tighten around the carved wood until his knuckles whitened.

"I don't," she said softly. "Not any more. I did once," she offered, knowing that it wasn't what he wanted to hear. "I followed my impulses and they led me right over a cliff."

"Doesn't have to be that way again."

"Maybe not." The more she talked, the stronger she felt. She continued, not knowing if she was trying to explain her decision to him—or to herself. "But that's not how I live. I like things… organized. Tidy."

"And I like 'em loose."

"I know. And God help me," she admitted, shaking her head, "that's part of your appeal."

One eyebrow lifted again.

"How do you do that?"

"Huh?"

"The one-eyebrow lift. How do you—" she broke off, laughing and hoped it didn't sound nearly as hysterical as it felt. "Never mind. Zack, a part of me wants to tell you yes."

"And the other part?"

Kim blew out another breath and lifted her chin. "That part's hoping you'll leave fast before the less-disciplined part takes over."

"Uh-huh." He let go of the bedpost and walked toward her, one slow step after another.

God, just watching him move made her mouth go dry. He was all lean muscle and sharp angles. He moved quietly, as if stepping through a mine-field and maybe, she told herself, he was.

There was nowhere to back up to. Nowhere to

hide. Kim knew if he touched her, all of her fine resolutions and discipline were going to jump out the window, shouting, "Hallelujah," as they went.

"I meant what I said." Zack was close enough now that she could feel the heat pulsing off his body. Waves of hunger and need reached out from him to find her own hunger and need, to stoke them, and they really didn't need any assistance in reaching bonfire proportions.

"Meant what?"

"You'll have to ask." He reached up, stroked her cheek with the backs of his fingers. His touch sent jagged bolts of something deliciously wicked to the center of her belly.

Oh, boy.

"I can't."

"Not now, I see that," he whispered, and he was so close, his breath dusted her cheek as gently as his fingertips had. "But you will."

She stiffened at his cool confidence, but if she were going to be honest, then she had to admit that he was right. Sooner or later, she was bound to cave in. Zack Sheridan at his most lethal was something no woman could resist for long.

Steeling herself against the dazzling light in his eyes, she met his gaze and tightened her grip on the quilt clutched to her and ignored the cool breeze slipping through the partially opened window. Wind chimes danced musically and, from somewhere down the street, a dog barked as though chasing away a horde of invaders.

"It would be easy to give in to what I'm feeling for you."

One corner of his mouth tipped up. "There's another 'but' coming, I can almost hear it."

She obliged him. "But I went with easy once and in the end, it was more difficult than anything I'd ever experienced, before or since."

"What happened?"

His voice was a hush. Like a whisper in a confessional and maybe it was that tone—maybe it was the quiet of the moonlight—that had her telling him what he wanted to hear.

"Charles Barrington the third," she said.

He snorted.

Kim appreciated the sentiment. "He gave me a big rush. Came to the house all the time to see me. Made nice with my brothers, my parents. He brought me flowers, took me to plays and," she said with a sigh, "in general, played the part of the perfect boyfriend."

"When?"

"Hmm?" She was staring at the past and hardly heard her present.

"When was Chuck your man of the moment?"

"Chuck?" Kim slapped one hand across her mouth to muffle the hoot of laughter. "Oh, my

God, Chuck. I never thought, but that's the official nickname for a Charles, isn't it?''

Zack folded his arms over his chest and nodded. His mouth tight, eyes narrowed, he said, ''Now imagine what nasty little four-letter word it rhymes with.''

A moment. Then Kim laughed again. ''Appropriate. Funny how I never thought of that before.''

''Doesn't matter. Tell me about Chuck. Since he's the guy standing between us at the moment, I figure I rate an introduction.''

Her smile slipped away. She felt it and didn't even try to retrieve it. Kim was long over the pain, but she had a feeling that the sting of humiliation, of betrayal, would stay with her to her dying day.

''He asked me to marry him.''

''You said yes?''

''Of course.''

He snorted again.

''What?''

''Nothing,'' he said. ''Just go on.''

''Not much more to tell.'' She shrugged and the quilt dipped near her shoulder. She tugged it back into place. ''We were engaged. Everyone was pleased. Such a good match. Old Savannah families. His father was a congressman, mine was thinking even then about a run for the Senate.''

''And?''

''And,'' she let her gaze drift from his. She

stared out the window into the moonlit backyard and looked instead at the moment that was still carved into her memory. "We were at a party, but I had a headache. Wanted Charles to take me home. But I couldn't find him. No one had seen him for a while."

She closed her eyes now and saw again the brilliantly lit dance floor, the acres of crystal glinting in the overhead lights. Saw the flash of diamonds around the necks of society matrons, heard the whisper of conversations drifting just beneath the dance music provided by a small orchestra at the end of the room.

Kim remembered making her way outside. She could almost smell the jasmine, feel the wet heat of the summer air.

"What happened when you found him?" Zack prompted.

Kim opened her eyes and strangely, she was comforted by Zack's presence, even though she was standing there in little more than her bed clothes.

"I heard voices coming from the gazebo. I walked across the grass, and heard Charles speaking, but I couldn't make out who was with him." She stiffened then, as the memory sharpened, like a cleaver, slicing through her heart again. Thank heaven, the slice it took this time was a lot smaller than it had been once. "When I was close enough,

I heard Charles, carefully explaining to Elizabeth Coopersmith—''

''Where do they get these names?'' Zack reached out and took her hand.

She chuckled at his exasperation and had to admit she felt better for telling him this story. His grip was warm and strong and steady and she was grateful for it. Stupid really, to still feel the sharp slap of humiliation, but there it was.

She swallowed hard and pushed the rest of the words out, wanting it said. ''Charles was telling Elizabeth that once he and I were married, he and Elizabeth could meet again. Seems he'd purchased her a condo outside Hilton Head and she was pouting because he hadn't been by to see what the decorator had accomplished.''

''Bastard.''

She smiled. ''Oh, yes.''

''Did you hit him?''

Kim sighed. ''Why didn't I think of that?''

''I don't know,'' he teased and she turned to look up at him. ''You didn't have any trouble dusting me that night you tried to sneak past me.''

Her lips quirked and the tiny stab of pain eased back into the shadows where it usually stayed. ''Yes, but I was too much the lady that night for anything so unseemly.''

''Too bad.''

''Yes, it is a shame.''

"So what did you do?"

"Oh, I walked into the gazebo, handed Charles his ring back—it was a gaudy thing—and wished him and Elizabeth well."

"Darlin', you let him off easy."

"Not so easy," she said with a shrug of nonchalance she didn't quite feel. "He married her. Believe me, he's paying."

"So you just walked away?"

"It wasn't that civilized," she said. "After all, Charles made a point of telling me he'd been counting on the Danforth money. And that was why he'd put up with the cold fish that I was." She lifted her chin in defiance to an old memory. "Elizabeth had a few things to say as well, since she too had plans for my money—not that her family was poor, you understand. Just—"

"Not as rich as yours."

"Exactly."

"Hmph. Who knew that rich people can come from the wrong side of the tracks, too?"

Kim gave him a small, tired smile. "Not wrong exactly," she corrected, "just less right."

"Oh, yeah, that makes sense."

"Oh, I never said it made sense." She folded her arms across her chest and gave herself a hug.

Zack's insides fisted even tighter than his hands. He wanted to hunt down the miserable bastard who'd broken something fragile inside Kim. He wanted to beat the son of a bitch within an inch of his life, then heal him and start all over again.

But he couldn't do any of that. Charles the third was out of Zack's reach. But Kim wasn't. Her expression and the old sorrow in her eyes pulled at him until it yanked something from him he hadn't really been sure existed.

Tenderness.

"Chuck was a moron."

She laughed sharply. "True."

"So consider the source when you think about anything the idiot had to say."

"Oh, I do. Usually."

"Good. Cold fish?" He shook his head. "You're no fish, peaches," he said and grinned when her mouth flattened into a firm line. She really hated it when he called her anything but Kim. So he'd tease her by giving her something to be mad at. Something to replace the misery of the memory she'd just lived through again.

Reaching over, he cupped her face in his hands and stroked her high cheekbones with the pads of his thumbs. The feel of her skin against his was a jolt of liquid heat that rolled through him like a summer storm sweeping across the ocean.

"Not a damn thing cold about you, darlin'," he said, swallowing hard to choke his own need back.

"If ol' Chuck couldn't find the fire, maybe it was because he didn't have good enough kindling."

She trembled under his touch, his words, and Zack felt that slight reaction shudder through him. This woman had some strong weapons. Weapons she was using effectively whether she was aware of it or not.

"Zack…"

"Me," he said, interrupting her quickly, "I'm a great little fire-starter. But I think your fires burn plenty hot enough without help."

She shook her head, confused now as his words swirled around her and his hands continued to stroke her face. Regret shadowed the want in her cool green eyes and he knew they wouldn't be doing what he'd like to be doing. At least not tonight.

"I can't do this," she said softly.

"I know that," he said, feeling his own aching regret reach up to grab hold of his throat. "I'm just saying, don't let that bastard be the ruler you measure yourself by."

"I don't. I haven't. Not for a long time."

"Good."

"You're not what I expected," she said, her voice as quiet and steady as the beat of her heart, pulsing at the base of her throat.

"Yeah?" he asked, smoothing his hands into her hair, pushing it back from her face. It felt cool and soft as his fingers threaded through the long strands. He wanted to wrap them around his hands, pull her tightly to him and kiss her until neither one of them could think. "Is that a good thing or a bad thing?"

She sighed heavily then chewed on her bottom lip. "I think…it's a dangerous thing."

He chuckled, though it was strained. "Lucky for you, there's a SEAL in the house. Nothing we like better than danger."

"Lucky me." She gave him a wry smile, then turned her green eyes to him. Her eyes were remarkable. Within their depths he could see her emotions and deep dreams. And he could see himself reflected there, too.

A part of Zack wanted to turn and bolt for cover. He'd never planned on being a part of someone's dream. Didn't know if he could. But damn, if she wasn't the one woman who could make him think about trying.

"I'm uh…gonna go back to my room," he said, congratulating himself on being able to speak at all.

She nodded as he stood back, letting his hands fall to his sides. "Probably safest that way."

"Not the most fun, though," he quipped and gave her another smile, hoping she couldn't see what it cost him to turn and walk away from her.

"Probably not."

"I'm not him, you know," Zack said, his voice

a low scrape of sound. "I don't give a good damn about your money or your family or, God help us, *society.*"

She laughed lightly and it sounded like the crystal ring of the wind chimes hanging outside her window. "I know."

"Okay then," he said, backing up another step and then another until he'd rounded her bed and was safely at her door. "There is one thing you could do for me," he said, one hand on the doorknob, ready to shut himself out and away from her.

"What's that?"

His gaze dropped to the quilt she still held like an ancient shield in front of her. "It's been killing me for a week now, wondering just what you sleep in."

Surprise lit her eyes and, just for a moment, he saw a flash of excitement. "That's probably not a good idea."

"Probably not."

She thought about it for a long moment, long enough to have Zack imagining all kinds of wonderful things. Then she shook her head and that long, black hair flew back from her face. "Why don't we just leave it to your imagination, okay?"

He didn't know if he was disappointed or relieved. Though he'd love to get a look at the woman behind that quilt, he was willing to admit that if he did, it would make sleeping even harder than it was already.

"Doc," he assured her, "my imagination's what's killing me."

"Good night, Zack."

"For some of us," he said, shaking his head. Then, groaning, as the imagination she'd sentenced him to took over, he closed the door with the last of his strength.

Eight

To say things were a little tense around Kim's house would be like describing Mount Everest as a nice little hill.

It had been three long days since Kim and Zack had stood opposite each other in the moonlight, separated only by an antique quilt. And every minute of every one of those days, Kim's mind had reminded her of what she'd turned down.

And Zack wasn't helping any.

She felt him watching her. Felt his gaze on her as surely as she would his touch. He hadn't made a move on her since that night, and she wasn't sure if she was grateful or not. Which was so absolutely contrary, it infuriated her.

But she was walking a fine line between desire and logic. She felt on edge, as if every cell in her body was humming with an electrical charge. Her brain kept telling her that this would pass, and her body wanted her brain to shut up so it could get busy.

Bottom line though, neither of them was happy.

"Nice to find out at the ripe old age of twenty-eight that you're schizophrenic," she muttered to herself, staring unseeing at the landscape whizzing past the window of Zack's shiny black SUV.

"You say something?"

"No." Nothing she wanted to repeat.

"So why are we doing this again?"

She glanced at Zack and really tried not to sigh. But even her stoic mind had to allow her body to respond to Zack Sheridan in dress whites. In the dim light of the dashboard, he looked…way too good. She'd been attracted to the man in jeans and T-shirts. That same man in a dress white uniform was enough to make her want to stretch herself across the hood of the car and shout, "Take me now!"

"It's an engagement party for my brother Reid and his fiancée, Tina." And she'd almost forgotten all about it in the rush of hormones these past few days. What kind of sister did that make her?

"So it's a family thing, then?"

She looked at Zack and chuckled. "Oh, no. That's not the Danforth way, silly man."

"Yeah? What is the Danforth way?"

"Have a party, invite the world." Kim remembered too many of the stiff, formal affairs. Even as kids, she and her brothers had been expected to make an appearance at their parents' parties. They'd troop into the ballroom dressed to the teeth, smile, look like happy, all-American children, pause to be admired briefly, then be trotted off by the nanny, sent back to their rooms to have dinner on a tray.

Even birthday parties had become business deals. Mergers were made while professional clowns entertained society's children. Tonight, Kim knew, would be a different kind of circus— but just as crazy.

"It's a family celebration," she said, "but with dad running for the Senate, he's not about to miss the chance to do a little fund-raising. Reporters will be there and probably a couple of TV cameras." She looked at Zack. "The movers and shakers of Georgia will be filling Crofthaven tonight."

"So," he said, shooting her a quick grin, "I shouldn't be expecting a keg out on the patio?"

She laughed and some of the dread for the coming ordeal fell away. Kim loved her family, but she loathed these performances. She'd always hated the formal gatherings at the Danforth mansion.

Small talk with people you didn't like and wouldn't see again until the next "must" appearance…smiling when your feet hurt, holding a single glass of champagne but not drinking it because it wouldn't do for a Danforth to drink too much. Strained dinner conversations with strangers. No matter how many times she'd done it, she'd never felt comfortable.

"No kegs, but we'll raid the kitchen." She reached out and laid one hand on his forearm. "Joyce, the housekeeper, is a magician. She'll find us a couple of beers."

"Us?" he asked, smiling, moving one hand off the wheel to give her smaller hand a squeeze. "One night of beer and pizza with a bunch of SEALs has turned you off fine wine?"

The heat of his touch slipped right through her flesh and into her bones. It skimmed up the length of her arm and burned warmly in her chest. Reluctantly, she pulled her hand free of his and told herself to pay no attention to the sudden chill she felt.

"Not completely, but I will admit, there's a lot to be said for beer and pizza."

"There's still time to head to Pino's instead."

"Tempting," she said, thinking of the small pizza parlor not far from her house. She sighed inwardly. Oh, yes, Pino's sounded wonderful. "Unfortunately, I'd never hear the end of it."

"Okay," Zack said, shooting her a glance. In the pale light of the dashboard and the occasional flash of oncoming headlights, she looked tense—as though her innerspring had been wound way too tight.

He felt anxiety rippling off her in cool waves. Whether she knew it or not, she was building fences between them. Correction, he thought. She was adding height to the fences already there. The closer they got to the Danforth family mansion, the more reserved she became. It was as if she were slowly turning into a different person. Retreating from the Kim he knew to become the Kimberly who would probably never think of entering a run-down pizza joint.

"Turn right here," she said, and he noticed her voice had dropped another notch.

He steered the car right and passed through an open set of scrolled iron gates with a twin *D* in the center of each. Zack shook his head and guided the car through a long, tree-shaded drive. Moonlight speared down through the trees like an overhead spotlight focusing on a stage. Long, naked fingers of the trees seemed to reach out for the car, and the sheets of moss hanging from the gnarled limbs looked like ghosts, fluttering in the cold ocean wind.

"Impressive," he muttered, keeping his gaze locked on the illuminated path created by his headlights, slicing through the darkness. Far in the distance, he made out the golden sheen of lamplight winking from windows.

She sighed. "You ain't seen nothin' yet."

"Bet this used to intimidate the hell out of your dates back in high school."

"It would have, I suppose, if I'd had any. I went to an all-girls' school. In Switzerland." Her hands clenched more tightly, her fingers pressing against each other until her knuckles whitened. "Not a lot of dating there."

"Pillow fights, though, right?" he asked, grinning, trying to make her smile.

Her mouth lifted briefly and he felt like a hero. "Do all guys think like you?"

"The lucky ones," he said, then shifted his gaze back to the road.

And slammed on the brakes.

"What?" Kim flew forward, was stopped by the shoulder harness, then flopped back against her seat.

"You okay?" Zack asked, even as he unhooked his belt and opened his car door.

"I'm fine. What're you—"

"Don't you see her?" He lifted one hand and pointed to the woman standing at the side of the road. She'd moved out of the center of the drive, where she'd been only moments before. She'd scared hell out of him. Now she was just standing there, her long, black dress sweeping the ground, her pale face turned to them, her dark eyes watching.

"Zack…" Kim glanced at the woman, then back at him. "Let's just go on, okay?"

"Can't just leave her here," he said sharply and climbed out of the car. "Ma'am," he called as he stepped a little closer to the woman. "We'd be happy to give you a ride up to the house."

She gave him a small, brief smile and swayed slightly, as though buffeted by the breeze shooting down the long, tree-lined drive. She was illuminated by the moonlight, but his car's headlights seemed to shine right through her. The woman's long, dark hair lifted in the cold wind and swirled around her face. She lifted one hand to smooth it down, then stared at Zack through eyes dark and shadowed with pain so staggering, he felt the weight of her agony.

Zack's heart jumped to his throat and he wasn't sure why. Something was wrong. The hairs at the back of his neck lifted and sent an icy roll of dread trickling down his spine.

She opened her mouth and spoke. But she made no sound. Zack saw her mouth moving as she tried repeatedly to tell him something she obviously felt was important. She wrung her hands and a solitary tear snaked its way down her cheek as she realized he couldn't hear her.

And the more she tried to make Zack understand, the more her dark eyes filled with frustration. A sense of sorrow so strong reached across
the distance to Zack and shook him right down to
his bones.

"Zack," Kim said quietly, from behind him.

He couldn't tear his gaze from the woman in
front of him, but a part of him clung to the sound
of Kim's voice. "You see her, right?"

"Yes."

That was something, then, he told himself. He'd
faced guns, mines, storms at sea and more life-
threatening situations than most people ever encountered. But standing here in the cold night air
watching a ghost made him grateful to have company.

As he watched, the image of the woman wa-
vered, her eyes wept. She shimmered in the dap-
pled moonlight, then slowly disappeared.

Kim would have seen that, too, he told himself.
So at least he wasn't headed to the loony bin alone.
If they locked him up, maybe Kim would get the
cell next door.

He lifted both hands and rubbed them briskly
over his face. Then he turned and looked at Kim
as she climbed back into the car. She didn't look
the least bit surprised by all this. In fact, he remembered, when they'd first seen the woman,

she'd told him just to drive on. She'd known that woman was—what...*dead?*

Zack cut that thought off, moved quickly to the car, jumped in and latched his seatbelt. Then, gripping the steering wheel in both fists, he shot her a level look. "What the hell was that?"

"That," Kim said, "was Miss Carlisle."

He thumped the heel of his hand against his ear as if he couldn't quite believe what she was saying. "You know her name?"

"That's all we know about her," Kim told him as he fired up the engine and put the car back into Drive. "Well, that and the fact that she's been dead about a hundred years."

Zack snorted. This was turning out to be one interesting assignment. A gorgeous fish geek, mansions, stalkers and ghosts. And the month wasn't even half over.

Gritting his teeth, Zack blew out a breath and tossed one last look at the drive behind him—at the spot where the woman had disappeared. Nothing. He sent Kim another quick look before starting down the long road again. "So far, it's a hell of a party."

The gathering was everything Kim had expected it to be. Music drifted through the house, a lovely, soft layer just beneath the murmur of well-bred conversations. People wandered across the marble

foyer and gathered at the foot of the circular staircase that led to the upper floors. Crowds loitered
in the sitting room where a fire danced and leaped
in the stone hearth. A few people were clustered
in the music room, sitting at the Steinway, while a
very untalented man sat plinking out a melody that
was jarring in contrast to the orchestral melodies
floating on the air. Dozens of silent servers
threaded their way through the crush of people,
carrying silver trays filled with champagne flutes
and elaborate finger foods.

Kim headed for the ballroom, smiling at people
as she passed, but always conscious of Zack's hand
at the small of her back. She concentrated on the
warmth of his fingers, burning through the black
silk of her dress to imprint themselves on her skin.
The feel of him, so close, reminded her that she
wasn't here alone. That she needn't be resigned to
a corner tonight. That the plants surrounding the
polished teak dance floor would have to find someone else to talk to them.

"Lot of people for a family party," Zack muttered, leaning forward until his breath brushed the
back of her neck.

She shivered at the sensation and glanced back
at him. He was close enough for her to feel as
though she were falling into his eyes. Close enough
that a kiss was only a heartbeat away. Kim swal-

lowed hard and did a quick mental retreat. "No Danforth party is ever just family."

He slid his hand around her body to rest on the curve of her hip. Kim sucked in a breath and held it before letting it slide slowly from her lungs. She savored the sensation of his hand on her body even as she spotted envious stares from the women they passed.

Tall and lean and gorgeous, Zack Sheridan was every woman's fantasy in that naval uniform. And for tonight, at least, he was hers.

They paused at the threshold of the ballroom. Zack tensed behind her. She couldn't blame him. She'd grown up in this place and the ballroom could still take her breath away.

A cavernous room, the pale blue walls were decorated with paintings her family had been collecting for generations. In the spring and summer, the French doors on the far side of the room would be thrown open, allowing the scents of roses and jasmine to flavor the air.

But February was chilly even in Savannah. Light from the crystal chandeliers dazzled the crowd and seemed to sparkle through the room as brightly as the diamonds glinting around the necks of some Danforth supporters to sparkle. The music was louder here, but still a lovely accompaniment to the conversations. A few elegantly dressed couples swirled around the dance floor but most of the

guests were clustered around the small tables and
chairs set up along the perimeter of the room.
Nerves fluttered wildly in the pit of her stomach,
but Kim silently ordered them to calm. She'd had
years to perfect that ability.

"Do you know all these people?" Zack asked,
astonished.

"No. Just a few." Nodding her head, she said,
"The tall guy there in the navy blue suit, with his
arm around the short woman with the great hair?
That's my brother Reid and his fiancée, Tina."

"Uh-huh."

"Beside him," she continued, "are Ian, Adam
and Marcus, my other brothers."

"Big family."

"That's not even counting cousins," she said,
then grinned. "Like Jacob, there on the dance
floor."

She pointed out a tall man with short black hair
dusted with gray. He was laughing and spinning a
much shorter woman in a wild version of a jitter-
bug in the middle of the ballroom.

"He looks like he's having fun," Zack said.

"Jacob has fun anywhere," Kim said on a sigh
that was only slightly envious.

"So what do we do first?" Zack took her hand
and threaded it through the crook of his arm.

"Find my father, I suppose," she said, her gaze
already raking the crowd for one face in particular.

She found Abraham Danforth on the far side of the ballroom, deep in discussion with three other men. He didn't look happy. Kim felt a quick jab of anxiety. If Abraham Danforth wasn't smiling at a fund-raiser, there was a problem.

Kim led the way, but kept her hand on Zack's arm. It felt good to have all that barely contained muscle and steel beneath her palm. It made her feel invincible. Almost.

As they approached her father, his voice, lowered to a mere rumble, reached her despite his efforts to keep quiet.

"I don't care what they said, I won't have it," Abraham muttered, his gaze narrowed on the tallest of the three men in black suits.

Kim didn't recognize any of them, but that didn't mean anything. There were always plenty of strangers at these events. But she did spot a flicker of annoyance in the black eyes of the man her father was focused on.

"I assure you—" the man said, his voice colored by an accent she couldn't quite place. Spanish?

A tall, robust man with silvering black hair and sharp eyes that rarely missed anything, Abraham Danforth was not a man to be taken lightly. And judging by the flash of surprise in the black eyes watching her father, Kim thought Abraham's opponent was just realizing that.

"No," Abraham said sharply, cutting the man off midsentence. Moving in closer, Kim's father narrowed his gaze on the man in question and lowered his voice even further. "No one threatens my family, is that understood? If my son Ian has any more trouble, I'm going to take it very personally. Are we clear?"

The other man's mouth tightened into a grim slash across his darkly handsome face. *"Sí."*

Before Kim could wonder what was going on, Zack muttered, "Stay here," and stepped up beside her father. "Anything I can help you with, sir?" he offered, sliding a warning glance to all three men.

Abraham shot Zack a quick, approving glance, then looked back at the other man. "Thank you, but no. I think we're finished here, aren't we, *señor?*"

A short nod was his only answer.

"Fine. Thank you for coming, sorry you have to leave so early." Abraham lifted his left hand, crooked a finger and almost instantly, two equally grim-faced men stepped up to his side. "Show these men out, please."

"Yes sir, Mr. Danforth," one of them said, then turned to the visibly fuming dark-eyed man. "This way, sir."

Kim stepped up to her father's side. "Dad? What's going on?"

A heartbeat or two of thick silence passed before Abraham's features cleared, like storm clouds lifting to reveal a sunny day. "Kim, honey. Don't you look lovely?" He turned and held out one hand to Zack. "And you must be Zack Sheridan. You look just like your father did twenty years ago. Great to meet you."

"Dad," Kim said again, tugging at her father's coat sleeve. "Never mind introductions. What's going on?"

"Nothing for you to worry about," he insisted, before beaming at Zack again. "Thanks for your offer of help."

"Not a problem," Zack said, letting his gaze slide briefly to Kim's furious eyes. "SEALs stick together."

Abraham sighed and smiled. "My SEAL days were long ago, I'm afraid."

"Once a SEAL," Zack said, "always a SEAL."

Abraham grinned. "Hoo-yah, Commander Sheridan."

"Exactly."

"If you two have finished your bonding dance," Kim said, her voice low enough, tight enough, to demand their attention, "I wonder if you might spare me a moment for the 'womenfolk'?"

Her father frowned slightly, then shook his head. "No more unpleasantness tonight, Kimberly. It's your brother's big night."

She sighed. "Dad, Reid doesn't know half these people."

"It's still his engagement party. Let's not forget that, hmm?"

"But what about Ian?"

He frowned again, deeper this time. "Please keep your voice down. There was a threat made. Some Colombian drug lord was rattling his saber. I've taken care of it."

"Drug lords?" she repeated, eyes wide.

"Shh." Clearly exasperated, he grabbed Zack's arm and said, "Commander, dance with my daughter."

"A pleasure, sir," Zack said and took Kim's hand, closing his fingers around hers when she would have escaped. "Come on," he whispered, leading her onto the dance floor. "No point in fighting a battle you're not going to win."

Still fuming, she tossed a look back at her father. "What kind of thing is that for a SEAL to say?"

He swung her into his arms, pulling her tightly against him. Smiling down into her grass-green eyes, he shrugged and said, "Honey, you're no SEAL, so give it up. Your old man doesn't want to talk about it and you're not going to change his mind."

"But—"

"Always a 'but' with you," he said, smiling, and swayed to the rhythm of the music soaring through the huge room. "Just for once, let that go and just dance with me."

She opened her mouth as if to argue, then, still staring up at him, deliberately snapped it shut again.

"That cost you, didn't it?" His whisper was for her alone.

"More than you know," she admitted, sliding her left hand up to his shoulder as she moved in time with his steps.

"Well then, here's something to take your mind off it."

"What?"

"You're beautiful."

She blinked up at him.

"Remember," he said, seeing the doubt flash in her eyes, "I don't lie."

She nodded slowly, keeping her gaze locked with his. "Thank you."

"You're welcome." Around them, couples moved in time to the music and conversations were being carried on from the sidelines. Deals were being made, promises crafted and lies exchanged. But here, with Kim in his arms, Zack felt as though they were alone on the planet. It was just the two of them, locked together.

He felt her breath shudder from her lungs. Felt the solid beat of her heart against his chest and the pure pleasure of her thighs brushing along his.

The short, black dress she wore fit her like a lover's caress. It hugged her curves and defined every tidy inch of her. The high heels on her small feet did amazing things for her legs. Her long, midnight-black hair was braided close to her skull, then fell in a long straight rope to the middle of her back. All he could think of while the end of that soft rope brushed over his hand was undoing the braid, threading his fingers through the mass of hair and pulling it all over him like a cool, black curtain.

Mouth dry, heart pounding, he somehow kept moving, swaying to the music that seemed to be pumping inside him. When she laid her cheek on his shoulder, he inhaled the soft, flowery scent of her hair and knew he was a dead man.

Everything about this woman called out to him on so many levels. He wanted her. Wanted to be inside her. Wanted to hold her and be held.

And he didn't think he'd be able to wait for her to come to him.

Zack reluctantly gave way as an older gentleman cut in and spun Kim into a waltz. She smiled at him over her new partner's shoulder and Zack held on to that smile while the next hour crawled by.

He mingled, feeling uncomfortable and wondering what the hell he was doing at this kind of a party. The whole place reeked of money and it hit Zack hard to realize that Kim was used to all of this. That she'd grown up in circumstances he would never be able to relate to. They were from such widely different backgrounds, they could have been from two different planets.

And yet, he couldn't keep his gaze off her.

She moved through the crowd with an ease and grace he admired all the more because he could see the discomfort in her eyes. No one else did, though, and he was proud of her. She handled strangers and friends alike. Always a warm smile and a few kind words. Zack stayed on the periphery of the party, where he could watch and still keep to himself. And his view of Kim kept his blood pumping. He couldn't seem to quell the rush of his blood when she was near. Couldn't seem to stop the desire that pumped through him every time he looked at her.

So he quit trying.

He listened to speeches, and even paid attention when Abraham, reacting to a request from a guest, retold the story of Miss Carlisle, the Danforth ghost. Comforting to know he wasn't the only one who'd been surprised with a visit from the dead.

But after an hour or more of smiling and fielding stupid questions about the military, Zack was near the end of both his rope and his patience. Sidling onto the dance floor, he stole Kim from the arms of yet another old Southern gentleman and quickly whirled her to a corner of the room. His hand slid up and down her spine and she smiled up at him.

"Having fun?"

"Oh, yeah," he said wryly, pulling her more tightly to him. "Haven't had this much fun since the last time our chopper went down in the desert."

One corner of her mouth tipped up. "If it makes you feel any better, my feet are killing me."

He glanced at the pointy-toed heels. "They may not be comfortable, but they look great."

"Small consolation."

"Not from where I'm standing."

"Are you always this smooth?"

Zack grinned. The whole damn party was tolerable now that he had her in his arms again. "Do you really have to ask?"

"I'm glad you're here, even if you're having a lousy time," she said.

"Right now, I'd have to say I'm enjoying myself."

"Me, too," Kim admitted and swayed with him as he kept time with the music.

She slid her hand higher up on his shoulder and leaned into him. Zack tightened his grip on her right hand and tucked it next to his chest. "You know, Doc," he said, "I was thinking we could—"

"Kimberly, is that you?" A deep voice cut him off neatly.

Scowling, Zack shot a glance at the man who'd interrupted them. But when Kim stiffened in his arms, his protective instincts went on full alert.

She pulled away from him slightly and might have stepped out of his arms, had he allowed it. But Zack kept her pressed close to him even as she turned to look at the couple who'd stopped alongside them.

The shorter man had thick blond hair and small blue eyes. His smile was picture-perfect, but Zack thought his chin looked weak. The woman beside him was a stunner, from her dark red hair to the tips of her bloodred polished toes. A beauty, Zack thought, but a little cold around the eyes.

"Hello, Charles," Kim said.

Ah, Zack thought. The idiot.

"You're looking…well," Charles said, "isn't she, Elizabeth?"

His wife, though, hardly glanced at Kim. Instead her gaze locked on to Zack as she asked, "And you are?"

"Grateful," Zack said, tightening his grip on Kim and sliding one hand down her spine in an intimate caress that couldn't be missed.

"I'm sorry?" Charles said.

"Yes, you are, aren't you, Chuck?" Zack said.

A stunned silence ticked past.

"Charles, Elizabeth," Kim said, speaking up to fill the void, "this is Zack Sheridan."

"I'm glad we got a chance to meet, Chuck," Zack said, deliberately using the name that had the other man flinching. He ran one hand idly up and down Kim's arm in a proprietary gesture the other man didn't miss. "Wanted to thank you for being such an ass."

Charles's eyes popped in insulted surprise. "I beg your pardon?"

"No need," Zack assured him, fighting down the urge to plow a fist into that weak chin. This was the man who'd hurt Kim? Hell, he wasn't even worth hitting. He'd go down too easy. "You're forgiven."

"I don't—"

"Zack," Kim said, glancing at the other dancers as if afraid someone might overhear.

But Zack kept his voice pitched at a level directed solely at Barrington. "After all," he said, as if Kim hadn't interrupted him, "if you hadn't been such a chump, I wouldn't be here with Kim. So thanks again. Now, good night."

With that, he swung Kim into a wide circle and kept them moving until they were on the far side of the floor.

"I can't believe you just did that," she said, staring up at him, a smile dazzling her eyes and tugging at her mouth.

"I can't believe you're surprised," he quipped.

"Me, either," she said with a laugh that made him feel as though someone had just pinned a medal on his chest. "Thanks."

His hand swept up and down her spine again and he watched as flames of desire lit up her eyes. "Trust me on this," he said. "My pleasure."

"Zack…"

"How long do we have to stay at this thing?" His voice was low and tight, aching with a need that was suddenly so sharp, so vicious, it clawed at him.

"I don't—"

"I need you, Kim," he said, forcing the words past the knot in his throat that threatened to suffocate him on the spot. "I can't wait for you to come to me." He tightened his arm around her waist, pulling her flush against him until she was bound to feel the thick, hard proof of his desires pushing at her.

Her eyes slid closed and a whisper of air slipped through her lips. "Zack, I…"

"I admit it, Kim. I want you." His gaze moved over her face and his heart pumped furiously. "I want you so bad, I may not be able to walk out of here."

She lifted her gaze to his and stared hard at him for a long moment. Then she licked her lips, inhaled sharply and said, "Can you run?"

Nine

Zack kept his foot on the accelerator and took every red light like a personal insult.

Jaw clenched, gaze narrowed on the road in front of him, Zack fought down the urge to pull the car over to the curb and just have her right there. It was all he could do to keep his hands on the wheel—when he wanted them on her. He'd never wanted anything in his life the way he wanted Kim Danforth. Her perfume filled his head. Heat from her body reached out for him across the bucket seats and seemed to singe him, even with the open space separating them. Every short, strangled breath she drew rattled through him, leaving him just a little more shaken than he'd been before.

His heart hammering in his chest, Zack told himself it was ridiculous, that he was acting like a teenager about to get lucky with a cheerleader.

It didn't seem to matter.

His blood raced in time with the SUV as it swerved in and out of traffic. He heard Kim gasp when he took a corner a little more sharply than he'd planned. "Sorry, sorry," he muttered. "I'll slow down."

"Don't you dare," she whispered tightly and those three words were enough to have him floor the gas pedal and pray for green lights.

"Right. No slowing down."

The Danforth mansion was far behind them now. The crowds, the music, the inane chatter that had swelled to the ceiling, trapping them both for far too long in polite society—it was all gone. Now, it was just the two of them and nothing else mattered. It was as if the desire that had crouched between them so hungrily had suddenly erupted, tearing at them both with vicious tugs and pulls that couldn't be denied any longer.

Zack didn't even care that he had been the one to break first. Didn't mind that she hadn't come to him. All he cared about now was having his hands on her. His mind filled with images, one after the other. Visions of them tangled together on her bed. His hands sliding up her long, sleek legs, fisting in her hair. His mouth on hers as he entered her.

He groaned tightly and ordered his brain to shut down. All he needed was to wrap the damn car around a telephone pole. If he died in a wreck before he'd had a chance to bed Kim, he'd be one pissed-off ghost.

Taking the right turn onto her street, Zack emptied his mind of everything but parking the damn car. He pulled into the driveway, threw the car into Park, yanked up the brake, turned the engine off and reached for Kim.

She was on the same page.

Unlatching her seat belt, she leaned into him, moving into his embrace as if the only thing that had been holding her back was the canvas strap.

Zack pulled her across the gap between the seats and pinned her on his lap. She scooted around until she was comfortable, grinding her hips and bottom against his already hard, tight body.

"Doc," he murmured, between brief, hot tastes of her mouth, "you're killin' me here."

"No," she said, sliding her hands up to cup his face, "not yet. I want you alive and well and…I just want you."

"Good, babe, that's good." He took her mouth completely this time, giving in to the need to taste her. To feel her sighs slide into him, to feel the warmth of her.

He savored her, drinking her in and giving himself the pleasure of this first discovery. This wonder of mouths and tongues and breaths, mingling, blending, becoming one. And he felt the slam of something powerful punch at him as he held her tighter, closer, pressing her body against his until he felt her hardened nipples pushing into his chest like tiny firebrands.

Zack slid one hand up her thigh, under the hem of that short black dress and groaned when he found the tops of her sheer black thigh-high stockings—a wide, elastic band of lace. Instantly, his mind filled with the picture of Kim, wearing only those stockings and the roaring in his ears told him his blood was pumping wild and hot.

She shifted in his grasp, sliding around on his lap again as his fingers drifted higher, higher.

"Zack…"

"Just let me touch you, darlin'," he murmured, bending his head to kiss her neck, nibbling at her flesh with lips and teeth.

"Oh, boy," she whispered, tipping her head to one side, giving him easier access.

"Oh, yeah," he said, his breath dusting her skin. She was all. She was everything. She fit in his arms as though made for him. The way she turned into his chest, the way she curled her arms around his neck and pressed her lips to his throat—she was so much more than he'd ever found before. So much more than he'd expected or hoped for.

Outside the car, Kim's neighborhood was dark

and silent. Homes were locked up for the night and the only sound other than their own breathing was that of a dog, somewhere in the distance, howling at the moon. Zack knew just how the mutt felt. Hell, he wanted to howl, too.

He slid his fingers higher up her thigh, close, so close to the center of her heat.

She lifted her hips and her head fell back as she gasped, a quick, sharp intake of breath. ''Zack, I want—''

''Me, too, darlin','' he said, lowering his head to kiss the base of her throat. ''I can't wait. I have to touch you now.''

She lifted her head to look at him, and in the wash of moonlight, her eyes looked impossibly dark and full of secrets. Their gazes locked and she cupped his face in her palms. ''I don't want to wait another minute, Zack,'' she said softly, each word hitting him like a velvet bullet, slamming into his chest, his mind, his heart. ''Touch me, Zack,'' she whispered, leaning close for a kiss. ''Touch me now.''

Her mouth came down on his as his hand moved to cup her heat. She moaned and shifted uncomfortably, but he held her still. A man on a mission now, he swept his hand up her thigh, grabbed the edge of what felt like lace panties and gave them a quick twist. They tore easily and just like that, he had his hands on her.

In her.

She sucked in a gulp of air and kissed him again, hungrily, mating her tongue to his, and Zack's heart thundered in a heavy rhythm that rattled his ears and shook him to his bones. Lifting her hips for him, she groaned from the back of her throat as he pushed first one finger, then two, into her damp, waiting heat.

He tore his mouth from hers and breathed like a man coming up from twenty fathoms. She arched in his grasp and her legs fell apart, wider, wider, offering him more, offering him everything. He took. His thumb dusted the small nub of flesh at the heart of her and she cried out, her voice breaking on his name.

"Zack, it's too much, it's too—"

"Not enough, babe," he whispered, his own voice cracking on the hard knot of lust lodged in his throat. "Not nearly enough." His fingers dipped in and out of her heat, pushing her, driving her, higher and higher. Her hips pumped, her breath quickened and danced in and out of her lungs on a frantic beat.

"Feels good. Feels…" She stiffened, and a low, keening moan slid from her throat as her body dissolved into a starburst of sensation.

"Right," he murmured, staring into her eyes as the first explosion ripped through her body. "It feels right."

* * *

Heart pounding, throat tight, Kim felt every cell in her body go soft and gooey and slide into a near-liquid state. If he hadn't been holding on to her, she probably would have *oozed* off his lap and onto the floor of the car.

The car.

Oh, boy. She'd just had the best orgasm of her life in the front seat of a car parked in her driveway.

Her brain whispered that she should be ashamed of herself.

Her body told her brain to shut up and enjoy the ride.

''That was,'' she said as soon as she thought she could speak without whimpering, ''amazing.''

''Wait until I have more room to maneuver,'' he said, one corner of his mouth tipping into a smile that tugged at her heart.

''Wow.''

''That about covers it,'' he agreed and smoothed the hem of her skirt down her thighs. ''Now how about we get inside and finish what we started?''

''You bet,'' Kim said, eager now for more. Her body still humming from his touch, she wanted more. Needed more. Needed to feel him filling her, his body sliding into hers, pushing her up that glorious peak one more time.

He opened the car door and stepped out, carrying her with him.

"I can walk," she said.

"And I can carry you," he told her, bending his head for a brief, hard kiss. "I like this way better."

Her, too, Kim thought. She felt like the heroine in a romantic movie. The handsome naval officer sweeping her off her feet and carrying her off for a long night of lovemaking.

How, she wondered, had this happened to her life? How had she gone from being a lonely marine biologist to having a sexual experience in a parked car, in less than two weeks? And how could she ever go back to the way her life was before Zack had entered it?

He stepped up onto the porch and promptly slung her over his left shoulder as he dug for his keys.

"Hey!" She pushed herself up by planting her hands on his back. "This is slightly less romantic, Sheridan."

He unlocked the door, then reached up to smooth the palm of his hand across her bare bottom. His fingers kneaded her soft flesh, sparking new needs, new desires. Kim shivered at the intimate caress and nearly melted against him.

"Give me a chance, Doc," he said as he carried her into the tiny house, "I'm just getting started."

"Promises, promises." She swung the door

closed behind them and Zack headed straight for her bedroom.

He walked through the open doorway and stepped up alongside the bed. Then with one smooth flip, he had her on her back on the mattress, staring up at him as he tore at his uniform blouse.

"Peaches, you want romantic, you've got it." He grinned as he got rid of his clothing in record time. Then he was naked, standing in front of her and all Kim could do was stare.

She couldn't take her eyes off him. Moonlight speared through the bedroom window and shone on him, defining every muscle, every hard edge and scar. He took her breath away. His eyes gleamed as he watched her and Kim's stomach jumped when desire flashed across his eyes.

"Now you, darlin'," he said.

Nodding, Kim scooted to the edge of the bed. Then she turned around and said, "Unzip me?" She could have done it herself, but she wanted his hands on her. She wanted to feel the whisper-soft touch of his fingers along her spine.

The zipper pulled free with a sigh of sound and his hands followed it down, smoothing along her back, curving along her hips.

"No bra," he said, turning her in his arms as he pushed the fabric of her dress down, letting it fall to the floor in a chic black puddle.

"No," she said and hissed in a breath as his hands cupped her breasts, his thumbs and forefingers tweaking her already rigid nipples into hard buds of aching need. "You have magic hands," she whispered.

He chuckled. "You ain't seen nothin' yet."

Kim swayed into him, then bent slightly to tug her thigh-high black stockings off. He caught her hands in his and shook his head.

"The stockings stay."

A curl of something wicked and delicious unwound in the pit of Kim's stomach. "Yeah?"

"Oh, yeah," he said, his gaze dropping to sweep over her with a long, approving look. "Babe, you are a fantasy."

"I'm real enough," she said, lifting her hands to encircle his neck.

He stared at her and Kim tried to read the emotions dazzling across the surface of his eyes, but they came and went so quickly, she couldn't be sure of any of them. All she knew was that she felt good in his arms. She felt beautiful and sexy and wild and free.

She'd never been any of those things and knowing that she could be, with Zack, was so liberating, she could hardly catch her breath.

"Lie down," he said softly, tipping her back onto the mattress. "Now you get your romance."

"Be inside me, Zack," she said. "I want to feel you deep inside me."

His jaw clenched and he inhaled sharply. "Me, too, but first I want to kiss every inch of your body."

She shivered and lost herself in the dark gleam of his eyes. "Zack..."

"Trust me."

"I do."

He smiled and leaned over her. He started at the base of her throat, trailing damp, hot kisses down to her breasts. Then he took her nipples, first one, then the other, into his mouth. He suckled her, drawing and pulling at her sensitive flesh until Kim could hardly be still. She writhed beneath him, twisting with the building fires within. His breath caressed her skin and fanned the flames until she thought she might spontaneously combust. She didn't really care, as long as he kept doing what he was doing.

He moved, nibbling his way down her stomach, across her abdomen and to the juncture of her thighs. Kim stiffened and inched back instinctively. But Zack's strong hands grabbed her hips and held her in place. She looked down at him as he knelt between her thighs and she managed to say, "Zack, you don't have to—"

"I said every inch, babe." He smiled, winked

and lowered his head to take her in the most intimate kiss she'd ever experienced.

Kim sighed and she was pretty sure she whined a little, too. It was just so perfect. So wonderful. So wicked. His tongue moved over her most tender flesh and she arched wildly, moving into him as he took her higher than she'd ever been before. His breath puffed against her, his lips and tongue and teeth tortured her with a sweet relentlessness that pushed her ever closer to the edge of madness.

And when the first tremors shook through her, he tasted her surrender, holding her gently, lovingly, until she drifted back to earth, still in the cradle of his strong hands.

Head still swimming, Kim looked at him and watched as he sheathed himself before covering her body with his.

"You make a hell of a picture, darlin'," he said, "wearing nothing but moonlight and those stockings."

"You make a hell of a picture yourself," Kim said, smiling as her blood sizzled and popped, "wearing nothing at all."

"All I want to be wearing is you," he murmured, dropping a quick, hard kiss on her mouth.

"Be in me," she said, cupping his face between her palms. "I want to feel you, Zack. I want to feel you inside."

"Now," he agreed and pushed his way home.

Kim gasped and arched into him, lifting her legs to lock around his hips. She pulled him tighter, closer, wanting to feel as much of him as she could. His hips rocked as he buried his face in the curve of her neck. She felt the rhythm quicken, felt her blood do a dance of welcome and her heart sing. He filled her. Completely. Totally. He pushed himself high enough inside her that she thought he actually touched her heart.

Kim lifted her arms to hold him to her and she relished the pounding of his heart against her chest. He lifted his head to look down at her and as their eyes met, that slow rush to completion flashed between them. Kim felt it first, then saw the same explosive shudders lance across Zack's eyes.

And this time when she fell, he was right there, taking the fall with her.

Ten

Zack knew he should move. Unfortunately, he'd forgotten how.

Every muscle in his body was lax. Yet at the same time, he felt energized. His blood rushed through his veins, his heart raced in a wild, frantic beat and his mind was busily trying to find a way to explain what had just happened.

But explanations weren't easy.

It wasn't just sex.

What he and Kim had shared went way above and beyond the simple easing of need. If it had been only lust, the urges in him would have been satisfied. He could have gotten out of bed, dressed and walked away—as he had so many times before.

But now, for the first time, he wanted to stay. That thought alone was usually enough to have him rolling away from her. Putting both emotional and physical distance between them. He stared blankly at the ceiling like a shell-shocked survivor of a fiercely pitched battle.

Beside him, Kim yawned, stretched languidly and sighed as she slid one foot along his leg. New need zapped him, sizzling along his veins like an out-of-control skyrocket. Then she pushed her hair back from her face and said softly, ''That was...''

''Yeah,'' he said, congratulating himself on being able to talk. ''That about covers it.''

She turned into him, curling her body along his, burrowing her head into the curve of his shoulder. His skin tingled, as if lit from within by thousands of sparklers. The scent of her hair reached him and enveloped him completely. Would he ever again be able to notice the smell of flowers without thinking of her? Of this moment?

She ran the flat of her hand across his chest and fires quickened inside him. Moments before, he'd been sated, now, new hunger rose inside him again, demanding satisfaction. He'd never felt this before. This all-encompassing need for one particular woman.

And a part of him pulled back from that acknowledgement.

Zack closed his eyes and captured her hand in his, holding her still, hoping it would be enough to rein in the desire pumping afresh through his body.

"I have to say," Kim said softly, her voice a low hush in the moonlit room, "I've never enjoyed the end of a party so much."

"I aim to please." His voice was light, his words casual, in an attempt to convince them both that what had just happened wasn't as mind-boggling as he seemed to think it was. But whatever he said, it wouldn't be enough to chase away the stray thoughts still bulleting around his brain.

Several long moments passed in silence and Zack's mind took that quiet and ran with it. Image after image filled his mind and they were all of Kim. Kim laughing, Kim walking along the river, the wind in her hair. Kim tonight, surrounded by her family and the immense wealth she'd grown up with.

That image stung.

He couldn't stop the sudden doubt. He'd grown up in a solid, middle-class family, the only child of hardworking people who'd lived the same kind of military life he now led. Their family had been small, but tight. Right now, his parents were off in an RV, discovering the country, and Zack was pretty much on his own. The navy was his family. His team members his brothers. That had been enough for him.

Until recently, his mind taunted.

He'd built a life he loved. One that didn't lend itself well to sharing. Zack scowled up at the ceiling. He'd tried once before, hadn't he? But his lack of a fortune—and the fact that he didn't give a good damn about making pots of money—had ended that before it could begin.

So, he thought now, if he hadn't been enough for *her,* how could he possibly think that he would be enough for Kim Danforth? She hadn't been born with just a silver spoon in her mouth; it had been the whole silverware set.

People with that kind of money simply weren't interested in anyone outside their own realm.

Not that he cared or anything.

Not that he'd been thinking of doing anything so crazy as proposing.

Not that he was in love.

Oh, man.

He scraped one hand across his face, hoping to wipe away the thoughts crowding his mind. But it didn't help. Nothing could.

He was in deep and he knew it.

"What're you thinking?"

"Hmm?" Kim's voice had startled him out of his train wreck of a thought process. For which, he told himself, he was grateful. Quickly, he searched for something to say. "I was uh, remembering that little speech your father gave."

She laughed a little, her breath dusting across his chest like a whisper. "Which one?"

"The one about the ghost."

"Poor Miss Carlisle." She shook her head and her hair shifted like warm silk against his skin. "Imagine arriving for a job as governess, only to be run down on the drive before you could reach the front door."

Ghosts. A safe topic, he thought.

"You'd think she'd quit trying to get in," he said. "After a hundred years or so of attempts."

"She's determined to make it into the house," Kim said softly. "Almost as determined as I was to get out of it."

She'd made it, he thought. Out of that house and into this bungalow that seemed light years away from the mansion they'd visited hours ago. She'd made her own life, apart from the Danforths. She'd carved out a world of her own. But that didn't mean that she wasn't still a part of that influential family.

"Some things," he told her, his voice thoughtful, "just aren't meant to be."

"You believe that?" She tipped her head back to look up at him.

Zack met her gaze and tried, this time, not to

notice just how green her eyes were. Just how hypnotic it was to stare into those depths and feel them draw you deeper, closer. And somehow, he knew that he'd be seeing those eyes of hers in his dreams for the rest of his life. She'd branded him somehow, and even when he left her—as he knew he would—he'd never really be free of her.

Zack held her closer and with his other hand, smoothed her hair back from her face, letting his fingertips glide along her cheek. The smooth slide of flesh against flesh warmed him, comforted him. "Sometimes," he said, "it's better to walk away."

"I don't believe that."

"I never used to," he admitted and wondered if she realized that he was already pulling back. He wouldn't admit to what he was feeling for her because there would be no point. There was no future for them.

"But now you do?" She went up on one elbow and looked down at him.

"Now," he said, staring up at her and feeling the raw pulse of need reach up and grab him by the throat. "Now I don't know what I believe."

"Do you know what you want?"

His mouth lifted in a brief twist of a smile even as a cold, unseen hand squeezed his heart until his chest ached. "At the moment...you."

She lowered her head to his, her thick, black hair hanging like a curtain of midnight silk on either side of them. "Then for now, let the wanting be enough."

"Doc," he said, already reaching for her, "I like the way you think."

He closed his mind to thoughts of tomorrow. To the warnings his brain tried to send. Because all he cared about right now was Kim's warm flesh pressed to his. The shine in her eyes and the curve of her mouth.

Zack had seen enough in his life to know that it was important to enjoy what you had while you had it, to appreciate the moment because that moment might not come again.

He scooped her up, pulled her on top of him, then wrapped his arms around her, pinning her to him. Their bodies brushed together, length to length, hard to soft. His hands skimmed up her spine, defining every line, every curve, his fingers exploring, carving the feel of her into his memory. He wanted Kim so deeply in his heart, his mind, that she was always there, just a thought away. Zack knew that in some distant future, the memories of this night, this moment, might be all he had left to remind him that once he'd held a woman who was everything to him.

She kissed him, her mouth on his aroused him so fiercely, he devoured her in response. Taking her head in his hands, he held her mouth fused to his, taking, demanding what she offered and giving all that he had to give. She sighed and he felt the ripple of it course down to his soul. Her breath became his. Their hearts beat in tandem. Blood raced and pulses skipped.

He wanted her as he had no other. But more, he needed her as he'd never expected to need anyone.

Rolling to one side, he tipped her onto her back and indulged himself by caressing her body in long, slow strokes. She damn near purred as she arched into him, digging her head back into the pillow, fanning that black silk hair beneath her.

This was good, he thought, dipping his head to taste first one of her breasts and then the next. She groaned and the flames within him licked at the corners of his heart. This was right, he thought, trailing kisses up the column of her throat and across her jaw before reaching her mouth. This was all, he thought, as once again, he tasted her, invading her warmth, letting himself slide into the heat and magic that was Kim.

''Zack,'' she whispered, her breath warm on his face. ''If we keep this up, we're going to kill ourselves.''

''Hell of a way to go though, peaches,'' he said, taking another kiss, then one more.

''Yes,'' she said on a sigh of wonder, ''yes, it is.''

Her hands skimmed up his back and he felt the strength in them. Short, neat nails scraped at his flesh and he felt the stroke of each one as if she were carving her initials into his heart. Marking him as hers.

That thought drove him, plunging through his mind like a runaway train. Need swept through him like a tidal wave, relentless, unavoidable, devastating.

Zack rode the crest of that wave and moved over her, sliding up the length of her. He watched the flash of desire snap across the surface of her eyes. Felt her desperation as she grabbed him, held him, lifting her hips in a silent, ancient welcome. And giving himself up to the flames within, he entered her again, claimed her again, and in the act of completion, found more need.

He linked his fingers with hers, needing that extra connection. He stared down into her eyes, and saw himself mirrored there. He watched her watch him and gazes locked, they reached the shattering end that somehow signaled a beginning.

The days marched past, one after the other, measured in sunrise and sunset. The hours in between were filled with sex and laughter and a freedom that Kim had never known before.

In Zack, she'd found a man who understood her love of the sea. A man who was more than willing to spend an hour or two scuba diving on the off chance they might see something spectacular.

Around Zack, she didn't feel like the nerd she'd always been. She felt…beautiful. And smart. And interesting.

And most importantly, at least to her, she felt…wanted.

He touched her and her skin sizzled. He looked at her and her blood raced. He kissed her and she melted. Since the night of the party, they'd been together. Every night, he came to her bed and in the morning, he was still there. Her heart was entwined with his, her life felt fuller and richer with him in it. And she wasn't at all sure what she would do when he left.

She'd accepted long ago that she wasn't going to find that one man. That she wouldn't have the family, the children, she'd dreamed of having when she was a girl. After that mess with Charles, she'd simply acknowledged to herself that she wasn't the kind of woman men fell in love with. She was, as she'd always been, too smart, too practical, too uninterested in the things other women seemed fascinated by.

She'd much rather spend the day underwater, charting fish, than spend hours wandering through a crowded mall searching for just the right outfit to wear to a society luncheon. She was happier keeping her long hair in a braid rather than face the nightmare of regular visits to a salon. She didn't enjoy small talk, and she'd rather have her fingernails torn out than be forced to sit through terminally boring board meetings.

There was a price to be paid for living the kind of life she preferred, and she'd long ago come to grips with the fact that her price would be solitude.

And then Zack Sheridan had marched into her nice, neat, solitary world and splintered it.

Sitting at the kitchen table, surrounded by her books and the paper she was supposed to be working on, Kim glanced over at the tall crystal vase that held what was left of her first Valentine bouquet. A week ago, Zack had brought her two dozen yellow roses, a box of truffles and, she thought with a smile, a new valve for the oxygen tank she used on her dives.

What woman wouldn't fall in love with a man like that?

"Love?" She whispered the word as though afraid that Zack would hear her. But he was outside in the backyard, mowing her tiny patch of grass. Pushing up from the table, she tossed her pen onto an open book and watched as it rolled right off the table. *Love?*

Her breath huffed in and out of her lungs. Her head took a wild spin that had the room tilting for one brief, fascinating moment and she was almost positive her heart had lurched to a stop.

She was in love.

Really in love, for the first and last time in her life.

"I should have seen this coming," she said, still half-stunned by her own discovery. "But even if I had," she reasoned, starting to pace now while her thoughts raced to keep up, "how could I have stopped it?" More importantly, "Why would I have?"

Well, because, you idiot, she told herself silently, life would be a lot less complicated if you hadn't let your heart get involved.

"But complicated can be good." She stopped pacing. "Can't it?"

Sunlight poured through the front windows and painted gold slashes across her furniture and the polished wood floor. From outside came the sound of the hand mower in the backyard, Zack's colorful cursing and, just beneath those homey sounds, the quiet music of the wind chimes hanging from the roof of the house. Kids skateboarded along the sidewalk, the wheels on their boards growling like caged beasts let loose for a much needed run.

The world was just the same as it had been ten minutes ago. And yet, she thought, wandering down the hall to the back door where she could stand and watch Zack, it was all so different.

He'd taken his shirt off as he worked on the yard and in the direct sunlight, his tanned muscles gleamed with sweat. The scars marking his body stood out a bit paler than the rest of his flesh, but somehow made him look *more* perfect rather than less so. Sunglasses shielded his eyes and a day's growth of whiskers dotted his face. His large, strong hands gripped the handles of the ancient mower and something inside Kim *pinged* in appreciation as she watched him tighten that grip.

What was she supposed to do about this, she wondered. How could she keep loving him to herself? But how could she tell him when she knew he was only here because it was his duty to protect her? They'd said nothing about tomorrow. They'd made no plans for anything beyond the month that was nearly up.

She laid one hand on the cool glass of the window half of the door, and watched, smiling, as he cursed the mower that continued to fight him. Her heart turned over and Kim knew that she had to do something.

She couldn't simply stand by and watch him walk out of her life as easily as he'd walked into it.

After dinner, when the phone rang, Zack reached for it first. Hell, he'd lunged for the phone as if it were the last lifeline in a churning sea.

He'd tried to keep busy. Tried to stay so wrapped up in one project or another that his mind wouldn't have time to torture him with thoughts of leaving Kim. But it seemed that no matter how busy he was, his brain was free to wander. And it did. Constantly.

Their month was nearly over, and soon he'd be shipping out again. Though a part of him knew that was a good thing, another, more hungry part of him dreaded it as he had never dreaded anything.

His career had been built around deployment. One mission fed into the next and he'd always liked it that way. New people, new countries, new problems to solve. New dangers and adventures. Him and his team.

But things were changing.

Three Card had a wife, for God's sake.

Hunter was still laid up in the hospital.

And Zack had found Kim.

"Yeah?" He damn near growled into the phone. An instant later, a chill swept over him as he listened to Kim's brother Ian tell him about the latest threat delivered to their father.

When Kim came up beside him, he reached out and took her hand. Feeling the chill in her skin, he folded his fingers around hers, trying not to notice how fragile her hand felt in his.

"What is it?" she whispered.

"Any leads?" he asked Kim's brother Ian, ignoring her.

"Nothing," Ian said. "Just the words, 'I'm still watching you,' signed by Lady Savannah."

"The woman needs a new routine."

"The woman needs to be locked up," Ian countered, his voice tight.

"I'm with you there," Zack said, letting go of Kim long enough to drape one arm around her shoulder and pull her in close.

Ian continued a moment later. "The cops think they've got a lead, so just keep an eye on my little sister, huh?"

"Don't worry about her," Zack said. "I'll take care of her." Until the navy pulled him away, his brain screamed. And then what? Who would look out for her then? Who would be with her when he was off halfway around the world doing God knew what?

Mind seething, he hung up, setting the phone receiver back into its cradle much more gently than he wanted to.

"It's my father again, isn't it?" Kim asked.

"Yeah," he said, turning to her, pulling her close to him. "Another threat."

"When is this going to stop?"

"Ian says they have leads."

"I hope so," she said, tipping her head back to look up at him.

"You're safe with me." Zack stared down into her green eyes and felt that magnetic pull working on him again. He smoothed her hair back, letting the thick, soft strands sift between his fingers.

"I know that." She slid her hands beneath the hem of his T-shirt, then wrapped her arms around his middle.

Her touch slammed into him and carried the same force it had the very first time. He wondered if it would always be like that between them, then immediately crushed the thought, since he would never know the answer to that question. Their time was almost up. And when it was, they'd each return to their own worlds, with nothing more than a few damn good memories to cling to.

Cupping her face in his palm, he bent his head for a kiss and when she nibbled at his bottom lip, Zack felt a jolt of desire spear up from deep within him.

Deliberately, he put the world aside and forgot about the threats and leaving her and anything else beyond this one moment.

"I want you again," he whispered, his breath dusting her lips, her cheeks.

"You can have me again," she said, going up on her toes to press her mouth to his. "And again and again and again…"

Zack smiled as he kissed her and felt the first wave of longing rise up to drown him in her magic.

Eleven

Two days later, they were that much closer to the end of the month and no clearer on what would be happening next.

There'd been no more threats made against Kim's father, the man who would be Senator. And as far as Zack was concerned, the actual threat to Kim herself had never been a viable one. The idea of her having a bodyguard, was, as she'd said, more to make her father feel better than because of a real need for protection.

He'd been there nearly a month and he'd seen no real danger to Kim. If anything, she'd proven to be a danger to *him*.

Zack frowned as he listened with half an ear to the rush of water from inside the house. He turned his mind away from imagining Kim in the shower, her long black hair clinging to her wet body. But it wasn't easy. He had some fond memories of that cramped, tiled shower. And those memories were going to have to last him a lifetime.

Neither of them was talking about the end of the month, only a few days away now. They each seemed determined to avoid the subject. And if that was cowardly, well, it was the only damn cowardly thing he'd done in his life, so Zack was willing to live with it.

Beat the hell out of being miserable about something that couldn't be changed.

And for now, at least, he had a distraction. Hula had stopped by and while Kim showered, Zack and his friend took a couple of beers to the backyard.

"You must be ready to get back to the action, huh?"

No. For the first time in more than ten years, no. But he couldn't admit that. Not even to Hula. Zack shot his friend a quick look and lifted one shoulder in a shrug. He took a long sip from the beer bottle, then cupped it in both hands between his up-drawn knees. "You get any word on what's up next?"

"Nothin', man." Hula grinned and winked.

"They don't tell me a damn thing. You're the team leader, brudda."

"Right." Stupid question. Hell, he knew as well as Hula did that none of them would get their next assignment until they'd reported back in for duty. God, even his brain wasn't working anymore.

"So what about the doc?"

"Huh?"

Hula shook his head, reached out and clinked the neck of his beer bottle against Zack's. "Man, you got it bad, don't you?"

"I don't know what you're talking about."

He snorted. "Yeah, I believe you."

"Shut up, Hula."

"I'll shut up, soon as I tell you that you're bein' a damn fool."

Zack scowled at him, even knowing that it wouldn't affect his friend. Hula had stopped fearing Zack's wrath years ago, and fear wasn't about to kick in again now.

"Damn, Shooter," the man said quietly, "that's a hell of a woman."

"You think I don't know that?"

"So, if you love her, tell her."

"Nobody said anything about love," Zack countered tightly. The word had been rocketing around inside him for weeks, but he'd be damned if he'd admit that to Hula if he couldn't get himself to say it to Kim. "Besides, who're you? Advice to the lovelorn?"

"Yeah, that's me. Just ask Three Card."

True enough. Just the summer before, Hula had been the one to give Three Card that last push that had landed their old friend a gorgeous wife. But that situation had been different. Three Card and Renée had had a history. They'd been together before and now they were together again.

Zack and Kim didn't have history. Hell, they didn't have anything beyond a month-long blip in their lives.

"Back off," he said quietly.

"Okay," Hula said, leaning back into a patch of shade thrown by the roof of the old house. "What happens to the doc when you go back into the field?"

"What d'ya mean?"

The other man shrugged. "I mean, if she's in danger still, what'll her old man do? Assign another SEAL to keep watch?"

Everything inside Zack tightened until he thought he just might break apart and the pieces go spinning off into space. Another SEAL? He hadn't thought of that. Hadn't considered it. Of course her father would pull some strings and get someone else to protect her. Of course there'd be another man assigned to this house.

To Kim.

His hand on the beer bottle clenched spasmodically until his fingers ached and he thought he might have felt the glass shatter. His brain got busy. Drawing up images designed to torture him. Another man, some faceless navy man, pitching his seabag into this house, making himself comfortable, sleeping in the tiny room that had been his when Zack had first come here. That same son of a bitch would flirt with Kim, accompany her on her long walks along the river. Maybe take her diving or out on her boat. *He'd* be the one to see her last thing every night and first thing every morning. *He'd* be the one to stand between Kim and danger. *He'd* be the one she turned to when she was scared.

Zack's heartbeat thundered in his ears.

His breath caught in his lungs, frozen until he saw black dots fly in front of his eyes and was forced to draw in air again. His back teeth ground together and a skim of pure fury danced along his bloodstream.

Some nameless, faceless bastard was going to be moving into the bungalow, taking his place. The place he belonged. The one place in the whole world he wanted to be.

How the hell was he supposed to live with that?

Hula chuckled and drew a sharp, steely-eyed

glare from Zack. "Oh, yeah," the man said, with a slow shake of his head, "who said anything about love?"

"Shut up." Zack snarled and got up to walk off his mad while one of his best friends laughed his ass off.

Kim tried to relax, though it wasn't easy.

Even being here, walking along the riverbank, wasn't easing her mind as it used to. But then how could it, with Zack walking beside her? How could she relax knowing that in a few short days, the man she loved would be walking out of her life?

What she needed was to be able to talk about this, about what she was feeling, about the emptiness that leaped to life inside her whenever she thought of Zack leaving. But there was no one she could go to. She'd never had a lot of girlfriends. She couldn't talk to her brothers about this, and her cousins...well, she didn't know if they'd understand. Besides, a selfish part of her wanted to keep this all to herself, despite the need to talk. Which was totally contradictory, of course, but that didn't seem to matter.

A cool breeze lifted off the water and danced past her, touching her with icy fingers that didn't come close to matching the frigid temperatures around her heart. The river water gleamed black and cold in the starlit sky, with no moonlight to glance off its surface. It looked as dark and empty as her heart felt.

She shoved her hands deeper into her pockets and tipped her face up into the wind. That way at least, if her eyes teared, she'd have an excuse for it.

Beside her Zack sighed, reached out and grabbed her arm. Turning her around to face him, he stared down at her through eyes she could see shone with regrets. A pang twinged in her heart, but Kim tried not to let him see it.

"I'll be reporting to base in three days. From there, I'll be shipping out," he said tightly, and she was so surprised, she would have staggered back if he hadn't been holding on to her.

Not that she didn't know he was leaving. Her heart had been ticking off the days for weeks now. Still, neither of them had mentioned it. Like an unspoken agreement, they'd avoided all talk of what would happen when he left.

Now that it was out there, lying between them like an unscalable wall, Kim steeled herself. "I know."

He tore his gaze from hers and stared out at the river, rushing past them as quickly as the days had flown by. "I don't know where I'll be going," he said, his voice almost lost in the muted roar of the water. "But I do know that it's a good thing for me to be going."

"What?"

He looked at her again and either didn't see the sparks flashing in her eyes or chose to ignore them. "Yeah, really. A SEAL shouldn't be tied down, Doc. Shouldn't leave behind people who might... care for him."

"Is that right?"

"Yeah, that's the way it is."

"And what about Three Card? Isn't he married?"

"Yeah, but..."

"And your father was a SEAL, right?"

"True," he said, and shifted position, like a boxer on the ropes trying to find his balance again.

"So basically what you're saying is that it's better for *you* if no one cares about you."

"Look, Kim," he said, reaching out and grabbing hold of her upper arms. He lifted her up onto her toes and met her gaze with wild, frantic eyes. "I was assigned here. It wasn't supposed to be permanent. I wasn't supposed to be anything more than a bodyguard."

The heat of his hands shot straight through the fabric of her jacket and down into her bones, easing away the chill that had been clinging for days. "And is that all it turned out to be?"

He let her go so abruptly she staggered back. "That's not the point."

"It's exactly the point." Her voice lashed at him like a bullwhip. He winced and she was glad to see it. Just as glad to see the coiled tension snaking through his body. "Do you love me?"

"What?" He swiveled his head and stared at her as though she'd popped a third eye in the middle of her forehead.

Shaken, Kim took a deep breath, huffed it out again and repeated the question, though it cost her. After all, what if he said "no"? "Do you love me?"

"For God's sake, Kim—"

"That's the second time you've actually used my name. I like the sound of it."

"Great. Here it comes again. Come on, *Kim.* I'm taking you home."

She pulled her arm out of his grasp and shook her head. "Not a chance. We're staying right here until we get this said."

His mouth firmed into a thin, straight line and his eyes narrowed dangerously. But that wasn't going to deter her any.

"You've already said enough," Zack told her.

"And you haven't answered my question."

"The answer doesn't matter."

She gasped, stepped up close and jabbed her index finger at his chest. "It matters to *me,* you jerk."

"It shouldn't." Zack grabbed her hand and told himself not to feel the sweet rush of heat that swamped him. "Love doesn't solve problems, Doc. It creates 'em."

"Don't do that," she said, her voice filled with a pain that seemed to reach out for him. "Don't start calling me Doc or darlin' or some other cutesy name in some cowardly attempt to pull back from me."

"Cowardly?" Zack stiffened and his fingers around her hand tightened reflexively. "I'm no coward, *darlin'.* And I say what I mean."

"Oh, for—"

But he wasn't going to be stopped now. If she wanted to have this out, then here was as good a place as any. It had to happen at any rate, and they were fast running out of time. In three days, he'd be back to his life and she'd be moving on with hers without him. Best to get this all said now.

"You really think I'm going to stand here and tell you I love you? How can I do that, Kim? That *would* be cowardly—to say that and then leave."

She flinched. "I didn't mean—"

He let go of her hand and reached for her shoulders again. Even through her jacket and the sweatshirt beneath, he felt the warmth of her skin and he knew he would be dreaming about her forever. "I'm telling you I *can't* love you. I'm a SEAL. You're a damn heiress. Never the twain shall meet, darlin'. Understand?"

She slammed one balled fist into his midsection and since he hadn't been expecting it, she managed to punch the air out of his lungs. He let her go and she took a step back. While he fought to regain his breath, she snarled at him.

"Are you serious?" She walked a wide, angry circle around him and Zack turned, keeping a wary eye on her. "You don't want me because I'm a Danforth?"

"I didn't say—"

"Yes, you did." She cut him off and held up one hand, warning him to silence. "This is amazing," she muttered thickly as her long, inky black hair was lifted by the wind to twist around her head like snakes, each of them ready to strike him down.

Zack thought about interrupting, but the truth was, he didn't think she'd hear him.

"All my life," she was saying, nailing him with a gaze sharp enough to draw blood, "people have wanted to be near me because of what my family might be able to do for them. Charles wanted to marry me because I'm a Danforth. And now you *don't* want me for the same reason?" She shook her head and scooped her hair back out of her eyes. "This is some kind of cosmic joke or something."

If it was a joke, she wasn't laughing and, damn it, neither was he. He'd never meant to hurt her. Never meant for this to happen. And now that it had, he wasn't sure what to do. "Kim…"

"You just be quiet." Her voice broke and that tore at him.

He hadn't really looked at it from her perspective. And now that he had, he could see that by trying to keep from hurting her, he'd brought her pain anyway. Chuck had wanted her money. Zack *didn't* want her money. So from where she was standing, both men had looked at her family's bank accounts rather than at her.

He didn't really care if her name was Danforth or Jones. Behind him, the river rushed on, slapping at its banks, murmuring like a disapproving crowd.

She finally stopped stalking him and when she did, she fired him a look that would have fried a lesser man. Zack figured she was due some temper, so he met her gaze steadily.

"One question, Sheridan," she said, her lips hardly moving, her voice no more than a low murmur. "Do you love me?"

His heart fisted in his chest, became a ball of ice. His lungs strained for air and his hands ached to grab her, hold her. For the first time in his life, he was really in love. The forever kind that he'd never expected to find. But instead of giving in to his own wants, he avoided her question by saying, "I'm a bad risk, Kim."

"You idiot," she said, the curve of her mouth taking the sting out of the words. "Loving somebody is a risk. It means that you're willing to take a chance that will make everything else in the world worthwhile."

The ice around his heart cracked a little and was almost painful. Willing? Hell, his whole life had been a series of calculated risks. Could he really cheat himself out of what might be by refusing to take the biggest risk of all? No, he couldn't. "You sneaked up on me, Kim."

She stiffened slightly, braced herself and asked, "What's that mean, exactly?"

He sucked in air, blew it out and taking his first risk, stepped closer to her. She was awesome. She was strong and brave and willing to risk her own pride for the chance at love. How could he do any less? And how had he ever thought he could live without her?

Zack looked at her and knew he'd been a dead man for nearly a month. He'd been hers the moment she'd opened her front door and fired her first sarcastic shot. She made him laugh, made him think, made his skin sizzle and pop with a single look.

She was everything.

And he had to have her.

He chanced the fury still flashing in her eyes and rested his hands on her shoulders. "It means that I never meant to love you."

Kim swayed a little, then locked her knees to stay upright. She stared into his blue eyes and even in the darkness, she saw the gleam of something warm and wonderful in their depths. Her heartbeat quickened and fluttered in her ears like dozens of birds lifting off the ground at once.

Shaking his head, he admitted, "One look into those grass-green eyes of yours and I was a goner. And still I fought it. I fought against loving you every day since the moment we met."

"Gee, thanks."

"It wasn't easy, darlin'. You're a hell of a temptation." He smiled and moved his hands to cup her face. "I never counted on you, Doc. Hadn't thought a pair of green eyes could slam into me and make me think about white picket fences and home and hearth."

She swayed into him, couldn't help it. The light in his eyes, the smile on his face all combined to make her knees do a slow, lovely melt.

"And kids?" she asked, one corner of her mouth quirking.

"God yes," he said, chuckling. "Kids, too."

Kim's breath slid from her on a sigh of pleasure. She reached up and covered his hands with her own. "I fought against loving you, too, you know. You weren't exactly in my plans."

"Yeah?" he grinned.

Kim's heart turned over, as it would for that smile for the next fifty or sixty years. "Yeah."

"So you love me, huh?" he asked.

"I asked first," she reminded him and felt as if the stars were shining down from Heaven just for them.

"So you did," he said, nodding. "I do love you, Kim Danforth."

She smiled up at him. "That didn't hurt, did it?"

He grinned. "Not so much. I think I could get used to saying it."

She hugged the words to her, knowing she would always remember the very first time he'd said them. "Glad to hear it, because I love you, too, Zack Sheridan."

"God, Kim," he whispered.

Then he pulled her close, wrapping his arms around her, pressing her tightly to him as if half afraid she might try to escape him. But Kim wasn't going anywhere. She'd finally found the one place she wanted to be.

"So," he said against the top of her head, his breath ruffling her hair. "We've got three days left before I ship out."

Her so-full heart gave a little twinge, but she told herself that it was just something she'd have to get used to. Saying goodbye to the man she loved—and looking forward to being reunited. She'd be a good military wife, she thought. He'd never see her cry. He'd never feel her worry. All he would feel was her love. Always.

"And…"

He pulled back so he could see her eyes. "What do you say to a quick Vegas wedding and a two-day honeymoon?" He winked and promised, "I want to be married to you, Kim. And I don't want to wait. We won't have much time together now, but I swear, we'll make every minute count."

"Vegas?" Would he never stop surprising her?

He shrugged and grinned again, and Kim knew she'd go anywhere with him.

"It worked for Three Card," he said.

An elopement, just the two of them. What could be more romantic?

"Then it'll work for us." Kim reached up, grabbed his face and pulled him down for a brief, hard kiss. She couldn't even remember what her life had been like before this amazing man had crashed into it. A Danforth getting married in Vegas. Oh, she couldn't wait to tell the family. "What're we waiting for?"

"Atta girl," Zack said, grabbing her hand and heading for her house. "Oh, and just so you know, if you still need protecting while I'm gone, I'm sending one of my friends to watch over you."

"Another SEAL?" she asked on a laugh, hurrying her steps to keep up with his long-legged stride.

"Oh, no way." Zack stopped suddenly, pulled her into his arms for a brief, rib-crushing hug and then gave her a lopsided smile that stopped her heart. "Not a chance, peaches. From here on out, I'm the only SEAL in your life, got it?"

The only SEAL.

The only man.

The only love she would ever need.

"Hoo-yah."

* * * * *

SIN CITY WEDDING

KATHERINE GARBERA

One

———

Larissa Nielsen had imagined how she'd look when she saw Jacob Danforth again. None of her ideas involved wearing her oldest pair of leggings and a tie-dyed Florida T-shirt. But the early-morning call from Jasmine Carmody, a reporter with the *Savannah Morning News,* had left Larissa no choice. She needed to talk to Jake before Jasmine told the world who Peter's father was.

Now Larissa was sitting in her car in front of Jake's Savannah town house like some crazy ex-girlfriend stalker. She wished she were just waking up back at her house in Riverside. She wished their morning routine wasn't disrupted and she and her three-year-old son could welcome the day on their dock overlooking the Savannah River. Instead, she was about to do something, her conscience reminded her, she should have done a long time ago.

She shone the light of her tiny flashlight on the pages in front of her. A collection of Robert Frost poetry had always been her saving grace. She'd used it to escape from life more than once and this morning, while she waited for time to creep by, it provided the escape she desperately needed from her chaotic thoughts.

A rap on the car window startled her. She glanced up to see the faint outline of a man. The man leaned down and she looked into dark brown eyes she'd never forgotten. His tough-guy look faded, replaced by a welcoming smile when he recognized her. She unlocked her door and Jake opened it.

Larissa wasn't a person anyone would call timid. But suddenly she felt like the Cowardly Lion. And it wasn't anything like the green floating head of the Great and Powerful Oz that scared her. She knew the man behind the curtain and she knew he would be royally pissed when she told him he had a three-year-old son.

Peter slept quietly in his car seat and she double-checked that his favorite blanket was tucked next to his chin before getting out of the car. The March morning air was chilly. She shivered a little and rubbed her hands on her arms, praying the tinted windows wouldn't reveal her son until she had a chance to tell Jacob herself.

"What are you doing parked in front of my house at seven in the morning?"

Jake was dressed in running shorts and a sleeveless T-shirt that was stained with sweat. He must have left before she'd arrived. She smoothed her hair down, wishing she'd had the time to make herself look more presentable.

He looked as good as she remembered. Would he feel as good? Somehow she knew he would, despite the fact that it had been almost four years since she'd had sex. She forced her gaze from his muscled chest to his face.

"It's a long story."

"About four years long?"

"You have no idea."

"Well, then let's get comfortable. Come inside and I'll make you some coffee. You know I'm famous for it."

She couldn't help but smile. Even when they'd been nothing more than friends, Jake had always been able to make her laugh. But she couldn't leave Peter sleeping in the car.

"Actually, I have something to tell you."

"And you can't do it inside?"

"Well…no."

She leaned back against the driver's door and tried to find the right words. She swallowed once then licked her lips. "Um…this is harder than I thought it would be."

"I wish I could help you out, Larissa, but I have no idea what you're trying to say."

She shook herself. She'd be matter-of-fact. She was known for her practicality. "Remember that night at the reunion."

"How could I forget?" he asked, running the tip of one finger down the side of her face. Shivers of awareness coursed through her. Jake had always elicited a response from her even when he wasn't trying to.

"I haven't forgotten it either," she said.

"Is that why you are here?" he asked. He leaned closer toward her, surrounding her with the heat of his body and his earthy scent. His dark eyes focused on her lips and she felt them tingle. Without thinking, she licked her bottom lip and he tracked the motions with his gaze. Dammit, this was getting out of hand. His touch on her face moved to her mouth, stroking her bottom lip with his thumb.

"Larissa Nielsen on my doorstep. I can't quite figure out why. Why now? Why are you here, Larissa?"

"A reporter contacted me about your uncle's senate bid." Larissa knew the only way to the truth was through the story of what had happened. Because the reason she'd been keeping Peter a secret hadn't changed and if Jasmine Carmody hadn't called her, Larissa would still be at home in Riverside watching the sun rise and drinking D&D Coffee's special morning blend.

"Those damned reporters. They won't leave any of us alone." Jake ran his fingers through his thick curly hair in a gesture she'd seen her son make when he was on the verge of a meltdown.

"I'm sorry," she said, knowing Jake treasured his privacy above just about anything else.

"Hey, babe, it's not your fault. So why are you here?"

"She knows about our one-night stand," Larissa blurted out.

"I wish you wouldn't call it that. I wanted to see you again."

He'd called her several times, but she'd dodged his calls. Eventually she'd moved to Atlanta with her college roommate to make sure Jake never found out their one night had consequences.

Jake hadn't been ready for fatherhood then. D&D's, the coffeehouse Jake had co-founded with his cousin Adam, had been about to go national and Jake hadn't really changed all that much since college. He was still the fun-loving, Saturday-morning-soccer-playing guy he'd always been. And she knew from bitter experience that a woman who tied a man down became a burden. She'd vowed long ago to never become a burden.

"I had my reasons for not meeting you in Cancun." She nibbled her lower lip. *Just tell him.*

''Our one night together isn't really that newsworthy, honey. Don't worry about that.''

''Actually, it is,'' Larissa said.

''Why, did the reporter have pictures?'' Jake asked with a bad-boy grin that brought that night back in vivid detail. It had been a steamy summer night, and in his arms she'd felt like the most beautiful woman in the world, not the plain Jane she'd always been.

''Yes, but not of us.''

''Then who?'' he asked, becoming exasperated.

Oh, God. ''Our son.''

Jake staggered back from her. ''Did you say son?''

''Yes, his name is Peter, Peter Jacob, and he's three years old.''

Jacob reached for the back door but it was still locked. ''Unlock it.''

She did and he opened the door and looked down on their sleeping son. Peter's curly hair was the same dark shade as Jake's. He reached out for Peter's head with a touch so gentle that she knew she'd made a mistake in not telling him sooner.

But the past had taught her a bitter lesson, and she'd always dreamed that her life would be sit-com perfect. Instead reality was very different. All the excuses she'd made to herself for the past three years sounded lame now and when Jake glanced up at her, she knew he'd think so, too.

''My son,'' he said, looking down on Peter with a wealth of emotions that she hadn't suspected Jake could feel.

* * *

His son. He still couldn't really take it in. Parenthood was an alien concept to Jake. He reached for the buckle on the car seat but couldn't figure out how to operate it. Nothing in his life had prepared him for this. He'd have to give his brother Toby a call later; he was the only expert on fatherhood he knew.

"Get him out," he said to Larissa. His hands were shaking. He was a father.

She brushed past him. Her slender body had remained unchanged over the years since they first met. Her clear blue eyes had always struck him as the most honest he'd ever looked into—until today.

Larissa put her hand on his back and leaned into the car. One of her breasts brushed against his side and arousal moved through him like lightning. He felt the heat from her hand on the small of his back burn through his shirt.

She pushed against him as she leaned into the car, balancing herself with the touch on his back. Reaching out, she ruffled Peter's hair. "Morning, sleepyhead."

"Morning, Mama," he said.

They had a bond. A bond that Jake had never wanted but now suddenly envied. Maybe this was what he'd been searching for lately. Maybe this would fill the restlessness that his work and partying couldn't.

Jake reached for his son and the boy recoiled, pulling a ragged-looking bear and a tattered blanket closer. Tucking the edge of the blanket between his lips, Peter looked at Larissa.

"It's okay, baby. Jake's a friend." Larissa turned toward him, her breath brushing across his cheek. Her mouth was fuller than he'd remembered.

"He's kind of shy around new people," Larissa said.

"The word *Dad* is foreign to him?" Jake asked, to remind himself that Larissa wasn't the sweet girl from his memories. She was the woman who'd had his child and kept it a secret.

"He's only three. Some things take time to remember."

"Did you have a problem remembering too?" he asked sarcastically.

Jake had always loved women. He'd never had any trouble with them. Women were meant to be protected, he knew, even though his track record on this front wasn't great. But how did you protect someone who had betrayed you?

She sighed. "If you're going to treat me the way I deserve to be treated, I'm going to take Peter home and come back by myself. To him you're a stranger who's mad at his mom."

He realized she was right. For better or worse, Peter's entire world revolved around Larissa. And making Larissa cry or angry probably wouldn't help Peter to like him. He straightened from the car and took the two steps back to the sidewalk.

She lifted their son out, brushing a soft kiss against the top of his head and rubbing his back before setting the boy on the sidewalk. It was obvious how deeply Larissa cared for her son. He shouldn't be surprised. She'd always had a nurturing quality about her. Originally it was what had drawn him to her.

Peter clung to the back of Larissa's leg, watching Jake with the same intensity that his mother did. Why hadn't she trusted him enough to tell him he had a son?

"Did that reporter follow you?" he asked.

"I don't think so."

"Let's go inside just to be safe."

She nodded and bent to pry her son's hands from her thigh. She took the small hand in her own and as Jake watched them, he realized the two of them were watching him. Waiting to see what he'd do. Frankly, he was out of his element.

He bent down on one knee and held out his hand to his son. Peter hesitated, then handed Jake the bear. "Oh, he's giving you Mr. Bear. That means he likes you."

"I'm glad one of you does," Jake said.

Larissa watched him with those soulful eyes of hers. And he felt like a big mean bully. He tried to get past his anger so he could remember all the reasons he liked her but he couldn't.

"Oh, Jake this isn't about liking you," she said, softly.

He glanced up at her. "Then what is it about?"

"Me not being the right woman for you."

"Well, I do tend to like a different sort of woman."

"I know. Tall, blond and built."

"Nice opinion you've got of me, Rissa. But I'm not that shallow. I meant honest. I like my women to be honest."

She flushed. He knew that anything else he said now would be mean and sarcastic, but sending her away with the son he'd just discovered wasn't an option.

He pivoted on his heel without saying another word. Unlocking the door to his town house, he turned left and entered his living quarters. The living room was sleek and sophisticated. All chrome, glass and Italian leather. The entertainment center was top of the line and he'd just had a new large-screen plasma TV installed on Friday.

Larissa and Peter stood in the doorway as if afraid to enter. How old was his son? He knew she'd told him, but he'd been trying to grapple with the fact that he was a father and hadn't paid attention. It had been almost four years since he'd seen Larissa so Peter would have to be about three. What did kids that age do?

"Does he watch TV?"

"Yes. But only PBS."

Figures, Larissa would be all about educational television. He looked at the serious little boy.

His son. He felt a stirring so deep inside that it made his anger pale. This was his son. His future was tied to this little boy, and he knew he had to make the situation right.

He knelt in front of Peter again. The boy had his eyes. He studied Peter until the boy reached out and touched the stubble on his chin. "You're prickly."

"I didn't have time to shave yet."

Peter glanced up at Larissa. "How come you don't feel like that?"

"Girls don't," she said.

"Girls are different," Peter said, turning back to Jake.

"They sure are."

"You got any food?" Peter asked.

"Peter."

"It's okay. Come on, I'll fix us some breakfast." He stood and led Peter down the hall to the kitchen. "Then your mom and I need to talk."

Jake seated Peter at the large butcher-block table and checked the pantry for something a little boy might want to eat. He had two jars of martini olives and a box of water crackers. The fridge held several bottles of wine, a six-pack of Coors and an opened bottle of champagne. Maybe Wes had eggs in his fridge. His best friend lived upstairs.

"I probably should have found a sitter for Peter," Larissa said.

He turned to look at her. Peter was occupied at the table with an electronic book that Larissa must have had in that big purse of hers.

"I'm glad you didn't," he said.

She was so close he could smell the fragrance of her shampoo. She wore no makeup. But then she rarely did. Her skin was smooth and fine, creamy looking. Lust surged inside him, which further enraged him. He didn't want to want her.

She swallowed and he knew that she still wasn't sure letting him know his son was a good idea. He wondered how much of it stemmed from his reputation and how much of it came from her knowledge of him.

He'd never really taken responsibility seriously. Everyone in the family knew it. And thanks to the media coverage of his uncle's senate bid, most of the public knew it too. He was the fun-loving, thirty-year-old millionaire with the Midas touch. But Larissa should know better, especially when she'd found out she was having his son.

"What do you want to eat, sport?"

"Pancakes."

"Uh…let's see what I've got." Jake had no idea how to make pancakes. He could scramble eggs but there weren't any in the fridge. "I can run upstairs to see if Wes has some eggs."

"Your college roommate Wes?"

"Yeah, you remember him."

"Don't bother. Surely you have some cereal."

"Frosted Sugar Os and Captain Crunch."

"He'll have toast with butter."

"Educational TV and healthy food. Larissa, does our boy get to have any fun?"

"Of course, he does. Just not bad influences."

"Is that why you never called me?" he asked.

"What?"

"Am I a bad influence for our son?"

"No. Never."

She closed the distance between them, reaching up to touch him and then dropped her hands. "The reasons are complicated. Let's get Peter settled, then we can talk."

He nodded. He'd wanted her to touch him. Needed her to in a way that made him feel vulnerable, reminding him that he was just a man and had more weaknesses than he wanted to acknowledge.

The toast was buttered and eaten in short order. Jake grabbed a soccer ball from the closet, and now that the morning sun was shining brightly, they took it outside. Peter kicked the ball, chasing it from one end of the yard to the other.

He gestured for Larissa to sit down on the chaise and dragged over one of the Adirondack chairs he'd made last summer.

He watched his son running after the ball on pudgy legs. Larissa had taken something from him that he could never get back. Though deep inside he allowed he probably wouldn't have been ready for fatherhood three years ago, he still felt betrayed.

Jake suddenly thought of his father. God, the old man was going to be extremely disappointed when Jake told him he had a three-year-old son. Just one more screwup from a son who never measured up.

Larissa sat there looking much the same as she had in their college days. A sweet innocent who didn't really fit in at Georgia Tech. He'd befriended her because she'd reminded him of his younger sisters and he would've wanted Victoria and Imogene to have found a guy who'd do the same.

But all of that faded when he glanced at their little boy. "I'm so angry I want to shake you."

Two

Larissa had been hoping that Jake would just jump on the problem with the reporter, but she should've known better. He was a detail man who liked to get all his facts in order before making a decision. Many times during their college days, he'd used her as a sounding board for his theories and ideas before drawing a conclusion. She leaned back in the lounge chair and took a sip of her coffee.

"Stalling is not going to make me less angry," he said.

"I know." She watched her small son chasing the ball across the yard and tried to find the words to tell Jake that she'd kept Peter a secret for herself and for him. She hadn't wanted Peter to grow up in a household similar to the one she had.

Her parents had married because her mother had been pregnant. From her earliest memories Larissa was aware that if she hadn't been born, her parents wouldn't have been married. Theirs was an unhappy house. So she sought refuge in a world of books, creating her dreams from the stories she cherished. Tales of epic love and vanquishing heroes.

But the real world wasn't full of those epic love stories she'd dreamed of for her life. And instead of being a fair lady waiting in her tower to be rescued, Larissa's fate had become her mother's.

"I'm waiting," Jake said, his voice quiet and deep with suppressed emotion. Her heart ached because she knew how hard it had always been for Jake to express his emotions. To the outside world he presented his devil-may-care bachelor image but Larissa knew that Jake's emotions ran deep. He was anything but carefree.

She studied Jake's face. He was so familiar to her, not just because of his resemblance to their son. But because she saw his face every night in her dreams. Even before Peter was born, Jake had been the one man she'd never been able to forget.

Perhaps it was because of their friendship. She'd survived her college years at Georgia Tech because of him. Unlike the other guys who'd looked right through her, Jake had seen her.

He'd been her first male friend. The first man she'd trusted. The only man she'd ever really been comfortable with.

She couldn't tell him that she'd kept their son a secret because she'd been afraid that one day he'd leave her for a more glamorous woman and perhaps take their son with him.

"Everything about Peter is complicated."

Jake sat on the edge of her lounge chair and touched her face carefully. She knew in that instant that however Jake saw her, it wasn't the way other men did. "It doesn't have to be. Just level with me."

When he touched her she couldn't think. Shivers of awareness spread throughout her body and she'd never been more aware of Jake's maleness.

The fact that he was filled with rage at the secret she'd kept for too long didn't make it any easier to stop her skin from tingling, her nipples from tightening, or the warmth from pooling between her legs. She closed her eyes. But that only intensified his touch. It brought the entire focus of her world down to the two of them and the warmth of his fingers on her face.

"I'm waiting, Rissa."

Rissa, Jake was the only person who'd ever cared enough to call her by a nickname. To the world she was the serious librarian who could find any fact in record time, but to Jake she'd always been…she wasn't sure what she'd been to him. Or what she would be now.

She opened her eyes and his face was barely an inch from hers. His breath brushed her cheek and she knew if she leaned the tiniest bit toward him, he'd take control of this unexpected embrace. His lips would touch hers and she'd give up reason and sanity to experience again the magic they'd shared on that long-ago night.

She cleared her throat and leaned away from him. He rubbed his fingers, which had just been touching her face, and looked at her with regret.

"I'm not sure where to begin. The reasons are long and complicated. And you're too angry to really listen."

"Any man would be."

"I'm not saying you shouldn't be. I just don't want to become a victim in your quest for vengeance."

He watched her for a moment then stood in a rush, cursing under his breath. She realized she was right.

She should have known better. She'd never been more than a rather average looking woman and Jake...well, Jake was used to prime cuts of womanhood. Tall, leggy blondes with D cups and flawless complexions. The closest she'd come to a D cup was after Peter had been born and her milk had come in.

"Then let's get this talk about our son over with."

She took a deep breath. She felt even more vulnerable than she had when she'd arrived at his house this morning. "I don't know what to say."

"For God's sake, woman, you graduated from Georgia Tech with honors. How hard can it be for you to find the words?"

"I wish it were easier, but it's all tied to my feelings."

"About me? I didn't force you that night."

"Jake, I was there, remember? It was an incredible night. I don't have any lingering resentment from that."

"I knew it."

"Good thing we're outside."

He quirked one eyebrow at her in question.

"So that your swelled head has room."

"Start from the beginning. I thought I used a condom."

"I think it broke."

"What?"

"I was a little sticky the next morning. So I took a test as soon as possible."

"You knew when I called to ask you to go to Cancun?"

"Yes."

Jake turned away from Larissa, intent on leaving before he said something he'd regret. Larissa was watching him with tears in her eyes and his head told him there was no way she'd intended to hurt him with her decision. But right now his heart told him he didn't care.

He felt betrayed because he'd always trusted Larissa. If any of the other women he'd slept with had shown up on his doorstep with a child in tow, he'd know they were there for money. He was always careful about protection because he knew that his name and his money left him vulnerable to ambitious women.

But Larissa was the sweet girl he'd felt comfortable talking to in the late hours at the library. The woman who'd come back to their five-year reunion looking like the embodiment of every female fantasy he'd ever had. The woman who'd come to him today for help whether she admitted it or not.

And he was in no mood to help. He had to shake the fury pumping through him with every beat of his heart.

"I'll be back," he said, and walked into his house.

He headed down the hall to his tae kwon do workout room. In the corner was a bag he used for kickboxing practice and for sparring when Wes wasn't available to work out. He closed off his thoughts. Centered himself and focused all of his energy on the punching bag. Twenty minutes later he was dripping with sweat and still not sure he was ready to talk to Larissa. But they didn't have the luxury of time. There was a reporter who was determined to flash his face across the front page of every paper with the word *father* in the headline. He had to step up to the plate. He had to drop the safety of his carefree existence and really make his life count.

He bit back a savage curse. He wasn't ready for this. Didn't know that he ever would be. But Peter—that little boy—and his family deserved better. His uncle had enough to worry about with his campaign and some vaguely threatening e-mails. Jake wasn't going to add Larissa and Peter to the mix.

Grabbing a monogrammed towel from the rack near the door, he walked through his house. His town house had been featured in *Modern Architecture* as the ultimate bachelor pad. He grabbed a bottle of water from the fridge before stepping out on his patio. He wasn't sure what he expected to find when he returned.

He knew it wasn't Larissa sitting on the grass with their son in her lap. Both of them had their eyes closed and faces turned to the sun. He thought they were sleeping but then realized that Larissa was speaking softly. The words were familiar to him. Robert Frost's poem *Stopping by Woods on a Snowy Evening*.

He'd never felt more inadequate for the task before him than he did at this moment. Sure, *Fortune* magazine had called him and Adam the golden boys of the coffee bean world, "taking a tried and true idea and making it new and fresh."

But fatherhood was different. It involved emotions

and all kinds of variables that didn't work in a solid business plan. And emotion was the one thing he'd always felt most uncomfortable with.

He guessed that was partly why he had a son with Larissa. The night of the reunion he'd realized she'd become more than just a smart girl who'd listen to him ramble on about what he wanted to do with his life. And he'd been uncomfortable with all she'd made him feel. Except for the passion she'd evoked in him. Passion was one area he was extremely comfortable with. So he'd seduced her under the stars.

Watching mother and child now kindled a desire for something that he hadn't realized was missing from his life. He wanted to be a part of that golden circle of light. Of that deep bond between mother and son. He wanted to insure that Rissa and Peter could always find a patch of sunlight to sit in. He set his towel and water bottle down on the table and crossed to them.

Not questioning his actions, he sank to the ground behind Larissa and settled himself around her. He left a couple of inches of space because he knew that in spite of his feelings of betrayal, he wasn't above using sex to manipulate her. He wanted her like hell on fire. And if he touched her again, he wasn't going to be able to control himself.

He put his hands over Larissa's and felt her stiffen. Peter's small hand moved to rest on his wrist and Jake felt something close to peace for the first time since he'd been old enough to know that he was a Danforth.

He liked the sound his deep voice made added to Larissa's soft tone and Peter's childish one.

"The woods are lovely, dark and deep
  But I have promises to keep
  And miles to go before I sleep
  And miles to go before I sleep."

They finished the poem together and Peter leaned around his mother to watch him with wide questioning eyes.

"How did you know the words?" Peter asked.

"Your mom taught them to me," he said, softly. The boy continued to watch him with a focus that was unnerving.

Peter broke into a wide grin and said, "Cool." The boy hopped to his feet and ran across the yard toward the ball.

Jake turned his head a quarter and met Larissa's clear blue gaze. For a moment they were back in the uncomplicated days of college. Life was just about doing what felt right and making each moment count. Victoria had still been safely at home, and he hadn't yet fathered a child. But times had changed and Victoria was gone—disappeared at a concert so long ago. And though everyone warned them she was dead and would never return, Jake's family kept hope alive.

Larissa smiled at him and his groin tingled. She

was so close that her scent filled his nostrils with each breath.

"I did, didn't I?" She licked her lips nervously and he leaned closer to her. Her mouth had always fascinated him. Her lower lip was fuller than the top and he knew from that one brief night how sumptuous her mouth would feel under his own.

He leaned farther toward her, but Peter used his wrist for balance as he stood and then raced across the yard to the soccer ball.

"Yes, you did," he said to Larissa.

"That seems like so long ago."

"It was a different life," he said.

Peter kicked the ball over to them with more energy than skill. Jake had always been very good at soccer and his son showed…none of Jake's aptitude.

"Where'd you go before?" Peter asked, coming over to them.

"To my workout room. I needed to clear my head."

"Is it clear now?"

"Almost," Jake said, ruffling his son's hair.

He stood and helped Larissa to her feet. He still wanted to know why she hadn't told him she was having his child, but he'd save that conversation for later when they were alone. Right now they needed to figure out what to do next.

But Peter was watching him and he didn't want to have an uncomfortable conversation in front of the boy. "Let me show you how to kick the ball like the pros do."

"What's a pro?" Peter asked.

"A professional player. You know someone who gets paid to play the game."

"You can get paid to play?" Peter asked.

"Only if you're really good."

Jake showed his son a few basic kicks and then got out his practice goal net and left his son playing.

Larissa had returned to her lounge chair and watched him warily as he walked toward her. He didn't like the look on her face. He didn't like it at all.

Larissa tried not to stare as Jake walked over to her, but she couldn't help it. Sweat glistened on his neck and she knew that if she got close to him, he would smell earthy. She wanted to indulge herself in him once more. But he needed answers and she'd come here this morning intent on giving them to him.

She closed her eyes. While Jake had been gone, she'd found the words she needed to tell him. She'd have to sacrifice her pride, but Peter was more important than pride.

Jake returned and sat on a chair facing her. He braced his elbows on his knees and leaned toward her. She took a deep breath.

"Jake, I—"

"Larissa, I—"

She laughed. In the old days when they'd been friends, often they'd both started talking at the same time.

''You first,'' Jake said.

Knowing that Jake had never been anything but good to her, she sorted out the pieces of her troubled past and took a deep breath. ''The reason why I didn't tell you about Peter is that I wanted to manage parenthood on my own.''

''You always were pretty stubborn about that. Why don't you save the rest of the tale for a time when we are alone? Let's talk about what we do now.''

She appreciated the reprieve, but she was curious. ''What made you change your mind?''

He shrugged massive shoulders. ''Something about you looking at me like I was an ogre.''

''I didn't.''

''Sweetheart, you have the biggest, most innocent eyes I've ever looked into, and it only takes one instant for you to make me feel like a bully.''

His words made her feel special. ''I didn't mean to.''

''I know. Let's fix this reporter problem and then we'll talk. We'll find a sitter for Peter and we can learn each other's secrets.''

''I don't have any secrets.''

''Peter's it?''

''Yes, just Peter. I felt so…panicked when Jasmine Carmody called and said she knew you were Peter's father. There's nothing I can do to protect him from anything she writes for her newspaper. At least he can't read.''

''How did she find out about Peter? Am I listed on the birth certificate?''

''No. She said she'd talked to Marti Freehold. Do you remember her?''

''She's the biggest gossip I've ever met.''

''Yes, she is. Marti mentioned she'd seen us leaving the reunion together. And that we'd looked, well, like we needed to find a private room and quick.''

''Sounds like Marti,'' Jake said.

''Jasmine Carmody has Peter's birth certificate and she knows you're not listed on there, but she also has a picture of you when you were the same age as Peter. They're practically identical.''

Jake leaned back in the chair and Larissa tried not to stare at him. She knew that he was trying to solve a very sticky problem. And she shouldn't be lusting over him at a time like this.

Finally he cleared his throat. ''I think I may have come up with a solution that will take the sting out of any article Jasmine Carmody writes.''

''What?''

''We'll live together as a family.''

''Will that work?''

''Sure it will. What she's doing is just a step above blackmail. If we acknowledge it and move on, then she can't hurt us with whatever she writes. I think it's the perfect solution."

"But living together? I don't think that's necessary."

"I do. I want to get to know my son. We'll be a family unit and once she knows I've acknowledged Peter is mine, she won't be able to hurt us."

"Jake, we hardly know each other."

He raised his eyebrow at her. "I'd say we know each other pretty well."

"That was just one night."

"Rissa, I was talking about all those late-night conversations in the library."

She flushed, knowing good and well what he'd been referring to. She wasn't sure what had changed while Jake had been gone, but his workout had brought back the man she knew. The man she was comfortable with. The man who wasn't so angry at being left in the dark where his son was concerned.

"Still, we've never lived together. I mean, where would we live?"

"I don't have every detail planned. I'd like to live here because I'm close to D&D's and I go into the office every day when I'm not traveling."

"Well, your place isn't much farther than mine from the library. But I don't know that I'd feel comfortable in your house."

"We'll hire a decorator to do the place over."

"I don't know. That seems like a big expense for…"

"For what?"

"For camouflage."

"Camouflage?" he asked.

"We aren't in a relationship. Are you sure about this?"

"One-hundred percent certain."

"Would we be like roommates?"

"What did you have in mind?" he asked, waggling his eyebrows at her.

She didn't know if she could live with Jake and not give in to the lust surging through her. This was probably the dumbest idea ever but deep in her heart it felt right.

"Not what you're thinking. I mean we're both adults. We can keep our hands to ourselves. We're living together for Peter's sake, not for ours."

"It's precisely because we are adults that I think we're going to have a hard time living together and not sleeping together."

"Jake, are you trying to say I can break your will-power?"

"Sweetheart, do you really want to start a battle over this?"

"Why, don't you think I could win?"

"Not if I put my mind to it."

"It's not your mind that tempts me, Jake."

He threw his head back and laughed. Her heart

clenched and her entire body ached. She wanted to be in his arms again. But she knew better than anyone did what a relationship based on a child was like. She also knew that when it came to lasting relationships, the odds of her and Jake making it work were very slim.

Her only chance at sanity was to make sure he stayed out of her bed and her heart.

Three

Jake knew there was no way he'd be able to live under the same roof as Larissa and keep his hands to himself. But if she wanted to pretend a platonic relationship was all she wanted, he'd let her. Passion and proximity were two things that couldn't be ignored.

He'd been celibate for a while now. Though he still casually dated, sleeping with women he hardly knew had lost some of the excitement it had held. And his business took most of his time. Becoming a millionaire in his own right before he turned thirty had taken all of his concentration.

The spark that had been kindled at their college

reunion almost four years ago hadn't died after one night together. This morning had proved that the fire between them still burned strongly. But he was willing to bide his time until they had everything settled between them before he made any moves toward Larissa.

He knew that in time she'd be in his bed. Everything else about the future seemed uncertain, but there was a sense of rightness in his soul when he thought of the two of them together. Just to be certain that he never lost his son again, he made a mental note to call Marcus, his cousin and family lawyer.

"You can move in today. Do you need my help to get your stuff?"

Larissa got to her feet and paced around the patio. Peter was still playing by the soccer net Jake had set up. Larissa watched her son for a few minutes, then turned back to him. "Not today. Let me think about this."

Jake moved near to her. She crossed her arms over her chest and stepped back from him. What was she afraid of? "What's to think about? No sex and we'll live here."

She bit her lip. "For how long?"

Jake shrugged. His experience with relationships said that most didn't last longer than it took to get your stuff settled, but Peter guaranteed they'd be together longer. "I don't know. Why?"

"What if one of us falls in love with someone

else?'' Larissa asked. The wind caught a strand of her hair, which brushed across her face. Larissa reached up and tucked it behind her ear.

Love was the one thing he'd never really found with any woman. It seemed elusive to him somehow. He wondered sometimes if love and happiness were going to be forever out of his reach. He was jaded enough to know that he wasn't going to find love through the intense desire that he felt for Larissa. ''I doubt that would happen.''

''Why not?'' she asked, holding herself tighter while she waited for his answer.

He didn't like the barrier she'd built between them. Didn't like that she was comforting herself and that she was still hiding something from him. So he said the one thing sure to needle her. He remembered her soft heart and belief in happily-ever-after.

''Because love is part of the game that people play when they are searching for themselves. We're both secure in our place in the world.''

She fisted her hands and put them on her hips. ''That is the stupidest thing I've ever heard.''

This was the Larissa he remembered. Eyes shooting sparks when he pushed her buttons. She'd been so sure she was a plain Jane who no jock would ever look at twice. But she'd caught his eye and held it longer than any of her peers back then. ''Surely, you don't believe in love?''

"Of course I do. And I'm raising our son to believe in it, too," she said, gesturing to Peter.

"You're just preparing him for heartache."

"Is that what love means to you?" she asked. Despite her argument, he didn't think she believed in love, either. Because any woman who had a romantic look on life would have contacted her baby's father.

He didn't like the direction this conversation was taking. "I don't know what love means to me. I can honestly say I've never really experienced it. Have you?"

"No."

"I don't think we'll have a problem with either of us falling in love. You're down-to-earth and so am I."

"I don't want to be a burden to you, Jake. I don't want to wake up one morning and find out you don't want us anymore."

"Why would that happen? I don't have time for anything else right now. D&D's keeps me busy and I'm not dating anyone."

"Right now, but you change women as often as you change your pants."

"That's not true. I haven't been with a woman in the last year and a half."

"Sure, you haven't."

"Believe what you want but I've never lied to you."

"Low blow."

"The truth hurts."

"I don't think this will work. Maybe I should take Jake and leave Savannah."

"You can leave if you want to, but you're not taking my son." Jake wasn't going to waste a single day of his time with Peter now that he knew he had a son. His dad, who'd always been busy with the shipping company, had made time for family. He wanted the opportunity to do the same.

She rubbed her eyes with the heels of her hands and then looked at him. He knew this was hard on her and he sympathized with her to a certain extent but they wouldn't be in this predicament now if she'd come to him when she'd first found out she was pregnant. "I don't know what to do. But I don't want to make things worse than they are now."

"I'll take care of everything for you."

"I'm not looking for a hero."

"Good, because I'm not much of one," he said. He'd always known his own faults.

He wanted to reach out and touch her. To take her in his arms and promise he'd shoulder her burdens, but he knew she wouldn't accept that. "Trust me on this, Rissa. I'll take care of everything."

"You aren't doing this for revenge, are you?"

"I don't follow."

"You know, make me move in here and then...do something to keep Peter and kick me out?"

"That's a nice opinion you have of me."

"Well, I wouldn't blame you if you tried it."

"You're important to Peter," he said. Larissa was the center of Peter's world and his son was the most important person to consider.

"People are going to say I trapped you."

"Let them talk. Anyone who knows you won't believe it."

"It's easy for you to say."

"Nothing about this is easy for me."

"I know. So we'd live with you until your uncle's campaign is over? Then the media scrutiny around your family will die down and we can go back to our normal lives."

"I'm not going to disappear after this reporter moves on to her next juicy topic." He realized the words were true as he said them. Larissa and Peter were his responsibility now and forever. And whether she lived with him or not, he'd always be involved in their lives. And that felt right to him deep in his soul.

"Promise?" The word was hardly out before Larissa bit her lip wishing she could take it back.

Jake closed the gap between them and cupped her face in his big hands. His brown eyes more serious than she'd ever seen them before, he leaned close to her. There were hidden depths to this man she'd scarcely explored.

She wondered what he'd do if she turned the tables

on him—if she held his face in her hands and looked down on him with something like tenderness.

"I promise."

She shivered. This was the secret dream she'd harbored since she was a young girl. That she'd find a man, a big, strong, attractive man who'd make her feel that she was the center of his world. But her dream had always been a bittersweet one, because time and experience had taught her that being the center of any man's world was a fleeting thing.

"Oh, Jake, don't say things you don't mean."

"Woman, I don't know why you have such a low opinion of me."

"I don't. It's myself I don't trust."

"What's not to trust?"

"You. Saying things that I'll take to mean something you aren't feeling."

"This isn't the love thing again, is it?"

"Don't be flip."

"I can't help it. You make me want to be a better man than I know I can be."

She was flattered that he thought she had any power over him. And saddened to realize that Jake thought he wasn't a great man to begin with. "Really?"

"Really."

"There you go again, making me believe you could be my knight in shining armor," she said, feeling her control shatter.

"I thought we both agreed I was no hero."

"When you touch me I can't think of anything but you."

"Rissa," he said. Lowering his mouth to hers, he brushed his lips back and forth over her own. It was a simple, gentle kiss, but it shook the moorings of everything she believed about herself.

She brought her hands to his shoulders, holding on to him for balance in a world that was suddenly spinning further and further out of her control. He traced the shape of her mouth with his tongue, running it over the closed seam of her lips. She knew what he wanted—what they both wanted. She opened her mouth on a sigh. And he teased her with his tongue. Teased her by giving her a hint of what was yet to come.

She leaned into him, resting against his strong body. She felt safe and in danger at the same time. Her breasts were heavy and she threw back her shoulders, rubbing their tips against him. He moaned deep in his throat, the sound feral and arousing.

Sliding his hands down her neck and then around to her back, his hold on her changed. He traced the line of her spine with his fingertips and she shuddered. She felt him tremble, too.

Jake pulled her more firmly against his body. His groin nestled into the notch at her thighs, her legs turned to jelly. She sank against him, totally caught up in his embrace. Jake supported her completely with one hand on her backside and the other behind her neck.

She moaned deep in her throat, tunneling her fingers through his hair to try to control their embrace. Or to at least be an active participant in it. He rubbed his tongue over hers and then pulled back.

Watching her intently, she couldn't help but wonder why she'd stayed away so long. But she knew the answer—because sanity was hard to come by and Jake threatened hers. She pulled away, tripping over her own feet in her hurry to put some distance between them.

Jake steadied her with one hand. His touch was warm but not soothing against her arm. She wanted to say the heck with her reservations and just indulge herself in a red-hot affair with this man. But there were too many barriers between them. Not the least of which was a little boy who deserved a happier childhood than Larissa had experienced.

She'd promised herself to protect Peter. No matter what the cost to her. Peter hadn't asked to be born and it was up to her make sure he had the best life had to offer. And Jake, for all his playboy ways, seemed genuinely interested in being a father to his son.

She knew she couldn't keep Jake and Peter apart. She'd have to make sure that Peter never knew the circumstances that had brought Jake and her together.

If things didn't work out between her and Jake, she didn't want Peter to feel it was his fault.

"Are you sure about the platonic part of this relationship?" Jake asked.

"You're the one who suggested it," she said. More than ever, she thought. Her blood was racing through her body. Her nipples were beaded and aching for his touch. And her center was wet with desire for him. She wanted to take his hand and lead him into the house where they could be alone. Only the knowledge that her son was a few feet away kept her from taking such an ill-advised action.

"Rissa?" he asked, running his finger down the side of her face.

"Yes," she said. She had to get out of this place. Figure out what was going on in her life and make a plan to protect herself from the vulnerability that Jake brought out in her.

He smirked. "Whatever you say."

She knew he could make her eat her words, just prayed that he wouldn't.

"Mama, can I have some juice?" Peter asked, racing over to them.

"It's *may* I, sweetie," Larissa said.

"*May* I have some juice?"

"Sure," she said, going into the kitchen to her oversize bag and pulling out a juice box. She paused in the doorway before returning to the patio. Jake and Peter were in front of the goal net again and this time

Jake was setting himself up as goalie. She watched the two of them together and realized she wasn't the only one who'd been missing a man in her life. No matter the cost to herself, she had to make this new arrangement with Jake work out. For Peter's sake.

"Here's your juice, Peter," Larissa said from the patio.

Jake ruffled Peter's hair, lifting up the boy to carry him back to the patio. It was the first time he'd held his son's small body. A surge of protectiveness roared through him.

This was his son. Peter rested his head on his shoulder and Jake met Larissa's gaze. Something passed between them and he knew she knew what he felt.

"We should get going. Peter needs a nap."

"I'll carry him out to your car. When will you be back?"

"I have to work this afternoon. I won't have time to get our stuff together until after I pick Peter up at the sitter's."

"Can he stay with me?" Jake asked.

"I...I don't know if he would. He doesn't really know you."

"I'm the boy's father. Isn't it time he got to know me?"

"Yes, it is. But watching him takes a lot of patience and attention."

"What do you say, sport?" Jake asked Peter. "Want to stay with me while your mom's at work."

"Are you my dad?" Peter asked.

"I am."

Peter looked at his mom and Larissa took a deep breath and nodded. "It's okay with me, sweetie."

"Can we play soccer some more?"

"After you take a nap," Larissa said.

"Okay, I'll stay with you."

Larissa gathered her things and Jake carried Peter out to her car. She buckled him in the car seat and put Mr. Bear and his blanket around his face.

Jake stood waiting by the car when she turned around. "I'm not due at work until three. I'll bring Peter by around two-thirty."

"Why don't I come to your place for lunch? I can help you pack up your stuff. Peter can help me bring your stuff back here."

"Okay. Are you sure about this living together thing?"

"Yes. I have to do it because I'd feel like less than a man if I didn't."

"Why don't you think about it? I couldn't bear it if you had regrets."

"I wouldn't have asked if I wasn't positive this was the best course of action. Now that I know I have a son, nothing less than living under the same roof will satisfy me."

"Somehow I knew you'd feel that way."

"Knew it this morning or when you first discovered you were pregnant?" he asked.

He still wanted to know why she hadn't come to him to begin with. He would have done the honorable thing then. Even though she'd said she'd wanted to manage motherhood on her own, Larissa wasn't one of those staunch feminists. Sure she'd believed women deserved equal pay and equal opportunity, but she'd always had a sort of dreamy vision of what family life should be.

A vision that included a mother and father and two kids. A cute little cottage on the river. A big yard with room for soccer practice and a dock to fish from. Somehow his vision and hers had blended together in the early-morning hours when they'd talked about the future.

She'd always made him want to talk about the future and maybe he realized that was why her answer now was so important. He wanted to believe that she'd known he would have done the honorable thing three years ago, not because of what society would say, but because of the woman she was.

"I've always known it," she said, quietly.

Without thinking, he reached out and pulled her close in a bear hug. He held her tightly to him and knew deep in his soul he wasn't letting this woman or their son walk out of his life. "I hope this isn't a mistake."

Jake let her go. "It's what's best for Peter. So are you going to stop arguing and move in with me?"

She stared at him. Her eyes were wide and questioning, still holding secrets that he wondered if he'd ever uncover. "I will."

Satisfaction flowed through him. She belonged to him and so did their son. The sooner he had them under his roof the more settled he'd feel. "Good."

She crossed her arms over her chest again and he realized she was trying to put a barrier between them. She didn't realize that running only made him want to chase her. And catch her. His mind filled with images of what he'd do when he caught her. When he coaxed her willingly to his bed.

"I'm going to call Nicola, Uncle Abe's PR person and advise her of this current situation. My folks are going to want to meet their grandson. So after you get off work tonight, we'll head over there, if that's okay with you."

"I'm not sure I want to meet your parents."

"Why not?"

"They're bound to be mad at me."

"They're nicer than I am."

She hadn't even considered the family that Peter would now call his own. Her own dad hadn't spoken to her since she was six and her mom had died during her first year of college, so he'd never had any grandparents. "I doubt that."

"Don't worry about it. I'll take care of everything. Trust me," Jake said.

"You keep saying that."

"I'm going to continue to until you finally believe in me."

"I wish I could, but it's not that easy."

"What's not?"

"Trusting a man."

"I'm not just any man. I'm the father of your child."

"I know," she said. He couldn't know that made it even harder for her to trust him.

Four

After Larissa and Peter left, Jake called his lawyer and had a lengthy conversation to put in motion a bid for custody of Peter. The first thing Marcus had suggested was a paternity test to give them a legal leg to stand on. Jake didn't doubt that Peter was his son. He knew Larissa. And he'd looked into his son's eyes. Peter was his. But he liked the idea of having the documentation to prove it.

Nicola had been out of the office so Jake had left a message for her to call him. Then he drove to Larissa's house. Riverside was a nice suburb of Savannah and as he neared Larissa's house he realized she wasn't just eking out a living. She'd made a life for herself and their son that was comfortable.

He felt a little bad about the plan he had put into motion with Marcus. But he wasn't going to give up his son now that he'd found out about him. Being a father felt right deep in his soul and if he had a few doubts that he wouldn't be up to the job, he'd get over them. There had never been anything he couldn't achieve when he put his mind to it. Except for gaining his father's respect.

Mindful that Larissa said she was going to give Peter a nap, Jake avoided the front door and walked around to the backyard. As he approached the side of the house he heard soft Asian music playing. He rounded the corner to the back of the house and found Larissa lying on a yoga mat in a shady area.

He watched her change poses. He admired her grace and style. But from his position he could also see her cleavage and any altruistic thoughts he had were banished by the rush of desire.

He waited until she finished her routine by sitting in a meditative pose. She looked peaceful and serene—untouchable. And she evoked in him a savageness he'd always tried to tamp down and hide.

Clearing his throat, he climbed the steps of the deck. Her eyes snapped open and she stared at him. There were beads of perspiration on her neck and chest. His first impulse was to lick them from her skin. His eyes narrowed. His breathing changed and he felt arousal spread throughout his body. Damn.

This reaction to her didn't fit into his well-ordered plans for Larissa.

She scrambled to her feet when she realized he was watching her. The formfitting leggings and snug sleeveless shirt left little of her body to the imagination. It was the first time he'd seen her in anything that wasn't loose and concealing. Even that night they'd made love, she'd insisted they leave the lights low.

Her legs were long and curvy. Her hips a real woman's and not a model's. Her breasts were pert and, he knew from experience, just the right size to nestle in his palms.

The spandex shirt clung to the full globes and Jake had to swallow when her nipples budded against the cloth under his gaze. She stopped moving and he glanced up at her face. A pink blush covered her neck and cheeks, but she didn't cross her arms over her chest.

"Are you sure about this platonic thing?" he asked, his voice husky with need.

"No, I'm not sure."

He took two large steps toward her, closing the gap between them. She didn't smell sweaty the way he did after exercise. It reminded him of how different the two of them were. How different men and women were and how exciting those differences could be.

Unable to resist, he traced with his finger a bead of perspiration that rolled down between her breasts, disappearing under her shirt. She shivered when he reached the border where skin and fabric met. He watched goose bumps spread over her skin and, hesitating only a second, he dipped his finger under her shirt.

She was just as soft to the touch as he remembered. Her breasts appeared a bit bigger than before and he let his finger slide under one of them. She bit her lip and tilted her head to the side, watching him with hooded eyes.

She swayed and he brought his other arm up around her waist, holding her the way he'd dreamed of since he'd opened her car door this morning. He pulled his finger free of her shirt and lifted it to his lips.

Her pupils dilated as she watched him and her breath rushed in and out as if she'd just completed a five-mile run instead of a yoga routine.

The salty taste of her on Jake's tongue only whetted his appetite for more of her. He leaned toward her. She gripped his biceps and rose on her tiptoes. Her breath fanned against his cheek.

He bent and captured her mouth. She opened for him with a sigh that told him she'd needed this embrace as much as he had. Her fingernails bit into his arms as she returned his kiss.

He cupped her bottom and brought her more fully against him. Her hardened nipples pushed into his chest. He swallowed her moan as he deepened their embrace. He reached again for her breast, sliding his hand up under her shirt this time. She shuddered when he palmed a nipple.

He slid his mouth from hers, down the slope of her neck until he could trace the V-neck of her shirt with his tongue. She trembled again in his arms, her hands clutching at his head.

The phone rang inside the house and Larissa pushed him away, stumbling, her eyes wide and wounded. She hurried into the house to take the call and he cursed under his breath. Pivoting on his heel, he walked to the edge of the deck.

He braced his hands on the railing, bowing his head and breathing deeply, searching for his control. Hell, what was he thinking? He hadn't come here to make love to Larissa. In fact, considering their situation it was the last thing he should be doing. Further evidence, as if he needed it, that he wasn't cut out for responsibility. Maybe he should rethink the custody suit. He knew it was male pride motivating him.

He heard her return, sensed her standing in the doorway watching him. She cleared her throat and he glanced over his shoulder at her.

She'd put on a large sweatshirt while she'd been in the house and crossed her arms over her chest. He didn't know what to say to her and he had the feeling if he opened his mouth he'd say something stupid instead of acting like the rather suave guy he liked to think he was.

Finally she said, "Peter's still sleeping. Why don't you come inside and I'll make us some lunch."

"I'm not hungry," he said.

"Oh. Okay."

This wasn't working out the way he'd planned it. "Larissa, sit down."

"Why?"

"We have to talk."

"I guess we do. Are you sure you don't want any food? How about some iced tea?"

"No. Nothing."

She sat down on one of the wrought-iron chairs around a small café-style table. He took one of the chairs, spun it around and sat facing her.

"What'd you want to talk to me about?"

"A couple of things. First off, I'd like to take Peter to get a paternity test."

Larissa laced her fingers together and stared at Jake. He was so familiar to her, yet at the same time a stranger with steely determination. This was the man who'd made D&D's coffeehouse the success it was today. And though Larissa had spent some late nights with Jake in college, he'd been more of a dreamer then than the man he was today.

The calm she'd tried to find through yoga had disappeared as soon as she'd seen Jake. She'd gone into his arms remembering the man she'd left earlier today. The man who'd told her she could trust him. This didn't feel like trust. This felt…this felt like betrayal.

"You don't think he's your son?" she asked at last.

He watched her with that intense dark brown stare that penetrated through the layers she used to protect herself. She flinched under his scrutiny, tucking a stray strand of hair back into her ponytail.

"I didn't say that," he said, running his hands through his thick black curly hair. She could still feel the texture of his hair in her hands. She clenched her hands and tried to concentrate on his words.

"Yes, you did. If you believed me then you wouldn't need a test." She'd known he'd be angry at her for keeping the truth from him but had never expected him to doubt he was the father.

"Don't make this about you and me, Rissa. This is a matter of practicality. I can't provide for Peter until I'm legally recognized as his father. Only a paternity test can prove that."

Practicality. She'd spent a lifetime being practical, realistic and sensible. She understood those things, but just once she wanted the fantasies she still harbored to come true. A million thoughts ran through her head. Jumbled and confused—a chaotic disarray of her view of reality. She pulled her legs up in the chair and wrapped her arms around them. Of all the things that Jake could say to her this was the one thing she'd never expected.

She wished now she'd run away this morning when

Ms. Carmody had called. That she'd taken Peter and disappeared. Anything so she didn't have to go through this. She'd created a mess of complications she'd never considered when she'd kept Peter a secret.

Complications that had made her regret her actions a few times—things like medical history; Peter had asthma. Things like who would take care of her son if she died; Larissa had no family. Things like being a part of a wealthy family; Larissa made enough to provide for her son, but was she denying him the opportunity for more?

"Everything is so…" She trailed off, afraid of revealing too much to Jake. It would be different if they were just friends, if there wasn't that spark of sexual attraction buzzing between them.

He raised one eyebrow at her in question.

"Complex," she said at last.

His lips quirked and he reached across the small table to pull her hands off her legs. He twined their fingers together. "We'll take it one day at a time—together."

Together. The word scared her. She'd grown used to being independent, to being solely responsible for Peter. It was strange to think that Jake would have some say in Peter's life. Not necessarily in a bad way, she realized, which also scared her.

"I'm still not sure that us moving in with you is a good idea."

"Now that I've seen your place, I'd be willing to move here."

She didn't want Jake here in her house. This was her sanctuary from the world. The one place where it didn't matter that she'd never really had a father. "No, we better stay at your house."

"This is a nice place," Jake said after a while, gesturing to the house.

"Thanks. It suits us. We spend a lot of time out here or on the river."

"I never pictured you as an outdoorsy person," he said. He shifted her hands in his, his thumbs making lazy circles on her palms.

"Probably because I'm so bookish."

"Bookish?"

"What would you call me?" she asked.

"Intelligent but in a sexy way."

"I had no idea brains were a turn-on for men."

"I don't know about other men."

She smiled at him, unsure where this was going. She tugged her hands away from his and looked out at the Savannah River. She loved this house even though she'd inherited it from a man she'd scarcely known.

"Did you move here after Peter was born?" he asked.

"Yes, my grandfather left the place to me."

"I'm sorry for your loss."

"That's okay," she said. Her grandfather hadn't

ever spoken to her when he'd been alive. The old man had disowned her mother when she'd first found out she was pregnant. "We weren't close."

"I remember your mom died when we were in college. Do you have any other family?"

"I have Peter."

"This must have been some fun place to explore as a kid."

She shrugged. She'd never visited here until the day they'd moved in. She'd sold her condo in Atlanta and moved here. Her grandfather hadn't kept any pictures of her mom or herself in the house. She'd found a drawer in the mahogany desk in the den filled with unopened letters from her mom. Only one letter had been opened—the one she'd sent to her grandfather telling him he had a great-grandson.

He'd never contacted her, but Larissa often wondered if that was why he'd left her this place. Not for her and for the sins of her mother, but for Peter. The great-grandson he'd never let himself know.

"I know you're an only child, but did you have cousins to play with?" he asked.

"Not every family is like yours, Jake. Some of us are only children of only children."

He put his hands up. "I didn't mean anything by it. This is a great place to raise a son. When you said he only watched PBS, I was scared you were turning him into a little brainiac."

"I'm trying, but he has your genes," she said, trying for a lightness that she didn't really feel.

He grabbed his chest. "Ouch."

She chuckled.

"I'll take that lunch you offered now," he said. Something had changed in his eyes that made a ray of hope blossom in her chest. She realized that there was no one else she'd rather share parenthood with than this man.

Larissa's kitchen reminded him of Tuscany. It was painted rich warm colors. He could tell she'd remodeled since she'd moved in. The houses in this neighborhood had been originally built in the fifties. But her kitchen was very modern. The large butcher-block island where she assembled lunch had a new look to it.

"Is salad okay?"

Not really. He'd still be hungry when he was done. But they'd reached a kind of truce on the deck and he didn't want to rock the boat. "Sure. What can I do to help?"

"Can you cook?"

He laughed. "No. But cutting up veggies isn't that hard."

"No, it's not. I'm making a Greek salad, so you can cut up olives and peppers for it."

She put on a Jimmy Buffett CD while they worked in the kitchen. The first time he'd noticed Larissa in college had been at a Buffett concert. She'd been the only one in their group without a grass skirt or Hawaiian shirt. And she'd turned eight shades of red when Buffett sang "Let's Get Drunk and Screw."

"I love this CD. I remember the first time you heard some of these songs."

"Me, too. I wanted to die, I was so mortified that ya'll were singing it at the top of your lungs."

"Wasn't long before we'd corrupted you and you were singing along. Remember the next concert less than a year later?"

She gave him a saucy grin, one he'd forgotten. For all her shy ways in a large group, one on one, Larissa was a sassy woman. "You always were a bad influence on me."

His track record with women wasn't the best. He'd gotten Larissa pregnant and not known it. In his defense, he'd been going through a lot then. His sister Victoria had disappeared and D&D's was starting to go big time. Jake didn't cut himself any slack for those things. Some men were inherently flawed when it came to women and he was beginning to believe he was one of them.

"Yeah, I guess I was," he said.

He felt her hand on his arm and realized he'd stopped cutting. "I was joking."

He put the knife on the counter, leaning his hip against it and staring down at her. Damn, he'd forgotten how small she was. He felt big—too big for her and for her kitchen. He also felt too hard for the woman who'd blushed at provocative song lyrics. "But there is an element of truth to your words."

She cupped his jaw. Her long fingers were cold against his skin. "Not really. You've never made me do anything I regretted."

There was something in her eyes that convinced him of her sincerity. He leaned down to kiss her. A quick embrace that held shared memories and the hope of finding some sort of peace for the future. She pulled away too soon for him.

"We better get back to work or we'll never eat," she said lightly, stepping away from him and moving around the island.

Did she really think one butcher-block countertop was going to stop him? He'd let her back away earlier when her phone rang but he knew they were going to have to come to terms with this sexual attraction between them before she moved into his place. "Maybe I'm not hungry for rabbit food."

"What are you hungry for?" She tilted her head to the side and watched him with eyes that knew their effect on him.

"Do I really have to tell you?" he asked, coming around the side of the counter and closing the gap between them. He backed her up against the countertop, not stopping until their bodies brushed against each other.

She tipped her head back, exposing her long elegant neck. He lifted one large blunt finger and stroked the length of it. She trembled under his touch and her pulse started to beat more heavily. Her eyes narrowed to slits.

"The only thing on the menu is Greek salad, Jake."

She wasn't ready for anything other than teasing, he thought. Right now, maybe that's all he was ready for too. Marcus had made some interesting points on the phone. A paternity test was only one of the things he wanted from Larissa. He also needed to know why she'd kept her pregnancy a secret.

He stepped away and went back to chopping olives. "Too bad. I had my sights set on something mouthwatering."

She said nothing but assembled the salad and led the way out to the deck overlooking the Savannah River. She was still nervous around him, afraid to trust him, and she was right to be. He had his own plans and she was only a means to an end. As cruel as that sounded, he couldn't curb his gut instinct, which told him an eye for an eye.

"Thanks for lunch," he said while she cleared the plates.

"It was only a salad," she said.

"It was delicious."

"Thanks. I'm not really much of a cook."

"Me either. Luckily I know how to dial for take-out."

"I can't eat take-out every night. And it's really not good for Peter. Or you."

"I run five miles every morning and play soccer on Saturdays."

"I...I've seen you."

"When?"

"Last fall. Peter and I were having a picnic at the park. We were packing up to leave when you guys arrived for your game."

"Why didn't you say something?"

"I was scared."

"Of what?"

"My reasons are personal, Jake."

"Honey, surely not too personal to share with the father of your child."

"Sarcasm doesn't become you."

"Neither do lies you."

"I'm not lying to you."

"Not today, right? It's funny how truth seems to be your ally when you need one."

"Ally? Are we enemies?"

"Only in your eyes."

"When did I make us enemies?"

"When you kept my son a secret," he said savagely.

"I can't believe we're going through this again."

"I'm waiting to hear these reasons of yours, Rissa. Because I have to tell you I can't believe the sweet girl I knew in college would keep this from me. What other secrets are you hiding?"

Five

Larissa stood and walked into her house, unsure what to say but needing to escape. She paused inside the living room. Portraits of Peter lined the wall. She had spent a small fortune in film developing since he'd been born. She'd filled this empty old house with pictures of her son.

With pictures of the small family that she'd finally found. She scanned the pictures, stopping on one taken only two weeks ago, Peter on the dock with his fishing pole in hand. He'd been aggravated that he hadn't caught anything and he stared down into the water with the same determination she'd just seen in Jake's eyes.

She hurried past the photos and entered her kitchen, where she started cleaning. Cleaning had always been a chore that soothed her. It was simple and straight-forward, and when she finished she could look back and see what she'd accomplished.

Unlike life, which seemed never to run smoothly. Every time she thought she and Jake had a chance at getting past her deception, his anger reared its ugly head. And she knew he deserved some answers, but the last thing she wanted to do was bare her soul to him.

Jake had always been the one guy she'd wanted. The one guy who'd made her feel like it was okay to be herself. The one guy who…she'd never been able to forget.

She sensed him behind her. She put the rest of the dishes in the dishwasher and turned to face him. He had that bulldog angry look on his face and his arms crossed over his massive chest that told her he wasn't budging until he got some answers.

She swallowed, twisting the dish towel with her hands. "You're right. I do have some secrets that I don't want to share with you."

"I'm trying to understand. But your lack of trust makes it damned hard."

"I know. Remember earlier when you asked me about my grandfather?" she asked, sorting through her past and finding one of the things that seemed safest to tell him. Jake came from a wealthy family with history and pride. And she'd never had a real family until Peter. She'd never felt she'd missed out until she'd had her son and realized what life could've been like.

He leaned against the doorjamb, no less intimidating in the more relaxed pose. ''Yes.''

His black T-shirt stretched across his chest and she wished she'd never left his arms earlier. He was too handsome for his own good. He could be dirt poor and he'd still have a legion of women after him.

If she'd stayed in his arms earlier, nature would have taken its course and she could have avoided this conversation. But she was vulnerable where Jake was concerned. She didn't want to create any further bonds between them and risk the chance that she'd be hurt when he left. And she knew he'd leave. No man had ever stayed. Starting with her grandfather, before she was even born.

''Well, I never knew him. He and my mom had a falling-out before I was born. He disowned her over her choice of husband.''

''Your father?''

She nodded. No way was she ever going to call Reilly Payton her father. The man had made it clear that society may have demanded he do his duty by her mother, but father was one role he'd never wanted to play. She'd legally changed her name to Nielsen when she'd turned 18.

"What's that got to do with you keeping Peter's birth from me?"

She took a deep breath, mentally crossed her fingers and bowed her head. She'd learned early on that if she was going to tell a half-truth it was easier if she wasn't looking the person in the eye. "I didn't want your family to disown you because of me."

"Sweetheart, look at me," he said.

She glanced up at him, hoping he'd let the subject drop. "Yes?"

"That's the biggest whopper I've ever heard. You know Wes and I are brothers and he liked you. My family could care less about your past or where you came from."

She'd forgotten about Jake's college roommate and friend, Wes. Wes was still like a second son to Jake's parents. But she knew that his parents would have minded having a daughter-in-law who'd done the same thing to their son that her mother had done to the Payton boy twenty-five years earlier. And Savannah society would have remembered it too. The Paytons were old money and her parents had been the talk of the town. If there was one thing those Southern ladies liked, it was scandal and gossip. Larissa had decided long ago she'd had her fill of being fodder for them.

"I'm sorry. The truth is my mom got pregnant to trap my..." She didn't know what to call the man who'd married her mom and then refused to have anything to do with the child they'd created. Certainly not father. Never father.

"...her boyfriend into marriage. I couldn't do that to you."

Jake cursed savagely under his breath. He pushed his hands through his hair and watched her. He entered the kitchen, walking toward her with a slowly measured gait. He stopped when there was about six inches of space between them. But she still felt dwarfed by his physical presence. She tried to step back, but the counter stopped her.

"Did you get pregnant on purpose?" he asked her.

She couldn't gauge his mood. Suddenly she felt very small and awkward. Wrapping her arms around her waist, she stared at his chest and whispered, "No, I'd never do that."

Jake took her chin in his large, warm hand, tipping her head back until their eyes met. "Then why would I think you had trapped me?"

She couldn't think when his breath brushed over her cheek like that. When his eyes looked down on her with a tenderness she'd thought never to see in them again. When he pulled her into his embrace and wrapped his arms around her. Oh, God, this was what she'd been afraid of. Leaning on Jake felt right in the seat of her soul and she knew that he wouldn't stay, but she couldn't help herself.

Didn't want to step away. They didn't move from

each other's arms until Peter came into the kitchen, rubbing the sleep from his eyes.

Her heart was heavy with fears and hope swirled together. She wanted to believe the promise Jake offered her, but she feared as soon as she did, she'd end up getting hurt.

Jake sat on the couch with Peter reading Jake's favorite book *Lord of the Rings: Fellowship of the Rings* to him. Peter was fascinated by the world of Middle-earth and was rapt in his attention.

Jake glanced at the mantel clock. What was taking Larissa so long? "I'm going to check on your mom. Do you want to watch some TV?"

"Yes, please, Daddy," Peter said with a smile.

They'd had a lot of fun this afternoon together. He and Larissa had told Peter that Jake was his father. Peter had been overjoyed at the news and had started calling him "Daddy" almost immediately. He said the word so often, Jake realized how much his son had missed having a father.

Jake turned the television on and left his son watching *Arthur*. Larissa had provided a long list of acceptable television programs on a laminated four-by-six-inch card for Jake when they'd moved in. He also had cards on acceptable words to use—apparently *shut up, stupid* and *idiot* were forbidden, as well as every curse word. There was an approved food list, which Jake had noticed was lacking his favorite cereal. He'd added it to the list with a Sharpie pen and put it on the kitchen counter where she'd see it when she fixed breakfast tomorrow morning.

He went down the hall to the guest bedroom he'd given Larissa. He didn't question it, but there was a sense of rightness to having her under his roof. And for him being responsible for her and their son.

It felt right in his gut. He sensed this was what his father must feel when the entire family was assembled at their home. It was the first time he'd ever felt anything in common with his dad and it felt…weird.

He rapped on her door. "You ready?"

"I don't know," she opened the door, and nervously stepped back.

"How do I look?" she asked.

She looked too damned good to be someone's mom. Her dress was a feminine bit of silk that teased him with its demureness. Teased him with the hint of sexuality beneath that flounced skirt ending just above the knees and the scoop neckline that hinted at her cleavage.

"You look fine."

"Just fine?" she asked, hurrying back over to the mirror and patting her hair once more.

"What's wrong with fine?" he asked, lounging against the door frame. He was fascinated to see the normally unflappable Larissa so unsure of herself. He'd never known her to worry about what she was going to wear.

"I'm meeting your family for the first time. Plus I'm bringing scandal down on them. I think I should look better than fine."

She did, but he wasn't going to reveal anything more to her. Her features were drawn and she looked more nervous now than she had in the doctor's office earlier when they'd had the paternity test done.

He left the doorway and entered the room. The bed was piled with discarded clothing. He wondered if this went back to what she'd said the other day about her grandfather. How did knowing your family had rejected you before you were born affect someone? For all his problems with his father, he knew the old man loved him and would always be there for him.

"What's this all about, Rissa?"

She sighed and sank down on the clothes strewn on the double bed. "I don't want to go."

He sat down next to her. Her perfume was faintly floral and sexy to him. But then everything about Larissa was. He reached for her hands, which she had clenched tightly into fists on her lap. He pried her hands open and held them loosely in his own.

She tipped her head to the side and looked up at him. It was a beseeching look that made him want to give her whatever she asked for. But at the same time, they were in this predicament because of her actions. He lifted one eyebrow in silent question.

She licked her lips and then turned her head toward

her lap again. "It was hard enough telling you about Peter. I don't think I can face your family."

"There's no other choice. You have to go with me so we both know how to handle the media. Nicola was clear on that point."

"I wish Jasmine Carmody had never called me," she said, looking up at him again.

"I'm glad she did despite the trouble she's caused. Jasmine Carmody has given me my son."

Larissa said nothing, but her eyes revealed the truth. And the truth wasn't a pretty and nice thing. It was that this woman would have rather run away than face him with the news of his own son.

He cursed under his breath and stood, walking away from her. Every time he thought he'd forgiven her, he was reminded he hadn't. Spending two hours in the toy store with his son had gone a long way toward showing him what he'd missed out on all these years. And now she was telling him again that she regretted telling him the truth.

He clenched his fists and walked toward the front door. "Get your purse, Larissa. We're leaving."

"Jake…"

He didn't pause or turn to look at her. She'd made her decisions. Now he'd made his. He'd see Marcus tonight at Crofthaven and set the custody suit in motion. It was obvious to him, no matter what Larissa said, she couldn't be trusted where Peter was concerned.

He was willing to cut her a little slack because of her upbringing, and he understood that she'd had a rough shake early in life. But Jake wasn't responsible for another man's mistakes and he wasn't going to keep paying for them.

Her hand on his arm stopped him and he pivoted to face her.

"I'm sorry," she said suddenly.

He realized she was trying to tell him something else. But he'd never been good at reading minds and didn't think he was suddenly going to get better at it.

"For?"

"Everything."

"Don't be sorry for everything. That's too big a burden for your shoulders. We're both responsible for this mess and I'm not going to let you continue to carry it alone."

Larissa felt small and very out of place in the grand foyer of Crofthaven. Peter leaned closer to her and she stooped to pick up her son as Jake gave their coats to Joyce Jones, the housekeeper. Jake exchanged pleasantries with the woman and then cupped his hand under Larissa's elbow, leading her down the hall.

"Where are we going?" Larissa asked.

"To the library. Relax."

"I can't. This place is intimidating."

"It's just a house," he said.

"It's not just a house. It's a historical landmark. It's your family's mark on Savannah and I feel like an interloper."

"Relax," he said again. "I didn't grow up here."

He rubbed Peter's head and their son glanced up at him. "Ready to meet your family?"

Peter didn't answer, just stuck his thumb in his mouth and held tighter to her neck. "Maybe I should have gotten a sitter."

"We don't need a sitter," he said. "What a couple of cowards you two are."

"Am not," Peter said, squirming in her arms to be put down. "I'm just as brave as Frodo."

Jake ruffled his son's hair. "I knew you were."

Peter glanced up at Larissa. "Mommy's not so brave."

"Then we'll be brave for her," Jake said, stooping down to Peter's eye level.

Peter nodded and slipped his hand into hers. He gripped hers tightly and smiled up at her. And she felt an infusion of love for her son and for his father. Jake was taking this task of being a father very seriously and she regretted that she'd waited so long to let him know he was a dad.

"Ready?" Jake asked.

She nodded and followed Jake into the library. The librarian in her was in awe. Private collections like this one were the stuff dreams were made of. She almost forgot her nerves. Despite his courageous

words in the hall, Peter seemed to have picked up on
her apprehension and now clung to her leg. She
rubbed his back, focusing on Peter and not the others
in the room.

There were five people in the room. Jake's uncle,
Abraham Danforth, and Wesley Brooks were at the
computer desk on the far side of the room. She knew
Wes from college, ''Honest'' Abe from the articles
she'd read in the newspaper about him and his family.
Abe was the patriarch of the Danforths, a retired Navy
Seal who was currently running for the senate.

There was a couple on the couch who stood when
they entered. They had to be Jake's parents. There
was too much emotion in their gazes for them not to
be. They both eyed her and Peter with curiosity. The
other woman with gorgeous red hair and bright green
eyes was taller than she was and Larissa was no
shorty at five-seven. She had to be Abe's PR manager.

''Is this our grandson?'' Miranda Danforth asked,
crossing the room. Jake's mom had blond hair worn
in a sleek bob. Her eyes were a warm blue that made
Larissa feel safe and comfortable.

''Mom, this is Larissa Nielsen and my son,'' Jake
said.

Peter clung tighter to Larissa and wouldn't turn
around and meet his grandmother at first. ''I'm
sorry,'' she said. ''He's not used to meeting new people.''

''That's okay,'' Miranda said, running her hand

down Peter's back. "Why don't you come sit down with me?"

Larissa followed her across the room, conscious of all the others there. Wes Brooks, Jake's college roommate, looked up from the desk where he was working on the computer. He gave her a friendly smile and a wink. Larissa smiled back. She knew Jake's not officially adopted brother from their college days. And it was nice to see a familiar face in this sea of Danforths.

Miranda seated herself on a leather sofa and Larissa sank down next to her, pulling Peter onto her lap. Harry Danforth stood on the other side of the room. Jake had followed them and he sat on the other side of Larissa. He dropped his arm over her shoulders and she felt comforted by his presence.

As he'd said earlier, she wasn't alone in carrying this burden. But Peter had never felt like a burden to her. He'd always been her joy. And these people, Jake's clan, were lucky to have her precious son in their family.

"Jake called me earlier about your situation—" Nicola said.

"Pardon me for interrupting, Nicola," Miranda Danforth said. "Peter, would you like to come to the kitchen with me for some cookies and milk?"

Peter lifted his head from Larissa's shoulder. "What kind?"

"Peter."

"That's okay, Larissa. Double chocolate chunk, I believe."

"Mama?"

"You can go, sweetie. Mrs. Danforth is your grandmother."

"Wow. A daddy and a grandmother."

Miranda smiled down at him. "You've got a grandfather as well as a bunch of other family."

"Really?" Peter asked.

"Really," she said. "I'll tell you all about them while we have our cookies and milk."

"Okay!" Peter said, taking Miranda's offered hand and following her from the room.

Larissa felt naked without her little boy on her lap. She laced her fingers together and tried not to pretend that she was the cause of an uncomfortable situation for this very important family.

"I've been thinking about this all afternoon and I've come up with a solution that I think will take the heat out of anything Ms. Carmody writes."

"Great, I'll help in any way I can," Larissa said.

Jake rubbed her shoulder, and she leaned back to smile at him. He didn't smile at her, but a warmth entered his eyes that made her acutely aware of every place where their bodies touched.

"Perfect. I think you two need to get married as soon as possible."

Jake surged to his feet. "No way."

For Larissa, the next few moments seemed to happen in slow motion and there was a ringing in her ears. She wasn't sure what she'd expected, but being forced to marry the man whose child she'd had wasn't it. She had the first inkling of what her mother may have felt all those years ago when she'd faced Reilly Payton and his family—trapped and doomed.

''Excuse me,'' she said, standing. She walked from the room, down the long hall and out into the night.

Any chance of forever happiness with Jake was gone in an instant, because no man could ever love a woman who'd forced him into a marriage he didn't want.

Six

Jake knew he'd screwed up even before he'd felt Larissa leave the room. But one look at the condemnation shining from his father's eyes was all it took to make him feel about fourteen again. Dammit.

He turned away from his father and focussed instead on Nicola.

"Is a marriage going to be a problem?" she asked.

Jake had no idea. He suspected that he was the last man Larissa would marry right now, after hearing his reaction to the suggestion. But the suggestion had taken him completely off guard.

"No, it won't be a problem, will it, Jacob?" His father, Harry Danforth, said. There were maybe two moments in his life when Jake had felt as if he'd pleased the old man. Once when he was six and won the all-city soccer kickoff, and once when he had made his first million with D&D's Coffeehouses. But for the remainder of Jake's life, he'd seen his father with the same look he had on his face now: one of disappointment.

Even Uncle Abe and Wes were looking at him like he'd screwed up. But he knew what his father meant. He'd made this mess, now it was time to clean it up.

"I don't know that Larissa wants to marry me," Jake said. Not much of an excuse but the only one he had.

"Then convince her," Harry said.

"I'll try." Jake stood and exited the room. He paused in the hallway and leaned back against the wall. His hands were shaking and he had that gut feeling that life was changing in a way he hadn't anticipated.

The hallways were lit with wall sconces and Jake figured Larissa hadn't gone out the front door, but out the back into the gardens. He pushed away from the wall and moved slowly through the house. Crofthaven was a showplace, unlike his parents' more modest house.

He stepped out into the spring evening and paused. What if he couldn't convince Larissa to marry him? He'd learned a long time ago that running away from problems wasn't a solution. But marriage? It wasn't as if he had anything against the institution, but he wasn't sure it was the right move for them.

He heard the rustling of leaves and a soft fall of footsteps. He followed the sound until he found Larissa. She was walking around one of the smaller formal gardens in the backyard. Hedges surrounded it and there was a very European feel to this garden. A marble bench was tucked off to one side and Larissa paused next to it, then sank down on the bench. He stayed in the shadows to watch her.

The full moon and landscape lanterns provided soft lighting to the area, revealing the woman who was bound to him in ways he didn't understand. It was more than that they shared a child. It was more than sharing college memories. It was a soul-deep feeling that made him flinch and that he found difficult to ignore.

He didn't know what to say to her. He wasn't really sure what he wanted from her. But he knew what duty demanded and he'd give it his best shot.

He was about to step from the shadows, when Larissa turned her head to the right and brought the blossom of a hibiscus close to her face, inhaling deeply. What was she thinking?

"Can I join you?" he asked.

She turned toward him. He stepped from the shadows and waited for her permission to join her.

She shrugged and crossed her arms over her chest. He sat next to her, leaving space between them.

Though it was only a few inches, he knew the gap here was miles wide. His next words would have to build a bridge over it. But he wasn't ready. He was still angry that she'd never told him about Peter before now. He knew he needed to get past the anger and thought he'd been making some progress in that direction.

But sitting in his uncle's library and knowing those closest to him knew the mother of his child didn't think he was good enough to be a father—well, hell, it hurt. And he'd reacted the only way he'd ever learned—by lashing out and hurting back.

Hurting the one woman he wanted to protect. She looked fragile sitting here in the garden. But he knew she wasn't fragile. Larissa was a survivor. She rolled with the punches and kept plodding along with life.

She cleared her throat. "I'm sorry I ran out like that. I…"

Suddenly everything was clear and he knew, despite the anger and need for vengeance still pulsing through him, that marriage to Larissa wasn't just a right choice; it was a necessity.

"I'm sorry."

"It's okay. I know you don't want to marry me."

"The thing is, I'm not sure I don't."

"What are you saying?"

"I wasn't prepared to have everyone know you thought so little of my fathering skills."

"Oh, Jake, I didn't."

"Of course, you did."

"Didn't you hear anything I said to you earlier?"

"About what?"

"My family. I never thought about you as a father, Jake. I thought about you as a man trapped by circumstance. And I was right, wasn't I?"

He cursed under his breath and stood, then paced away from her. He was a man trapped, but not so much by circumstance as by his past. By all the lousy decisions he'd made to get to this point. All the time when he'd put feeling good and having fun in front of responsibility.

It was time to get his act together in his personal life and he knew it.

He turned back to Larissa, who watched him with wide, wet eyes. He knew he'd hurt her. Somehow he hadn't expected her pain to cut him. But it did.

He strode back to her and took her hands in his. He sank down in front of her on one knee and looked up into those pretty blue eyes. Those eyes that usually showed her wit and intelligence, but tonight were guarded and vulnerable.

"Larissa Nielsen, will you marry me?"

Larissa wasn't sure what to say. Marrying Jake, well honestly, it was what she'd been secretly dreaming of since she'd first met him in college. But she'd also dreamed they'd have a huge wedding in Savannah so the old gossips wouldn't be able to talk. She'd wear an elaborate white gown similar to Princess Di's and she'd be the most beautiful woman on that day.

It was a fantasy she'd devoted too much time thinking about. Despite Jake being down on bended knee, Larissa knew that responsibility was motivating Jake and not love or eternal devotion. And she knew that he was a good man. He'd already proved he could be a good father. And sometimes in life you had to take what was offered and kiss goodbye the secret dreams you'd harbored.

"Are you going to keep me hanging forever?" he asked, his voice low and husky. When she looked into those devastating dark brown eyes of his, she wondered if she'd ever be able to deny him anything.

She shook her head. He was doing his duty—darn it. She had to remember Jake was still angry with her for keeping Peter a secret for three years. Jake wasn't in love with her, and no matter what else happened, she had to protect her emotions from him. Because she knew from watching her mother's bitter experience that falling in love with an illusion was never a good thing.

"You don't have to do this," she said at last, forcing herself to look away from him. She looked instead out at the well-tended gardens. She and her mom had had a window box at the small duplex they'd lived in most of her life. One small box that they'd filled with annuals every year. And though Crofthaven wasn't Jake's childhood home, she knew this kind of garden—the kind that took a small army to maintain—was what he was used to.

Their lives were worlds apart and she wondered in her heart if they could ever make anything work between them. Even his original idea of them living together now seemed doomed. But marriage—marriage was sacred to her because she knew that when it wasn't right, too many people got hurt. Innocent little people that had no right being hurt by choices that adults made.

"Do what?" he asked, shifting closer to her on the ground. His arms circled her hips and tugged her closer to him. He didn't leave any space between them. She remembered what it was like to be in his arms and wanted to be there again. She'd never thought of herself as sex crazed until she met Jake. He made all her senses go on hyperalert.

He was so close and she remembered their earlier embraces. She still ached for him in this most basic way. She needed something from him that she wasn't sure she should take, because it would make her even more vulnerable.

"The down-on-one-knee proposal thing."

"It's for me as much as for you."

"Yeah, right. I heard you in the library, Jake. You don't want to marry me."

"Dammit, Rissa, you piss me off," he said, pinching her butt.

She swatted his hand away. "I know I do. So why are you asking me to marry you."

He wriggled his eyebrows at her. "You also turn me on."

"Is this a joke to you?" she asked.

He cursed under his breath and then hugged her tightly. "I can't explain it, but there's something about you I've never been able to forget."

Her heart melted a little at his words. He let go of her hands and cupped her face, bringing her face toward his. He brushed his lips over hers, softly, gently…seductively. Making her yearn for deeper contact between them. But she knew what he was doing, what he was trying to say with this kiss. And she returned it. Took control of the embrace, kissing him deeply.

Jake stayed at her feet and it was a heady feeling to dominate him. He was totally at her mercy. His head tipped up to hers; his body was under hers. Her emotions swirled out of control. She wanted more from him than this. She wanted—no, needed—something that he wasn't offering.

Something more than duty. She broke the kiss, taking deep breaths to try to remember that despite the garden and the moonlight, this wasn't a love story. She wasn't the heroine in some happily-ever-after tale. Reality was that Jake hadn't wanted to marry her. It was only the pressure of the media and his family that had sent him out after her.

And despite his sweet words, she knew it was too soon for Jake to feel anything but anger toward her.

"What's going through that head of yours, Rissa?"

"Nothing you'd want to hear."

"I know I've screwed up one thing after another, but marry me and let me make this right."

"If we got married it'd be more business than romance, wouldn't it?"

"It would be what we made it. There's no one else in our relationship but us and Peter."

"I'm scared, Jake."

"Of what?"

"Of making the wrong decision and ruining Peter's life."

"I told you earlier that those shoulders of yours are too small to carry everything. Share that burden with me, Rissa, I'm not going to let you down again."

Promise? She wanted to ask but didn't. Normally she wasn't this needy. Normally she wasn't this timid. Normally she made her decisions and lived with the consequences. But it was time to stop clinging to girlhood fantasies and start living in the real world. A world that included more than her and Peter.

"Okay, Jake. I'll marry you."

Jake figured it probably wasn't the best acceptance in history, but he knew it was good enough for him. He stood, pulled Larissa to her feet and took her in his arms.

But her fingers over his lips stopped him. "No, Jake."

"Why not?"

"I want this marriage to work for Peter's sake."

"I've never heard that sex screwed up a marriage."

"I think it would screw up ours. I can't think straight when you kiss me."

"Good," he said, lowering his head again. But she turned away from him and his lips barely brushed her hair.

"Dammit, woman."

"You're not listening to me."

"You're not saying anything I want to hear."

"I'm sorry, but I think keeping things platonic between us is for the best."

"Woman, who are you kidding?"

"Maybe myself. But it's important to me."

"Hell," he said, letting her go. She took a step away from him, but it didn't change the way his blood was racing. He was still aroused and could tell from her shallow breathing and flushed skin she was too. If he pushed her, he could convince her she was wrong. He knew it. And he suspected she knew it.

Why then was she saying no?

"I'm not letting this go. Honestly, I don't think we can live together without sleeping together."

"You may be right. But I'd like us to try it."

"I don't understand."

"It's because we have to get married," she said softly.

He waited, sensing there was more she had to say. Here was the Larissa he'd known in college. The quiet and contemplative woman who'd spent hours discussing world politics but had never said a word about her upbringing. Would he ever understand this woman?

Finally she bit her bottom lip and looked up at him. "I don't want to start thinking there's more between us than obligation."

He knew she was being serious. He wanted to respond to that, to take this discussion even deeper, but instead, all he could think about was her lips. The bottom one she kept nibbling on as she thought about what she was going to say next. He wanted to suckle on it, to tease away her solemn mood with a lighter one. A safer one. Because he didn't like where this conversation was going.

"More? Like what?" he asked at last.

She crossed her arms over her chest and tipped her head to the side, watching him with those wide expressive eyes of hers. "Like love."

Oh, no, not love. If the topic didn't change soon, he'd have to say to hell with it and force matters back into the physical realm, where he was more confident. "Just love?"

"The in-sickness-and-in-health, until-death-do-us-part stuff. I don't want to buy into this fantasy that I've had in my head for so long a time.''

"What fantasy?'' Did he have a starring role in this image in her head or was he a walk-on replacement? He suspected the latter.

"Oh, Jake. Don't make me tell you this.''

He held his hands up. Far be it for him to force anything from her. "I'm not making you tell me anything.''

"I know. Let's go inside and tell Peter we're getting married.'' She started walking out of the garden. Jake wasn't really ready to rejoin his family. Even though he'd convinced Larissa to marry him, he knew his dad still wouldn't be pleased.

"I'm not sure how much he understands,'' Jake said, letting her change the subject.

"He's pretty smart for his age. But you're right, I don't think he realizes we aren't married.''

She kept walking and he had no choice but to follow her. Dammit, when had he become a coward? He took her elbow and led her up the path to the house. "He took to me being his dad really well.''

"I'm sure the two shopping carts of toys you bought him didn't hurt.''

"Hey, the kid had never been to Toys "R" Us, Rissa. I think that constitutes neglect,'' he said. Jake had never been to one, either. He and Peter had enjoyed their afternoon in the store immensely.

She pulled away from him and stopped. "Peter's not neglected."

"Hey, I was kidding. You've done a great job with our son. I'm proud to call him my boy."

"Sorry about that. Must be the single mom in me."

"Well, you're not a single parent anymore."

"No, I'm not. That's going to take some adjusting for all of us. And for all his easygoing nature, you wouldn't believe how stubborn he can be about things."

"Sure I would. He's your son."

"I'm not stubborn."

"What would you call it?"

"Determined," she said with a faint smile.

They'd reached the house, but she didn't enter. She stood there with her hands twisted together and waited.

He pulled her close for a quick hug and then opened the door to the house. Even though he'd never had any trouble sweet-talking women, suddenly he couldn't find the right words to use with Larissa. He was out of his element here and he didn't like it.

He led her back into the library. His folks were sitting on the floor with Peter, helping him put together a puzzle. Standing with Larissa at his side and watching his parents and son together, Jake felt like everything in his world had finally come together.

Seven

Larissa was glad to leave Crofthaven behind. She'd put Peter in the new car seat in Jake's big Suburban while he went to have a few last words with his father and Wes. It was odd to see Jake and Wes at Crofthaven, but they fit in there in a way she'd never imagined.

Nicola had recommended a Vegas wedding and would contact a few of the bridal magazines to come and photograph her for their spreads. Jake had taken over when they'd reentered the living room and she'd been happy to take a back seat to him. This whole marriage thing still felt very surreal.

She knew she was never going to sleep tonight.

Too much had happened and she needed time to herself to figure it out. She'd never imagined that having a child with a man could make things so complicated. There were some papers she had to sign before they were married. The family lawyer, Jake's cousin Marcus, had recommended she get her lawyer to read them. Unlike the Danforths, she didn't have a lawyer. But she had a friend from college who'd become one.

According to Marcus, the papers were straightforward—your run-of-the-mill prenuptial agreement without too many complications. She understood why Jake had wanted a paternity test after reading it. Jake had more money and assets that she'd ever imagined.

She rubbed the bridge of her nose. She felt she was getting a migraine. She took Mr. Bear from her purse and tucked him into the car seat with Peter.

Though the hour was late, Peter was still awake. Meeting his family hadn't intimidated him at all. He was practically buzzing with excitement. She sat next to him in the back seat of the car.

"Did you know my daddy has two brothers and two sisters?" he asked her.

She pushed his hair back from his eyes. "Yes, I did."

"But one of my aunts is missing."

Victoria. Jake had told her a little bit about it earlier. They'd found a body in the attic at Crofthaven and the family refused to believe the remains might be Vicky's. But so far no proof had been offered. ''I'd heard that as well.''

''My grandmother—she said I could call her Granny—told me all about them.''

''I'm glad. Do you like having all this family?''

''I guess. I'm tired, Mama.''

''I know, sweetie. Why don't you close your eyes?'' she suggested. He leaned against the side of his car seat. She had the idea it was going to take him a long time to settle down.

''Are they always going to be our family?'' he asked.

She wondered at that. But she knew Jake well enough to know that he wasn't going to let Peter out of his life now that he'd found him. ''They'll always be your family, kiddo.''

''What about you?'' he asked. He reached for her hand and she gave it to him. He tucked it between his face and the car seat, leaning on her hand.

Though the angle was awkward, she didn't pull her hand back. She loved these moments when he just needed to be touching her. ''What about me?''

''Aren't they your family?'' he asked.

Family. It was the one thing that had always eluded her. She'd created her own little safe unit with Peter, but anything larger scared her. ''I guess so. When your daddy and I get married, they will be my family, too.''

"What's married?" Peter asked as Jake opened the door and climbed behind the wheel.

"I'll explain more in the morning."

"Okay, Mama."

"You want to climb up front with me?" Jake asked.

"Sure," she said. She leaned over and kissed Peter whose eyes were finally beginning to droop. She got out of the car and moved to the front seat.

As she closed the passenger door, she heard Peter's sleepy voice. "Thanks, Daddy."

"What for?"

"For my family."

Larissa felt a pain deep in her heart. Of all the gifts that Jake had given Peter, he wasn't impressed with the money he'd spent at the toy store. He'd been impressed by the one thing she'd never been able to give him. And it hurt to realize that she'd been depriving him of it all along because of her own fears.

"You're welcome, buddy," Jake said, his voice low and husky. He reached into the back seat and ruffled Peter's hair.

They started the car and drove back toward Savannah in silence. Larissa's thoughts troubled her. She'd never thought of herself as selfish, never realized that she'd put her needs in front of her son's. She never acknowledged that the fear she'd always secretly harbored had driven her to isolate herself from others.

"I know this is kind of rushed, but I promise we'll have a nice wedding."

She knew Jake was trying to ease her mind. But she was having a hard time acknowledging her past behavior and dealing with the guilt it now caused her. "I'm sure whatever you decided on will be fine."

He turned to look at her, his features stark in the dashboard lights. "I want it to be better than fine, Larissa."

She hugged herself, feeling more vulnerable than ever, even more so than when she'd given birth to Peter alone in the hospital. "I'm not sure I deserve that."

"Why not?" he asked. He'd turned his attention back to the road and she was glad. She didn't want him to look at her.

"I just suddenly feel very selfish."

He didn't say anything, and she waited until they'd driven at least a mile before she spoke again. "I've been so afraid of getting hurt that I didn't think of Peter."

"You said it earlier—he's not neglected."

"Who's to say what constitutes neglect? I'd never realized how my own fears were shaping him. He really took to your mom."

"Yes, he did. She took to him, too. She offered to watch him when we go to Vegas," Jake said.

"I'm sure he'd love that."

"Good. That's settled." He reached across the seat

and took her hand, holding it in his for a minute before placing it on his thigh. She felt reassured in ways
she shouldn't because she'd promised herself that she
wouldn't let herself care for Jake.

It was more important than ever that she make this
marriage work. If she didn't, then they'd all end up
hurt. And she wasn't going to be responsible for caus-
ing the men she loved any more pain.

It was midnight a week later and Jake was wide-
awake. So he got out of his bed and wandered down
the hall to the kitchen. He tried to pretend it was
family concerns that disturbed him. Wes had been out
at Crofthaven all week trying to stop a computer virus
that Uncle Abe had downloaded with his e-mail. His
father hadn't called once but Jake knew the old man
was disappointed. His mom had dropped by twice and
Larissa had disappeared each time.

Too much had happened lately. It wasn't every day
that he found out he had a son. And that was partly
the reason for his restlessness. But he knew the true
reason was the sweet blonde sleeping in the room
next to his.

Larissa was more of a woman than he remembered.
It wasn't as if he'd forgotten her in the almost four
years since he'd last seen her. She'd always elicited
a blend of bittersweet memories. He'd thought he'd
scared her away that long-ago night with his love-
making. Larissa had always been so innocent—hav-

ing a one-night stand would have been enough to scare her.

He opened the fridge and stared at the contents. Larissa had brought groceries on her way home. He reached past the soy milk and grabbed the six-pack of Coors that had been pushed to the back of the fridge. He took the six-pack outside. He stretched out on one of the loungers, feeling the moisture that had developed from the night air saturate his T-shirt. He pulled it off and tossed it on the ground next to the beer.

Tipping his head back, he watched the stars. He remembered one time when Larissa had talked him into going to the observatory. They'd spent the night listening to *Dark Side of the Moon* and watching constellations.

Damn, that was a long time ago. Sometimes he felt years older than he was.

He heard the scrape of footsteps on the ground and turned to see Larissa silhouetted in the doorway. She wore a nightshirt that buttoned down the front. It wasn't meant to be sexy even though it did leave her long legs bare, but he found it so. To distract himself he took a long draw on his beer bottle. As a distraction, it was a piss poor one.

Jimmy Buffett had the right idea when he'd written ''Why Don't We Get Drunk and Screw.'' Just mindless sex with Larissa was what he needed tonight. But he knew in the morning it would have consequences.

He ached for her. And having her here in his house made that ache deepen. He'd never had a woman here overnight. With all the traveling he'd done in recent years, there really hadn't been time for a relationship. Hell, that was an excuse. He could have had a woman the night before and he'd still want Larissa with this gut-twisting need.

He knew he wasn't going to sleep or have anything resembling comfort until they'd spent a few hours in bed together. But he'd agreed to a platonic marriage. He intended to try to honor it.

"Can I join you?" she asked. Her hair hung in waves around her shoulder, tousled and disheveled from sleep. He knew she was a natural blonde, but there were so many different shades in her hair that he used to suspect she dyed it. But dying her hair wasn't something that Larissa would do. She was always very genuine.

"Sure. You want a beer?" he asked, gesturing to the six-pack at his feet.

She shook her head and hesitated near his chair. "Are you getting drunk?"

What would she do if he was? "Nah. Just passing time."

"Are you okay?" she asked. She glanced around for somewhere to sit. The other chairs were damp with moisture. She picked his shirt up from the ground and used it to wipe down the seat of one of the lounge chairs. She dragged it closer to his lounger and put her feet on the bottom of his.

Such small, feminine feet. His looked big and rough next to hers. He wanted to explore all the ways they were different. To strip them both naked and take his time with the exploration.

"Why wouldn't I be okay?" he asked, to distract himself from her sweetly curved body and the images of her body dancing in his head. One night years ago wasn't enough.

"Well, it's after midnight and you're sitting in the dark drinking. Something about that doesn't seem like the confident man I've come to know." She ran her toe up his calf, teasing him. Her toenails were painted a deep luscious red that confirmed what he already knew. There was more to the prim librarian than she wanted the world to see.

He glanced up and realized she'd been watching him stare at her legs. "I can't sleep."

She ran her toes back down his leg and then tucked her feet under her and tilted her head to the side. "Why not?"

"You don't want to know," he said, draining his bottle of beer. He leaned over to replace it in the carton and get a fresh one. He twisted the cap off and offered it to her.

She reached forward and took the bottle. Her shirt gaped open and he had a glimpse of the inner curve of her breast. His body hardened a little more, and he shifted his legs to find a more comfortable position.

She took a long sip of the beer and then handed the bottle back to him with a smile. "I wouldn't have asked if I didn't want to know what was keeping you awake."

"I'm hard with wanting you," he said baldly.

"Oh."

"I had a feeling you'd say that. Go back to bed, Larissa, before I forget my good intentions and seduce you."

She stood up and he felt a twinge of disappointment. "Who seduced whom the last time?"

She walked away before he could respond to her. And he watched the smooth swaying of her hips.

Larissa double-checked her seat belt and waved goodbye to Peter in Miranda Danforth's arms as they drove away. Ten days had passed since she'd let Jake know he was Peter's dad. Tears burned the back of her eyes and she stared out the window until she had her emotions under control. Jake drove away from his parents' home through Savannah and headed to the airport.

Jake's family home was just as luxurious as Crofthaven, but a little smaller in scale. It was also homier. The walls in the family room had been covered with pictures of Jake and his siblings at various ages. And there was a display that was practically a shrine to the trophies Jake had won playing soccer.

"What happened with Victoria?"

"She disappeared at a concert."

"When?"

"Years ago. We all feel responsible. She was our baby…"

"You can't protect everyone."

"I know. I just—I bought her those tickets, Rissa. *Me*. The big brother who always spoiled her."

"It's not your fault."

She waited for him to elaborate, but he didn't. He'd been like this since they'd gotten up this morning. Was he having second thoughts? She wouldn't blame him if he did—she had a few doubts herself that this marriage was the right thing to do.

"Have you changed your mind about our wedding?" she asked.

He fiddled with the radio dial, tuning in a rock station. "No."

He turned the volume up and Three Doors Down sang about being Superman. She tried to relax against the leather seat, but she couldn't. She tried to tell herself that this marriage wasn't their kryptonite, but it felt like it.

She tried to tell herself it was the fact that she was leaving the Southeast, something she'd never done before. She tried to tell herself it was the fact that she'd left Peter with her soon-to-be in-laws. She tried to pretend it had absolutely nothing to do with the man sitting next to her.

"I've never been out of Georgia, really. I mean, I've been to Hilton Head, but that's practically Georgia, it's so close."

He didn't turn the volume down or even glance her way. She remembered last night when he'd put her hand on the top of his thigh. "You're rambling."

"Yes, I am. I wonder why?" she asked. She wanted to touch him again. Even though they had an early flight, he'd still taken time to go for a run this morning. His legs were muscled and solid. Her fingers tingled with the remembered feel of his leg under her touch.

"Nervous?" he suggested.

"I wasn't until you started acting like some darned robot this morning."

"Robot?" His tone was disinterested. He'd practically ignored her at his parents' house.

"Listen, Jake, I'm not in the mood to play word games with you. If this is what our married life is going to be like I don't think we should go through with it."

He turned the radio off and removed his sunglasses, glancing over at her. There was something unreadable in his eyes that warned her that he was not in a pleasant mood. "It's too late for that."

"No, it's not."

He didn't say anything else and Larissa knew she

should have remembered the lesson she'd learned a long time ago. That she couldn't really depend on anyone but herself. Despite what he said, she knew her shoulders were strong enough to carry the burden of single-parenthood. She wanted to take Peter and her grandfather's Bayliner and take to the sea. They would find a place where the two of them could live together—maybe an island somewhere.

But she knew her son wasn't going to be happy leaving behind his new family. And Larissa could never live without her son.

"I don't want to live my mother's life, Jake," she said quietly.

"You don't have any family to disown you," he said.

Nice of him to point that out. She wrapped her arms around her waist and hugged tightly. "I have Peter."

"We have Peter," he said.

"We don't have anything except a media blitz between us."

He cursed under his breath. One of his less flattering habits was that tendency of his to curse when she made him mad. She made a mental note to lecture him on that at a later time.

He pulled the car to the side of the road and turned to face her. "I'm not sure what you want from me."

"Courtesy would be a nice start."

"I'm not being rude."

"Well, I don't understand these one-word answers."

"I can't be your best buddy, Larissa."

"Why not?"

"Because we're living together and I want that to be real. And you don't."

"It's not that I don't want it to be real."

"Then what is it?"

"What if I start believing this is real and you decide that I'm not the right woman for you to spend your life with."

"I'm not that flaky, Rissa. I know my mind."

"Right now you think you do because of Peter."

"Woman, are you trying to drive me insane?"

"No, I'm not. I just don't want to end up like my mom did."

"Alone?"

"Yeah, alone."

"Where was your dad?"

She took a deep breath and looked into Jake's eyes. There was no way she wanted to get into this conversation with him. But she wasn't prepared to spend the rest of her life or the rest of the weekend with Jake while he gave her the cold shoulder.

Taking a deep breath, she said, "I don't have one."

Eight

"No dad? I don't understand," Jake said. He rubbed the bridge of his nose with two fingers and tried to assemble everything she'd told him of her past. He knew she'd had a rough childhood and he didn't really want to be responsible for her having to relive it now. But he had to understand her.

He hadn't been able to sleep last night and his future evenings looked just as restless unless she gave up her idea of a platonic marriage. The only idea he'd had that might work was keeping a distance between them, but even that was next to impossible.

"Explain it to me," he said at last. She was seated next to him in a pretty pink dress that made her eyes seem even bluer. With her blond hair free around her shoulders she looked too feminine for him. Too soft and gentle and he was very afraid that his baser instincts would overwhelm him, despite his mother's best efforts to make him into a gentleman.

"There's not much to say. My mom trapped herself a husband, but Reilly wasn't interested in being a dad, so he refused to have any contact with me. When I was four, he ran off with his secretary, leaving us nothing."

"I'm sorry, Larissa. But I don't see how our marriage resembles your mom's. I've already told you I don't feel trapped. We were both there the night Peter was conceived."

She smiled at him—the first time she'd done so today, and though he knew he shouldn't let it, he felt that smile all the way to his soul. It made him feel bigger than he was—like a man who wasn't a disappointment to his dad. A man who hadn't spent most of his adult life dodging responsibility. A man who could be hers for the rest of his life.

"Thanks."

"You're welcome. Do you feel better now?" he asked.

She shrugged and glanced out the window of the car. Jake leaned back in the seat and thought about all Larissa had told him. He suspected she was leaving out some very important details. He realized suddenly that perhaps her own father's treatment of her had influenced her decision not to tell him about Peter.

"You kept Peter a secret because you thought I'd treat him the way your dad did you," he said.

She turned to look at him, but she didn't say anything. Her silence confirmed his suspicion. This was why he'd never dated a woman for too long. He knew he wasn't good at building relationships.

"I'd never hurt our son," he said at last. He meant it too. Realizing that made him doubt he should continue with his custody suit. Because the one thing that would really hurt Peter was not having Larissa in his life. And though he justified his suit as insurance that Larissa could never cut him out of their lives again, he knew it was more about payback. Suddenly payback didn't seem justifiable. He'd keep it on the back burner if this marriage didn't work out.

Larissa bit her lower lip, tears glittering in her eyes. "I know that. Believe me, Jake, I wouldn't have made love with you that night if I thought you were anything like Reilly was."

He should put the car back in gear and do what Nicola had suggested this morning before they left— pretend they were actors and show the world a couple in love. Jake knew he was going to have no problem pretending to be in lust with Larissa. His real problem was going to be remembering it was a charade.

"Then what did you mean by not wanting to end up like your mom?"

"Just that Reilly resented her."

"I don't resent you," he said, drawing his finger down the side of her neck. She shivered under his touch and leaned just the tiniest bit closer to him.

He leaned down and kissed the base of her neck. She trembled under his touch, her fingers coming to hold his head. He glanced up at her. Her eyes were closed and she held him with a fierceness he knew she'd deny.

They were both masters of hiding. But he didn't intend to let her hide anymore. She didn't want a platonic relationship with him and they both knew it.

He raked his teeth down the column of her neck and she moaned deep in her throat. He felt the vibrations against his lips.

"This is crazy," she said.

"This is right," he said, pulling her more fully into his arms. She wedged her hands between them and pushed away slightly.

"What now?"

"We said we'd try to keep this nonsexual."

"God, woman, how many times are you going to bring that up? I think it's obvious we're fighting a losing battle."

"I know."

"Then why'd you bring it up?"

She took a deep breath. "Because I'm not the type of woman who is going to make a good Danforth wife."

"Why not?"

"You need someone of your own class. Someone who comes from money and is used to eating on bone china and drinking from Waterford crystal glasses."

"I don't live like that."

"No, but your family does. And they're going to realize I'm not worthy of the Danforth name."

"I'm not sure I'm worthy of the name. But it's mine and once we're married it'll be yours. I don't want to hear any more about it from you."

"Yes, sir," she said.

"Woman," he growled at her.

She laughed. It made him feel lighter in that moment than he'd have thought possible. The more he learned of Larissa's childhood, the more he understood why she'd kept Peter a secret. Understanding wasn't the same as forgiving, though.

"Now, let's get back on the road. I don't want to miss our flight," he said, putting the car in gear.

"Want a drink?" Jake asked once they were seated on the plane in Atlanta. There hadn't been a direct flight to Vegas from Savannah.

"Yes, something strong."

"Still wigged out from the landing of our flight from Savannah?" he asked, waving the flight attendant over to them.

"I'd like to say no," she said.

He ordered two bottles of Corona. He handed her

one and Larissa played with the lime and bottle while other passengers filed past them, taking their seats.

"It felt like we were on a roller coaster. I hate roller coasters," she said.

"I love 'em," he said, tilting his bottle back and taking a long drag.

Was there a better example of all that was different between them? "You would. I'm not like that."

"Like what?"

She thought about it for a minute. "Adventurous."

"I'd disagree with that. In some settings you are extremely adventurous."

"Which ones?" she said.

He leaned closer to her. His spicy cologne surrounded her and then she felt his breath brush against her cheek. "Intimate ones."

She gave him a secret smile. Every time she was convinced they were an ill-suited match, this physical spark flamed back to life. There was a bond between them that went way beyond being parents to Peter, and touched on her secret fear of depending too strongly on this man.

"Drink your beer before I decide to test that adventurous spirit," he warned.

She took a sip of her beer and threw caution to the winds. "What if want to take that test?"

"You don't. Platonic friendship, remember?" he asked.

"Hoisted on my own petard," she said. She wondered if she'd merely issued Jake a challenge by insisting on a platonic marriage—a challenge he'd be helpless to resist. She knew him well enough to know he liked to win. Was that why she'd done it? So she could say he'd seduced her into changing her mind? So she could blame him if things went wrong?

She didn't dwell on that too closely, because it made her the worst kind of manipulator. She was only fooling herself. Jake wanted her and had made no bones about it. She was the one attempting to play it safe…and failing miserably.

"Indeed. Changed your mind?"

Time for honesty, Larissa. "About a dozen times but I always come back to the same decision."

"No sex?" He arched an eyebrow at her.

If she changed her mind it would make this ache deep inside her go away. For a little while, things would seem fine between them, but she suspected in the end she'd end up with a bigger ache. "Yes," she said quietly.

He finished off his beer. "In that case I'd better find something to distract me."

She took a sip of her beer and pulled the SkyMall catalogue from the pocket in front of her. Their time in the air passed quickly.

"The pilot has turned on the fasten-seat-belt sign signaling our descent into the McCarran International Airport."

Larissa nervously gripped her armrest. Once the

plane landed, everything would be out of her control. Jake had worked on his laptop through most of the flight. He'd scheduled a meeting for late this afternoon with the Vegas D&D's. She was a little in awe of his business persona. It was nothing like the frat boy she'd known in their college days or the man she'd come to know since Jasmine Carmody had forced them back into each other's lives.

He put his hand over hers on the armrest and pried her fingers free. "Nervous?"

"Yes."

"Don't be. I'm right here and I won't let anything happen to you," he promised. Lifting her hand to his lips, he brushed a soft kiss against her knuckles.

She bit her lip and looked away from him and out the window. That was the problem. Jake was here and she wanted to believe it was forever. It was getting harder and harder to remember that he was here because his family had forced him to marry her to save face.

He'd been solicitous during their flight—friendlier than he'd been in the car on their way to the airport. She'd been tempted to lift the armrest and scoot as close to him as she could, to rest her head on his shoulder while he worked. She wanted to pretend for a minute that they were really going to Vegas to marry because they couldn't bear not being man and wife any longer.

But she knew the truth and that knowledge had

kept the armrest firmly in place and her head on the back of the leather first-class seat.

He lifted the armrest and tugged her against his side. Leaning close to her, he whispered, "'The woods are lovely, dark and deep.'

She glanced up at him. God, this felt too right. Too good. But for this moment, while the plane was landing, she wasn't going to pull away. She was going to stay close to the only man she'd ever trusted and repeated the words of their poem to.

Together they recited the rest of Frost's poem. The last line echoed in her head...*miles to go before I sleep.* She'd felt alone on her journey for so long. But as she glanced up at Jake and saw him watching her with those brown eyes of his, she didn't feel alone anymore.

And in her heart she knew she'd never be the same. Because Jake wasn't just the right man to fix the mess Jasmine Carmody's report would create, he was the right man to fill the emptiness in her soul.

Every time he thought he had Larissa figured out, she did something that made him realize he didn't. He'd meant to keep his distance from her, but he'd been unable to. In all the years he'd known Larissa, he'd never realized how much of herself she kept from the world, and especially from him.

The one thing she'd never tried to hide was how much their son meant to her, and he had a few doubts about the wisdom of continuing with his plan to sue for full custody of Peter.

Larissa started to pull out of his arms when the plane pulled up to the gate. He stopped her with a quick kiss. She smiled up at him and he felt it in his groin. He didn't know if he could keep up the dual life that they'd decided on. Public touching and kissing, private hands-off.

Yet, she'd said again today she wasn't ready to make love with him. And he wasn't going to push her. He was going to sit back and let fate direct him. Hell, no, he wasn't. He was going to do his damnedest to make sure she came to the same conclusion he already had.

"Nicola has arranged for a reporter to meet us here."

"Jasmine Carmody?"

"No. Another one who will write up a piece about how in love we are and how circumstances kept us apart."

"What circumstances?" she asked.

"My traveling, your job. We'll be vague. The important thing is to appear totally in love."

"Totally?"

"Yes," he said. Nicola had said nothing about appearing to be in love, but Jake wanted to know what it would be like to have Larissa look at him with complete devotion.

"I'm not sure I can do this."

"Too late to back out," he said.

"I won't leave you hanging, Jake. That was just nerves."

"Would it be so hard to love me?" he asked.

She bit her lower lip and closed her eyes. They were so close she was still in his arms, but he felt a gulf open between them. He felt the space that Larissa used to protect herself from relationships open up. He felt her backing away and did the only thing he could think of to pull her back to him.

Storm her barricades. Lay siege to the fortress that was her body and win the battle. He brushed his lips back and forth over hers. "Don't fight it," he whispered.

"Fight what?" she asked, against his mouth.

"This," he said, angling his head and taking her mouth the way he wanted to take her body. With long thrusts of his tongue. Claiming every inch of her mouth with his own.

She opened for him and he felt her capitulation. This was the one place where they communicated with total honesty. Seducing her with tender pulls of her lips, he pushed his own hammering desires to the back burner and strove for patience.

He smoothed his hands down her back, bringing their chests together. Her heart hammered against his. She felt small and fragile in his arms.

Lord, she tasted better than he remembered. It felt like it had been years since he'd last held her like this. Then the dynamic of the kiss changed. Larissa lifted her hands to frame his face and tasted him with long, slow kisses.

Dammit, he was the one in control, he thought. But as she scraped the edges of her fingernails down the side of his neck, he gave up all pretense. He was putty in her hands.

Sliding his hands to her waist, he started to pull her onto his lap. He needed her over him now. He was hard and straining and he honestly didn't think he could wait another second to bury himself in her body.

"The captain has turned off the fasten-seat-belt sign, you are now free to gather your things and disembark."

Larissa jerked away from him. He cursed under his breath, dropping his head to his hands and breathing deeply to try to regain some control. He'd been ready to take her here in the damn airplane.

The other passengers began gathering their luggage and filling the aisle. There was no way he was going to be able to walk off the plane until he'd had a few minutes to forget about the incredible woman he'd just had in his lap.

He glanced over at her. She watched him with wide eyes that were full of confusion and possibly hope. She touched her lips gingerly.

"I'm not going to apologize," he said.

"Good. I'm not either."

He'd forgotten how sensual she was. Forgotten that night in Atlanta when he'd discovered that her passion for books and words extended to him as well. "I figured total lust would make better headlines than being in love."

"Good idea."

She gathered up her purse and unfastened her seat belt, preparing to stand. He put his hand on her arm, holding her in her seat.

"Aren't you ready to get off the plane?"

"No," he said.

She gave him a quizzical look. He gestured to his lap. Her eyes widened.

"I guess I do owe you an apology."

"Not on your life, Larissa."

She got that heavy-lidded look in her eyes and leaned toward him, but he held her back. "I'm an inch away from saying to hell with it and seeing if we can both squeeze in that rest room up there."

"Jake—"

He covered her lips with his fingers. "Not another word."

The last of the passengers filed by and Jake felt better under control. He picked up his briefcase and stood, keeping his hand on Larissa's elbow as they exited the plane.

She tugged her arm out from under his grip and took his hand. She slid her fingers through his. He glanced down at their joined hands and tried to not let it matter. Their holding hands shouldn't mean anything, but it did.

She trusted him. If she didn't want to admit that, it was fine with him. But he knew there was something between them now that hadn't been there before.

Nine

Larissa smoothed her hands down the sides of her simple wedding gown. She wasn't sure who had arranged for it, but there had been a small fortune in wedding gowns in the suite when Larissa had arrived. Jake had told her to pick one. He'd left her alone in the suite for the past four hours.

The hairdresser, makeup artist and photographer had arrived forty-five minutes ago and now she looked like someone she didn't recognize. Oh, God, what was she doing?

"Can I have a few minutes to myself?" she asked.

"Yes, ma'am." All three filed out of the room.

Larissa walked to the mirror staring at the woman

there. A woman who was sleek and sophisticated and not at all like the woman Larissa knew herself to be. She looked in the mirror like a woman suitable to be a Danforth wife.

She reached toward her reflection, touching the glass. This wasn't real. This was all pretend. Game face and all that.

But it felt real. It felt like the dreams she'd secretly harbored since she'd given birth to Peter. It's not real, she reminded herself again.

There was a rap on the door and Larissa went to answer it.

"Sorry, ma'am, but it's time to go upstairs for the ceremony."

She nodded. The hairdresser took the veil from her hands and placed it on her head. Tears burned the back of her eyes. She was alone with strangers, people paid to help take care of her because she had no family of her own to help with these moments. No mother to help her with her veil. No sisters to help pick out flowers or choose bridesmaid dresses. Just her. Alone. The way she'd always been.

The chapel was small and intimate. Jake stood at the front, talking to the photographer and Artie O'Neil, the reporter that Nicola had arranged to have write about their wedding.

Larissa tried to smile. Tried to pretend that this was what she wanted. That she was marrying a man who loved her. But she felt sick.

She turned and blindly ran down the hall. She heard voices and someone calling her name, but she didn't stop. She escaped through the fire exit and paused on the stairs.

She leaned back against the wall and wrapped her arms around her waist. She was crying. Crying for things that she'd never had. Crying for the dream that now seemed so childish and ridiculous. Crying for something that she'd never realized she wanted until now.

The door opened and she felt raw, exposed.

''Rissa, what's wrong?'' Jake asked softly.

She tried to swallow so she could speak, but she couldn't. She turned her head from him.

He closed the door and walked toward her. She put her hand up. ''Don't.''

He stopped and she tried to pull herself together. But her mind was filled with pictures of perfect families. The kind of family she'd been trying to create for Peter. What she wanted and what she would have were very different.

''Talk to me, baby. I don't know what you need.''

She didn't, either, and that was the problem. How was she going to be able to explain that she wanted something she'd never had? That today, when she was standing at the back of the chapel, she realized she wanted a mother? A real mother who would have noticed her daughter and not stayed mired in her own bitterness.

"I...I'm sorry."

Jake closed the gap between them and pulled her into his arms. "About what?"

She shrugged. When he held her like this she didn't want to leave. She wanted to believe the illusion they were presenting to the world was true. "This. Being so emotional."

Jake tipped her chin back and she stared up at him through the filmy lace of her veil. "A wedding is a big deal in a woman's life."

"What about a man's?" she asked.

"What?"

"Is this a big deal to you, Jake?" She should have kept her mouth shut, shouldn't have worried about what he was going to say, but she did. She didn't want him to answer unless he said the words her wounded heart needed to hear.

He pushed her veil up and smoothed it back away from her face. Without the barrier between them, his breath brushed her cheek and his eyes were very sincere. He leaned close to her and whispered, "You're the only woman I've ever asked to marry me. You know this is a big deal."

She sighed. She did know that. Jake was a good man. A good man who she was falling more and more in love with each moment she spent with him.

She realized suddenly that her tears had nothing to do with the family she'd never really had and everything with wanting Jake to marry her for love and not convenience.

He handed her a snowy handkerchief that bore his monogram. She wiped her face and saw the residue of the makeup she wore on it.

"I just felt so alone," she said.

"Well, you're not. We're in this together."

"Sorry I made a mess of my makeup."

"I don't care about that."

"You don't?"

"Rissa, you're the most beautiful woman I've ever seen."

Suddenly things didn't seem quite as desperate as they had earlier. "Thank you."

"You're welcome. Are you ready to get married now?"

She nodded. He gently kissed her forehead and lowered her veil once again. Then taking her hand firmly in his, he led her back to the chapel. When they exchanged vows, a part of her began to believe that Jake never would leave her.

Larissa smiled for the pictures after their wedding, and even though Jake knew that they were playacting, it felt real to him. A little too real, he thought uncomfortably. He'd always been a loner even though he'd been surrounded by siblings and cousins. There'd been a core part of himself he'd kept private. Larissa was the only person he'd ever let get a glimpse of it.

And now they were married. Jake moved away to have a few final words with the reporter.

Larissa was standing by herself. She'd clung tightly to his hand throughout the ceremony and he remembered promising her he'd help shoulder her burdens. He knew she didn't believe his words. But when he'd looked into her eyes and given her his vow, he'd realized he meant them. Legally she was his and there was a sense of rightness that accompanied that feeling.

Artie promised to send a rough draft of the article to Nicola for approval before his magazine printed it. Soon they were alone. Just him and his bride. The primitive part of Jake's soul was ready to claim her. To throw her over his shoulder and carry her upstairs and push aside her doubts. To prove to her that she'd made the correct decision when she'd pledged her life to him.

But he'd been raised with more sophistication than that. He'd arranged for them to have dinner on the rooftop of the hotel. Away from the prying eyes of any reporters.

Away from the intimacy of their suite. He crossed the chapel to her side.

"What else do we have to do tonight?" she asked nervously. He knew she hadn't liked the public part of their wedding—the pictures that would be sent to magazines and newspapers, the questions that Artie had asked and they'd answered.

"Nothing. The evening is ours."

She flushed a little and licked her lips. God, she was making all his good intentions hard to carry out.

"I've got a surprise for you."

"Really? What is it?" she asked, tilting her head to the side. He noticed she did that when she was in a contemplative mood. What was going on in her head?

He wished he understood her better. But he was honest enough to admit understanding Larissa or any woman had never been a top priority.

"A secret that I think you'll like. Now close your eyes and follow me."

"Okay."

He took her hand and led her to the elevator. He used the passkey he'd gotten from the casino manager to access the rooftop. When the doors opened, he pocketed the key and lifted Larissa into his arms. He walked to the table surrounded by candles and string lights. He set her on her feet.

"Open your eyes."

Larissa looked around at the romantic setting. A dining tent had been set up on the roof. It was draped in sheer gossamer fabric and lights twinkled from underneath it. She saw a table set for two. Beyond the dining area, the night sky was bright with the lights of the Vegas strip. But the smooth sounds of Jimmy Buffett poured from the speakers.

"Stars Fell on Alabama" was playing. It was their

song. The song they'd danced to at the reunion on the night they'd made love.

Jake led her under the canopy and they were secluded from the world. She felt that she was the wrong woman in the wrong place. This was a romantic dream and not at all anything that practical Larissa Nielsen had ever experienced. But she wasn't Larissa Nielsen anymore. She was Larissa Danforth. And maybe romance was what she needed.

"Dance?" he asked.

She nodded and he pulled her into his arms. Her head fell to his shoulder and he danced her around the rooftop. "It feels like a lifetime since that night," he said.

Jimmy Buffet sang...*did it really happen?* And it was a question that Jake had asked himself many times since he'd last made love to her. The memory of it was so vivid and so real, and yet unbelievable.

"I was so nervous about dancing with you," she confessed.

"Why?"

"Because you're a good dancer and I'm not."

"I didn't notice that."

"I didn't either. Once you took me in your arms, all my worries dropped away. It was...magical."

He didn't say anything, but he'd felt the same way. It had been a magical night. A moment out of time to be treasured for always. He lowered his head and dropped nibbling kiss down the side of her neck. She sighed and tipped her head to the side to give him greater access.

He sucked lightly at the pulse beating strongly at the base of her neck. She shivered in his arms. He soothed her with languid strokes of his hands down her back.

She pushed her fingers into his hair and pulled his head down to hers. Raising on tiptoe, she kissed him. Her lips moved over his with intent, arousing in him a need that had never been sated.

He wanted to let her take the lead so that later on there'd be no question of him seducing her. But he couldn't just stand there. He stopped dancing and lifted her in his arms with his hands on her buttocks and thrust his tongue deeply into her mouth.

He craved her. He doubted that anything less than total surrender would satisfy the ache that kept growing inside him.

She pulled back, gasping for breath and watching him with wide eyes. He dropped his hands and stepped away from her, clenching his fists at his side.

"Let's eat."

"Jake?"

"Not right now, Larissa. Food, first."

"I don't want food."

He paused and glanced over at her. "What do you want?"

"You," she said, and walked toward him purposefully.

* * *

Blood rushed through his veins, pooling in his groin as she walked closer. He staggered back and had to sit down on one of the dining chairs. He'd expected to have to woo her slowly. He had, in fact, arranged for total privacy for them on the rooftop by asking the hotel staff to wait for his request before coming upstairs.

She continued toward him, a smile spreading over her face. The music still played in the background— no longer Jimmy Buffett but some smooth-sounding classic jazz. Miles Davis. Not an artist that was his favorite but one that he knew Larissa loved.

She paused. "Miles Davis?"

He nodded.

"How'd you know?"

"Woman, you've got about fifteen different CDs of his."

"You're observant."

Only when something mattered, he thought. And Larissa mattered to him in ways he was only beginning to explore.

"I like that," she said, still moving toward him slowly.

"Good." He stood and crossed the small space between them in two strides. It had been an eternity since he'd last held her in his arms.

He'd been aroused since they'd stepped off the plane and no amount of work, exercise or cold showers had dulled it.

Her mouth opened under his and he told himself to take it slow, but slow wasn't in his programming with this woman. She was pure temptation. He slid his hands down her back, pulling the zipper of her dress down at the same time.

Her bodice loosened, and from his angle looking down at her, he could see the tops of her breasts and the barest hint of her nipples. He lowered his head, using his teeth to pull the loosened fabric away from her skin.

She wore a demure cotton bra under her wedding dress and that simple undergarment made something clench deep inside him. Her nipples stood out against the plain fabric. He ran the tip of one fingertip around her aroused flesh. She trembled in his arms.

He undid the front clasp of her bra and brushed the cups away. Lowering his head, he took one of her nipples in his mouth and suckled her. She gasped his name and held him to her with a strength that surprised him. He pulled back and blew lightly on her skin.

She shivered and tried to direct his attention to her other nipple, but he held back. Knowing that his control would shatter at any moment, he wanted to savor this feeling of anticipation while he still could.

Her other nipple pouted for his attention, growing harder under his stare. He lifted one hand to touch her and saw the differences between them. His hand was huge and her breast small, smooth...flawless.

He cupped her breast, rubbing her nipple with the palm of his hand. Rissa tilted her head back, her hands still clutching at his head. Her mouth opened and he heard her moan his name.

He took that other nipple in his mouth. Teased her with his tongue and then the edge of his teeth, scraping carefully against the nubby texture.

Her fingers drifted down his back and then slid around front to work on the buttons of his shirt. She took a half step back and pushed his shirt open. She growled deep in her throat and leaned forward to brush kisses against his chest.

He continued caressing her breasts until they were full and her nipples prominent. He slid his hands down her smooth skin. Everywhere he touched he wanted to linger, but tonight wasn't for extended love-making. They had been apart too long.

She bit and nibbled at his chest. His groin hardened so painfully, he could take his pulse between his legs. He felt like her plaything. He wanted to lie back and let her have her way with him. But there was no room here.

He pulled her to him and lifted her slightly so that her nipples brushed his chest. Holding her carefully, he rotated his shoulders and rubbed against her. Blood roared in his ear. He was so hard, so full that he needed to be inside of her body *now*.

Impatient with the yards of satin pooling at her hips and down to her toes, he shoved them up and out of his way. He caressed the long length of her thighs. She was so soft. She moaned as he neared her center and then sighed when he brushed his fingertips across the front of her panties.

The cotton was warm and wet. He slipped one finger under the material and hesitated for a second, looking down into her eyes.

Her eyes were lidded. She bit down on her lower lip and he felt the minute movements of her hips as she tried to move his touch where she needed it.

He was beyond teasing her or prolonging their torture. He pushed her panties aside and plunged two fingers into her humid body. She squirmed against him.

He lifted her and crossed to the table in two long strides. He sank to the chair and pulled Larissa over his lap.

He turned Larissa in his arms. "What are you doing?" she asked.

"Trust me," he said.

She murmured something he didn't catch.

"Rissa?"

"Yes, Jake. I trust you."

He guided her hands to his shoulders. "Hold on."

Reaching between their bodies he freed his erection and then pushed the satin of her skirt to her waist. He held her hips in his hands. She was soft and womanly. Their naked loins pressed together and he shook under the impact.

He had to have her. Now. She was naked to the waist and he used one hand to pluck at her aroused nipples, the other testing the readiness of her desire for him. He found her wet and ready. He adjusted his hold on her hips and then entered her with one long, hard stroke.

She moaned his name and her head fell forward, leaving the curve of her neck open and vulnerable to him. He bit softly at her neck and felt the reaction all the way to his toes when she squirmed in his arms and thrust her hips toward him.

A tingling started in the base of his spine and he knew his climax was close. But he wasn't going without Larissa. He wanted her with him. He caressed her stomach and her breasts. Whispered erotic words of praise and longing in her ears.

She moved more frantically in his arms and he thrust into her deeply with each stroke. Breathing through his mouth, he tried to hold back the inevitable. He slid one hand down her abdomen, through the slick folds of her sex, finding her center. He stroked the aroused flesh. She continued to writhe in his arms no closer to her climax than before.

He circled that aroused bit of flesh between her legs with his forefinger, then tickled it very carefully with his nail. She screamed his name and tightened around him. Jake pulled one hand from her body and locked his fingers on her hips, holding her still for his thrusts.

He penetrated her as deeply as he could. Suckling at the base of her neck, he came long and hard.

He held her carefully in his arms and cradled her to him.

This marriage that had started out as a media Band-Aid had just become very real. And Jake didn't know whether he liked that or not.

Ten

Aftershocks of pleasure still rocked her body. She closed her eyes and leaned fully into him. Jake held her with a strength that scared her. *What had she done?*

He was big and strong and more man than she'd ever known—the only man who'd ever seen the real Larissa and now she was his wife. And she wanted it to last forever. Not just until Abe Danforth won or lost his senate bid.

Forever…that elusive thing had always been just out of her grasp. She had Peter, but in her heart she knew one day he'd leave her as well. But Jake had never been hers and she had the feeling he never would need her as deeply as she needed him.

This couldn't happen again. And yet she didn't know if she'd be able to keep her hands to herself. One time wasn't enough. She still wanted him. She hadn't gotten to explore his body and relearn his shape. She doubted a lifetime would be long enough for that.

Her cheek rested on his shoulder and she never wanted to leave the circle of his arms. If only this moment could last forever.

''Well, Mrs. Danforth.'' Jake sounded much too pleased with himself.

He idly stroked her back and the hair on his chest tickled her nipples. She didn't want to want him again. She wanted him out of her system so she could move on with her life. A life that had been disrupted by him and the emotions he evoked in her.

''Well what?'' she asked, lowering her head and nipping his pec. The muscle flexed under her mouth and she traced a random pattern with her tongue. He tasted good. Salty and masculine like only Jake did.

He cupped her jaw and tilted her face up to his. His nostrils flared with each breath he took and she knew he was reaching the point of no return. She was already there. Her center was dewy and her body ached to be taken by him again. To have him fill her until she couldn't think of anything but the pleasure he gave her.

She licked her lips, tasting him on her. He leaned

down and spoke directly into her ear. "That was a nice appetizer. But I'm hungry for more of you."

Her heartbeat sped up and everything feminine in her melted. The night breeze was cool and she shivered as it brushed over her aroused body.

Her mind said to step away from him but her body ignored that advice. This was her wedding night and likely the only one she'd ever have. She'd face the consequences of this night tomorrow.

She rubbed her nipples against his chest and tugged his head down to hers. His pupils dilated and his breath came in short pants. His erection pressed urgently against her and she doubted they were going to make it off the rooftop tonight.

He thrust against her and groaned as he encountered layers of skirt. "Damn. I want you naked."

"Me, too," she said, bathing his chest with kisses. She slid off his lap and lowered herself to her knees in front of the chair. She took his hard length in her hands.

He held himself still. His hands in her hair moved in circles and his hips thrust toward her the slightest bit. She knew what he wanted. What she wanted. Taking his buttocks in her hands, she drew him forward until the tip of him brushed her lips. She breathed against him and heard him groan.

She tasted him with delicate licks, then took the tip into her mouth. He shuddered. She felt his hands tighten in her hair and he pulled her to her feet. He fastened his pants with quick, careful movements, then refastened her dress.

"We need a bed. Now."

"Yes," she said. Her voice was husky and barely recognizable to her own ears.

Scooping her up in his arms, he carried her across the rooftop to the elevator. "There's a key car in my pants pocket."

She fished around for it, deliberately fondling him before she found the key. He staggered back against the wall and she knew she was playing with fire. He took her mouth in a kiss that demonstrated his dominance. It was deep and carnal and left her quivering in his arms. The elevator car opened and he carried her inside.

"Push the button," he ordered.

She did. The ride was mercifully short and soon they were in their suite. Jake carried her to the king-size bed and put her on her feet beside it.

His fingers made quick work of the zipper running down her back and her dress slid from her body, pooling at her feet in a sea of white satin. Jake stood there watching her. Her breasts were full and heavy, her nipples stood taut and ready for his touch. Her panties were long gone and her thigh-high hose were her only garments.

"Get on the bed," he said.

She stepped delicately out of her dress and turned slowly to crawl up the bed. She heard him growl deep in his throat and then felt his warm hand on her ankle. He tugged her flat.

"Don't move," he said.

She heard the sounds of him disrobing and then felt his naked body pressed along her back. She was completely surrounded by him. He held her like that for long minutes. His hands sweeping down her sides, his fingers reaching under her body to tweak her nipples.

He turned her over and sat back on his haunches watching her. He ran his forefinger down the center of her body. Helplessly she watched her sensitized skin grow rosy under his touch and when he skirted the curls at the apex of her thighs, she moaned softly.

He gave her a wicked smile but continued his path toward her feet. He reached her ankles and chained each one in his loose grasp. Then he slowly pushed her legs back toward her body. She felt totally exposed and vulnerable. And more turned-on than she'd ever remembered being.

He slid up her body, lowering his head he tasted her hot center with his lips and tongue. His hands left her ankles and he reached up to fondle both breasts.

He rubbed and pinched her nipples until her breasts felt too heavy, too full. She needed him. His mouth on her most feminine flesh was driving her toward orgasm, but she wanted Jake's body over hers. She wanted to watch his eyes as he took her and experienced a shared climax.

"Jake," she said, pulling on his hair.

"Come for me, Rissa."

"I want us to be together."

"We will…later. Please."

She couldn't deny him or her body. She rubbed her hands against his scalp and waited for his intimate touch. His breath brushed her first and then his tongue. His slid his hands down her body, gripping her hips and maneuvering her so that he had greater access to her secrets. He thrust one blunt finger into her channel and she clenched around it. He teased her with that one long finger, reaching up and pressing on a spot beneath her pubic bone. He continued to tickle the nubbin between her legs with his tongue and the twin pressures on her forced her over the edge. Her climax was intense and powerful but still she wanted more. She needed Jake.

He moved up over and held her still. He entered her with one long deep thrust. "Ah, that's it."

He penetrated her so deeply she felt they really were becoming one being. She lifted herself, tugged his head down to hers and took his mouth the way he took her body. He tore his mouth from hers as his thrusts increased. He lowered his head and suckled on one of her breasts and she felt a change come over him seconds before he flooded her with his release. Her own followed closely and she held him to her with a desperation she'd deny in the morning.

* * *

Jake ordered breakfast while Larissa showered the next morning. The night before had put to rest any doubts he had about making their marriage a real one. He wasn't sure what had changed her mind about keeping their marriage platonic, and frankly didn't care. He was starting to feel he and Larissa had a real chance at happiness, and that scared him.

But he was willing to do his duty this time. With a wry grin, he realized that duty had never felt so good. Slowly he was beginning to trust Larissa again. He understood now why she'd kept Peter a secret.

He picked up the phone and dialed Marcus's office. It was time to stop his bid to win full custody of Peter. Marcus had handed the paternity suit off to Ted Larson, one of his co-workers who specialized in family law. Jake got Ted's voice mail. He left his name and the number at the hotel for a return call.

The bathroom door opened and Larissa walked across the room to her suitcase. She wore a hotel bathrobe and a towel turbaned on her head. She looked cute and sexy at the same time.

"Come over here, woman," he said.

She gave him a haughty look over her shoulder. "You gave enough orders last night."

He had. And she'd responded to them beautifully. "I'm ready to take them," he said.

"I'll bet you are."

She rummaged through her clothes, selecting a

pretty sundress and undergarments. She headed back toward the bathroom with her clothes.

"Where are you going?" he asked.

"In there to change."

"You can change here. I'll be a good boy and keep my hands to myself."

"Well, that's kind of why I was going back in the bathroom."

"You don't want me to keep my hands to myself? No problem, Rissa." He stood up and walked toward her.

"Stop, Jake. I need to talk to you."

He didn't like the sound of that.

"About what?"

"Our intimate relations."

Sometimes you could tell Larissa was a librarian. "You mean our sex life."

"Yes. I think I gave you the wrong impression last night."

"No, you didn't, sweetheart," he said. Last night had been raw and earthy. He crossed to her and took her in his arms. "I still respect you."

"Oh, Jake. Not about that. I...I want to stick by our original agreement."

"Which one?" he asked.

She sighed and tilted her head to the side as she looked up at him. "The platonic one."

He cursed under his breath and stepped away from

her. The woman was trying to drive him insane. "Why?"

"Because sex makes things complicated. I'm sorry, I should have spoken up sooner, but I wanted a wedding night to remember."

"Good. I did, too. But this doesn't have to end."

"Yes it does."

"Explain it to me," he said.

"This wasn't real. The wedding, the setting, the dress. Everything was playacting."

"It felt real to me when I took those vows that made you my wife."

She blanched and looked away from him. "Me, too."

"Baby, I'm not like your dad. I'm not going to do to Peter what he did to you."

She wrapped her arms around her waist, holding herself so tightly that he knew he wasn't saying the right thing. Hell, he had no idea what the right words were. It was like being in virgin territory; he knew how to seduce Larissa into his bed, but he had no clue how to keep her there.

"I'm waiting to hear you say you know I won't hurt Peter."

"Of course I know that, Jake. The first time I saw you with him, I knew I'd cheated both of you out of something."

"Then what's the problem?"

"Me," she said, softly. "I'm the problem."

"You know I won't hurt you."

"What if I hurt you?"

"I'm not that fragile," he said. What kind of wimp did she think he was?

"That's what I was afraid of."

"I'm not following."

"I can't hurt you because I'm nothing more than a make-believe wife to you. You don't care for me."

"Don't put words in my mouth. I care for you more than I do any other woman."

"Right now."

"Larissa, there are no guarantees in life. You know that and so do I. I'm not sure what you think you're going to achieve by not sleeping with me."

"I'm trying to keep from falling in love with you, idiot. I don't want to be vulnerable to any man."

"I'm not just any man, Larissa. I'm your husband."

She shook her head and turned away. There was a knock on the door and Jake didn't move to answer it. He wanted to hash this out to a conclusion, but Larissa was already retreating behind that wall of icy cool that she used to keep him out. "Room service," they both heard from the door.

"This isn't over," he warned as he exited the bedroom.

Larissa was dressed by the time Jake returned. She'd clipped up her hair and was fastening her sandals when he walked back into the room.

"In a hurry?" he asked.

"No. I just didn't want…"

"To appear weak," he said. Cursing under his breath he stalked to his suitcase and removed his clothing for the day.

"Go eat, Larissa," he said without looking at her.

She stood in the doorway. "Didn't you want to finish our conversation?"

He gave a derisive snort. "No. I don't think so. I've had enough of trying to convince you I'm respectable." He walked away from her without a backward glance.

She shivered and rubbed her hands over her arms, feeling colder and more alone than ever. She'd expected Jake to say many things when she told him she wanted to stop sleeping with him. But she hadn't anticipated the depth of his anger.

She picked at the breakfast he'd ordered for them, but could only manage drinking the coffee. The phone rang and she answered it.

"Jacob Danforth please," a male voice said.

"One moment. Can I tell him who's calling?"

"Ted Larson."

Larissa set the handset on the table and crossed their suite to the bathroom door. The shower had stopped. She rapped on the door and Jake opened it, shaving cream on his face and a white towel slung low around his lean hips.

She swallowed. His hair was damp and a bead of

moisture trailed down his neck to his chest. Unconsciously she lifted her hand to catch the drop. Jake caught her hand in his and held her captive. She glanced up into his eyes.

She could read nothing in his gaze. Had she just made the biggest mistake of her life by demanding a celibate marriage with this man?

"Change your mind already?" he asked.

Sometimes it was as if he could see straight to her soul. Had she changed her mind? It would be so easy to loose herself in the web of sensuality that Jake created, but in the end, she knew she'd have a tough time moving on when he was tired of her. And Jake had never stayed with one woman too long.

She shook herself. "You have a call."

He rubbed her hand over his chest before letting it drop. She flexed her fingers, raking her nails over his skin. His towel stirred. She wanted to stay. What had she been thinking to put the brakes on this? "Take a message for me."

Her hand tingled and her body said her mind was on the verge of insanity. She couldn't live with Jake and not be his woman. "Okay."

She pivoted on her heel, but her legs were weak and she didn't know if she was going to be able to walk away from him.

"Rissa?"

She glanced over her shoulder at him. "Yes?"

"You never answered my question."

"I'm afraid to," she said, and walked away, firmly closing the bedroom door behind her. She needed to regain her perspective. She needed to talk to her son. She missed him. She'd talked to him right before the ceremony yesterday.

She took a message from Mr. Larson and left the note on Jake's briefcase. She dialed the number to Jake's parents' house. The housekeeper answered on the third ring.

"This is Larissa Nielsen…Danforth. May I speak to Peter?"

"Just a moment, ma'am."

"Hi, Mama."

Tears burned the back of her eyes. God, she missed him. They'd never been apart before this. "Hey, baby. I miss you."

"Me, too. I'm having so much fun here. I'm going to see some horses today."

Peter's happiness was palpable on the phone. Realizing she'd given her son something he never should have been denied made all the sacrifices worth it. She had to remember her marriage to Jake was for Peter. It wasn't for her and it certainly wasn't for Jake. "Good."

"When will you be home?" he asked.

Larissa wasn't sure of the exact time since Jake had their tickets but he'd said some time this evening. "Before bedtime."

"I love you, Mama."

"Love you too."

They said their goodbyes and she talked to Miranda briefly about what time to expect them. It felt weird to be discussing her son with someone else. She hung up and sat on the edge of the coffee table where she'd taken the call.

"You okay?" Jake asked from the doorway. He wore a pair of chinos and a shirt in a flattering shade of blue.

She nodded.

"Who was on the phone?"

"Ted Larson. I took his number for you. I called to check on Peter."

"How's he doing?"

"Great. They're going to see some horses today."

"That would be the stables near the house. Does he ride?"

"Jake, he's three."

"So?"

"No, he doesn't ride."

"We'll have to teach him," Jake said.

"Is this going to work?" she asked without thinking.

"Yes, Rissa, it is. I'm angry right now, but I'll get over it and we're going to work things out," he said, and there was a promise in his voice that she trusted.

"For Peter?"

Jake crossed the room to her side and tipped her head back with his knuckle under her chin. "For us."

Then he slipped away to make his phone call. She cautioned herself not to believe him but she couldn't help it. Hope had been born and she believed they had a chance at forever.

Eleven

"**O**h, no," Larissa said as they pulled to a stop in front of his town house a little before ten that night. Peter was sleeping fitfully in the back seat and Larissa had been in a quiet mood since they'd left Vegas.

"What's the matter?"

"I recognize that car," she said.

Jake waited.

"It's Jasmine Carmody. What's she doing here?"

Jake reached over and patted Larissa's hand. "Probably checking up to see if our marriage is a real one."

"Let's go to my place. We can hide out until she leaves."

"I'm not hiding from anyone. Especially a reporter."

"I guess you're right."

"Of course, I am."

Jake pulled into the driveway and shut off the car. Larissa nervously twisted her fingers together. "Calm down. We're in this together."

He leaned across the seat and brushed his lips over hers. She sighed into his mouth and he hesitated, then deepened the kiss. He'd decided in the shower this morning to let Larissa set the pace for their marriage. She had too much sensuality in her to keep them apart for long. And once he'd gotten past his frustration, he'd realized she had a good point. Sex between the two of them was a convenient way to avoid talking.

Hell, he'd been the first one to use it that night in Atlanta when they'd conceived their son.

"Ready?"

"I guess."

"Chin up, Rissa. We're a team now and I don't think one determined reporter can defeat us."

She smiled at him and he felt ten feet tall. He climbed out of the truck.

"Mr. Danforth, I'm Jasmine Carmody with the *Savannah Morning News*. Can I have a few minutes of your time?" the stunning African-American woman asked.

"For what?"

"To discuss the circumstances of your recent marriage."

"What do you want to know?" Jake asked.

Larissa got out of the truck and walked around to his side. Jake pulled her close to his side and dropped a kiss on her forehead.

"Very touching," Jasmine said. "I'm curious about something."

"What's that?" Jake asked.

"How does it feel to know you're the second generation of wealthy Southern gentlemen to be deceived by a Nielsen woman?"

Larissa stiffened under his arm.

"I didn't deceive Jake."

"Of course, you didn't, Ms. Nielsen."

"It's Mrs. Danforth," Jake said. "And Larissa didn't trap me into marriage, Ms. Carmody. I trapped her."

"Do tell," Jasmine said.

"That's private and personal. I don't think we have anything further to say."

"I'm not giving up," Jasmine said. "I'm going to write this story with or without your cooperation."

"Then write this—Larissa and I have been friends for over ten years and our marriage has brought us the kind of happiness neither of us thought possible."

Jake lowered his head and kissed Larissa, hoping she'd understand from his embrace that he meant those words. Their marriage wasn't a temporary media fix, as it had started out—it was real and lasting. Because with Larissa, he'd found a place in his family. And a family of his own.

Peter stirred in the back seat of the car, coughing and crying out. Jake opened the back door and lifted out his son.

"Where's Mama?"

"Right here, sweetie," Larissa said, rubbing her hand over their son's head.

Peter squirmed in Jake's arms, leaning over toward Larissa. Jake let the boy go though he didn't want to. Peter coughed again and Larissa cradled him close to her.

"We better get him inside," Larissa said.

Jake closed the door and put his arm around Larissa. Jasmine continued to watch them and Jake had the feeling that they hadn't seen the last of her. But it didn't change the way he felt. He wasn't going to let a reporter hurt Larissa. She'd carved out a life for herself the only way she knew how.

"I didn't think she'd find out about your dad."

"Reilly Peyton isn't my dad. He was a sperm donor."

Jake laughed. She didn't sound angry with Jasmine. "You're okay that she found out."

"I'd rather she hadn't. But when you came to my defense I realized something."

Peter coughed again and Larissa rubbed his back. "I hope he's not getting sick."

"I'll call the doctor when we get inside," Jake said. He knew he should focus on Peter, but in the back of his mind her words lingered. "What'd you realize?"

"That having you by my side made all the difference in the world. Even if she prints her article—and I'm sure she will—it won't be me standing in front of Savannah society by myself. We're a family and together we'll decide what makes us Danforths. I've never really felt like I could fit in at home, either."

"Why not?"

"My father put a lot of pressure on me to be the responsible one. That eldest sibling thing, I guess. I've dropped the ball a lot, Rissa. You know I'm not perfect, but I'm not going to drop the ball this time."

"I know, Jake," she said. She reached up to touch him with her free hand.

"Let's get this little guy into his pajamas and then finish this conversation," Jake said.

"Mama?" Peter said, his breath rasping in and out. His chest was heaving with the effort to breathe.

Jake didn't like it. "Has he done that before?"

"No. Call the doctor," Larissa said. Though she tried to keep her voice calm, he saw her hands tremble.

Jake grabbed one of Larissa's laminated index cards and dialed the doctor's number. Larissa sat on the couch holding their son close and murmuring softly to him. But Peter kept struggling to breathe and

Larissa finally stood up. She paced around the room with their son in her arms. Jake was suddenly afraid that now that he'd found the happiness he'd always sought, he wouldn't be allowed to keep it.

Jake got the doctor on the phone and described Peter's symptoms. Dr. Gold instructed Jake to take Peter to the hospital, saying he thought Peter might be having an acute asthma attack.

Jake got his family out of the house and into the car, his heart pounding as he raced to the hospital.

Larissa had never been so scared in her entire life. Peter was hooked up to a drip IV and a nebulizer. His entire chest heaved with each breath he tried to take.

She clung tight to her son's hand and willed him to breathe easier, but she knew that wasn't possible. Jake rested his big strong hand on her shoulder, and she sensed he was urging her to share her burden with him but she couldn't.

She wouldn't be able to relax until Peter was off this machine and breathing easier, though she appreciated having Jake and his family around her. And she knew that Peter did as well.

Tonight she'd had her first taste of what being a Danforth meant. Instead of sitting in the waiting area until it was their turn, they'd been given a private room and admitted with little trouble. Dr. Gold had seen Peter once and this was the second breathing treatment that Peter had taken.

Jake's parents had arrived and were now in the waiting area. Jake hadn't left her side the entire time. He held her hand or Peter's and made sure they were very aware of his presence.

He was a solid support for Larissa and she realized she loved him. Watching him talk quietly to their son, and handle every detail that came up in the hospital had shown her what she'd secretly been afraid to admit all along.

Jake wasn't just her husband, he was her love. She also realized, when he'd talked to his family, that Jake kept the depth of his feelings a secret. It was humbling to know she might be the only one who realized Jake was so much more than the easygoing, successful businessman that he presented to the world.

Peter finished his breathing treatment and lay back against the pillows. He looked so small. Jake tucked Mr. Bear and Peter's worn blanket up next to him. Larissa leaned down and kissed him.

"Mama? Can we say our poem?"

"We sure can, baby."

Quietly she started Frost's poem and Jake and Peter joined in. By the time they'd gotten to the last line, Peter's eyes drifted close.

Larissa turned to Jake. "I feel so helpless."

"Me too."

She felt like crying. When she'd made her decision

not to tell Jake about Peter, she'd only had Reilly Peyton as an example—a man who'd never wanted to be a father. But from the first moment Jake had known about Peter, he'd proved that fatherhood was a natural part of him.

"Why are you looking at me like that?" Jake asked.

She didn't want to let him know how desperately she was coming to need him. "Like what?"

He shrugged and looked uncomfortable. "I'm not sure."

She slid off the bed and sat on his lap. Wrapping her arms around him, she held him tightly to her. God, she didn't think she'd survive if he left her.

"Thank you," she said against his lips.

"For what?" he asked, running his hands down her back and hugging her to him.

He smelled good. His cologne was spicy and woodsy, a direct contrast to the sterile scent of the hospital. "For being here. I'm so glad I didn't have to deal with this on my own."

He looked at her. His brown eyes were serious and she remembered all the promises he'd made her. Promises that she'd been afraid to believe. "That's my job now."

"Are you sure?" she asked, still afraid to accept his words.

He squeezed her tight and then tucked her head

under his chin. "Hell, yes. I'm not letting either of you out of my sight."

"Oh, Jake."

Jake kissed her with a passion that she sensed concealed hidden depths. She clung to him. For the first time in her life she really needed someone by her side and it scared her. Almost as much as her fear of being left alone. She watched Peter sleeping. Each exhalation wheezed a little.

Someone cleared their throat and she glanced up to see Harold Danforth in the doorway. Jake's dad was dressed in chinos and a button-down shirt. He looked tired and tense but his face filled with love when he glanced at his sleeping grandson.

"No need to ask how things are in here," Harold said.

Jake stiffened under her. Larissa got to her feet and walked over to the hospital bed to check Peter. She rested her hand lightly on his chest to feel each breath he took. "You know me, Dad. Can't keep my hands off a pretty girl."

"I do know you, son," Harold said. There was a pride in his eyes that Larissa realized Jake didn't see.

"Your mom and I wanted to check on Peter before we went home for the night."

"He's sleeping," Jake said.

"I'll go get your mother," Harold said.

Jake cursed under his breath and pushed to his feet, joining Larissa by Peter's side. Jake settled his hand over hers on their son's chest. "God, I hope he beats this thing."

"Dr. Gold said there's a chance he could outgrow the asthma."

Jake said nothing, but Larissa felt some of her anxiety wane. She knew that with Jake by her side there was nothing they couldn't handle.

"What's up with you and your dad?"

"Nothing," Jake said, pacing across the room.

"Jake?" She turned to face him, but he wasn't paying the least bit of attention to her.

"Leave it be, Rissa."

She crossed the room to Jake and wrapped her arms around him.

"Talk to me," she said at last. She'd been so caught up in her own feelings of inadequacy that she hadn't noticed the tension between Jake and his father before.

"I don't want to get into that. You've got enough on your mind with Peter."

She tilted her head back and met his eyes. "Peter's resting now. Tell me about your dad."

"It's nothing," he said, moving away. It seemed he couldn't stand still. "I've never been able to please the old man."

She stopped his pacing with a hand on his arm. "I don't get that from him. He seems really proud of you." That was the truth. Harold had taken her aside earlier and told her when the chips were down there was no better man to have by her side than Jake.

"Yeah, right. What dad wouldn't be proud of a son who can't keep his hands off his wife while his grandson struggles to breathe?"

"I'm sure your dad understands that we need each other now."

Jake shrugged.

Larissa wasn't sure what else to say. She thought Harold was probably relieved that their marriage wasn't just for the media, but she didn't want to open that topic of conversation. "It wasn't like that. And I think your dad knows it. You should talk to him."

"I don't think so."

She raised herself on tiptoe so they were almost eye-to-eye. "Well, I do. I think you should do it. And I'm not going to stop bringing the subject up until you do."

"We've only been married two days and already you're nagging me."

For the first time since they arrived at the hospital she felt like smiling. "Start out as you mean to go on, I always say."

"Good thing I know how to keep you quiet."

"How?" she asked, smiling teasingly up at him.

"Like this," he said, lowering his head and taking her mouth in a kiss that said things he'd never say with words. That embrace said thank-you and I'll be there for you. She clung to his broad shoulders and kissed him with the same intensity.

When his parents returned to the room, he reluctantly let Larissa go. A storm raged inside him. He'd never felt so helpless as he had on the drive to the hospital. He was used to focusing on a goal and achieving it. And tonight had shown him that life with Larissa and Peter was going to be anything but predictable.

Since they'd landed back in Savannah, he'd realized that the only thing he wanted was some peace and quiet with his small family. He wanted what his folks had always had, but he didn't know that he was worthy of that kind of bond. He'd played around with women for so long that, even though Larissa made him feel things that he'd never experienced before, he wasn't sure he could be the kind of man she needed.

She moved across the room toward his mother and Jake wondered how Larissa felt about suddenly having an extended family. He wouldn't give up being a Danforth for anything, he realized.

"How's Peter doing?" his mom asked.

"Better. He's finally sleeping," Larissa said.

"I hope this attack wasn't brought on by anything at our house."

"I'm sure it wasn't, Miranda. He had a great time visiting with you."

"We enjoyed having him there. God, I miss having a little boy in the house."

Jake loved his parents, but he wanted them to go so he could hold Larissa in his lap again and keep an eye on both her and Peter. "It's been a long night."

"Yes, it has," his dad said.

"I'm thirsty, I think I'll go down to the vending machine and get a Diet Coke. Want to go with me, Miranda?" Larissa asked.

"Sure, dear. Do you want anything, Jake?"

"Coke would be great, Mom."

Larissa followed Miranda toward the door. At the entrance, she paused and looked at Jake. *Talk to your dad,* she mouthed. Bossy woman, he thought as she disappeared.

His father leaned over Peter, brushing back his hair. "He looks so much like you."

Jake crossed to the other side of the bed and leaned down over his son. "Yeah, he does."

"This takes me back. Remember that summer you broke your arm?"

"Do I. I couldn't play soccer for six weeks."

"That's right. You missed out on winning that MVP trophy you'd had your eye on."

"I got it the next year."

"You were always good at winning."

"Yes, I was."

"You okay, son?"

Jake shrugged. It didn't matter that he was over

thirty and owned a successful business. He still felt like a boy in his dad's presence. His father was a man who had it all and made it look easy. Not even the disappearance of his youngest sister, Victoria, had phased Harold. He'd still held the family together and kept everyone focused on finding her. Jake didn't think he'd ever be the man his father was.

"Having a kid is a double-edged sword," his dad said suddenly.

"What do you mean?"

"Just that you do your damnedest to protect them and then out of the blue something you can't control happens." His dad reached out and touched Peter's forehead. In that moment he saw on his father's face the same vulnerability that Jake felt toward his son.

"Like with Victoria," Jake said. He'd never really gotten over the guilt he'd felt at her disappearance. And he'd never shared with his dad the responsibility he bore toward the incident.

"Yes," his dad said, running his hands through his hair. "Good news on that front. The body in the attic at Crofthaven isn't hers."

Jake felt a sense of relief at the news. No one in the family had given any credence to the theory that the body had been Victoria's. They all knew she'd disappeared in Atlanta, not in Savannah. "I never believed it was."

"Me either. God, I wish I knew where she was," Harold said. Another crack appeared in Jake's image of his dad. His old man had always appeared so capable and confident. Jake hadn't realized that underneath was a man who had as many vulnerabilities as Jake had.

"Me too. You know I've never forgiven myself for not attending the concert with her. I shouldn't have bought her those tickets."

His dad gave him a sad smile. "You never could tell her no."

That was the truth. He'd loved having younger sisters who looked up to him. Jake had always been indulgent with the women in his life. "It scares me sometimes to think that I might screw up with Peter that way."

"I wish I could tell you it ends, son."

"It doesn't?"

"No."

"How do you do it, Dad?"

"I lean on your mom. That woman is the best thing that ever happened to me. And you kids...well you're extensions of her."

Jake looked at his dad and for once didn't feel like a failure. "I hope I'm half the dad you are."

"I know you will be."

Before he could respond, the women returned with some cold soft drinks and a couple of bags of snacks.

"How's Peter?" Larissa asked.

"Still sleeping," Jake said.

Larissa crossed to his side and slipped her arm

around his waist. He held her close and watched their son sleep. A moment later, he glanced across the bed at his dad.

His dad winked at him and for the first time, Jake felt like a man that his dad was proud to know.

Twelve

The next evening Peter was doing much better, but Dr. Gold wanted to keep him one more night for observation. Larissa was tired—she hadn't slept in more than twenty-four hours. She was emotionally drained. Jake's family was wonderful, but they could be a little overwhelming. Jake's sister Imogene had breezed in on her lunch break wearing a power suit and looking totally gorgeous. Larissa had felt unkempt and frumpy by comparison.

Though obviously a workaholic, Imogene had spent part of her lunch break sitting at Peter's side and reading to him. Jake's brother Toby had called and Peter had talked to him on the phone. Wes had stopped by with a new electronic game for Peter, and all and all her son had seemed as overwhelmed as she'd felt at having so many people care about them.

But they were alone now. Jake was outside talking with his dad. She wasn't sure what had happened last night, but she felt like all the superficial reasons she'd been using for keeping Jake at arm's length had disappeared. She wasn't protecting her heart, because it was too late to do so. She'd fallen in love with Jake a long time ago and now that they were married she couldn't stop her feelings from deepening.

Peter had wanted her to sleep next to him, so she'd crawled into the bed with her son. Peter slept quietly, resting his head on her arm. She bent close and listened to his breathing. It was deep and steady. Relief flooded her and she hugged his small body close.

"Hey, lady," Jake said from the doorway. "How's our boy doing?"

She glanced up at him and felt her heart jump in her chest. Damn he looked good. Tired but good. He had two days' worth of beard stubble on his cheeks and he'd never looked more attractive. Sensual awareness flooded her body. Not now, she thought—I'm doing the mom thing.

"He's resting now. We were watching SpongeBob before he fell asleep. A show that Peter informed me you said he could watch. Correct me if I'm wrong but SpongeBob wasn't on my index card of approved television shows."

''Really? I'm sure I saw it on there,'' Jake said with a sly grin.

Peter loved having a daddy and it was just as clear that Jake loved being one. Jake had spent just as much time as she had at the hospital. He'd played games with their son and made plans to go camping this weekend down in St. Augustine. Listening and watching the two of them had convinced Larissa that Jake was in their lives for good.

''I'm going to let it slide this time, but once he's out of the hospital we'll go back to our normal TV schedule.''

''Whatever you say, Larissa,'' he said in the bland tone that told her he was going to do whatever he thought was best for their son. She had to admit Peter had bloomed since Jake had come into his life. Her little boy had always been quiet and reserved. But lately he'd come out of his shell.

''Why do I get the feeling you're placating me?'' she asked.

He shrugged, but there was a sparkle in his eyes that told her he liked sparring with her. ''I don't know. You always were a smart woman—you tell me.''

She prided herself on her intelligence, which made it even harder to believe that she'd actually thought she could live with Jake and not be his lover. Now she just had to figure out a way to bring the topic up so he'd know she'd changed her mind.

"Did your parents go home?"

"Yes. Mom said they'll be back in the morning when Peter is released."

Jake stopped at the side of the bed and ran his fingertip down her bare arm. She must look a mess. She reached up to tuck a strand of hair behind her ear but Jake brushed her hand away. "Leave it alone. I like it when you don't look all tidy."

"It's safe to say I'm not tidy at this moment." She carefully pulled her arm out from under Peter's head and stood up. Jake didn't back up and they were pressed almost body to body.

"No, you're not."

"Neither are you," she said, running her hands over his rough jaw. He felt earthy against her soft fingers and she wished they were alone. She leaned up and kissed him. Jake responded with a longing that took her by surprise. The kiss was carnal and deep and when he stepped away she shivered with desire.

"Rissa, is there something you're trying to tell me here?" he asked.

"Well, maybe I am."

"I'm not going to make any more guesses where you're concerned any longer."

"I'm sorry about that last morning in Vegas. I guess I freaked out."

"Our wedding night was incredible."

"Yes, it was. I don't want that to be our only night together."

"It won't be."

"Good, then we're on the same page."

"Larissa, we're not in a meeting with the library board."

She flushed. "I know. But it's easier to talk about it in business terms."

He shook his head. "Are you saying you want to be my wife, in every sense?"

"Yes," she said softly and cuddled closer to the man she'd given her heart to.

Jake felt he'd been through the ringer. He was used to blithely skating through life. Keeping his emotions in a nice safe place that was only breached by his siblings, parents and cousins. Over the past twenty-four hours he'd come to realize that Peter and Larissa had found their way into his heart.

Peter was naturally easy to love. The boy was a blend of Jake's rambunctious go-get-'em attitude and Larissa's quiet intelligence. It was an odd combination and it awed Jake to think that part of him was going to live on through Peter after he was gone.

And he'd realized he didn't want to lose this family he'd found, the family he'd created when he was still so self-involved that he'd never noticed. The family that he knew he'd never be able to survive without.

Larissa yawned behind her hand and her shoulder slumped with fatigue. She looked as if she was about to collapse. "Why don't you take the Suburban and go home and rest?"

He liked to think that he'd helped her through this crisis. And it had been a crisis. He could handle any major problem at D&D's, but nothing had made him sweat like watching Peter struggle to breathe. It had made him realize how fragile this life was. It had reminded him of all the reasons he'd started hiding his feelings when Vicky had disappeared. Only now he knew that hiding wasn't the solution. Celebrating life and remembering the reasons why it was good were important.

"Thanks, but I think I'd better stay here in case Peter wakes up."

"Don't you trust me to take care of him?" he asked. He had to wonder. She'd scarcely left him alone with Peter since they'd been at the hospital. Her quiet strength surprised him, but it shouldn't have. Larissa was a survivor.

She closed her eyes, hiding from him. As always, she was a mystery to him.

"Of course, I do. It's just I don't…"

"You don't what?" He wondered sometimes what she saw in him. She'd always been the one person that had slipped past his guard. The one person he could tell his dreams to who didn't make him feel like an idiot. The one person he'd always wanted to impress. And he had the feeling that sometimes he came close to doing that.

"I don't want him to need someone else," she said in a rush of honesty.

He understood. Sometimes it was easier to be everything to someone than to share the responsibility. "I'm not some stranger, Rissa. I'm his dad."

"You're right. I'm still not used to trusting men in general."

"Me in particular?" he asked. Hell, he sounded like a sap. Why did it matter if she didn't trust him? Because you love her, a voice inside him said. The thought staggered him.

She pivoted to face him. He couldn't read her expression, but he didn't care anymore. Now he was concerned with hiding his own weakness from her. He'd always been the strong one and he wasn't going to let anything—not even Larissa—change that. "I trust you, Jacob Danforth, more than I'd ever thought I could trust any man."

Her words went straight through him. The mantle of responsibility felt heavy on his shoulders and he vowed that he'd never do anything to make her doubt the faith she'd placed in him. God, he needed to be alone with his wife. He needed to know that his son was safe and healthy and then take his wife to bed and reaffirm the bonds they'd tentatively forged in Vegas.

"Come here, woman," he said.

"Why?"

Because I need you, he thought but didn't dare say. "Just get over here."

She gave him a flirty smile and walked across the room with slow hip-swaying steps. Each move she made seduced him. And made the barriers he'd thought he'd built around his heart crumble.

She stopped a good six inches from him. Her gaze skimmed over his body and he couldn't help it, he stood up straighter and flexed his muscles.

"Very impressive," she said.

"I know."

She laughed and he realized it had been too long since he'd seen Larissa smiling. He promised himself that from now on she'd have lots of reasons to smile.

He reached out and dragged her close. He wanted to clutch her to his chest but forced himself to just hold her loosely instead, carefully so not to reveal the intensity of the emotions swamping him. But deep inside he knew he'd never be complete without Larissa by his side. She made him a better man and he knew that if she ever left he'd be incomplete. How was he going to keep her by his side without letting her know?

Larissa left Jake and Peter at the hospital. She felt more certain than ever that she and Jake were going to make it. That they were going to be one of those couples that succeeded despite the circumstances under which they'd started their marriage. She returned to Jake's town house on autopilot and when she entered the house she went straight to his bedroom and crawled into his bed.

Surrounded by his scent, she fell into a deep sleep. The doorbell woke her four hours later. She stumbled from the bed and shrugged into Jake's robe.

She hoped it wasn't Jasmine Carmody again. Though she'd made a kind of peace with her past, that didn't mean she wanted to discuss it with that reporter.

A quick peak through the peephole showed that it was a man she didn't recognize. She opened the door.

"Can I help you?"

"Are you Larissa Nielsen?"

"I used to be. I'm Larissa Danforth, now." God that sounded right to her ears. She'd feared marrying into a moneyed family but she realized her fears were based on her father's attitude and her mother's marriage. Jake was so different than Reilly Peyton.

He handed her an envelope and walked away. She closed the door and reentered Jake's town house. That was strange, she thought. She went into the kitchen and put a cup of water in the microwave. She used her fingernail to open the envelope and pulled out the papers.

She skimmed them and lost feeling in her legs. Clutching the papers, she sank to the floor. Jake was suing her for full custody of Peter. He'd lied about the paternity test! He'd had it done so that he could take her baby away from her.

She pulled her knees to her chest and hugged them tight, realizing that her worst fears had been realized. She'd trusted him. And he'd betrayed her. The entire time he'd been playing a game calculated to hurt her in the worst way possible.

She staggered to her feet and went into the guest bedroom Jake had given her when they'd moved in. She took a shower and dressed with care. She didn't know what to do next but knew that she had to confront Jake. If he thought she was going to give up her son because he needed revenge on her, he had another think coming.

But she knew she'd never drag Peter through any kind of custody battle. She never wanted her son to feel as if his birth was something that brought regret to his mother and father.

When she was dressed, she got in her car and sat in the driveway while her hands stopped shaking. She leaned down on the steering wheel and tried to figure out how things could go from being close to perfect to a nightmare.

Finally she had her trembling under control and a slow anger began to build inside her. By the time she got to the hospital, she was ready to tear Jake Danforth apart. How dare he manipulate her that way? Didn't family mean anything to him? Didn't he realize how legal battles tore at a child's security?

She entered the hospital and rehearsed her words in the elevator on the way up. Then she thought about Jake's parents. Miranda had invited Larissa to call her Mom. Had she known that her son was planning to take Peter away? Had they all been in on the scheme to keep her from her son?

The elevator doors opened on Peter's floor and suddenly she was afraid to face the future. She knew that she wasn't going to be her usual levelheaded self. She knew that she was an inch away from tears and outright wailing.

She got off the elevator and walked slowly past the nurses station. It was early in the morning and the halls were filled with doctors making their rounds. She paused outside the door to Peter's room. Tucking a strand of loose hair back into her ponytail, she cautioned herself not to get emotional.

She pushed open the door and stepped inside. The room was dark except for a stream of sunlight coming through the gap in the curtains. Jake lay on the bed next to Peter. He cradled their son against his chest.

The scene looked so right. Too right. Maybe she should do the adult thing and back away. Let Jake have Peter. Jake could give him so many things that Larissa couldn't. He had a large family, plenty of money and most importantly, he loved Peter.

Tears burned the back of her eyes and she fought to keep them from falling but couldn't. They were hot on her face and when she lifted her clammy hands to wipe them away she caught a glimpse of her wedding ring.

She felt like a fool for ever believing that Jake would have wanted her for his wife. Maybe he'd just wanted to get her out of town so that he could build his case against her.

And she'd made it so easy by falling for him. By letting him manipulate her in the most intimate way.

A sob escaped her and she knew she wasn't in any shape to confront Jake right now. She turned to leave the room. She'd wash her face and get herself together.

"Rissa?" he asked.

She steeled her heart against the compassion she heard in his voice. Before, her lonely heart had been looking for love, but now she knew the truth. Jake was using his silky words and smooth ways to lull her into complacency. She glanced over her shoulder at him. Jake sat up, easing his arm out from beneath Peter and crossing the room to her.

"Baby, what's wrong?"

"I…" She couldn't get the words out of her mouth. How could she verbalize the hurt that had come on so unexpectedly? This was her worst fear and why she'd fought so hard to keep from falling in love with Jake.

"Did that reporter bother you again? I'm going to call my lawyers and have them take action against her."

Strangely those words were the ones that made her stop crying. "Call your lawyers?"

"Yes, my lawyers."

"You're good at that, aren't you?"

"What do you mean?" he asked, his eyes narrowing.

"That I'm well aware of how you've been keeping your lawyers busy—planning to take Peter from me."

Jake cursed savagely under his breath and Larissa took a few steps from him. Crossing her arms over her chest, she looked at him the way she would an enemy.

"Larissa—"

"Don't bother lying to me now, Jake. I've got the proof in my hands."

Jake shoved his fingers through his hair. A million excuses and defenses hovered on the edge of his tongue. He knew what to say and how to dance away from her. How to keep himself emotionally safe and protected from the vulnerabilities that only this woman could make him feel.

But seeing her hurting like this, knowing he was responsible, made him feel horrible. He didn't want to see her cry.

He pulled her into his arms. She struggled against him and he knew he only had a few seconds to say the right words. But what were they?

He caught her face in his hands and stared down

at her. He rubbed the tears from her eyes and leaned close to her. God, she was so small and vulnerable. "I'm sorry."

She started to speak, but he pressed his mouth to hers, stopping her words. She smelled so good and he knew he should be concentrating on making his mistakes right. She kept her mouth tightly closed but stopped struggling to get away from him. He lifted his head.

"I was angry when you first told me about Peter."

"I know. But I thought we'd gotten past all that. Dammit, Jake. I thought we were starting a life together."

"We are, Rissa. We have started a life together." He was hedging and she knew it. But if he told her what was in his heart and she didn't return his feelings, he'd feel like a fool. Better a strong man than a fool, he thought.

"It doesn't feel like this is much of a life. I wanted a real marriage, not one based on vengeance."

"I wanted revenge," he said honestly.

"I can't let you take Peter. You can offer him much more than I can when it comes to money and family, but you can't offer him the one thing that every child needs—love and nurturing."

"What makes you so sure?" he asked.

"Because you don't know how to love."

He shuddered. Jake shoved his hands through his hair and turned away from her. Was she right? Had he forgotten all he'd learned about loving relationships in trying to keep himself insulated from the pain that came with failing? He paced to the window and rested his head against the cold glass. There were no answers in the sky or in the densely crowded parking lot below.

The only place with the answers was inside him. And losing Peter or Larissa wasn't an option. He needed them in his life.

He straightened and turned back to the woman who didn't realize she held his heart in her hands. She watched him carefully, clearly not sure what to expect next. He realized it was time to stop running and stop hiding from the emotions that scared him the most and the woman who inspired them.

"I'm not going to take Peter away from you. Hell, woman, I don't think I could live without the both of you in my life. And I certainly can't live with the knowledge that I hurt you so deeply."

"I never could have gone through with the suit. It was my back-up plan. A safe way for me to pretend I could keep you under my control."

He opened his arms and she hesitated only a second before running across the room and jumping into his arms. He held her tight and whispered all the words he was afraid to say out loud.

"You are the breath in my body, the light in my soul and the beating of my heart. I can't survive without you. I love you."

"Oh, Jake. I love you, too."

He bent to capture her lips with his and this time she opened her mouth to his. The kiss was deep and sensual, but heavy with the promise of tomorrow. A promise Jake hadn't been able to believe in for a long time.

"Mama? Daddy?" Peter called from the bed.

Jake pocketed the legal papers Larissa had brought with her and they crossed the room to their son.

"Hey, baby. How do you feel?" Larissa asked, brushing his hair back from his forehead.

"Hungry," Peter said.

Jake laughed. His son was always hungry. "I'll go get you some food. What do you want?"

"Krispy Kremes."

"Peter, how do you know about doughnuts?" Larissa asked.

"Daddy told me about them last night and promised we could go as soon as I leave the hospital."

"Sounds like a good plan," Larissa said.

The doctor entered the room and in a short while Peter was discharged. Jake's parents arrived and Jake felt really worthy of being a Danforth for the first time since Victoria had disappeared. He realized that his coffeehouse business and his playboy lifestyle were just excuses to keep from staying still long enough to feel the guilt.

But he let go of the guilt. He knew his sister was

alive somewhere and he knew that they would find her.

"Mom and Dad, will you take Peter in your car? We're going to the Krispy Kreme."

"Sure thing, son," his dad said.

Jake took Larissa's hand in his and led her to the Suburban. "What are we doing?"

"I just wanted a few minutes alone with you, Rissa."

"I thought we settled everything."

"I'm going to call Ted Larson as soon as his office opens and drop the custody suit."

"I know."

"You sound pretty confident," he said.

"Honey, you told me I was the air you breathe. I think that gives me the right."

"Am I the air you breathe?"

She leaned up and kissed his jaw. "No."

"No?"

"You're the blood in my veins."

He scooped her up in the parking lot and spun around with Larissa in his arms. Then he bent and kissed this woman who'd given him more than he ever expected to have—love and a family.

Epilogue

Jake had decided that their honeymoon in Vegas had been too short and had surprised Larissa and Peter with a two-week trip through the Southeast following Jimmy Buffett's concert tour. This was their last night before heading back to Savannah. They were in Orlando in the parking lot at the TD Waterhouse Center. Jake and Peter wore identical unbuttoned Hawaiian-print shirts and khaki board shorts under grass skirts.

They were parked next to Courtney and Jen, two college girls they'd met at the concert in Miami the day before. They were grilling chicken and making margaritas. Jake came up behind Larissa and slipped his arms around her waist. He kissed her on the neck and whispered delicious promises in her ear.

Larissa leaned back against him and looked over at their son playing nearby. This was the life she'd been afraid to let herself dream of. But here it was nonetheless and it was so much more than she'd ever imagined.

"Mama, look," Peter said.

Their son proceeded to shake his hips and start singing fins. "Did Daddy teach you that?"

"Yes, come on, Daddy. Let's dance for her."

Peter and Jake did their hip-shaking dance for her and earned applause from the others in the parking lot. Larissa felt a sense of peace and belonging that she'd never thought to find. She closed her eyes. She realized that she was going to have to thank Jasmine Carmody for giving her the family she'd always dreamed of.

* * * * *

JOIN US ON SOCIAL MEDIA!

Stay up to date with our latest releases, author news and gossip, special offers and discounts, and all the behind-the-scenes action from Mills & Boon...

 millsandboon

 millsandboonuk

millsandboon

might just be true love...

MILLS & BOON

THE HEART OF ROMANCE

A ROMANCE FOR EVERY KIND OF READER

MODERN

Prepare to be swept off your feet by sophisticated, sexy and seductive heroes, in some of the world's most glamourous and romantic locations, where power and passion collide.
8 stories per month.

HISTORICAL

Escape with historical heroes from time gone by. Whether your passion is for wicked Regency Rakes, muscled Vikings or rugged Highlanders, awaken the romance of the past.
6 stories per month.

MEDICAL

Set your pulse racing with dedicated, delectable doctors in the high-pressure world of medicine, where emotions run high and passion, comfort and love are the best medicine.
6 stories per month.

True Love

Celebrate true love with tender stories of heartfelt romance, from the rush of falling in love to the joy a new baby can bring, and a focus on the emotional heart of a relationship.
8 stories per month.

Desire

Indulge in secrets and scandal, intense drama and plenty of sizzling hot action with powerful and passionate heroes who have it all: wealth, status, good looks…everything but the right woman.
6 stories per month.

HEROES

Experience all the excitement of a gripping thriller, with an intense romance at its heart. Resourceful, true-to-life women and strong, fearless men face danger and desire - a killer combination!
8 stories per month.

DARE

Sensual love stories featuring smart, sassy heroines you'd want as a best friend, and compelling intense heroes who are worthy of them.
4 stories per month.

To see which titles are coming soon, please visit

millsandboon.co.uk/nextmonth

LET'S TALK

Romance

For exclusive extracts, competitions
and special offers, find us online:

 facebook.com/millsandboon

@MillsandBoon

@MillsandBoonUK

Get in touch on 01413 063232

For all the latest titles coming soon, visit
millsandboon.co.uk/nextmonth